"Bestselling Australian author Victoria Purman is one of our nation's most valued storytellers . . . Rich in historical detail and filled with memorable characters, *A Woman's Work* is a book that I know will unite readers . . . A meaningful and authentic portrait of a bygone era."

—*Mrs. B's Book Reviews*

"*A Woman's Work* is a tender meditation on women of a bygone era, with issues as current as those we struggle with today: keeping it together in the balancing act of life, how to juggle a family, work, relationships while retaining and honoring yourself . . . [the book] reads like a love letter to our mothers, grandmothers, and aunts."

—*Better Reading*

"Nostalgic, compassionate, and beautifully written."

—*Woman's Day* on *A Woman's Work*

"Heartachingly raw yet filled with the beauty of the human spirit, this novel is a triumph that will linger in the heart and psyche."

—Karen Brooks, author of
The Good Wife of Bath,
on *The Nurses' War*

"Heartfelt, heartbreaking, emotional, and so very moving."

—*RBH Historical* blog on *The Nurses' War*

"Just as she did with her acclaimed 2019 novel *The Land Girls*, *The Women's Pages* draws inspiration for its storylines and characters from the Australian women who came before us, making it even more gripping and poignant . . . Thanks to its rich Australian history, multi-dimensional characters, and a story of love, ambition, and resilience that will sweep you away, *The Women's Pages* is the one new novel you need to share with your book club, family, and friends."

—Mamamia

"Post-war Australia is captured brilliantly in all its relief and celebration, as well as the struggle and heartache . . . Victoria's characters are real women—complex and compelling. Once again, Victoria reeled me in to a richly imagined (and meticulously researched) world. I loved the characters and slowed down in the final pages, reluctant to finish the book and leave them behind."

—Better Reading on *The Women's Pages*

"Victoria Purman's books are always well-researched; they never disappoint or leave you wanting more and are a pleasure to read . . . Five stars."

—Karen Reads Books
on *The Women's Pages*

"Seamlessly merging historical facts with fiction, Purman's focus is on exploring the post-war experiences of women in this enjoyable, moving, and interesting novel . . . Heartfelt and poignant, with appealing characters, *The Women's Pages* is an excellent read . . . An engaging story that also illuminates the real history of post-war Australian women."

—Book'd Out

"I consider Victoria Purman one of Australia's leading storytellers in the field of historical fiction . . . *The Women's Pages* is a rich historical fiction title that leaves a strong imprint on the reader."

—Mrs. B's Book Reviews

"A richly crafted novel that graphically depicts life during those harrowing years. A touching tale and an enthralling read."
—*Reader's Digest* on *The Women's Pages*

"A powerful and moving book."
—*Canberra Weekly* on *The Women's Pages*

"An engaging tale about family life and relationships at this turning point in Australian culture. Dealing with the legacy of the old whilst carving out the new. It valiantly shone the spotlight on the women who fought to break free of a solely domestic role in search of greater independence."
—*Great Reads and Tea Leaves*
on *The Women's Pages*

"This is an enjoyable novel to read . . . The historical research is invisibly sewn into the world building. Most importantly, the characters are vivid and believable."
—*Other Dreams, Other Lives*
on *The Women's Pages*

"An engaging tale from a foundation of extensive research that deserves its place in the canon of Australia's wartime-inspired fiction."
—*News Mail* on *The Land Girls*

"Moments of great sadness and grief, as well as moments of pure, radiant joy, unfold in this gentle, charming tale . . . The genuine heartfelt emotion and the lovely reimagining of the way we once were . . . makes *The Land Girls* such a rich and rewarding read."
—Better Reading

"A moving tale of love, loss, and survival against the odds."

—*Better Homes & Gardens*
on *The Land Girls*

"Purman's almost lyrical description of this particular point in Australia's history is a richly crafted treat veering cleverly through the brutal hardships faced at the time while also filtering in little moments of beautiful, historical nostalgia. It's a well-told story filled with multi-dimensional female characters."

—*Mamamia* on *The Land Girls*

"I would recommend *The Land Girls* for its historical significance, romance, and power to make the reader feel proud to be Australian."

—Chapter Ichi

"A beautiful story with rich characters, vivid settings, and the whole emotional range."

—*Beauty and Lace* on *The Land Girls*

"There is a wealth of detail woven into this novel . . . Victoria Purman just seems to be going from strength to strength with her historical fiction."

—*Theresa Smith Writes* on *The Land Girls*

"What a lovely tribute this book is to all the women of the Australian Women's Land Army . . . I enjoy her style of writing, the characters, and the in-depth description she gives to make you immerse yourself into her world."

—*Reading for the Love of Books*
on *The Land Girls*

"A heartwarming novel . . . The story of Bonegilla is a remarkable one, and this novel is a tantalizing glimpse into its legacy."

—*The Weekly Times* on
The Last of the Bonegilla Girls

"Victoria Purman has written a story about people exactly like my family, migrants to Australia . . . I came to this novel for the migrant story, but I stayed for the wonderful friendship Victoria Purman has painted between the four girls."

—*Sam Still Reading* on
The Last of the Bonegilla Girls

"A moving and heartwarming story [and] a poignant and compelling read, *The Last of the Bonegilla Girls* is . . . a beautiful story about female friendship and how it can transcend cultural and language barriers."

—Better Reading

"*The Last of the Bonegilla Girls* is a touching and compelling story of female friendship and celebration of what it means to call Australia home, no matter where the journey began . . . Beautifully told . . . with an ending that will leave you dewy-eyed and [with] a renewed sense of hope."

—Blue Wolf Reviews

"An enjoyable and well-written historical novel with tragedy, love, and friendship in a harsh landscape where the only option is hard work and survival."

—S. C. Karakaltsas, author, on *The Last of the Bonegilla Girls*

"A celebration of Australia's multicultural history, of love, friendship, tolerance, and building bridges . . . [and a] glimpse into a chapter of Australian history we normally hear little about . . . *The Last of the Bonegilla Girls* is an insightful, uplifting, and feel-good book that I recommend to all lovers of Australian historical fiction."

—*But Books Are Better*

"I couldn't turn the pages fast enough, but at the same time I didn't want it to end. It kept me guessing from the beginning."
—Rachael Johns, bestselling Australian author, on *The Three Miss Allens*

"Serious social issues, including the plight of unwed mothers, domestic violence, and the place of women in Australia's history are wrapped up in poignant romance."
—*Good Reading* on *The Three Miss Allens*

The
RADIO HOUR

ALSO BY VICTORIA PURMAN

THE BOYS OF SUMMER SERIES
Nobody But Him
Someone Like You
Our Kind of Love
Hold On to Me

STAND-ALONE NOVELS
Only We Know
The Three Miss Allens
The Last of the Bonegilla Girls
The Land Girls
The Women's Pages
The Nurses' War
A Woman's Work

The

RADIO HOUR

....

Victoria Purman

HARPER MUSE

Published by Harper Muse, an imprint of HarperCollins Focus LLC.

This book is a work of fiction. All incidents, dialogue, and letters, and all characters with the exception of some well-known historical figures, are products of the author's imagination. Where real-life historical persons appear, the situations, incidents, and dialogues concerning those personas are entirely fictional and are not intended to depict actual events or to change the entirely fictional nature of the work. In all other respects, any resemblance to persons living or dead is entirely coincidental.

Any internet addresses (websites, blogs, etc.) in this book are offered as a resource. They are not intended in any way to be or imply an endorsement by HarperCollins Focus LLC, nor does HarperCollins Focus LLC vouch for the content of these sites for the life of this book.

ISBN 978-1-4003-4803-9 (trade paper)
ISBN 978-1-4003-4805-3 (e-book)
ISBN 978-1-4003-4806-0 (downloadable audio)

Library of Congress Cataloging-in-Publication Data

CIP data is available upon request.

Printed in the United States of America

24 25 26 27 28 LBC 5 4 3 2 1

This book is dedicated to

Caitlin, Rhiannon, Victoria (aka Little Vic), and Matilda.
I love it that you ask yourselves WWVD.

What an honor it is to be your mentor and friend.

Literature cannot be the business of a woman's life, and it ought not to be. The more she is engaged in her proper duties, the less leisure she will have for it even as an accomplishment and a recreation.

LETTER FROM ROBERT SOUTHEY TO CHARLOTTE BRONTË, MARCH 12, 1837

Her word had no weight, her convenience was always to give way.

Persuasion, JANE AUSTEN

It's never too late to be what you might have been.

GEORGE ELIOT (ATTRIBUTED)

Chapter 1

MAY 1956
Sydney, Australia

IN WHICH OUR HEROINE—SPINSTER,
SECRETARY, AND LOYAL DAUGHTER MISS
MARTHA BERRY—DISCOVERS SHE'S ABOUT
TO EMBARK ON A NEW ASSIGNMENT.

Miss Berry, I'm sending you to work with one of our new radio producers."

Sitting across from Mr. Rutherford Hayes, Martha Berry could almost see her reflection in his gleaming mahogany desk. She'd made sure to shine it with furniture polish that very morning— just the way he liked it—and had double-checked that the black Bakelite ashtray onto which he tap-tap-tapped his ubiquitous pipe was empty too. It had been clean as a whistle first thing that morning but now resembled the ruins of Pompeii. The national broadcaster's head of drama was rather fond of his tobacco.

"I see," Martha replied, holding a smile on her face. She sat perfectly still, the way she'd been taught as a girl. Her hands were cupped politely in her lap, her legs crossed at the ankles just like the queen's. That way, there was no risk of her underwear ever being exposed. Her back was ramrod straight even without the aid of a corset. These were skills she had learned thirty-five years before at secretarial college. Don't fidget. Only speak when spoken to. Never, ever take a risk that someone might see your underwear. And always—always—remain polite.

While Mr. Hayes puffed and stared into the middle distance, Martha's attention drifted to the framed photograph of Her Majesty Queen Elizabeth II on the wall behind him. It needed straightening. How could she have missed that?

"This young chap is kicking off a new radio serial. Quentin Quinn's his name." Mr. Hayes sucked deep on his pipe, leaned back in his chair, and exhaled a locomotive engine's worth of smoke right across the desk and directly into Martha's face.

She swallowed a cough.

"Everyone at the ABC is in a permanent state of apoplexy about the arrival of television. It's only months away, Miss Berry. It's television this and television that. Personally, I don't think it'll take off here in Australia. People will always want their radios. You can bet on that." Mr. Hayes aimed his pipe at Martha as if to prove his point and then took another puff.

Martha had seen photographs of televisions. They were little movie screens in wooden cabinets with legs; fancy new pieces of furniture for living rooms that would soon compete with the radio cabinets that had until now taken pride of place. The British and the Americans had had television for years, of course, and while some in Australia had been pushing for it, others weren't quite sure about the whole newfangled medium.

"I myself believe it'll be nothing but a conduit for mediocrity and vulgar sensationalism," Mr. Hayes continued, staring up at the ceiling as he pontificated. "The very novelty of it will encourage people to look at anything, no matter the quality of what's served up to them. Goodness me, the television chaps are telling me that judging from what they've seen in America and England, they could broadcast a film of a cat licking its paws and people would watch. What about the children, Miss Berry? What if they develop an addiction and forget how to run and play? What will happen if people stop conversing with each other because they're too busy watching a box? Or if they stop going to lectures or musical performances or the theater or concerts. And, god forbid, reading. What if people stop reading?"

Martha almost forgot to breathe. Would people really stop reading? What would happen to their imaginations if they stopped reading books?

"And . . . and," Mr. Hayes spluttered, "worst of all, what if people permanently turn off their radios and start watching television instead? Where will we be then? No, Miss Berry, I don't believe this supposed balm for the masses will take off. Radio will always reign supreme. The good women of Australia won't be able to chop up their vegetables and fry up their chops for dinner while they're watching television, will they?"

"I don't believe they will, Mr. Hayes."

"Let us simply put aside all this television-will-be-king thinking. We can't let those chaps working over in the television department get the upper hand, can we? That's why we will continue to invest in original productions. Like this new radio drama."

"I can't wait to hear more about it."

He put down his spent pipe, leaned back in his chair, and linked his fingers together, resting them in a tangle in his lap. "Since Miss Jones returns from her holiday next Monday, I've been wondering what to do with you now your temporary assignment with me is over." He smiled. "I thought perhaps working with this Quinn fellow could be your next position. You've done a marvelous job looking after me while Miss Jones has been away, Miss Berry." He paused to search his memory. "Tasmania, I believe."

"Tasmania?"

"That's where Miss Jones has been. With a group of her girl-friends. On a bus trip."

"I see."

"Have you ever been?"

"On a bus trip?" Martha asked by way of clarification.

"To Tasmania."

"No, I haven't, Mr. Hayes. I hear Mount Wellington is a sight to behold. Especially when the peaks are kissed by snow as winter beckons."

Mr. Hayes gave Martha a curious look and held it for a long moment, then shook his head. "Yes, quite. Anyway, this Quinn fellow. He's very bright indeed. A wonderful writer, so I'm told. He's young, but aren't they all these days?"

Martha chuckled at the acknowledgment of their vintage. It had been no trouble at all working for the kind, gray-haired man. More than a decade older than she was, judging by the wrinkles around his eyes and his sagging jowls, he was an old-fashioned gentleman in the best of ways. He had a mature sensibility that she liked and a gravitas she both understood and appreciated.

"They are indeed, Mr. Hayes. But as they say, youth is often wasted on the young."

"Ah, Oscar Wilde," he replied with a knowing smile.

Martha was far too polite to point out that it wasn't Oscar Wilde. Or George Bernard Shaw either, as many thought.

"We want this young chap, Quinn, to come up with another *Blue Hills*."

Martha startled in her chair and gripped the armrests. "What's happening to *Blue Hills*?"

"Goodness, nothing at all, Miss Berry. That marvel Gwen Meredith has turned *Blue Hills* into such a success story that the powers that be"—Mr. Hayes pointed to the ceiling—"want something else just like it. But not *exactly* like it." He sighed. "The truth is, we had something else in mind to fill the fifteen-minute time slot after *Blue Hills*, but it's fallen in a rather deep hole, I'm afraid. We had such high hopes for *Detective Reeves Investigates*. Imagine—a real detective on the radio hosting his own program. But, unfortunately for all concerned, the detective"—Mr. Hayes cleared his throat—"has been assigned to a very important police matter and is now unable to host the program and share his true-life detective stories."

That wasn't exactly true, but Martha was far too polite to tell Mr. Hayes what she'd heard through the unofficial grapevine: Detective Reeves (Detective Smith in real life), a respected officer with a long career in the force, had been exposed as a bigamist. He'd apparently left a wife—and, shockingly, three young children—behind in Adelaide twenty years earlier and had never bothered to get divorced, or even tell his new wife, Faith, the very-much-younger-than-him shopgirl he'd met while buying socks. When the first Mrs. Smith read about the brand-new program featuring a real-life detective in *ABC Weekly* magazine, she was astonished to see a photograph of her missing husband. She had quickly turned up in Sydney with a long-overdue account in one hand for all she believed she was owed for raising their children on her own and a sturdy umbrella in her other hand. The new Mrs. Smith had been so horrified by the realization her marriage wasn't legal that she'd hopped on a train to Thirroul to her parents to await the arrival of her child.

Interestingly, the scandal had never made the papers. The police swept it under the carpet because Detective Smith was one of their own, and the broadcaster announced that radio's Detective Reeves had been called away on an important assignment fighting crime, and the whole thing had been shelved. Everyone in management and in the police force was confident the embarrassing episode would just go away. And funnily enough, it did. At her age, Martha couldn't be shocked that men's scandals remained secrets. It was the way of the world, after all.

"A policeman must always go where the crime is," Martha said, "even if the bright lights of radio are beckoning."

Mr. Hayes chuckled. "Indeed."

"So," Martha said, knowing he would be grateful for the change of subject, "the new serial will follow *Blue Hills*?"

"That's right. At a quarter past one in the afternoon and then again in the evenings. Gwen Meredith and her town of Tanimbla and her characters are staying put, but we feel there's an audience for another drama at that time of day. Do you know, Miss Berry, that Mrs. Meredith writes every single episode? Fifteen minutes of original drama. A bloody marvel. A terrific lady writer. She's one of a kind. A singular talent. I don't think there's another woman in the world who's as accomplished as she is in radio drama. We were lucky enough to find the only woman with the talent, determination, and grit to be that prolific and that clever. The letters we get from listeners about *Blue Hills*—why, you wouldn't believe it, Miss Berry."

Martha did believe it. She'd been an avid listener herself since the drama had first gone to air in 1949, and she'd been a fan of its predecessor, *The Lawsons*, which had started in the last years of the war. Mrs. Meredith was an accomplished playwright and emerging theater personality when she'd entered an ABC play competition in 1940, and even though the judges had selected someone else as the winner, Mrs. Meredith was the clear favorite in a listeners' poll. Of course, there had been grumblings that she was married and surely a married woman wouldn't have the time to devote her attentions to her job when she was busy devoting them all to her husband, but Mrs. Meredith had proved the naysayers wrong and *The Lawsons* and then *Blue Hills* became smash hits, and Mrs. Meredith became radio's brightest star.

Martha had never been able to listen to the daytime airings as she'd always been at work, but her mother, Violet, listened avidly at 1:00 p.m. over her lunch and never complained about hearing it all over again when it was repeated in the evenings, as had become a habit for Martha and Violet and households from Perth to Townsville and everywhere in between. After dinner, the nation would quiet, cups of tea would be made, and a biscuit or two would be consumed while the symphonic strains of the opening theme of *Blue Hills* filled the living rooms and kitchens of Australian households.

"I did a stint in the mail department last year. I saw the correspondence with my own eyes."

"Then you'll know they pour in from everywhere, from the back of Bourke to Western Australia. The powers that be want to surf on that success." Mr. Hayes leaned back in his chair and fiddled with his empty pipe. "We want to see what Quinn comes up with. He'll bring a younger perspective, you understand. We want it to be set right here in Sydney. In the suburbs. The ordinary suburbs. It will encompass all the things young people like these days, music and dancing and so on."

Martha nodded politely.

"Not that we want to lose the housewives, mind you. They love their sweep-while-you-weep dramas. *Portia Faces Life*. All those dramas on *Lux Radio Theatre*."

"*When a Girl Marries*," Martha added. She and Violet loved "radio's most appealing human interest romance," as it was billed.

"Yes, quite. And, of course, the commercial broadcasters have their lady lawyers and doctors, that sort of thing. As the national broadcaster, we very much see it as our duty to provide entertainment for the ladies of Australia. The men, of course, have their news and current affairs and discussions of serious literature, opera, and theater in the evenings when they get home from the office and are looking for some relaxation. But it's only right that we cater to the fairer sex too."

"It certainly is, Mr. Hayes."

"And you, Miss Berry, will be a vital cog in the new serial. I know you've worked with many of our producers, all those talented chaps who've gone on to bigger and better things. That young Peter Fellowes started here at seventeen, you know, and has flown the coop to London. He's writing for the BBC." Mr. Hayes's face lit up. "The original Auntie herself!"

"He was a prodigy indeed," she replied. And one who never once managed to land a screwed-up script in the wastepaper basket next to his desk.

"You know the ropes here. Show them to Quentin Quinn. Make sure he fills in all the right forms and so on. You'll be good for him." Mr. Hayes looked to the ceiling and she sensed a pontification coming on. "Miss Berry, you're one of a special breed here."

"Special?" She'd never heard herself described in such a way and was suddenly perplexed by the compliment.

"You're a female."

This was hardly news to her, but she was far too polite to interrupt Mr. Hayes's soliloquy.

"We have found, over the years, that female secretaries such as yourself are easier to supervise. You're very tolerant of routines—which men might find frustrating, if not a little boring—and you accommodate those routines with care and a certain equanimity."

"That's very kind of you to say, Mr. Hayes."

"Yes, we have found that the more creative types—the men—can be somewhat hotheaded and demanding. But you women? It's something to do with your natural tact, your patience, and your overall diplomacy that makes you excellent workers. You're so well suited to managing the men and transcribing their words, as typing at speed does seem to come naturally to you all. And, of course, we find that because women have helped their mothers with the household chores and with the task of looking after the men of the household, they develop a natural tendency to look after their bosses too." He narrowed his eyes at Martha and cocked his head to the side. "You've worked here many years, haven't you, Miss Berry?"

"Yes, Mr. Hayes."

"How many exactly?"

"From the beginning—1932."

"Goodness. The very year we began broadcasting." He picked up his pipe, made a huge fuss of lighting it, and puffed it back to life. "You must be thinking about retiring then."

"No thoughts in that direction, Mr. Hayes." Thoughts of retirement? She was younger than Mr. Hayes, and he still occupied his comfortable leather chair.

"No grandchildren to look after, then? No . . . knitting for them? Or baking biscuits, that kind of thing?" Wasn't the fact that she was still "Miss" any kind of clue to him? If she were married, she would not legally be allowed to work in the Commonwealth Public Service and many other places. She wasn't Mrs. Meredith, after all. No, she was the perfect working woman. She was husbandless. Childless.

"No grandchildren, Mr. Hayes. And I don't bake."

"You don't bake?"

"No. I'm terrible at it. Whatever I attempt I always seem to burn. I blame my oven."

"I see." The conversation had strayed uncomfortably into the personal, and Mr. Hayes's cheeks reddened in response to the transgression.

"When does Mr. Quinn begin?" Martha asked.

"Next week." He paused. "You've moved from place to place quite a lot, as I recall. Filling in for others, working on new programs, that sort of thing."

"Yes, Mr. Hayes."

"Why is that?"

Martha was far too polite to point out that despite all the assistance she'd provided to her male bosses over the years, she'd never been offered a permanent position with any of them. Perhaps she had been too hesitant to ask for one. Perhaps she had rubbed people the wrong way. She had never been able to figure it out.

"Moving from department to department has certainly kept me on my toes. No day is ever the same," Martha replied. "If there's nothing else, Mr. Hayes?"

"No, that is all."

"Thank you, Mr. Hayes." Martha stood to go, nodding ever so slightly in deference to her boss.

"There is one thing before you go, Miss Berry."

She waited.

"We have high hopes for *As the Sun Sets*."

"That's the title of the new drama serial?"

"Yes. Spot on, don't you think?"

"Yes, very catchy indeed." Martha paused. "Can I fetch you another cup of tea?"

"Why yes, that would be lovely. Thank you, Miss Berry."

Martha closed his office door as she left.

Chapter 2

IN WHICH MARTHA BERRY SHARES HER
NEWS ABOUT *AS THE SUN SETS*
AND RECEIVES SURPRISING ADVICE
FROM HER MOTHER, VIOLET.

Hello, Mum. Good evening, Mrs. Tilley. Mrs. Ward."

The three gray-haired women sat on Mrs. Tilley's front veranda in three identical wicker chairs sipping tea from bone china cups that were as old as they were. On a low table in front of them sat an empty plate with a scattering of telltale crumbs.

The three neighbors' homes in Randwick in southeast Sydney were identical: single-fronted, built from red brick, with hallways to the left that ran along three main rooms on the right and then opened to a kitchen, with a laundry and bathroom via a trip out to the back veranda. If the women were like peas in a pod, so were their homes.

"Hello, dear," Violet said with a warm smile. "Had a good day?"

"I did." Martha smiled back as she stopped on the footpath and looked up at the women. She could set an alarm clock by this scene.

"You're too late for any biscuits." Mrs. Tilley tut-tutted, checking her wristwatch for added dramatic effect. "We've been here for an hour waiting for you to walk up the street, and in the meantime your mum's eaten 'em all." Mrs. Tilley chuckled and patted Violet's hand.

"Get that bony thing away from me, Nance!" Violet burst into laughter and pretended to shove her friend.

Mrs. Ward rolled her eyes and set her cup on the tiled veranda. "These two are worse than schoolboys"—she winked—"fighting all the time."

In weather both good and bad, Violet, Mrs. Tilley, and Mrs. Ward gathered every afternoon—in that brief period of respite between preparing dinner and cooking it—to watch the world go by.

Mrs. Tilley and Mrs. Ward weren't blood relatives, but they were the closest thing Violet had to sisters. They had always been surrogate aunts to Martha, with their children more like cousins than her own. Martha had never really had the real thing, the blood kind. There'd been one uncle who moved to Brisbane after he served in the First World War and whose untimely death and small inheritance had enabled Violet and Martha to buy the house they'd lived in since. While her father had two brothers, Martha didn't know them and they had no interest in knowing her or Violet. Sometimes a person just didn't warm to their relatives. And if it wasn't estrangement, it had been the First World War and the Spanish flu. Those twin horrors had left a generation of Australians with missing branches on their family trees.

Martha still remembered the fear that swept through Sydney when the flu was detected, spreading almost faster than the contagion itself. Public places had been closed. She'd particularly missed the library and her precious books. Their neighbors and friends remained at home behind locked doors, and if they did have to venture out, they covered their faces with white hand-kerchiefs. Looking back, it seemed every second person had caught the flu in 1919, including Violet. Thank god she had survived it. Martha was only thirteen years old and, with her father already dead, she had never forgotten her bone-shaking fear of being left an orphan.

"If you didn't want me to eat all the biscuits, you shouldn't have baked them, Mrs. Tilley!" Violet laughed.

"If you didn't eat my biscuits, you'd have wasted away by now. We know you can't trust Martha's cooking." Mrs. Tilley winked at Violet and all three women laughed again with Martha joining them. It was no secret she lacked something vital in the kitchen department: interest.

Martha understood how important this afternoon routine was to her mother. It was the comfort of the familiar. She knew her daughter was on her way home, that Martha would prepare dinner—even if it was a simple meal—while they chatted about her day, that it wouldn't be long before they both retired to the living room, where they would bask in that lovely and com-forting radio hour while the sun was setting and familiar and friendly voices from the wireless filled their living room and their hearts. Mother and daughter would sit in companionable silence, sipping their tea, hanging on every word of the action and drama and romance of *Blue Hills* and the other serials Violet loved. After, they would dissect the characters' dramas as if they were real people, neighbors perhaps, instead of actors in a studio playing pretend. And later, when the music programs began, the orchestral strains would lull Violet into drowsi-ness, and after she'd urged her mother to bed, Martha would return to the living room, pluck the bookmark from one of her beloved worn volumes, and immerse herself in George Eliot or the Brontës or Jane Austen all over again until she, too, had to go to bed.

Violet and Mrs. Tilley and Mrs. Ward were a willing audience to life on the street. They were there for the slow and then hurried trickle of children hauling their satchels and cases home from school in groups of twos and threes, stopping to play marbles on the footpath, shouting in horror when one of them veered its way toward a drain before being rescued just in time by someone's nimble fingers. Girls played hopscotch on hastily scrawled grids on the road, knowing that nothing would remain permanent with Sydney's rain and car tires smudging their chalk-marked squares. In waves behind the children came mothers pushing prams, calling out, "Just on my way back from the shops, Mrs. Berry." Or "How are you, Mrs. Tilley? You baking, Mrs. Ward?" And the women would answer, "No complaints" or "Melting moments today," and they would exchange waves and smiles and the pudgy-cheeked babes in their prams would stare up in awe.

"Did you get some of the rain today? There was a downpour in Kings Cross." Martha opened the low gate and stepped onto the path bordered by beds of neatly trimmed lavender. Mrs. Tilley sewed the seeds into cloth bags to keep moths out of the wardrobes of every bedroom on the street. Martha smoothed a hand over the leaves and breathed in the wafting scent.

"Oh my word, we did. It is May after all and winter's just around the corner. Which reminds me. Mr. Tilley had better get up on his ladder and clean the gutters. No one wants overflowing gutters, do they, Mrs. Ward?"

Mrs. Ward nodded in agreement.

"I was planning to get all my washing done today, on account of my granddaughter bringing her little ones for me to look after on Monday while she has her hair set, but look at me now! All discombobulated, that's me." Mrs. Tilley raised her arms in mock exasperation and let them fall into her lap. She reminded Martha of Olive Oyl from the *Popeye* cartoon strip. She was almost six feet tall and as thin as a string bean. She was like Jack Sprat in the nursery rhyme—the one who could eat no fat—but she did and never seemed to gain a pound. She wore a headscarf tied at her forehead in a dainty knot, and for special occasions she twisted her hair into a low bun at her collar. Her daughter and grand-daughters were just like her. One of Mrs. Tilley's granddaughters had begun walking the catwalk as a model for the David Jones department store.

"Tell me, Martha," Mrs. Ward called with a hand cupped to her mouth as if they were fifty feet from each other, not five, "what's that Fleur up to now on *Blue Hills*?" She shook her head. "She's trouble, that one."

Martha shrugged. "I'm sorry to say I don't know any more than you do, Mrs. Ward. Mrs. Meredith writes that serial and she keeps things quite secret." If Martha had heard rumors about what was going to happen to Fleur, she was far too polite to spoil anyone's anticipation, not to mention she was bound to keep it confidential. "But I have some news, if you'd like to hear it."

Mrs. Tilley and Mrs. Ward were suddenly silent. After all these years, they knew better than to ask if the news involved a man. They'd asked her about her love life seemingly every day until she turned thirty-five, but when that birthday passed, asking the spinster next door about her romantic affairs must have felt less like curiosity and more like rubbing salt into a wound, so they'd stopped.

"I'm all ears, Martha," Mrs. Tilley said, leaning forward in her cane chair. She crossed one leg over the other, her limbs twining together like tendrils on a choko vine.

Mrs. Ward raised her eyebrows expectantly, her rosy cheeks as plump as new season apples.

"What's this news then, dear?" Violet asked.

"There's going to be a new serial. It will be on the radio every lunchtime and every evening just after *Blue Hills*."

"Oh, that's exciting," Mrs. Ward said with an appreciative nod. "I do like my shows. Especially that *Mary Livingstone, MD*. But goodness me. Her mother! Such a shrew. And that Mary herself, always putting her career before love. It only leads to loneliness, you know." She tut-tutted. "But really, Martha. Could anything be better than *Blue Hills*?"

Mrs. Tilley nodded firmly. "Nothing will ever top *Blue Hills*."

"Nothing ever will," Violet agreed.

Martha hadn't realized this was going to be such a hard sell. "I've been asked to be the secretary to the producer of the new show."

Mrs. Tilley suddenly smiled and reached over to nudge Mrs. Ward. "I'm sure if you're involved, Martha, love, it'll be almost as good as *Blue Hills*." She turned to Violet and winked. "You know how much I like that Dr. Gordon. Oh, that voice! He can put his shoes under my bed anytime."

Mrs. Ward gasped. "Mrs. Tilley! What would Mr. Tilley say?"

She cackled. "Who cares!"

Violet struggled to her feet and Martha went to her, holding her mother's forearm to steady her.

"That's all very exciting, dear. To be there at the beginning of a new program."

"What's it called, this new show?" Mrs. Tilley asked.

"*As the Sun Sets*."

Violet looked quizzically at Martha. "Is it set on a tropical island, dear?"

"Like *From Here to Eternity*," Mrs. Tilley added. "Remember Burt Lancaster and that Deborah Kerr rolling in the waves?" She fanned herself. "Mind you, they probably got sand up every which way."

Martha was sure their girlish laughter could be heard up and down the entire street and loved that they didn't seem to care.

"*From Here to Eternity* was filmed in Hawaii." Mrs. Ward sighed. "I'd love to go there one day. All those palm trees. And Burt Lancaster."

"*As the Sun Sets* will be set right here in Australia. In a suburb just like Randwick, as a matter of fact."

The older women exchanged confused glances.

"Here?" Mrs. Tilley said. "In a street just like this one?"

"That's right," Martha replied.

Mrs. Ward screwed up her face. "Don't know what they're going to put in the show. Nothing interesting ever happens 'round here. Except the horse races, of course."

"Who are the characters going to be, Martha dear?" Violet asked. "What's going to happen to them?"

Mrs. Tilley leaned in. "Will there be scandals? I love a good scandal."

As Martha guided Violet slowly down the steps and through the front gate, waiting patiently for her mother to negotiate her pain with every movement, she turned back to Mrs. Tilley and Mrs. Ward and flashed them a smile. "You'll have to listen to find out, won't you?"

"Ooh, you're a cheeky one." Mrs. Ward laughed. "If you don't behave, I won't bring my scones to your birthday party on Saturday."

"I would be heartbroken if you didn't." Martha smiled.

"Don't listen to her." Mrs. Tilley cackled. "She knows we can't leave you to the catering, can we?" Mrs. Tilley's and Mrs. Ward's laughter rang in Martha's ears as she and her mother made their way up their own front path.

"It's going to be a lovely party, dear," Violet said as she pushed open the front door. "I can't wait."

Martha dropped three peeled and chopped potatoes into a pot of water and lit the stove.

She was about to turn fifty years old. Martha thought it over for a moment as she covered the aluminum saucepan with its pale red lid. She hadn't planned to live out her life as an unmarried woman. She'd had girlish dreams once of marriage and children and a home and washing on Mondays and baking on Tuesdays and ironing on Wednesdays and roasting lamb on Sundays and all the rest. She'd held on to those dreams in the absence of anything else for a long, long time until she realized how foolish it was. Dreams could so easily be snatched away, and no matter how much she would have loved to have a husband and children, life didn't always bring what a person wished for.

There were worse things than being a single woman and looking after her mother. It wasn't a big life, but it was hers.

"Martha dear. You can't tell me anything else about the new serial?"

"Not yet. I'll find out more tomorrow when Mr. Quinn starts."

Seated at the kitchen table, a warm cup of tea in front of her, Violet smiled. "*Mr.* Quinn, did you say?"

Martha scoffed as she closed the cafe curtains above the sink. "You're worse than Mrs. Ward. Don't go getting too excited on that front. He's at least half my age, I understand. Possibly younger. Directly from university or some such. He's probably not even shaving yet. Or ironing his own shirts."

Violet laughed. "Since when has a man ever ironed a shirt?"

Another upside of being unmarried, Martha thought. She would never have to do her husband's ironing.

"All the young men these days, going off to university." Violet tut-tutted.

"And young women too."

"You could have gone to university, Martha. You were smart enough. You're still smart enough. But"—she shrugged—"things were different for girls like you back then."

"There's no point wishing for anything other than what we have," Martha replied. "I'm very content with my lot in life. We have a home that's ours, even if it needs new gutters. I have a job and we have food on the table three times a day. And treats on weekends."

"You're like a fried egg, you know that, Martha? Sunny side up, that's you. Always have been."

"And always will be." Martha went to her mother and squeezed her arthritic hand gently. "We've a lot to be thankful for, even though you have your challenges. But you don't have to worry. I'll always be here, Mum. Always."

Violet lifted her other hand and cupped her daughter's cheek. "You're the best daughter a mother could ever have, dear."

"I don't have much competition on that front, do I?" She kissed the top of her mother's head and then went to the sink to wash the carrots.

"I don't mean to be morbid, Martha, but when you're my age, you do look back over all the years and wonder . . . what would our lives be like now if things had turned out a bit different?"

"You mean if you and Dad had had the money to see a dentist?"

Violet sighed and shook her head. "He was as stubborn as a mule, our Perce. I would have sold all our silver to pay for the dentist if he hadn't been so . . . Anyway. Every penny counted back then." She dabbed at her eyes with a handkerchief. She always had one on her, whether tucked up a sleeve or secreted inside her bra or in a pocket of her apron. Had her stoicism come naturally or had it been ground into her, given the litany of burdens she'd been forced to bear throughout her life? She'd lived through two wars, had lost a brother in France in the first one and then her parents within a year of each other in 1946. No one really knew what they died of. They were just old, worn-out, and brokenhearted.

Violet had married at twenty and become a widow two days before her twenty-first birthday. Her husband—a father Martha didn't remember and for whom Violet would always carry a torch—had died from a toothache. At least it started out as a toothache. It wasn't long before that toothache became an abscess that led to Perce tugging the troublesome gnasher out with a pair of pliers he kept in the shed because "No point wasting money on a dentist, is there, love?" The truth was that they didn't have the money for a dentist in the first place. When the hole in her father's jaw became filled with pus, the trouble really began.

He'd died slowly and then all at once. The infection spread to his blood and was carried around his body in a few thousand heartbeats, and when the doctor came, Perce's shivering and moaning had stopped and he was lying dead as a doornail in the bed he'd shared with his wife since the day they'd married in 1905.

Violet had then moved baby Martha's bassinet into her own room and let the front room out to lodgers, insisting on only taking in single girls. There was a ready supply in those days, young women who'd traveled from the country into Sydney to work as shopgirls or to attend secretarial college. The girls' parents had been happy to discover that their daughters were lodging in a home with no husbands or sons, reassured they would be cared for by a mother figure.

Martha made the most of growing up in a quiet house of women. She'd liked her own company when she was young and didn't have any lonely times because books were her friends. Martha believed Jane Austen was right when she said that any person, be it gentleman or lady, who has not pleasure in a good novel must be intolerably stupid. At school, she'd been a perfect student. She was never in trouble for chatting in class, never had a wooden ruler slapped over her knuckles, and never scraped her knees because she'd been running across the asphalt yard when she wasn't supposed to. She'd liked etching out a hopscotch grid on the street outside her house and hopping and jumping up and down the squares, not minding if she was joined by other children from nearby homes. Her own company had always been enough.

Maybe that was where Violet had come up with the idea in the first place that her smart and bookish daughter should become a secretary. She'd certainly seen a cavalcade of girls with not half the wits of her own daughter take up positions in offices. Martha couldn't remember a discussion or a debate about it when she was growing up. Perhaps she'd simply agreed to go to secretarial college and then into the workforce with the full knowledge that her mother was scraping every penny together and had opened her home to strangers simply to put food on the table.

Life was life and Martha had coped with the slings and arrows of its misfortunes with a calm equanimity. What use were regrets? They couldn't bring soldiers back from the dead or fathers back from their early graves. Regrets wouldn't make her mother healthier. Wishing for something different didn't make it happen any more than praying to a god might.

She had made a life for herself. Others might judge it to be small or unimportant, but that didn't matter to Martha. She had her health. She'd been kissed more than once, although she had never made love to a man. That was one thing she did look back on with some regret. She would have liked to have known what it felt like to lie with someone, skin to skin, whispering words of love in the quiet dark of the late night or early morning. To share breakfast with someone while reading the papers and then take a leisurely stroll together in the afternoon. But never mind. She thought of all the widows from both wars who had faced the harsh reality that they would never again share such intimacies with the men they loved. There was much loneliness in the world. She wasn't an orphan in that regard, as the saying went.

She had her work. She still had her mother, which she would consider a blessing if she believed in the divine. It was luck, mostly, she truly believed. Did one make their own luck? Was luck being in the right place at the right time, or being in the right place for so long that eventually luck had to happen?

Martha fried the sausages and cut them—and the potatoes and carrots—into pieces small enough that Violet could manage them with a spoon, rather than having to negotiate a knife and a fork, something her arthritis rendered impossible. She could use a spoon quite nimbly, and Martha had adapted her tried-and-true recipes to suit.

Although Martha didn't like baking biscuits or cakes, she quite liked cooking breakfasts and lunches, which was fortunate because she'd been running the kitchen—and the whole house—for more than twenty years. When Violet had no longer been able to take in washing and mending, something she'd done in her later years when they'd simply had enough of having strangers living in their house, Martha had stepped up and the partnership they'd navigated together had slowly transformed into a one-woman band, with Martha conducting and playing all the instruments. The pain in Violet's hands and back and knees had slowly become more immobilizing, and she needed more rest than she ever had before. The doctors said she had simply worn out her body after so many years of physical hard work and it was time to stop. Martha believed it was the rheumatoid arthritis taking its ever-increasing toll, but she was too polite to point that out.

Violet was now unable to dress herself or comb her hair without pain. Walking was a struggle most days, and although she was made of stern stuff and had never complained about her lot in life, Martha saw her mother's discomfort and her agony. Violet's pain was in every exhalation, in the way the color sometimes drained from her face, in the sleep she needed during the day to make up for what she struggled to find at night.

"Getting old's not for the fainthearted, Martha dear." It had become Violet's mantra, and Martha's too. For in her mother's agony, Martha saw her own future, when her fingers might ache too much to type, when even lifting a telephone receiver might hurt. There had been no signs yet of the plight that plagued her mother, but Martha couldn't be sure she wouldn't be afflicted in the same way.

Sooner or later.

Chapter 3

IN WHICH MARTHA BERRY MEETS HER
NEW BOSS, QUENTIN QUINN, AND HEARS
SOMETHING SHE SHOULDN'T.

Martha Berry was quite used to people talking about her as if she wasn't there.

She just hadn't been expecting it on Quentin Quinn's first official day as the producer and writer of *As the Sun Sets*.

He'd barely introduced himself the next Monday morning before assigning Martha her first task. He had insisted on having a new nameplate created for the door to the office bearing the words *As the Sun Sets*, with *Quentin Quinn, Producer* in larger type underneath.

He was a compact young man, trim and boyish, with a smattering of pimples still scattered over his chubby cheeks. His short brown hair was slicked back neatly like all of Sydney's young men wore their hair, and instead of a long tie knotted sensibly in a Windsor, he wore a bow tie, no doubt believing it made him appear creative and interesting.

When he'd strolled into the office that morning swinging a

leather briefcase and sporting a deep brown fedora that matched his obviously new suit (he'd forgotten to snip the stitch holding the vents together at the back), he'd also immediately noticed that Martha was half a head taller than him. He'd slowly raised his eyes to the top of her neat hair, and she hadn't missed the blush in his round cheeks. It was a reaction she was familiar with, but she had long ago realized it was not her job to make men feel better about their shortcomings. He'd kept his hat on for the first half hour to maintain the illusion of a few extra precious inches.

"There's no point hiding your light under a bushel, Mrs. Barry," he insisted as he'd stood to admire the new door sign, rather like a governor might admire a city's plaques on which his name had been engraved on the occasion of something or other of great civic importance. Clearly, *her* light as well as her name were to remain hidden firmly under her bushel.

"Right." Quentin Quinn nodded in Martha's general direction and then turned his attention back to the door. "Now everyone who walks up and down this corridor on their way to Rutherford Hayes's office will know that this is the room where *As the Sun Sets* happens." He'd rocked back on his heels, pushed his hands into the pockets of his trousers, and smiled so widely that Martha thought he might split his chubby cheeks open right at the point where two boyish dimples pockmarked them.

He then stepped outside the main office door and peered all the way down the long corridor to the very end, where the office of the head of drama was located. It was lore within the national broadcaster that the closer one's office was to Mr. Rutherford Hayes's office suite, the more important one was in the general scheme of things. At the moment, the *As the Sun Sets* offices were situated opposite the noisy, clunking lifts.

"The sign certainly leaves no doubt, Mr. Quinn, about whose office this is," Martha replied with equanimity.

Martha hadn't known Quentin Quinn for more than two hours before she realized he would step over whosoever he needed to on his quest to be closer to Mr. Hayes. Martha understood—a result of many years of experience—the way power worked in organizations. Some believed there was no point in doing good work unless one's superiors were aware of it. There was only one group of staff members who seemed to think the opposite was true, and they were the reporters in the newsroom. The news-men worked hard to fly under the radar, rather like spies might, far away from interfering managers who were put on this earth to stymie every good yarn and reject every expenses claim. She'd always thought they were rather peculiar.

"Right. I shall get to work." Quentin Quinn fumbled in his pocket for a pack of cigarettes.

"I do believe they're on your desk."

"Goodo. Right. A cup of coffee, Mrs. Barry." It wasn't an offer. It was a request.

"It's *Miss* Berry, actually." While it would normally be impolite to point out his error, she also believed it was important to get things right in the beginning before they were set in stone and too hard to change.

He looked her up and down. "Rightio."

"One sugar?" she asked.

"Three. And make it black."

—————

The second thing Quentin Quinn had done on his first day at his new job was complain about Martha.

She'd made his cup of coffee and placed it in front of him on his desk when the telephone on hers rang. As it was for him, she'd put the call through before sitting down to her list of tasks. Martha hadn't intended to listen in on his conversation, but how could she not hear him when he hadn't bothered to close the door to his office and he was so loud? Perhaps he believed her to be slightly deaf as well as partially gray and slightly wrinkled.

"Thanks, old chap. This is my big chance, Ken. I'm going to blow *Blue Hills* out of the water. Gwen Meredith's a bit old hat, isn't she? All that country town stuff. I want that prime time slot, you know." There was a pause and Martha heard the clink of his cup in its saucer. "Casting? You think he'd be any good? Sure, I'll look at him. There are quite a few roles for men and, I think, two girls? Although we could perhaps get away with hiring just one woman if she's versatile and can play young *and* old." He cackled uproariously.

"Not grandmother old. I'm talking mid- to late thirties? She's the wife of the chap who runs the butcher's. I know. We're doing the common man in this one. No, not many. I must say I thought I would have more people. You know, a whole team. There's a secretary. Some old bat who's been here a million years, judging by the look of her. Stuck in her ways, like every other old woman I know. Hell, it's like working with my mother. But what can I do? I've been lumped with her." There was a long pause while he listened.

"What am I looking for? You know, the perfect secretary. One who types fast and walks slow." He cackled again. "I will. I'll march right into Rutherford Hayes's office and tell him, 'Look here, man. I don't know what you were thinking, but you've saddled me with someone who should be at home baking cakes and looking after her grandchildren.' She must be sixty, at least." He laughed and Martha heard his lighter flick open.

Martha's fists clenched of their own accord. She looked down at them. Her knuckles were white.

"Damn right. I mean, a bloke needs some pleasant scenery to help while away the hours when he's slogging over a typewriter, don't you think?"

Slogging over a typewriter? Quentin Quinn didn't even have one sitting on his desk. He liked to think out loud, he'd told her earlier that morning in between bouts of admiring his name on the door. She'd offered to find him a typewriter of his own, but he'd resisted.

"I like to hear the words floating through the air, just like they will float through the air from a listener's radiogram or transistor to their ears. It's an aural experience, Mrs. Barry. I'll dictate. If it's good enough for that woman Gwen Meredith, it's good enough for me."

Martha was familiar with the belief held fiercely by most men that typing was beneath them. Except for the newsmen, who treated the task like a brute endeavor, a battle of man against machine; the harder they pounded the keyboard, the more serious the story they were writing. The others seemed oblivious to the fact that women had spent hours and hours at secretarial college and then years more in the workplace perfecting such a skill.

"I'm waiting for her to crack under the workload. She won't be used to dealing with someone like me." Quentin Quinn laughed again, his voice a high-pitched cackle. "Anyway, must dash. I've got a script to write. And actors to cast. Gee, I like the sound of that. What about you? A radio commercial? What for? Antacid tablets? I know where I'd rather be, Ken. See you tonight. My treat."

Quentin Quinn slammed down the handset of his telephone as if his negotiations for world peace had just been cut brutally short and shouted, "Mrs. Barry! It's time to write."

Was he going to remain seated and bellow to her as if he was calling the cows home? She slowly got to her feet, smoothed down her skirt, and walked into his office.

"Shall I boil the kettle for another cup?"

"Good idea. Coffee will help get those creative juices flowing." He stood, removed his suit jacket, and held it out on two fingers.

She stared at him. He stared back.

"Yes, Mr. Quinn?"

"My jacket."

"I believe you'll find a hanger on the back of your office door."

When he continued to stare at her, she took the jacket and hung it on the aforementioned hanger on the hook on the back of his office door.

"What's this?" He tapped a finger on a manila folder in his in-tray. On it, Martha had written the word *Casting*. She'd compiled the biographies and headshots of the actors he was being asked to consider for various roles in the new drama. Mr. Rutherford Hayes had sent a memo to Quentin Quinn with his suggestions.

She lifted it from the tray and passed it to him. When he flipped it open, the photographs and papers slipped out onto the carpet. He made no effort to pick them up. As she gathered them together, Martha said, "You'll need to choose the cast. You will also need to book the studio to record the first week of episodes, working back from the airtime schedule. Our first episode goes to air on Monday, June 25. So we'll need to record the first week's episodes four weeks from tomorrow. That'll give us a week of post-production time."

No response. Quentin Quinn's Adam's apple bobbed at his throat like a sailboat on the harbor. "Four weeks from tomorrow? That's sooner than I expected. Especially since we don't have scripts. Or actors." He held a hand to his forehead as if a sudden headache were about to crack his skull wide open.

Martha had learned over the years, perhaps as a mother might from teaching her children, that most often it paid to let others discover things for themselves. Those who believed they had already mastered a skill or pastime or activity that they were in actual fact undertaking for the first time—those who believed that confidence alone would see them triumph—needed to understand from the outset exactly how much they *didn't* know. And how much they had yet to learn.

She was quite experienced in rescuing men who had been appointed far above their level of competence and had made a vow to herself on the tram into work that morning that she would let Quentin Quinn learn for himself. After all, she wasn't his mother. He had already spent far too much time skylarking about with nameplates on doors and complaints to friends about aged secretaries and not enough actually looking at everything in his in-tray.

But she was far too polite to point that out.

She sighed. "I suggest we book the studio and a technician for four hours to record five fifteen-minute episodes. Will that be sufficient, Mr. Quinn?"

Quentin Quinn's legs seemed to wobble and he leaned forward, gripping the edge of his desk. "Four hours, did you say? Four weeks from tomorrow? We can't push it out a little more? And we can make the episodes longer, I'm sure of it. I mean, fifteen minutes isn't long enough for a decent drama, is it?"

"Each episode is very strictly fifteen minutes, Mr. Quinn. Not sixteen, not fourteen minutes and fifteen seconds, not even fifteen minutes and thirty seconds, or there will be letters to parliament."

"Letters to parliament?"

Martha nodded. "Nothing must interrupt the timing of the program after ours. If that starts late, then the news might run late and it absolutely, positively must go to air at two o'clock on the dot. People set their watches by our news, you know."

He huffed. "Of course I know that."

"And once you've cast the roles, there will be contracts to draw up and get signed. It will be important to take into account that if some of our talent are working on other programs, which they often do because the actor's life is a peripatetic one, they'll have to juggle any recordings and rehearsals they might be committed to for the commercial radio broadcasters."

Quentin Quinn perched on the edge of his desk and lit a cig-arette with jittery fingers. He then swore creatively under his breath.

Martha was no longer upset by such fruity language. It was the lingua franca of hotheaded and demanding creative types. Every beautiful flourish and economical sentence that fell from the lips of a writer seemed to be accompanied, in the next breath, by a short, sharp exclamation. They were words that would never in a million years appear on the radio. Free-flowing language came with the territory, she had realized many years ago, having worked so long with men under pressure from deadlines and writer's block and complaints and sore heads from too much beer the night before and apparently demanding girlfriends or wives and bosses who'd never made a program in their life weighing in on creative decisions. Then there were the constant grumbles about pay, which amused Martha because they were paid men's rates, not women's, and in her opinion they should be more than happy about that. No, she'd come to believe creative types simply liked to complain.

"I suppose I'd better get to work."

Martha nodded to her desk in the adjoining room. "Ready when you are, Mr. Quinn."

....

Two hours, four cups of coffee (him), and one cup of tea (her) later, Martha was still sitting in front of a blank page.

For his part, Quentin Quinn had almost worn a running track in the carpet.

"I've got it!" He suddenly stilled and snapped his fingers, opened his mouth to speak. And then promptly lost his inspiration.

After another ten minutes, and against her better judgment, she threw him a bone. "There needs to be an opening announcement, Mr. Quinn. So people know what they're listening to. For instance, before *Blue Hills*, the announcer says, 'The ABC presents *Blue Hills* by Gwen Meredith' and then that lovely, stirring theme starts up. The music tells them it's time for *Blue Hills*. What do you have in mind for *As the Sun Sets*?"

Quentin Quinn chewed on his bottom lip. "'The ABC presents *As the Sun Sets* by Quentin Quinn'?"

"That's a start, certainly." Martha pressed her fingers to the keyboard and typed his first ten words. What a cracking beginning.

"And what do we do about the music . . . ?"

She sat back in her chair. "Perhaps you can search the music library for a piece that encapsulates what you imagine for *As the Sun Sets*."

Quentin Quinn's eyes widened as if a light bulb had gone off over his head. "I'll do just that." He paused. "How do I do that?"

"The music library is on the second floor. Ask for Mr. Pattison, and if you can't find him, ask for April."

"Right. Of course."

To men like Quentin Quinn, Martha was nothing but an old woman with her hair in a neat bun at her neck, a brown woolen suit, and sensible shoes. He would have no idea—and no curiosity—about the fact that she had worked everywhere and knew almost everything about how the broadcaster operated. No, he would not think that about her at all. How had she become invisible and indispensable all at the same time?

He snapped his fingers and then jabbed a finger in the direction of Martha's typewriter.

"Get ready," he announced.

"I'm ready," she replied.

"Type," he mumbled and then paused. "I need a cigarette," he said before scurrying back to his office looking like a young boy who'd just lost his puppy.

One of the most important jobs of the producer and writer was to actually write the scripts and run the production. It was as simple and as complicated as that.

And this was only day one.

By Friday, they had two pages of script, which would equate to— Martha worked it out at three words per second—four and a half minutes of drama.

It was becoming evident to Martha that Quentin Quinn was almost fatally ill-equipped for the job. She allowed herself to feel a pang of sympathy for him. No, it wasn't exactly a pang. A mere twinge, perhaps. He was a young man thrown in at the deep end and, given his lack of experience, both in drama and in life, it should have been no surprise to anyone that he was floundering.

Martha took a clean sheet of paper and slid it into the typewriter, turning the carriage until it appeared at the front. She hit the carriage return and began typing a list of all that still needed to be done—things she was certain Rutherford Hayes would ask about when he sauntered past the office and popped his head in, as he was wont to do, and which more often than not set the producers and writers into spasms of anxiety.

Budget breakdown
Cast
Auditions
Offers and contracts
Book studio
Rehearsing and recording schedule

And then she sighed and let herself feel a prickle of anxiety about the next one:

Scripts

"Miss Berry." Martha looked up from her typewritten list. Rutherford Hayes was standing in the doorway, his eyebrows raised and a question on his lips. She clutched a hand to her chest. Had she conjured him out of thin air?

"Yes, Mr. Hayes?" That prickle of anxiety became a shudder of doubt.

"Is Quinn in?"

"I'm sorry, no. He's at lunch."

Mr. Hayes checked his watch. Martha knew without glancing at her own that it was already half past two. Quentin Quinn had disappeared at half past eleven and hadn't returned to the office. He'd been in his new job for five days and had already made a

habit of the long lunch, and while it was none of Martha's business, he had taken to returning from lunch in his cups.

"Still?"

Martha neither confirmed nor replied.

"I see. I need to talk to him about scripts for *As the Sun Sets*."

She nodded.

"Just to have a look over them. See he's on the right track, that
sort of thing. Has he talked to those actors I recommended?"

Martha held an impassive expression. "I believe that's next on
his agenda."

Mr. Hayes pushed his glasses up his nose with an index finger.
"Right."

"Shall I make a note for Mr. Quinn to come to your office when
he returns?" Martha had covered for men so many times before
that the rules of being a secretary were ingrained in her. Pretend
to know nothing. Don't pass on any information that might get
you into trouble with those who had secrets to hide. Mum's the
word and all that.

Mr. Hayes cleared his throat. Since she'd worked for him when
Miss Jones was on her Tasmanian bus holiday, she'd learned it
was his way of masking his annoyance.

"Thank you."

"Have a good weekend, Mr. Hayes."

"You too, Miss Berry."

As soon as he'd walked into the corridor, Martha sat back in
her chair and wished she was religious so she could pray for some
progress.

Where on earth was Quentin Quinn?

Chapter 4

IN WHICH MARTHA BERRY CELEBRATES A SIGNIFICANT BIRTHDAY.

Happy birthday, dear Martha, happy birthday to you!"

A whooping cheer went up around the room, and then Mrs. Tilley started up again. "Why was she born so beautiful, why was she born at all?" And when Mrs. Tilley waved her encouragement to the guests crowded into the Berrys' kitchen, they all joined in for the final lines of the verse. "Hooray for Martha, hooray at last, hooray for Martha, she's a horse's arse!"

Martha laughed and laughed—mostly at the thought of Violet singing the word *arse*—and when she realized everyone else was, too, a wave of contentment settled over her. She felt happy. Friends and cake. What else was there to be had in life?

"Trust you, Mrs. Tilley," Mrs. Ward gasped, trying to catch her breath after laughing so hard. "You can't be singing that song in front of all these people."

"Oh yes, I can!" Mrs. Tilley slapped her friend on the shoulder. "It's Martha's birthday. The *big* one. And anyway, what's wrong with saying *arse*? Everyone's got one."

From her seat at the head of the kitchen table, Violet tapped a knife on a teacup to quiet everyone down. "It's time to cut the cake, Martha."

Violet passed the knife and Martha held it over the cake Mrs. Tilley had baked that morning: a Victoria sponge filled with freshly whipped cream and half a jar of Mrs. Ward's strawberry jam from the summer before. On top, the iced numbers five and zero sat plump and shakily drawn, slightly askew, and rosettes of icing decorated the edge. It wasn't fancy. Martha didn't want or need fancy to celebrate her fiftieth birthday. The cake was plain and simple, just as she was. She loved that Mrs. Tilley knew that about her.

Martha closed her eyes to make a wish and held the knife over the sponge.

"Don't touch the bottom!" May called out with a start. "It's bad luck."

"That's true," April added, twirling a curl around her finger. "Seven years of it."

"I'm sure that's an old wives' tale," June piped up.

"Would you risk it?" April replied, aghast. "I wouldn't. What if my bad luck meant I never found a husband?"

"You call *that* bad luck?" June huffed and crossed her arms over her ample chest.

Martha had only recently made the acquaintance of the three young women. The girls had walked into the staff cafeteria on their first day looking positively terrified. They had all started working at the broadcaster on the same day as part of a new intake of secretaries. There had been a recruitment drive to fill positions vacated by girls who'd either recently married or moved to the television department, in readiness for the beginning of television transmission in September.

Martha hadn't been offered the chance to move over to television. She supposed the powers that be had taken one look at her and judged that she would be retiring any day now. Or that at her age she wouldn't be able to come to terms with all the newfangled technology being installed to broadcast television signals around the country. They probably imagined she was also befuddled by the telephone, the typewriter, and the sewing machine.

She'd dubbed the young women the Calendar Girls because, well, it was obvious, really. April, May, and June were more than half her age, but that hadn't seemed to stop them from looking forward to her company—and her to theirs—when they met at lunchtimes in the staff cafeteria. It had done Martha good to hear the opinions and views of people so much younger than herself, those who hadn't lived through the war in the same way, who'd been at school when VJ Day had been declared.

Martha pushed the knife through the sponge and made her wish. Once upon a time she might have hoped for a husband and children. Now, she dreamed of a home library full of books and the time to read them.

"I didn't touch the bottom, May," she announced, and another round of cheering commenced before Mrs. Tilley and Mrs. Ward bustled about slicing the sponge, handing out plates, and pouring more cups of tea. The noise and laughter and chatting spun around Martha, and she took a breath to settle herself.

She was fifty years old today. In May 1906, she had come into the world silent and barely breathing and, according to Violet, had needed a good slap right on her bottom from the midwife to force that first cry from her lips.

"You were never a complainer," Violet told her whenever she reminisced about her daughter's childhood. "Even as a young thing. You never threw tantrums like some other children do, you know, flailing about on the floor in the butcher shop or at the grocer's. Oh, those poor mothers. You were such a good baby. I could always settle you with a story. How you loved your stories. And in the pram, you'd lie there and be perfectly entertained just looking up at the clouds. I always wondered what you were thinking. As soon as you could walk, you would stay right by my side and hold my hand the whole way. Later, when it was just the two of us . . . well . . . you seemed to grow up overnight. Bless your father." Violet still teared up at the mention of her late husband.

Every birthday, Martha wished her father was there to celebrate with them. There had been a hole in the Berry family and in their hearts for so many years. She had been so young when he died that she didn't remember a voice or the feel of his arms about her or the smell of his tobacco smoke or the greasy touch of his hair oil on the antimacassars or what his work shoes looked like when he kicked them off at the end of the day. His early and unexpected death had left Martha an only child when she was too young to speak.

"Happy birthday, Martha." Mrs. Tilley's daughter Dymphna, Martha's childhood best friend, sidled up to Martha with her husband by her side. "Do you feel like an old lady now?"

Martha threw back her head and laughed. "As a matter of fact, I do, especially on cold mornings."

"I'll be looking to you for advice. My birthday's coming up soon and then I'll be fifty too. And a grandmother not long after that!"

Martha's heart was suddenly full of joy for her old friend. "Beryl's having a baby? Oh, congratulations."

Dymphna looked proud as punch, and her husband, Cyril, the same. He stroked his mustache proudly and puffed out his chest. "It'll be a boy. I'm sure of it."

"How can you be sure?" Martha smiled. "It's all a matter of chance, isn't it?"

"It's tradition! Every firstborn in her husband's family since Federation has been a boy. And he's going to be named after me." He puffed out his chest even farther, if that was possible. "Cyril Hector. Now that's a name."

Dymphna rolled her eyes. "Love, no mother wants to call her boy Cyril these days. They want modern names, like Peter or Stephen or Andrew. David's nice too." Dymphna batted a hand as if to brush away the idea. "And anyway, it won't be up to us. It'll be up to Beryl and her husband. Although why the father should have a say when we do all the work having the baby, I'll never know!" She chuckled at her own joke. "Martha, you and your mum will be invited to the christening, of course. It wouldn't be the same if you both weren't there."

"I wouldn't miss it for the world. When's the baby due?"

"February next year. Just think, 1957! I can't believe how the years have flown by since we used to play hide-and-seek up and down the street."

"And Mr. Lane used to run out of his front yard waving his broom at us shouting about the Huns." They shared an understanding look. It had been funny when they were children but wasn't now that they were older with an adult understanding of what Mr. Lane might have been forced to see and do during the first war.

"It seems like yesterday," Martha said. How had so much time passed in the blink of an eye?

Dymphna chuckled. "I've already started knitting, and so has Mum. You know what she's like."

"I do indeed. I'm sure she'll smock up the most beautiful christening gown imaginable."

"I'll be sure to send that invitation, Martha. Happy birthday." Dymphna and Cyril moved to the kitchen table for more cake and Martha turned to see April, May, and June standing before her, smiling nervously.

"Did you all have enough to eat?" Martha asked.

April patted her flat stomach and then primped her blonde locks, looking around to see if anyone had noticed a hair out of place. "If I eat any more cake or scones, I'll be bursting out of this girdle."

Martha pretended not to notice June rolling her eyes.

"Would any of you like to take something home for later?"

"Oh no, we couldn't," May replied, looking shocked at the mere suggestion. "We wouldn't want to put you out."

June huffed. "Speak for yourself. I'd love a butter biscuit or two."

"Please take whatever you like. There's so much food left."

May cleared her throat as if she was about to make a grand announcement. "We'd just like to say we were so glad to be invited to your party. It's been ever so lovely."

April nodded her agreement. "I don't know anyone else who's fifty years old. Other than my grandparents, I mean, and I've only got two of those left. I used to have four."

"Everyone has four grandparents, April." June rolled her eyes again.

"You're very welcome, all of you," Martha replied.

"I hope you like your present," May said, her eyebrows lifting into her hairline. "It's *Sense and Sensibility* by Jane Austen. It reminded me of you because, well, you're just so sensible, Miss Berry. You always have the best advice. I hope you like it."

"May!" June frowned. She always slumped her shoulders but

she was still the tallest person in the room. "It was supposed to be a surprise! That's why it's wrapped up in paper."

Martha smiled. Of course she liked it. She'd read it once a year for forty years. But she was far too polite to tell the girls that and, anyway, her well-thumbed copy was almost falling to bits. As Austen herself had written in that very book, it isn't what we say or think that defines us, but what we do. And what the Calendar Girls had done was very thoughtful indeed.

"You couldn't have chosen better," Martha reassured them. "I'm an Austen devotee."

"We know how much you like reading," May said, smiling broadly. "Remember when we saw you in the cafeteria that first week we started at the ABC? There you were, sitting in the corner all by yourself, reading your book. And you didn't mind at all when we asked if we could join you. You seemed like the only friendly face in the place."

Martha remembered. She had been reading *Middlemarch* by George Eliot.

"Thank you for the very thoughtful gift, and thank you for coming. I expect I'll see you on Monday."

"I hope your new position on *As the Sun Sets* is going well," May said with barely concealed awe. "You're so lucky to be working on a new serial."

April giggled. "Is Quentin Quinn *very* handsome?"

"Won't *quite* handsome do?" June added.

Martha thought it polite to be diplomatic about such things. She could never find someone so incompetent the slightest bit attractive. And besides, he was young enough to be her son.

"You'll have to stop by my office and judge for yourself."

The Calendar Girls smiled broadly—even June, which Martha

thought was a breakthrough. She was most certainly a glass-half-empty kind of girl, and Martha couldn't help but wonder why so young a person seemed to carry all life's miseries on her broad shoulders. As they moved to go, June cast a yearning gaze toward the still-abundant display on the kitchen table.

"Please take some cake before you go, all of you," Martha said. "We seem to have enough for the whole street."

June let herself smile and her cheeks blushed beetroot red.

Chapter 5

IN WHICH MARTHA BERRY PROVIDES SOME
SAGE ADVICE TO HER YOUNG FRIENDS.

By the end of his second week, Quentin Quinn still hadn't completed any scripts.

Martha wondered if he understood the principle that words were a vital part of the process of creating scripted drama. Without words, there would be no need for actors to speak, and without words and actors, well, there would be a whole lot of drama but not the kind that would be broadcast over the radio.

On Friday, she had waited at her desk all morning for Quentin Quinn to arrive so they could get to work, but by lunchtime he still hadn't appeared and hadn't left any kind of message for her as to his whereabouts. Every man she'd ever worked for had been time-challenged. And they had all been men, of course, those producers.

The ABC employed a handful of women in senior roles, but Martha had never worked with any of them. They were clustered in areas management considered most suited to their talents— women's programming and education—and she had never been sent to those departments to assist. The powers that be most likely believed that because they were women they could do their own typing and make their own coffee without the need for extra secretarial help. Martha's best chance of seeing those elusive women in the flesh was in the staff cafeteria. She'd never spotted Kay Kinane, the very experienced producer who had recently set up the ABC's television training school. Rumor was that she was heading off to produce a new program for women to be called *Woman's World*, hosted by Mary Rossi. It sounded very exciting and Martha knew by its title alone that it would be a program her mother would very much enjoy. Once they'd bought a television, of course.

Therése Denny, whom Martha had shared a lift with once or twice, had sailed off to London in 1949, after years of working as a stenographer, to learn all she could about radio production. There were rumors that she was going to return to work in television, but they were only rumors and, anyway, Martha wondered how anyone could tear themselves away from the bright lights of London to return to Australia.

And who in the organization didn't know about Joyce Wiggins? She had become something of a legend, causing some kind of scandal everywhere she went. The men in the ABC were simultaneously envious of her illustrious career—writing for the British Army's Psychological Warfare Division during the war and working for international broadcasters—and then furious that she was clearly so much more experienced than they were. A secretary was never going to be a threat to them. Someone like Joyce Wiggins was always going to be.

Once, Martha had been reading *The Mill on the Floss* when Joyce had stomped across the cafeteria wearing a pale-colored fur coat and a jaunty straw hat. Little wisps of her fringe could be seen under the brim and she wore a scowl on her thin lips. She had clattered her cup of tea onto the next table and sworn under her breath. Martha had looked up in shock. She'd never heard a woman swear.

"'We don't give those jobs to women,'" Joyce had huffed. "I've never heard anything so ridiculous in my life. 'You might get married.' Not on your life."

Martha had leaned over. "Are you all right?"

Joyce had narrowed her brown eyes at Martha. "Don't you ever get sick of the incompetent men who run this place?"

Martha had been far too polite to reply. Her lack of reaction seemed to take the wind out of Joyce's sails. Of course, Martha had those frustrations but she expressed them to no one. One didn't go around criticizing one's superiors, no matter how much one might have felt like it. It simply wasn't done.

"Oh, never mind." Joyce had shot her a scowl and grumpily bitten into her sandwich.

Martha knew her place. She was there to assist those who made the big, important, creative decisions. She—and the new crop like April, May, and June—was a secretary and would always be a secretary. It was only the most exceptional women—like Gwen Meredith and Joyce Wiggins and Kay Kinane and Thérése Denny—who would climb the ranks. In all her years, Martha had worked for a succession of men, each younger than the last, most coming directly from Sydney University with a degree in something or other, usually English or philosophy, and a relationship with radio that extended to listening to it in the homes they still lived in with their parents in a leafy part of Sydney with a view of the harbor.

Of course, they didn't need typing skills or management credentials or any familiarity at all with a studio, a script, or even a microphone. They were young men with promise and intelligence and, most importantly, the immense good fortune of knowing just the right person—a neighbor, an old school chum's father, an old school chum—who would, at the appropriate time at the club or the Members' Stand at the Sydney Cricket Ground, whisper something in the right ear just as the broadcaster was inducting a new intake of producers. It was believed that these young men were supplied with the intelligence and acumen and broad minds needed to work on programs that soothed the souls of the masses, as well as educating and entertaining those same souls.

But they couldn't do that alone. Every producer needed a girl to assist him with the more mundane office tasks such as typing, creating schedules and casting lists, searching out telephone numbers and addresses, fetching lunch from the staff cafeteria when he was far too busy to do it himself, buying his cigarettes, picking up his freshly pressed shirts from the dry cleaner, and sometimes even lining up to buy tickets for a play.

Martha had done it all in all the years she'd been at the broad-caster. She'd raced from the ABC's headquarters in Kings Cross to David Jones on Elizabeth Street to buy last-minute silk scarves for those who'd forgotten their wives' birthdays or bottles of French perfume when they remembered their mistresses' (except for during the war, when French perfume had been as scarce as hen's teeth). She'd brewed perhaps a million pots of tea and made endless cups of coffee to dull the thud of the morning-after hang-overs. She'd called the front bar of the local watering hole more times than she could count to let the front barman know that so-and-so was wanted urgently and if he happened to be there (which he always was), would the barman be so kind as to please suggest he finish his drink and return to the office promptly.

At work, she had mothered one baby-faced producer after

another. At home, she daughtered. Lunchtimes in the cafeteria
with April, May, and June were a respite she looked forward to
more than she could say.

She glanced at her wristwatch. It was half past twelve and there
was still no sign of the elusive Quentin Quinn. Martha decided it
was time to head to the staff cafeteria for lunch. A cup of tea or two
and a chapter of *Jane Eyre* might help settle her annoyance.

"Miss Berry!"

Martha glanced across the cafeteria and their three smiling
faces shone back at her from over the heads of the other diners.
She smiled to herself. There would be no chapters today, but she
found herself not minding at all. She made her way to the table,
and as she skirted around other tables and chairs diners never
pushed in, she picked up snatches of conversations about the
Cold War (the news department), the impending flood (the rural
department), the Olympics (the sporting department), clouds of
cigarette smoke, and off-color jokes (all of the men). May stood
quickly and pulled back the chair next to her, urging Martha
to sit.

"Hello, Miss Berry," she said. "We were hoping we might see
you for lunch today."

"Hello, girls," she replied. Seeing them was the balm she
needed. When she was seated, she undid the clasp on her handbag and brought out a waxed paper bundle. It crinkled as she
opened it. Inside were four neat triangles of sandwich.

"Cheese and pickle again, Miss Berry?" June asked, peering
at the sandwich over her cat's-eye glasses. The thickness of the
lenses magnified her eyes in such a way that people were always
startled by how huge they appeared to be.

"Yes." Martha took a polite bite. "I find it the best combination
when I have to prepare my lunch in the mornings. Two thin slices

of cheese with pickle spread between them. Ham and tomato is a bit of a disaster, I'm afraid. The bread becomes rather soggy. What's that you're having, April?"

April sighed. "Two Ryvita biscuits and a boiled egg. I'm watching what I eat."

"Oh, pffft." June huffed. "As if *you* have to."

April looked affronted. "I *do* have to. I read somewhere that the Dior models all eat crispbread before they glide down the catwalk. It's the only way they manage to fit into those dresses."

"That and corsets, of course," Martha added.

"But look at your waist!" May exclaimed. "It must be only twenty-two inches, if that."

"Exactly! And I need it to be eighteen at the absolute most." April propped her hands at her belt. Her fingers almost met in the middle. Martha wondered how much smaller April could actually get before she was unable to breathe or digest any food. "These are perfectly fine, but I read about a slimming biscuit in the *Weekly*. I thought I might try it. It helps you lose unsightly, distressing fat."

From the corner of her eye, Martha noticed June rearrange her cardigan where it pulled tightly over her bosom. She sincerely hoped June wasn't comparing herself with the genetically blessed April, but it was a vain hope. It would be impossible not to in her shoes.

April continued, oblivious. "It's specifically made for overweight sufferers. It's slimmed thousands of women, apparently. All you have to do is eat the biscuit with a cup of tea or coffee and it takes away all your cravings for anything sweet."

"Can you clarify?" Martha said. "You eat a biscuit to slim down?"

April brightened. "Yes! And all those horrible cravings for the

fat formers, like sweets, cakes, and bread, go and all your unwanted fat disappears!"

"I'm guessing it's not a *chocolate* biscuit then," June said with
a grumble.

"I expect you're right," May replied, looking dejected.

"Or I might try Ford Pills," April added. "Or there's Beecham's
too."

"My grandmother takes those," May said. "They help her with
her bilious attacks and stomach upsets. And her headaches too.
She gets a lot of headaches. My father says that's because she
complains so much. She says it's because she lives with us."

June leaned across the table and pinched April's arm just above
her elbow.

"Ouch!"

"According to my pinch test, there is absolutely not even one
extra pound on you. All I felt there was skin. So stop it with this
nonsense. You're perfectly fine the way you are."

April shook her head adamantly. "No, I'm not."

"I wish *I* could have a piece of cake." May dropped her chin in
her hand. "Or two."

Martha turned to her. "Why can't you have a piece of cake?"

"Because my problem is, Miss Berry, that I can never stop at
just one. One slice becomes two and then two becomes five, and
I feel so terrible about having scoffed all that cake that I go to bed
feeling sick and find myself having to start dieting all over again
the next day." May leaned close to whisper and April and June
came in closer, too, as if their friend was about to reveal a secret.

"And I simply have to stop scoffing cake because . . ." She paused
and looked around to ensure no one was listening in. "Chubby
girls don't get themselves engaged, do they?" She was trying ever
so hard not to cry, but her trembling lower lip gave her away.

April gasped. "You have a sweetheart?"

"No. And that's the problem, isn't it?" May was so dejected. Martha tried to remember what she had been like as a nineteen-year-old in that decade between the beginning of the Depression and the war. It seemed a lifetime ago. So many dreams had come and gone since then, but she didn't recall that any of them had involved sporting a smaller waist.

"My father says I'm too chubby to get a bloke, and if I can't get one, how will I ever get a fiancé or a husband or a home of my own with all this unsightly fat?" May poked the soft folds of the fabric of her skirt and her belly underneath. "That's what the magazines call it."

"I'm sure your father means well," April said kindly.

"He only wants what's best for you," June added.

Martha finished her sandwich and cleared her throat. Men could be so horrid and unthinking. Even fathers. "Sometimes men don't think before they speak, May. What he should have pointed out to you is that you're a smart and sensible young woman with your whole life ahead of you. You have a kind heart and a generous disposition. You have a gay laugh and a beautiful smile. Anyone who meets you can't help but be taken in by those admirable qualities."

May sniffed and dabbed at her eyes with a neatly pressed handkerchief she'd tugged from inside the sleeve of her cardigan. "That's very nice of you to say, Miss Berry, but . . ."

Martha lowered her chin and met May's watery eyes, hoping some of the wisdom she'd accrued during her own fifty years on earth was evident in what she was about to say. "Wouldn't we all like to be something we're not? Taller? Shorter?" She tried not to look at June as she said it because June was almost five foot ten inches and Martha knew she was already self-conscious about towering over most people she met. Martha wanted to reassure her that she would become used to being so tall for a woman and that one day she might find it quite effective when dealing with men's shortcomings. "If we're a brunette, we want to be a blonde. If we're a blonde, we want to be a redhead. If our hair is as straight as candles, we want a wave. We hate our freckles and our toes and our long fingers or our short ones."

June held out her hand and splayed her ringless fingers. "My mother always said these long fingers were perfect for playing the piano."

"Do you play?" Martha asked.

June slipped her hands back under the table. "We couldn't afford a piano. Or lessons."

"But they're excellent for typing, June," April told her with an encouraging smile.

"What did you want to be when you were young, Miss Berry?" May asked. The three women waited while Martha thought.

She didn't take any offense. She was well aware she wasn't young anymore. Her childbearing days—if she had been in any position to have children, that is—were almost over. She had in the past few years discovered gray strands in her mousy-brown hair, which she didn't fuss with trying to hide or disguise with one of the new at-home hair-coloring treatments that were becoming the fashion for young women who wanted to see what it was like being a Marilyn Monroe platinum blonde or a Rita Hayworth brunette. Now that she'd been prescribed reading glasses, she had discovered hitherto invisible lines on her face and wiry hairs on her chin, and sometimes her knees creaked when she got out of bed in the mornings. She looked on at the fancies of the young ones with a bemused curiosity: the new songs from America that dominated the hit parade and the adoration with which young women admired flamboyant local singer Johnny O'Keefe. Martha didn't pay much attention to the latest fashions in clothes or shoes, either, as a fifty-year-old unmarried woman shouldn't.

But there was a time when she had.

Her first crush had been Len Booth from up the road, who'd been six years older than her and as handsome as any crooner she swooned over on the radio (for she imagined they were all as tall, dark, and handsome as the men depicted in the short stories in the *Women's Weekly*). Len was tall, taller than she was, and as she stood at five foot seven inches, that was very important to her. She'd swooned when he'd knocked on their front door in full AIF uniform in March 1918 to say goodbye to her and her mother, for he was shipping out to France that day.

"Be brave, love," Violet had told him after he'd leaned down and kissed her on the cheek. Martha had only lifted her eyes from her saggy socks and her dirty knees to look up at him, and he'd grinned at her and winked. Just at her. Not her mother. All the blood had whooshed from her head down into her shoes, and she'd had to grip her mother's hand for she felt as if she might faint.

"Bye, Len," she'd managed to whisper.

And as he'd walked away, he'd paused and turned back and doffed his hat to her.

He was killed a month later. Martha had never forgotten the sound of the sobbing from next door, and not just from Len's mother. A shadow had been cast over the house that had never lifted. People came and went with food and flowers, and when it came time for a memorial service for Len—for he'd been blown to bits and since his bits couldn't be sent home, there would be no funeral—Martha was forbidden from going because everyone thought a funeral was no place for a child. She couldn't complain for she still felt like a child then, with an innocent's confusion about what had happened. Len's mother and father never got over the loss of their only son, and soon after getting the telegram they moved to live nearer their second daughter and her children in Bowral.

That was when Mr. and Mrs. Tilley moved in next door and re-placed the grief in the street with laughter and the sound of new children's voices and hopscotch squares on the street and a billy-cart that zoomed so fast at the hands of the Tilleys' oldest boy that Martha had always been too afraid to ride in it. The other children called her a scaredy-cat and meowed at her, but she wouldn't be persuaded to put her life in someone else's hands or in their cobbled-together contraption. Her own father's death had taught her that she didn't need to sail to France to be blown to bits and die. She could just as easily get a toothache and die right there in Sydney.

Then there'd been Ern. Martha had just started work as a sec-retary at an import-export business at Millers Point and had taken to stopping by Mack's Butchers on Hastings Street on the way home to pick up something for dinner for her and her mother. Ern had just been taken on as an apprentice butcher and he had such a charming way about him that every evening the counter was three deep in ladies. Martha's height had been an advantage—one she hadn't appreciated until then—as she was more easily able to peer above all the hats and waving gloved hands to cast her eyes on Ern's easy smile.

Perhaps that was why he'd noticed her in the first place. Be-cause she was so tall. It couldn't have been anything else. Martha had always thought of herself as rather plain looking. Her hair was an ordinary brown, cut in a short bob like every other woman's, which meant the ends poked out from the bottom of her cloche hat just like everyone else's. Her nose was ordinary. Her brown eyes were ordinary. She had neither full, romantic lips nor thin ones. Her nose was neither too prominent nor turned up like a pug's or aquiline like a Roman's. She had never had to worry about eating too much cake back then, as Violet always teased her about having the appetite of a bird, which was her good fortune during the Depression years. But perhaps it had been a collection of all the ordinary things about her that had caught Ern's eye.

"Hello, love," he'd called out with a wink. "What can I get you today?"

She'd asked for four sausages but he'd given her five, which she'd only realized when she walked into the kitchen and unwrapped the butcher paper to see the fifth sitting there alongside the others, like a handful of fat little juicy fingers. When she opened her purse to check her change, she realized with a heart beating faster that he hadn't even charged her extra.

It hadn't been long—three weeks, perhaps—before Ern had asked Martha if she was free to see a picture the next Saturday night. She didn't have to double-check if she already had plans because she never had plans, and she said yes and was certain she was blushing when she answered because her cheeks suddenly burned.

That Saturday night they'd gone to see a picture at the new Century Theatre on George Street and he'd kissed her and she hadn't minded because she'd never been kissed before and he was so handsome and she felt important somehow that Ern from Mack's—the best butcher in Sydney, or so the sign on the window said—had chosen her out of all the young ladies who walked into the shop. And she'd liked kissing; the strange tingle of it, the graze of his freshly shaven cheek against hers, the smell of his hair oil, the worn wool of his suit jacket under her fingers as she held on to his lapels to stop herself from floating into the air right there in the cinema and butting her head against the dusty chandelier hanging from the ceiling.

For three Saturday nights in a row, they'd gone to the pictures and he'd kissed her. Martha couldn't even remember what the films were, and when she returned home each evening and Violet asked her what the picture was and if she'd enjoyed it, Martha made something up and hoped it was enough to satisfy her mother's curiosity. She didn't like lying, but a lie was easier than the truth. She knew Violet would worry if her daughter admitted to kissing a man she barely knew in the back row of a cinema. It was all Martha could do to fend off her mother's insistence that there be a chaperone, or at least another girl on a double date with a friend of Ern's.

On their fourth date, Ern had slipped a hand up between her legs and pushed his fingers against her underwear and she'd gasped and he'd said against her mouth, "It's all right, love," and it was then she had an inkling that he couldn't actually remember her name.

On Tuesday of the next week, as she was waiting in line for mincemeat to make a meatloaf, but really to see Ern again, a woman entered the shop screaming in fright and all the customers collectively gasped and turned as one, and the woman, who was Martha's mother's age and still wearing her apron and slippers, gasped, clamped a hand against her heart, and shrieked, "Ern! The baby's on its way!"

Ern turned white as a sheet before scrambling to untie his apron and racing out of the shop faster than someone could say "Fire!"

That was the end of Ern.

There had been one other man since then, just in time to stop

Martha from giving in to the idea of never finding love. Trevor from the payroll department at work had asked her out for afternoon tea and she'd happily said yes. He was a quiet man in his midthirties who'd worked his way up to having the responsibility of handing out the pay envelopes to staff each payday. On Thursdays, Martha queued up at the pay department as all the employees formed an orderly line with great anticipation. Some of the male staff would whoop and head straight out to the pub. Martha wondered how many pounds, shillings, and pence would make it home to their wives for the household essentials and how many pounds, shillings, and pence would be poured down their throats before closing time, because standing in a smoky bar was preferable to going home to a houseful of children and a harried wife. Martha rarely ventured into such establishments. The ladies' lounge and a glass of sherry held little appeal.

When Martha received her pay envelope, her name typed neatly on the front (Berry, Martha, Miss), she would thank Trevor with a smile, return to her desk, and slip the envelope into her handbag.

It was only later that night, after dinner at the dining table, that she would divide her money into piles for the household (groceries and bills), saving (one pound each week, which she could manage because she and her mother weren't paying rent), and sundries. Martha would never think of them as luxuries—luxuries were fur coats and silk scarves and handmade shoes—but she liked having a little left over to buy the *Women's Weekly* every Wednesday, the personal items she needed from the chemist, new stockings when hers could no longer be repaired without looking shabby, a small bag of candies for a Saturday evening treat for her mother, and the occasional cinema ticket for herself.

Nowadays, the Calendar Girls went to the cinema at least once a week, even on their meager wages, and occasionally they were able to entice Martha along to see the latest Frank Sinatra or Bob Hope film. There was always another *Road to* somewhere. James Stewart was Martha's favorite. She'd had a crush on him since *Mr. Smith Goes to Washington* back in 1939. There was something about his voice she'd always loved, and although she had no idea of his height in real life, he seemed to lope along, which indicated to Martha that he must be quite tall.

Trevor had been quiet in a friendly sort of way, had always been neatly dressed in a three-piece suit, even on the most humid of Sydney's summer days, and had been lovely company. He even enjoyed spending the evening at home with Martha and Violet playing cards and listening to the radio. He always brought along a bunch of flowers for her mother and a bottle of sherry to share.

But it hadn't been long before that first flush of attraction had faded into more of a friendship than anything else. Martha tried her best but she couldn't feel much of anything when he kissed her, although she wasn't sure how she was expected to when his kisses were mere pecks on the cheek and a quick squeeze of her hand. At their age—she was twenty-nine and three-quarters and he was thirty-two—she couldn't be expected to feel as she had when Len had winked at her before he was killed by the Germans, or when Ern had pressed his fingers up against her underpants at the cinema.

Trevor was nice but that wasn't enough. She had too much to give up to settle for nice. Martha had decided that she'd lived a long time without a man in her life and settling for nice wasn't enough to resign from her job for, because she would have to if she let things run their expected course and married Trevor. Women in the Commonwealth Public Service couldn't keep their jobs if they were married. She might have given it all up if Jimmy Stewart had proposed to her, but not for anyone else she'd ever met.

She sometimes wished there had been grandchildren for Violet to coddle. Her mother would have made a wonderful grandmother. Violet had missed out not only on the love they would have shared with her, but on all those little rites of passage for women of her age. She would have knitted layettes in the palest of yellows or blues or pinks or mint greens. She would have spent hours hunched over her ancient pedal sewing machine re-purposing old clothes into overalls for little boys. And how she would have baked. Biscuits by the dozen and cakes too. Martha may not have lived a traditional life for a woman of her age, but she had lived a life nonetheless.

Her mind was still sharp and she had a job she enjoyed. There were worse things.

And as for the dreams she'd had when she was younger, for her own life?

Girls like Martha Berry couldn't afford to have dreams back then. But things were surely changing, weren't they? She looked at the three young women at her table. April wore all her fears about people not thinking she was pretty enough on the furrowed brow of her very pretty face. May, with cheeks that demanded pinching and the disposition of a diplomat, sat in the middle as she always did, hanging on every word of the conversation. And June, hiding something that seemed to have sucked all the joy out of her. What troubles they had for such young women.

"Think big dreams, girls," Martha said. "As Charlotte Brontë says, you are free human beings with independent wills. You never know what fate has in store for you."

Chapter 6

IN WHICH MARTHA BERRY FEARS THE SUN
MAY NEVER RISE ON *AS THE SUN SETS*.

As the Sun Sets. Episode one."

The next Monday, Quentin Quinn returned from lunch at a quarter past three and with a loud hiccup wheeled his leather chair out of his office, propped his feet on the edge of Martha's desk and crossed them at the ankles, and lit up a cigarette. He clearly fancied himself as Australia's answer to Cecil B. DeMille. He'd given up pacing the carpet—"The ideas simply aren't flowing, Mrs. Barry"—and was now alternately staring at the ceiling and bellowing sentences into the air before changing his mind and calling out, "No. Cut that," with a snap of his fingers.

Martha smelled beer on his breath and tried to lean ever so slightly in the opposite direction. She looked at the sheaf of butcher paper interspersed with carbon paper rolled around the carriage of her typewriter—a line of XXX covering his deletions—and waited.

Martha had already poured him five cups of coffee, with two heaped teaspoons of granules in each plus two sugars.

Unfortunately the caffeine was failing to have the desired effect, and neither were the ten cigarettes he'd already smoked.

"Episode one." Her fingers hovered over the keys of her typewriter like a seagull might hover over a child's sandwich on the sand below, just in case another flash of inspiration should hit him.

In the two short weeks Martha had been working for Quentin Quinn, she'd come to know his habits. He was always ten minutes late for work, and when he pushed the door to the office open, the waft of smoke from a Camel cigarette drifted three paces behind him.

"Good morning, Mrs. Barry," he would announce theatrically as he shrugged off his suit jacket and held it on a finger for her to take and hang up for him. He would spend the first hour of his day thumbing through that day's newspapers and that week's magazines for inspiration for the traumas that *As the Sun Sets* might put its characters through. If it had characters, that is. Lunch was at midday and when he returned at two in the afternoon—or mostly later—she would be directed to put a new page into her typewriter and wait because inspiration was sure to hit any moment.

"Writing is thinking," he'd said authoritatively in response to a question she hadn't asked. "I need time," he'd added, tapping a forefinger to the side of his head as if the movement might rattle the ideas out. "To plot and plan and think, Mrs. Barry."

"Of course, Mr. Quinn," she'd replied.

For the first week, she'd corrected him—"Actually, it's *Miss* Berry, Mr. Quinn"—but had finally given up because her pointing it out didn't seem to make any difference. It was easier not to make a fuss. There was something about her that meant every boss she'd had seemed not to hear her. She'd decided her voice was simply too soft. She'd always been soft-spoken, her words whispers on her lips, and could no more shout across the office to ensure they heard her than she could fly to the moon.

Instead, she had studied the men she'd worked for, and Quentin Quinn wasn't that different from any of the twenty other male bosses she'd had across almost every department in the twenty-four years she'd worked at the ABC. It took many men to make a radio network operate and she'd served them all, from her recent stint working for Rutherford Hayes to answering phones for the boys in the garage, who worked on the newfangled outside broadcast vans.

Some of them were kinder than others. Some swore more than their predecessors and she'd heard so many *bloody buggering bastard*s over the years that she found herself completely immune to it. Words that would make a sailor down at Millers Point blush were like water off a duck's back to Martha. For every churchgoing teetotaler there was a churchgoing nasty drunk; for every enthusiastic young producer plucked fresh from university with a newly minted degree in English literature or history, there was a cynical old man in a neatly tailored suit whose dreams of a stellar broadcasting career had been stifled by something or other they could never accurately define.

"Damn it." Quentin Quinn jumped to his feet and fumbled for a cigarette from the crumpled pack he'd excavated from the pocket of his trousers. A match scraped the matchbox three times, and on the fourth attempt it finally caught. For the life of her, Martha couldn't figure out how the man could never light a match on the first attempt. He was always too hasty, too impatient to settle his shaking hands or even stop pacing behind her chair to press the match to the box with just the right amount of pressure to light it the first time.

His footsteps started up on the carpet, the soft thud of his brown brogues pressing into the flattened strip he'd created

with his relentless pacing behind her. Alongside that thread-
bare path, like spots where weeds might have been freshly dug
out in a garden, cigarette burns were scattered randomly. One
particularly drunken afternoon a week ago, he'd set a rubbish
bin ablaze when he tossed a lit cigarette into it. Martha's just-
brewed cup of tea had extinguished the flames and surely saved
the entire ABC building from burning to the ground.

Or at least that was apparently how Quentin Quinn had retold
the story while bending an elbow at the Burdekin Hotel, earning hoots of laughter about how lucky he was to have a secretary
with quick reflexes and a handy cup of tea. She'd heard all about it
from Ann from Accounts.

That was when Martha discovered she was being referred to in
some circles as Quentin Quinn's Tea Lady.

"The first scene, Mr. Quinn?" Martha asked.

"What was that, Mrs. Barry?"

She swiveled in her chair to face him. "We need the first scene."

"Rightio. Let's start this." He pointed at the typewriter as if
she might have forgotten how to type in the interregnum while
he gathered his thoughts. "Episode one. Scene." He hiccupped.
"Colon."

Martha typed, wondering what all that beer was doing to his
liver at such a young age.

Episode One
Scene:

Quentin mumbled to himself as he lit up another cigarette and
flipped the pages of a folder. While they still didn't have a script,
he had actually done some work in writing up descriptions of
the characters he'd mapped out for the show, its location, and

some future storylines. When he'd been missing from the office in the mornings, Martha had read the story bible cover to cover, familiarizing herself with the characters—their names, personalities, and occupations.

As the Sun Sets was to center on the Percy family. Jack, the patriarch, was the proprietor of a butcher shop and dispensed wisdom to all the customers who came into his premises. He was going to be a stalwart of the community with his shop at the center of it. He was married to the lovely and kind Vera, and their only child, a daughter named Betty, was at secretarial college. Unlike *Blue Hills*, which was set in the fictional country town of Tanimbla, *As the Sun Sets* was to be set in the city, in a fictional suburb that would be recognizable to city dwellers.

So far, so good.

Except that was all there was. Characters. There was no hint of any of the trials and tribulations that might befall them and no evidence yet that Quentin Quinn had plans to introduce any other characters. A fifteen-minute drama that was to air five days a week would need more than three people in it.

Martha glanced at her watch, trying not to be too obvious about it. Creative types didn't like to be reminded that minutes or even hours were ticking by while they procrastinated. She didn't dare mention it either. In her experience, it only tended to make those creative types less creative. She'd worked on a number of radio serials, most of which hadn't lasted more than a few months. They'd lacked a certain kind of magic—and there was only one Gwen Meredith.

The producers and writers liked to believe themselves to be always creating, even if there was no evidence of it on the page. Whether they were walking down the street or eating lunch or taking a shower, they were constantly thinking and plotting and creating. Some mapped out a drama quite intricately, scene by scene. Some pondered and paced and then when they serenaded her with an "aha," they would *click-click-click* their fingers, as if the perfect idea had just popped into their head, and begin to dictate in a rush, speaking so fast it was all Martha could do to keep up. Some acted out the scenes, recreating the voices of the actors as near as they could manage while they were dictating. Martha's typewriter keys *click-clacked* like a speeding train on its tracks as the words were spoken at a million miles an hour, turning words into rhythms, and when she swept her hand across to the carriage return, she felt like the conductor of the Sydney Symphony Orchestra.

Some liked to begin the day early and would have dictated that week's episodes by midday, after which they would retire to the pub and not be seen again until the next morning. Others procrastinated in the mornings before kicking into gear at about three o'clock in the afternoons, which meant long days for Martha waiting and then long nights typing and retyping the scripts to create a clean copy. Some—the lucky ones—came to the office with plot lines and ideas firmly established in their imaginations, while others seemed to find inspiration as hard to come by as a four-leaf clover. She wondered why men like that chose radio as a profession when they clearly found it so exasperating and injurious to their livers.

Quentin Quinn sighed and flipped the pages of the story bible back and forth, as if he was searching for a lost phrase.

Martha sat back in her chair and put her hands in her lap. If they were to hover too much longer over the keyboard without doing any typing, she risked a cramp. "Would you like another cup of coffee, Mr. Quinn?"

"Hell no, Mrs. Barry. I can't think when I have too much coffee.

Let's see. No, I've got it." He clicked his fingers. He tapped the side of his head and the ash from his cigarette drifted to the carpet like softly falling snow. "I'm thinking." He muttered to himself between puffs. "Start typing. Now!"

INT: *Office. Just after lunch. Betty sits behind a typewriter. Her boss, Mr. Rogerson, is sitting on the edge of her desk lighting up a cigarette.*

BETTY: *I can't think, Mr. Rogerson. I simply don't know what to do.*

(BETTY *slumps down on her desk, head in her hands, and begins to cry.*)

ROGER: *There, there, Betty. Don't be such a silly girl. It can't be all that bad.*

BETTY: *But it is! I've been saving for six months to buy that coat and it's . . . (sobs) it's sold out.*

ROGER: *(chuckles) I'm sure there are other coats in the shops.*

BETTY: *But I wanted that coat. You don't understand.*

ROGER: *(tut-tuts) You're correct in your thinking in that regard. I don't understand how young ladies like yourself can become such slaves to fashion. Personally, I blame those silly women's magazines that you're all so attached to. For goodness' sake, Betty. It's time to stop crying over a silly coat. Why don't you make me a cup of tea? You're sure to feel better if you just get back to work, young lady.*

Quentin Quinn paused his pacing to butt out his cigarette in Martha's coffee cup before lighting another one, a triumphant smile almost splitting his face and highlighting his boyish dimples.

Martha wriggled her fingers and took a sip of her now-lukewarm tea. She scanned the lines she'd typed. Faultless, as always. Did any of these creative types understand how difficult it was to set up the margins correctly so their scripts appeared in a readable format for the actors? She bet not. While her lines were exact and the margins just as they should be, there was a problem. More than one, she thought. This couldn't possibly be episode one, scene one. Where were Jack and Vera? Where was the butcher shop? Why was the action taking place in an office when Betty Percy was supposed to be at secretarial college?

Quentin Quinn hadn't started at the beginning. And most important of all, why was the wretched girl sobbing over a new coat?

"Mr. Quinn, shouldn't we perhaps begin with a scene introducing listeners to Jack and Vera Percy and the butcher shop? So listeners become familiar with them as the main family?"

"*We?*" Quentin Quinn replied with a supercilious chuckle. "There's no *we* about what we're doing, Mrs. Barry. I'm the one coming up with the lines of dialogue. You're merely the typist. And last time I looked, typing wasn't writing."

And pacing up and down and continually lighting cigarettes wasn't writing either, she wanted to say, but she was far too polite to point that out.

"Of course, Mr. Quinn."

"But if you must know, I want to get Betty right up there front and center from the first episode. We need to hook younger listeners, get them addicted to something more than the hit parade. You know, young people, with the same interests and preoccupations as, well, people like me." He looked Martha up and down. "You people already have *Blue Hills* and *When a Girl Marries* and what's that other one called? *Portia* something?"

"Might you be referring to *Portia Faces Life?*"

"Yes. That one. Never listened to an episode. Not that tired old *Blue Hills* either."

Tired? Martha bit back words that sat on the tip of her tongue. Such disrespect. How proud he seemed to be of the fact that he didn't listen to the most popular radio dramas. Martha thought he should be appalled rather than triumphant. She glanced at him and despite her best efforts to disguise her feelings, they must have been written all over her face, for he went on as if to justify himself.

"Younger listeners, Mrs. Barry. If we hook them in young"—he mimed casting a fishing line and then reeling in a fish—"we'll have them forever. And I'll have a very long career indeed." He waved a hand above his head as if he were seeing something up in lights. "'Quentin Quinn. The man who saved the radio serial.' I've been brought in to attract younger listeners. To show—to show modern people with ordinary lives doing modern-day ordinary things. That's the mandate from upstairs." He pointed to the ceiling and Martha was so relieved. She might not have understood where upstairs was if he hadn't.

"The broadcaster wants younger listeners, not those on the verge of retiring." He looked at her just a little too long. "It's my job to create some energy and pizzazz. You know, young people and their problems."

Perhaps he might like to start with a script, Martha thought, but she was still far too polite to point that out.

Chapter 7

IN WHICH MARTHA BERRY FINDS INSPIRATION IN HISTORY.

In the hallway of the Randwick house she'd grown up in and had never left, Martha took off her coat and hung it on the coatrack. She reached around and withdrew the pin that kept her hat in place and set the hat on the hallstand. She smoothed down the gray strands in her hair, which seemed to be thicker and more independent than what remained of her natural brown, and primped her hair at her crown to give it a bit of life where it had been flattened.

So many women had abandoned the wearing of hats in recent years, but she'd persisted. She liked the ceremony of it, the comfort it provided when walking along the street that her hair would not be blown every which way by the winds that whipped up off the harbor and swept down through Kings Cross on a brisk autumn day. Or any day of the year, for that matter. She still wore white gloves, too, and liked that they protected her from touching the same seats and handles and coins as other Sydneysiders who caught the tram with her every day.

Many women in Sydney were like her. Women of a certain age in the same brown suits and the same sensible low-heeled shoes. Women who were still clinging to hats and white gloves as they stepped onto buses and ferries and trains to make their way into work in the city, who would spend their days typing and filing and answering phones and making cups of tea and doing all sorts of errands their bosses demanded. A sea of spinsters enveloped Sydney like a tidal wave. A sea of spinsters who, truth be told, could probably run the businesses they worked in, if they were ever taken seriously. And alongside this sea of unmarried women was a flood of younger women, fresh out of secretarial colleges and high schools, who were being trained to fill the void left by the just-married junior girls who'd walked down the aisle and accepted their final paycheck at almost the same time.

It was the women in their late twenties and thirties and forties who were missing from the morning and evening brown-suited, low-heeled office migration. Those women were at home with their children, forcing sheets and clothes and towels through a vicious mangle on Mondays and ironing on Tuesdays and baking on Wednesdays and cleaning on Thursdays and scrubbing floors every day and shopping when they could snatch time in between walking children to school and washing diapers and looking after husbands. They were the ones who turned on the radio and hushed their households every lunchtime as a way to preserve their sanity, longing to hear adult voices in that long, lonely void between breakfast and dinnertime.

"That you, Martha dear?"

"Won't be long, Mum," Martha called out. "I'll just put on my slippers." Her bedroom, second on the right, had always been dim, and was even more so now that winter had arrived. She flipped the switch and the light flickered temperamentally for a moment or two before it finally glowed.

Her room had been the same for as long as she could remember. A print of snow-covered alps she assumed were European, but she'd never been to Europe to confirm for herself, hung on one wall. On the fireplace mantel sat a selection of objects she'd collected over the years: a seashell, fragments of glass she'd found on the beach when she'd taken her mother on a holiday to Coffs Harbour just after the war. They were a dull bottle green and pale blue and had been battered by sand erosion so they were smooth at the edges. Her dark wooden wardrobe, its brass key sitting in the lock, was tucked beside the fireplace on the left and her dressing table was wedged on its right, its mirror on a swivel so if she positioned it just so, she could see either her bottom half or top half reflected back at her.

The dressing table was decorated with an embroidered duchesse set—a set of three linen pieces with scalloped and crocheted edges, one large and two smaller, hand-embroidered with tulips and peonies in blues and purples and yellows. She'd packed items in her glory box for years, filling it with Irish linen tea towels she imagined might hang proudly in her sparkling clean kitchen along with the new pots and pans she'd bought on sale at David Jones one year. She'd stitched and sewn numerous items too: linens and napkins and doilies, and she'd even knitted a tea cozy. She'd bought a sauce boat and a saucer with twenty-five Robur Tea coupons, as well as some delicate crystal dishes and a silver cake server.

When she'd turned forty, in that long and somber year after the end of the war, she'd cleared the cobwebs from her glory box under her bed, thrown out every single one of the old tea towels in the kitchen drawer, and begun using the linen ones. The pots and pans were finally put to use (her mother's original aluminum set had long been due for a replacement), and the kitchen felt marginally like one they shared rather than her mother's alone.

Her chenille bedspread, a new indulgence, was a pale mint green, and when she sat on her bed, she caressed the soft ridges of the swirling pattern and let her eyes flutter closed. She knew her mother was waiting and would be eager to talk, having spent most of the day on her own, but she needed a minute or two. Perhaps five. She was tired in a way that was new and unfamiliar. She found herself growing more and more nervous at the progress of *As the Sun Sets*. Or, rather more accurately, its distinct lack of progress.

She'd met some procrastinators in her life, but Quentin Quinn might well yet be crowned king of them all. Everything about him revealed that he was nervous about his new role, but he seemed oblivious to it. He seemed to believe the scripts would magically appear one day in his in-tray without any effort on his part; that actors would be cast; that the show would be recorded and go to air all on its own. And her biggest fear was that she would be tainted with the brushstrokes of his failure in Rutherford Hayes's eyes.

She lifted her hands and stretched out her fingers, one hand at a time, and waited for any telltale signs of the ache she knew all about from her mother, examining them for the appearance of any bony lumps on her knuckles that might indicate the onset of the debilitating illness that had plagued Violet for decades. Her hands ached from typing, to be sure, but not from anything else. Her fingers were still long and nimble. She pulled at the laces of her brown brogues and kicked them off. She wriggled her toes, debated if she could get away with stripping off her suit and blouse—and especially her corset and her bra—and slipping into her nightie and dressing gown before preparing dinner. She wished.

She put on her slippers and shuffled to the kitchen, where her mother sat reading *ABC Weekly*. Martha rounded the kitchen table and kissed her mother on the cheek.

"I'm sorry I'm late."

"It's no trouble, dear. I sat with Mrs. Tilley and Mrs. Ward until Mr. Tilley and Mr. Ward got home from work. Mrs. Tilley gave me some fruitcake. It's on the cupboard."

"That'll do for dessert then." Martha smiled. There was nothing on earth like Mrs. Tilley's fruitcake.

Her mother's gnarled fingers rested on her arm and attempted a squeeze. "I don't want you to work yourself too hard. What with everything you do here at home . . ."

"I do it willingly, Mum. I always have."

"But you're not a spring chicken anymore yourself."

Martha planted her hands on her hips. "I'm only fifty!"

"I know, I know." Violet chuckled. "When I married your father, I expected he would still be with me in these twilight years. And then he could have looked after me. And I had hoped . . . oh, never mind."

"Hoped for what?"

"I'd hoped that you'd be off and married with children of your own. I wanted you to have a daughter of your own as wonderful as you are to me. Wouldn't that have been nice? You see, dear, I didn't want you to have the lonely life I've had. Being alone, I mean. Of course, I had you and the two of us have battled on, haven't we? And we had a stroke of luck with this house. I can't think about what would have happened to us if we'd been at the mercy of a landlord. Imagine where we'd be if we'd had to pay rent all these years? And with me not being able to work?"

"Mum, you mustn't worry. We're lucky in so many ways. I satisfy myself with that." What other choice was there but to accept what life offered?

Violet dabbed at her eyes and sniffed. "Sometimes I have too much time to think, that's all. But it's a mother's job to worry about her daughter, no matter how old she is."

Martha felt a pang. It was something she would never know.

"What about we have soup and toast for dinner? I ate a few too many of Mrs. Tilley's biscuits. I'm not that hungry, really. There's a tin of tomato soup in the cupboard."

"Are you sure, Mum?"

Violet raised a hand full of swollen knuckles and crooked fingers and waved Martha's concern away. "There's no hurry, dear. You look dead on your feet."

"Nothing some warm soup won't fix. How are Mrs. Tilley and Mrs. Ward? What mischief were they up to today?"

Violet chuckled. "Mrs. Tilley's very excited about Beryl's daughter's baby. A great-granddaughter. Can you believe it?"

Perhaps that was why Violet had been ruminating and feeling sad. Martha couldn't deny that it had her feeling pangs of sadness too. Did it stem from the realization of her own childless state, or the knowledge that her poor mother was never going to know the joys of having grandchildren or even great-grandchildren? Theirs was a withering family tree.

One day, this home would belong to another family. Who would they leave it to when they were both gone? Another set of stories and memories would be created within these four walls. The scents of someone else's baking would fill the kitchen. Different clothes would be strung up on the Hills Hoist and perhaps different flowers would be planted in the front garden. Children would be born and people would die. That was the simple story of life. And if a person was lucky enough to have some meaningful years in between with family and friends they loved, they were fortunate.

"She must be terribly excited. Has she started knitting already?" Martha splashed the contents of the tin of condensed tomato soup into a saucepan and added the milk and water. While she stirred, watching the red swirls, she thought on the advice from some experts she'd read in *Women's Weekly*, men who bemoaned convenience food like tinned soup and packet mixes. Those men lectured that such things would make women lazy and children unhealthy. Martha thought they were the best thing to happen in the kitchen since the invention of cooking over an open flame.

She had a list of other things she believed would improve a working woman's life, and at the top of it was bringing back sliced bread. Before the war, bakers were allowed to slice it and put it in a paper bag if you asked, but during the war the government warned against the practice. Apparently, it was a waste of time and paper. It seemed like a small thing, but not having to find the bread knife or use a cutting board, and afterward not needing to clear up enough crumbs to feed a murmuration of starlings . . . Well, a lot of little conveniences added up to time and energy saved. And she wished for meals that cooked themselves and clothes that washed themselves and didn't need ironing.

"As a matter of fact, dear, Mrs. Tilley asked me to go with her to the haberdasher's tomorrow. I said I'd see how I'm feeling, if I get a good night's sleep. She wants to buy some wool so she can get started on a layette for the little one. Yellow, I think she said. Hedging her bets, she said."

"That's a good idea. It'll be nice for you to have an outing."

"And anyway, I need some dress elastic for that navy skirt. Since you put that elastic in the waistband of the brown one, I've never found it so easy to get off and on. Those buttons were such a nuisance." Violet lifted her hands and tried to flex her fingers. They barely moved.

"I don't know why there aren't clothes available that are made of some kind of material that stretches wider than its shape, so we can eat as much fruitcake as we like and not have to worry about our waistbands getting too tight. That would be especially useful after a big Christmas dinner, don't you think, Mum?"

"Mrs. Ward says she's going to give up her girdle."

"Is she now?"

"Don't tell her, but I don't think she can find one to fit her anymore. She does love her sweets."

Martha laughed. "At her age, she should eat all the cake she wants."

"There's truth in that," Violet said. She turned her attention back to the *ABC Weekly* on the table in front of her.

"Oh, look at this, Martha." Violet grasped the magazine and slowly turned it to her daughter. "It's an article about a woman writer in the sixteen hundreds."

Martha leaned closer and read out loud. "'Buried in Westminster Abbey, Aphra Behn was the first Englishwoman ever to earn her living as a writer in equal competition with men.' Well, imagine that. Born in 1640 and a writer."

"Well, I never," Violet said with a bemused chuckle.

"I've never heard of her. Judging by the dates, she was born after Shakespeare died. Why don't we know any of her novels or plays?"

"I don't know, dear."

When Martha heard the soup bubbling, she turned off the flame and ladled two bowls full and set them on the table. The strains of the overture of *Blue Hills* filled the room, but Martha couldn't think about Fleur and Dr. Gordon and the other characters as she sipped her soup.

She knew about the Brontës and Austen and George Eliot, of

course, and Mary Wollstonecraft Shelley (*Frankenstein* had always scared the socks off her) and Louisa May Alcott and Miles Franklin.

Aphra Behn had been published almost two hundred years before them, but how was it that her name had been lost to history all this time? It had been a hostile world for women who wrote. Charlotte, Emily, and Anne Brontë had not used their own names when they were published, going by Currer, Ellis, and Acton Bell. Austen had been known as "A Lady" on the title pages of her books when they were published. George hadn't even been George Eliot's real name, and Miles was really Stella Maria Sarah Miles Franklin.

Why had Martha not realized this before? The writers she loved, those who had shaped her world, who had filled her hours and continued to do so, had to hide who they really were to be taken seriously in a world of letters ruled by men.

Her spoon scraped the bottom of her soup bowl.

"Thank you, dear," Violet said. "That was delicious."

Martha gave her mother a distracted smile. All she could think about was Aphra Behn.

Chapter 8

IN WHICH CASTING FOR
AS THE SUN SETS BEGINS.

Why, Miss Berry. It's been positively ages."

Martha looked up from the contract she was typing and subtly flipped the top page over so it couldn't be seen by prying eyes. There was nothing Kent Stone (real name Cyril Pervis) loved more than gossip and the trading of it. She admired him tremendously despite that flaw.

"Mr. Stone. I'm delighted to see you again. It's been a while. Not since—"

Kent clicked his fingers. "*Summer of the Seventeenth Doll* back in '54."

"Wasn't that a huge hit?" Martha replied. "Not everyone can go to the theater, even if they do live in the city. I think a radio version of a popular play is the next best thing, don't you?"

"I don't know where half the actors in this town would be if we didn't have the radio serials. They've always helped pay the bills. And don't we all have bills to pay?" Kent Stone raised one eyebrow. "Money doesn't bloom on trees, no matter how hard we wish it. Some of us have to put the axe to the grindstone to make a living."

"We do indeed. I hope you've been well? And busy?" Martha asked.

"Yes to both, I'm very glad to report."

"I very much enjoyed your performance in *Inspector Brittain Calling*, Mr. Stone. Do you think there'll be more episodes?"

He took a deep breath and sighed. "Canceled, I'm afraid. Twenty episodes in and we got the axe. It seems no one gave a hoot if Inspector Brittain was calling or not."

"Oh, that's such a shame."

"Such is life, as they say."

Kent Stone was the closest thing Australia had to acting royalty. Martha had first seen him perform when she was a child, as he had been, and he was known as Cyril Pervis. He'd trodden the boards alongside his performing parents in shows created by the theater impresario J. C. Williamson and was a child star barely four feet tall who could sing like a nightingale and tap-dance the night away. Crowds all over the country had been captivated by the talented little gentleman. Back then, when he'd gone by the name of Little Singing Cyril (a name she had since learned he'd loathed), he'd once been the supporting act for Nellie Melba. But his singing career turned out to be short-lived. Cyril's parents had a falling out with J. C. after he opposed a bid by Australian actors to form a union in 1913 to fight for better pay and conditions. They were never again offered work and Little Singing Cyril's days on the stage were suddenly over.

Years later, Little Singing Cyril—no longer little or a singer—resurrected his career courtesy of a new name, Kent Stone. By turning to radio, he'd become one of Australia's most famous actors and had been a star of the stage and the airwaves since the 1940s.

"You know, Martha"—Kent removed his hat and brushed its brim for imaginary dust, then flipped his silk scarf over his shoulder and rolled his eyes—"this life is not for the fainthearted. It's a little tiresome to be in one's thirties"—he paused and waited for Martha's reaction. When she smiled knowingly at him, he grinned and continued—"and be at the beck and call of radio producers like"—he pulled a folded piece of paper from the pocket of his suit and held it at a distance, squinting at it—"Quincy something? Never heard of him."

Kent had many vanities and refusing to wear glasses was one of them. "Quentin Quinn." Martha paused. "He's new."

The actor sat himself on the edge of Martha's desk. "Oh, god forbid. How new, darling?"

Martha lowered her voice and leaned in. "This is his first drama. In fact, it's his first radio production of any kind. He's perhaps twenty-two years old. I believe you might be the first professional actor he's ever auditioned."

Kent leaned in, too, because he was far too professional to be so indiscreet as to be overheard, especially when pitching for a job. "Is it too much to ask to audition for someone who actually knows something about drama? About acting? About the creative process?" He thought about it for a moment. "What part am I up for? Your message didn't say."

When Quentin Quinn had asked Martha to arrange auditions for Jack, Vera, and Betty Percy, she had made sure to include Kent Stone on the list. He was her favorite Australian actor. Not only was he handsome for an older man and the possessor of a beautifully deep and versatile voice, but he also happened to be a nice person. Forever courteous to both producers and secretaries, he always turned up on time, was never inebriated when they were recording, and prepared his lines by actually reading through the entire script at least once before recording days. If Kent Stone was cast as Jack Percy, Martha's life would be so much easier.

"You're reading for Jack Percy, the owner of the Percys' butcher shop. The main male character."

"A butcher." Kent paused dramatically. He was well-practiced, after all. He stroked his clean-shaven chin. "I can do a butcher. I could play a baker and a candlestick maker, too, if I had to."

"Jack Percy is to be elder statesman of the suburb."

Kent Stone startled. "*Elder?*"

"Mature," Martha corrected. "A wise counsel and a pair of listening ears. A sage, if you will."

Kent raised his eyebrow. "That's better, Miss Berry."

"Jack will be the linchpin of the serial. He's got a lot of life left in him."

"How many episodes a week?"

"Five fifteen minuters. Upstairs"—she pointed to the ceiling—"wants *As the Sun Sets* to be the new *Blue Hills*."

"Doesn't everyone?" He chuckled. "I auditioned for Gwen Meredith once. No, make that twice. She didn't like me."

"I'm sure it wasn't that. You know as well as I do that some actors are better suited to certain roles. Just like you are the perfect fit for Jack Percy, Kent. I'm sure of it."

"Why, if it isn't Kent Stone." Miss Katherine Connors stood in the doorway, one hip cocked, a handbag in the crook of one bent arm and the other hand primping the back of her hair. A little hat sat perched on her head at a jaunty angle, and a net covered her face down to her perfectly aquiline nose.

"Katherine, darling. How delightful to see you!" Kent stood

and gave a little bow, as if Miss Connors were a princess. She nodded back at him solicitously.

"You're looking as handsome as ever, Kent."

He adjusted the silk handkerchief in the breast pocket of his suit. "Why, thank you. And look at you. Ravishing as always." He held out a hand and she placed one of hers in it. He dramatically kissed the back of it.

A little thrill rippled through Martha at being with actors once again. Somehow their presence made the fact of *As the Sun Sets* real. Up until then, it had seemed like the entire idea for the show was still floating in a bubble somewhere in the space above Quentin Quinn's head. And given his procrastination, Martha feared the bubble would eventually burst and everyone would discover what she had suspected since the first day she'd met him: that there was nothing inside his head but false hope and an ego with grand delusions. He simply wouldn't agree to anything. As it was, they wouldn't be casting at all that day if Martha hadn't put the sessions in Quentin Quinn's diary without consulting him first. "Things need to be done," she'd wanted to scream at him, but she was still far too polite to ever do such a thing. So, instead, she had begun to work around him.

Miss Connors, as she was known to almost everyone—never Katherine, except to her nearest and dearest—seemed to float into the room. She was pure glamour, from the black patent stiletto heels so towering that Martha had no idea how she managed to stand, to her slim ankles and her perfectly proportioned calves, her girlish hips, her tiny waist, and a bust nestled under the most perfectly pale décolletage. Her hair was maneuvered into a chignon with not one strand out of place, and her gloves were always the purest white. Her handbag was made from the shiniest patent leather and matched her shoes, of course. Her pale blue wool suit clung to her curves as if she'd been sewn into it. Her lips, always slicked with the reddest of red lipstick, looked immaculate. Martha supposed famous people had to maintain their appearance at all times lest people gossip that they were on the booze or something.

"And, Miss Berry. I'm so pleased to see you. I'm glad you're running the show."

Martha felt heat flare in her cheeks. "Oh, I'm not, Miss Connors."

"My mistake." Miss Connors winked at Martha before turning to Kent. "Who are you up for? Jack Percy, I hope?"

"The heart and soul of the show. The wise sage behind the butcher's counter who doles out advice along with his sausages and tripe. And you?"

"Your wife."

"Oh, wonderful. Look at us. Have we ever played husband and wife before?"

"I don't think so," Miss Connors replied. "Any script I can have a look at, Miss Berry? To get a feel for this woman?"

Martha took a deep breath. Her loyalties may have been split but she had to protect the show. "Some of the characters aren't quite fully realized," she explained, crossing her fingers in her lap, out of sight of the two actors. "But they will be by the time we finalize casting and start recording. Please don't concern yourselves."

"I've heard that before," Katherine scoffed. "I can't count the number of times I've received a script in casting and then watched as my lines were progressively cut to almost nothing by the time we got into the studio to record the show. For one drama, I went from eight lines to a mere 'Hello, Doctor.' That was it! I became patient number three. I didn't even get to tell him what was wrong."

"Was it a tragic disease?" Kent offered.

Miss Connors laughed. "I like to think it was an unwanted pregnancy."

"Wash your mouth out with soap," Kent proclaimed. "You know we can't say the word *pregnant* on air."

"Oh, I know, but a girl can dream about playing such drama, can't she? What about you, Kent? Wouldn't you love your butcher to have some terrible ailment from which he is slowly wasting away? I just know you'd milk that until listeners all over the country were weeping over their lunch."

"Only if it's a very slow death, my dear. An actor needs to pay the rent. Perhaps Jack could slowly get sick and then years later, when he's on his deathbed, lingering tragically, a miracle cure might be discovered that saves his life. I could be on the show forever! Look at Queenie Ashton. She's been playing Lee Quentin in *Blue Hills* from the very first episode. And Gordon Grimsdale's the same. He's been Dr. Neil Gordon all that time too. That's what I'm after, my dear Miss Connors. Longevity. I can't be the only one who's heard the rumors about television."

"No," Miss Connors replied.

"I haven't heard the rumors. What are they?" Martha asked.

"When television began broadcasting in America," Kent started, "it virtually killed off radio drama. Actors who'd been working for decades, getting decent work, were suddenly having to scrape by doing radio ads for hemorrhoid cream or indigestion pills. Only the youngest and most attractive types made the move over to the box." He shivered. "It would be unbearable. I mean, what else but radio and the occasional piece of theater work will keep me in the manner to which I've become accustomed? It's not an option for me to marry well. Unlike some, my dear."

Miss Connors and Kent exchanged glances. Martha understood perfectly, although they hadn't included her in their silent conversation because she wasn't an actor. But she understood better than they realized. If Martha was of a certain vintage, so were they. Kent's biography conveniently didn't mention his age but noted he could play "thirty to sixty." Martha had seen him onstage years and years ago and knew they were of similar age. Fifty. And Miss Connors must be nearing the same age, judging by how long she'd been in the business. Pancake makeup wasn't always applied just for the theater.

"I'm sure that won't happen here," Martha said, trying to sound reassuring. "People love their radio serials. And anyway, televisions will be so expensive."

Miss Connors didn't have so much to worry about, as indeed she had married well, to a businessman, and Martha knew for a fact that she wouldn't be rendered homeless if she didn't win the role as Mrs. Percy. Kent, on the other hand, was a bachelor, although he did share the rent on his Bondi apartment with his longtime chum, Sebastian, who was French. Or Hungarian. Or perhaps White Russian. Martha couldn't quite remember.

"From your lips to god's ear," Miss Connors announced theatrically. Honestly, everything she did was theatrical. Martha could barely take her eyes off the woman. "May she be listening." She winked at Martha as if Martha was a member of her secret club, and Martha couldn't hide her pleasure at the idea of being in any club with Miss Connors.

"Here he is now." Martha looked up as Quentin Quinn entered the room, somehow looking more disheveled than ever. He'd shed his suit jacket and his bow tie was loose at his neck. Martha stood. "Mr. Quinn, may I introduce you to Mr. Kent Stone and Miss Katherine Connors."

They all shook hands politely. Out of Quentin Quinn's line of sight, Kent raised an eyebrow at Martha and mouthed, "He's a child."

"They're here to audition for Jack and Mrs. Percy," Martha announced, just in case Mr. Quinn had forgotten.

"Rightio," he said, sweeping a hand through his hair and pushing the unruly strands back from his forehead. "Please come into my office."

This time he shut the door.

Chapter 9

IN WHICH MARTHA BERRY WITNESSES TERROR FROM THE SKY.

The next day, between morning tea and lunch, Martha heard a commotion in the hallway.

She looked up from her typing and cocked an ear. Some kind of indistinct shouting was growing louder and louder, along with stomping footsteps. They were a woman's, Martha judged, by the *click-clack* of heels on the linoleum floor.

"Pedantic bloody bureaucrats!"

Martha went to the open office door and looked out. Other secretaries were doing the same from each doorway. It was so uncommon to hear a woman's voice raised to full volume that they couldn't help but try to see what the ruckus was about, just in case someone had gone mad. Ann from Accounts, standing in the doorway opposite, looked across at Martha and whispered, "What's going on?"

Martha shrugged. "Your guess is as good as mine," she whispered back. Then all the secretaries turned as one to see a woman stomping in their direction, her face beet red, her arms swinging as if she were a soldier on a long march.

It was Joyce Wiggins, the producer.

"I'm bloody well fed up!" Miss Wiggins suddenly stopped at the door to the *As the Sun Sets* production office. As she did, every secretary stepped back and slowly closed their own office doors. They may not have been watching any longer, but Martha could bet they had their ears pressed to the doors trying to catch every word.

Miss Wiggins looked Martha up and down, taking in her sensible low-heeled brown brogues, her sensible brown suit, and her sensibly styled brown hair, sitting just at her sensible collar, and no doubt made assumptions about who she was and what her capabilities were. She wouldn't be the first, although Martha had never been appraised in such a way by a woman in such a senior position. To be perfectly frank, there weren't any women in senior positions.

"We've met," Miss Wiggins said, tilting her head to one side. "In the cafeteria."

"I believe we have," Martha replied.

"What's your name?"

Martha met her gaze. "Martha Berry."

"Joyce Wiggins." Miss Wiggins extended a hand to Martha, and Martha stared at it. She wasn't sure for a moment how to respond. Women didn't shake hands with each other, and they especially did not shake hands with men. It was a man's ritual, one that cemented business deals and agreements and the entry to a club that kept women out as fiercely as if it were guarded by a steel door.

Martha extended her hand, and Miss Wiggins shook it firmly.

"How do you do, Martha?"

Handshakes and first names? "I'm pleased to meet you, Miss Wiggins."

"For goodness' sake. Call me Joyce."

"Joyce," Martha replied. "I hope you don't mind me asking, but . . . is everything all right?"

"As a matter of fact, it's bloody well not." Joyce fisted her hands and propped them on her hips. "How long exactly have you worked here, Martha?"

"Twenty-four years." She couldn't quite believe it herself. It was almost half her life.

"Such loyalty," Joyce snickered, "to a cadre of men who don't deserve one iota of it."

Martha still remembered the day she'd walked into the ABC building all those years ago, having applied for a job she didn't really understand. She wasn't the only person in Australia wondering how it was possible for sounds to be broadcast through the air and come out of a small box in someone's home.

"Tell me, Martha. In all that time, have you ever worked for a woman?"

"No, I haven't."

"And why is that, do you think?" Before Martha could think of a response, Miss Wiggins provided it. "Because there aren't any women in such positions, that's why. Here I am, with all the skills necessary and more, and all they'll let me do is work on the women's sessions to advise the housewives of Australia how to make lamb chops or how to make mince go further or . . . or how to save money by upholstering your own bloody sofa! Do I look like a woman who cooks, Martha?"

Martha assumed she wasn't. "I take it you have spent your time much more wisely."

"Exactly. And do you think they'll let me put those skills to use?" Joyce's cheeks flushed with frustration. "And you've been a secretary all these years, Martha, I take it?"

"How did you know that?"

"Because you're a woman and that's what this place does. It hires young women as secretaries because they're *willing* to do it at lower salaries than the men. *Willing*," she scoffed. "As if they have a choice in the matter. And then when they marry, management gets rid of them and brings in a whole new crop of girls to ogle and train up and then get rid of all over again. You're not married, I take it?"

"No," Martha replied.

"A war widow?" Joyce's voice softened just a little.

"No. I've never married."

"Which explains why you're still working here. The old marriage bar. We got rid of that for the civil service back in England in 1946, but this country still stubbornly clings to it. Women won't make good workers if they're married. They'll be too distracted by their homely duties and raising children to devote themselves to their jobs. If women work, they'll raise a brood of delinquents. Funny, isn't it," Joyce said, looking to the ceiling, "that men can freely marry and father children and no one thinks them any less capable of doing their jobs or raising children. So, tell me. Have you ever had a promotion?"

"No."

"Not once?"

"No. Not once."

Joyce muttered something under her breath that Martha had only ever heard newsmen say.

"And who are you working for now?"

"Quentin Quinn. The producer and writer of *As the Sun Sets*."

Martha pointed over her shoulder at the sign affixed to the office door.

Joyce harrumphed. "Oh, I've heard of him. As wet behind the ears as a newborn puppy and just as useless. And yet, there he is. Producing and writing his own drama. It's absolutely bloody infuriating!"

Martha could see how, from Joyce Wiggins's point of view, it might be absolutely . . . infuriating.

"I cannot believe that. Young. Men. Like. Him. Get. Jobs. Like. This. Before I do!" Joyce stomped her foot in a rage. "And when I come up with fresh ideas of my own, they're handed to the men!"

"Goodness." Martha didn't want to say anything that could be construed as being disloyal to her employer, so she said nothing.

"I bet you'd run rings around all these hopeless chaps you've worked for all these years." She lifted her chin, clearly hoping any so-called hopeless chap in the immediate vicinity might hear. "Let me guess, Miss Berry. I bet you've worked in every department in this place. You would know better than almost anyone around here just how this decrepit old institution works." Joyce took a step closer and lowered her voice. Was she about to share a confidence? Martha was all ears. "You probably know where all the bodies are buried."

As a matter of fact, Martha did, but she was far too polite to admit it.

"Have they even deigned to promote you to script girl, or are you still being paid as a secretary?"

Martha didn't respond but realized from the suddenly soft expression on Joyce's face that this stranger hadn't really been waiting for an answer. She knew it already. Could Joyce also see the shame and embarrassment there in her pale green eyes? Twenty-four years. It sounded like a lifetime because it was. She had never imagined that when she started out as a secretary all those years ago, back in 1932 when the Great Depression was at its worst and neighbors had poured scorn on Martha for taking up a job when one in three men in Australia couldn't find one. The world still hadn't recovered from the stock market crash three years before and men were knocking on doors, begging for work. It was the year the Sydney Harbour Bridge officially opened and the year Phar Lap died far away in California, after which the country wept in collective grief.

She'd been twenty-six years old, well on her way to being the spinster she would inevitably become. Whatever grief she'd felt at that age was long gone, had metamorphosed into resignation and an acceptance of her fate. When she was in her midthirties, she'd been a witness to the reports of death and destruction that had flooded into the newsroom directly from reporters in the field, in Africa and France and England. Even though the worst of the details had been slashed by a censor's pen, the reports were still devastating. She had felt relieved in those years not to have had a brother or a husband or a sweetheart who had never come back from the war.

Yet she was still a secretary, constantly overlooked, never feeling the confidence or ambition to push to be more than she was, to rise higher, to learn more, to do more.

She found her voice suddenly. "I've never been promoted. I've never had a pay raise for doing more work. I've been shifted sideways my whole working life, filling in for so-and-so who's on holidays or so-and-so who's feeling poorly or the vacancy created by so-and-so who's just been married and left."

Joyce raised a fist to the ceiling. "Don't let them do it to you, Martha!" Joyce stepped to the office door and reached a hand out to the sign that read *As the Sun Sets, Quentin Quinn, Producer* and ripped it from the door before tearing it into little pieces, which settled at her feet like snow.

And with that final exclamation but no further words of advice about how she might in fact not let them do it to her, Joyce brushed past Martha, strode through the office door to Martha's desk, and looked at her teacup, her sharpened pencils, and the little blue crystal vase filled with daisies Martha had cut that morning from Mrs. Tilley's front garden.

She turned back to Martha. "Do you know I've been asking since the day I got here—six months now—for a new typewriter to replace the broken one they gave me?"

"That must be frustrating." Martha went to her desk. "Can I get you a cup of tea or perhaps a coffee? I might even be able to rustle up a biscuit or two."

"No. Thank you. Your typewriter looks old too."

"I suppose it is."

Joyce went to the window. She opened it wide and leaned out.

"Miss Wiggins!" Martha exclaimed and ran to her.

Joyce turned back to look at her with a wicked smile. "Don't worry. I'm not going to jump, Martha. I wouldn't give them the satisfaction." What she did do was stride to Martha's desk and haul the ancient black Remington typewriter into her arms. She struggled but made it to the window.

"Miss Wiggins. What on earth—"

Without another word, Joyce groaned and heaved and pushed the typewriter out of the open window.

"Stop!" Martha ran to Joyce's side just as an enormous metal crash echoed throughout the office. There was a high-pitched scream. Martha and Joyce pressed their shoulders together and peered down onto the footpath three stories below. There, on the street, a crowd of onlookers stood stunned. As if in slow motion, they looked up to the window and then studied the scattered remains of the Remington. One man raised his fist and shook it angrily up toward them.

"It came from up there!" a woman pushing a pram shouted. "You could have killed my baby!" And then she promptly fainted.

The typewriter was a collection of unrecognizable parts. The cylinder was rolling into the gutter. The frame lay on one side. The keys had separated from one another and would never form another word. Joyce Wiggins had killed Martha's typewriter—and narrowly avoided killing someone in the process.

"Miss Wiggins . . ." Martha couldn't speak. Her chest was tight, her head was pounding, and when she gripped the wall to steady herself, she realized her hands were shaking.

Miss Wiggins leaned farther out the window, cupped her mouth, and yelled, "Sorry! It slipped."

She then turned to Martha, put her hand out, and they shook. "They've ignored me and stolen my ideas one too many times. Nice to have met you, Martha. I'd best go and pack my things."

....

"Miss Berry. Do come in."

Early the next morning, even before her first cup of tea, Martha sat down opposite Mr. Rutherford Hayes. She crossed her legs at the ankle and wound her fingers tightly around each other and set the bundle of nervous digits in her lap. She needed a deep breath to try to settle her heartbeat. She still hadn't recovered from Miss Wiggins's sudden and dramatic appearance the day before in her office and in her life. She hadn't stopped shaking for at least an hour—all those poor people frightened out of their wits on the street below—and had barely slept a wink that night. It had been the most terrifying—and exciting—thing to ever happen to her.

"May I introduce you to the head of personnel, Mr. Duffy?"

Mr. Duffy stood, looking at Martha over the rims of his glasses, which sat so low on his nose that she expected them to slip off any moment. He held a clipboard in front of him in an attempt, Martha deduced, to hide his enormous girth. He appeared to be one of those men who couldn't commit to wearing his trousers and belt either underneath or at the top of his belly, so he'd settled for right in the middle and, since that didn't constitute a natural waist, he'd attached to his trousers a pair of braces as mud brown as his suit.

"How do you do," Martha said. As she sat, and the men followed, a wave of heat shimmered up her body from her torso to her head and her teeth. She was desperate to wipe beads of perspiration from her top lip but didn't want to perform such a personal gesture in front of the two men.

"Now, Miss Berry. We've called you in this morning to discuss this . . . trouble yesterday." Mr. Hayes shook his head in sad resignation. "With Miss Wiggins. The producer."

"The *former* producer," Duffy added from the corner of his mouth as he scribbled notes on his clipboard with a pencil.

"A most unfortunate business all around. She's been charged with destruction of government property and will be fined one hundred pounds."

Martha swallowed hard. That was a very large sum of money indeed. She wondered how Joyce would pay it on a woman's wages.

"The general manager has demanded a full report for the board, no less, and we are compelled to ask you some questions about the series of events that led up to the incident. Since you are the only eyewitness."

Martha nodded. She wasn't surprised in the slightest that Miss Wiggins had been sacked. The lady with the pram on the footpath had been absolutely correct. Joyce could have killed someone with her reckless behavior. It was only pure luck that there had been a green light at the pedestrian crossing and people were crossing the road instead of lingering on the footpath waiting. As it was, the attendant at the front desk had barely managed to hold off an angry mob of men who had tried to storm the building to make a citizen's arrest. He'd had to call the police to quell the furious mob, and Martha had heard from Ann from Accounts, who'd heard it from another secretary, that the woman who'd been pushing her baby in the pram, the one who'd fainted, was in the hospital being treated for shock.

The whole building had been in an uproar.

"I can't stress enough, Miss Berry, that management is treating this matter with the *utmost* seriousness."

"Of course," Martha replied. Mr. Duffy continued writing notes even though Martha had barely said a word.

"We've been trying to get to the bottom of what happened. We've talked with Miss Wiggins, and she's made certain . . . admissions."

Mr. Duffy huffed. Martha wondered why someone who worked in personnel seemed so impersonable.

"Since you were a witness to the whole dreadful affair, can you enlighten us as to what happened?"

Martha steadied herself. "I was working at my desk and heard some sort of commotion in the corridor. I went to investigate and Miss Wiggins walked right toward me. She introduced herself."

"Yes, yes. What else did she say to you, exactly?" Mr. Duffy lowered his clipboard and turned his gimlet eyes to Martha.

"She made mention of Mr. Quinn when she saw his name on

the office door. I told her that we were working on a new radio serial and she inquired after the characters. And then, without warning, she went into my office and opened the window. At first I thought she was simply trying for some fresh air. But she went back to my desk, lifted the typewriter with some difficulty, and threw it from the window. Before I realized what she was doing and before I could stop her."

Both men muttered and Mr. Duffy wrote furious notes.

"Did she give you any warning about what she was about to do? For instance, did she say, 'I'm going to throw your typewriter out of the window'?"

"No, Mr. Hayes."

"She didn't explain at all the reason for her course of action?"

Martha hesitated. While she could never condone what Joyce had done, she had understood immediately her frustrations at the way she'd been treated: being overlooked, being passed over, being ignored. Martha blinked and everything became clearer. She had kept mum for more men than she could count during her working life. It was the least she could do for Miss Wiggins. She shook her head.

"Well then." Mr. Hayes stood. "Thank you for your assistance, Miss Berry." Mr. Duffy kept scribbling. Martha stood and turned to leave the office. Something held her back. Suddenly her feet seemed glued to the tatty floral carpet.

She turned back. "While I'm here, Mr. Hayes. There's something I've been meaning to raise with you."

Mr. Duffy looked up from his scribbling.

"Yes, Miss Berry?" Mr. Hayes said.

She steeled herself. She had heard Joyce Wiggins's words over and over in her head all through the night while she'd tossed and turned: "Don't let them do it to you, Martha."

Martha had resolved that morning over her toast with marmalade that she couldn't afford to *go* mad as Joyce had done. So she had to *get* mad instead.

"It's been brought to my attention that people such as myself, who help with the preparation of scripts and all manner of tasks associated with the recording of radio serials, are designated as 'script girls.' I also understand they receive a higher salary than someone performing purely secretarial duties. Despite the extra workload I've picked up in working for a new producer in Mr. Quinn, I continue to be paid as a secretary. Yet I'm doing so much more."

Mr. Duffy stared at Martha openmouthed.

"I see," Mr. Hayes replied.

"As a matter of fact, in all the years I've worked at the broadcaster, I've never had a pay raise or a promotion."

Mr. Hayes looked at her quizzically. "Really?"

"Really."

"Well. I'm sure we can do something about that, given how discreet you've been about this whole Wiggins business. Duffy, see to it, will you?"

Mr. Duffy huffed and straightened his back. "I don't think so, Mr. Hayes. We can't just go around willy-nilly giving pay raises to all the girls. I mean, what if she tells the others and they all come demanding—"

Mr. Hayes cut him off with a wave. "Oh, for goodness' sake, just do it, man. I'm the head of the drama department. It's my call. And while you're at it, see to it that Miss Berry gets a replacement typewriter."

"A *new* typewriter," Martha added. It felt rather strange to be so bold, but she quite liked the sensation.

"Done," Mr. Hayes responded.

Mr. Duffy cleared his throat. "Does she really need one? The newsmen get priority and they—"

Mr. Hayes cut him off with a brisk, "Of course she bloody well does. Do you even have a clue what we do here in the drama department?"

Mr. Duffy averted his eyes and scribbled some more on his notepad.

Mr. Hayes reached a hand out to shake Martha's. She looked at it in surprise and then remembered Joyce Wiggins's firm hand-shake and copied it.

"Thank you, Mr. Hayes." She nodded at Mr. Duffy. "Mr. Duffy."

Martha walked down the long corridor back to her office, a place that would always remind her of Joyce Wiggins's spectacular act of self-sabotage and revenge, and smiled.

"So long, Joyce Wiggins," she murmured to herself. "It was very nice meeting you."

Chapter 10

IN WHICH MARTHA BERRY WONDERS WHAT THE ARRIVAL OF TELEVISION MIGHT MEAN FOR *AS THE SUN SETS*.

M iss Berry, did you know the word *television* means seeing at a distance?"

"How very interesting, June. I suppose it's from Latin or some such." Martha passed the young woman the sugar bowl, and June heaped two teaspoons into her tea.

Martha, June, April, and May were sitting together in the staff cafeteria for lunch. Martha had made a promise to herself—and to the girls—that she would tear herself away from the office once a week, on Mondays, to have lunch with her friends. And she had kept that promise, even though there was only one week left before the first episodes of *As the Sun Sets* were to be recorded, and there were still no scripts.

Martha had spent the morning checking her watch every minute in the hope that Quentin Quinn might arrive and start dictating to her, but that hope had been in vain. She simply had to get out of her office, and lunch with the Calendar Girls was the best distraction she could think of.

April sighed and tut-tutted. "I don't know how you can possibly have that much sugar, June. It'll rot your teeth. Not to mention what it's doing to your waistline."

June dropped her gaze to her tea and said nothing.

"I'm sure June knows that," May said in the conciliatory way she always said things. "She might not need reminding every time she has a cup of tea, April."

"Well, someone has to look out for her figure, and clearly June doesn't care."

"April," Martha said, and the tone of her voice silenced her three young friends. She hadn't meant it to sound like a warning, but perhaps it had come out that way. She couldn't bear the way April scrutinized June. What must it be like to be the same age and constantly in the beautiful April's shadow?

Where April was petite and slim as a reed, with soft blonde hair that wasn't from a bottle of hair dye, June was tall, broad-shouldered, and big-busted, with wiry hair that she battled to tame into a chignon with curls bursting out from her pins and creating a halo effect around her head. Violet might have politely described her as a big-boned girl.

Martha turned to April. "I know you're very careful with maintaining your own figure, but that doesn't mean others are inclined to do the same, no matter how much you remind them."

April sighed and put her elbow on the table and her chin in her hand. "I'm sorry, June. I didn't mean to be so horrible."

June looked up from stirring her tea and gave April a weak smile. "It's all right."

"It's not, honestly. It's all I can think about. Staying like this." April waved a hand in front of her face and down her torso. "My whole life, all I've ever heard from my mother was to watch what I eat. To do my hair just so. To never leave the house without at least lipstick and rouge and freshly polished shoes or what on earth will the neighbors think? To double-check my stockings in case there's a run. And if I have a single stray hair on my jumper, well, it's as if I was walking to the bus stop stark naked. 'You'll never find a husband looking like a fishwife,' she says. She won't be happy until I'm married off to someone—anyone—and out of her house, raising more children than I know what to do with. She wants me to be just like her." Tears welled in April's eyes.

Martha reached over to cover April's hand with her own. "I'm sure she wants what she thinks is best for you."

"But what if I never get married? What if no man wants me? What will she think of me then?"

"She'll want you to be happy," May said. "Whatever happens."

April sniffed. "I try so hard. Look at me. I have a tiny waist, but that didn't stop Bruce Potter from breaking up with me."

June sipped her sweet tea. "Who's Bruce Potter?"

May leaned in to whisper, "The man April was going to marry."

"You were engaged?" Martha asked.

"No, not exactly. But we would have been if he hadn't met Sylvia Frizell. He's stepping out with her now."

"She couldn't possibly be as pretty as you," May said. "No one could."

"And if he could be so easily distracted by Sylvia Frizell," June said with a determined nod, "then he wasn't the right chap for you."

"I'm beginning to think there's no right man for me. I'll end up an old maid. A shriveled-up old spinster. My mother will be furious."

All three young women turned to look at Martha.

"There are worse things than ending up an old maid," she said.

April gasped and covered her mouth with a hand. "Oh, I didn't mean—"

"It's all right, April. I know it's important to you. But keep in mind what Jane Austen said, that happiness in marriage is entirely a matter of chance."

Martha was no longer offended at such assumptions. How was it that if a man was a bachelor, he was thought to be footloose and fancy-free, too busy romancing a string of ladies to settle down, but an unmarried woman was destined to die poor and alone, like Miss Bates from *Emma*. Poor Miss Bates. Overall, Martha found herself quite content.

"Miss Berry's right," May said enthusiastically. "Being married doesn't mean you'll automatically be happy, and being a spinster doesn't mean you must end your days wizened up like a raisin. Or humorless like my great-aunt Bernice. The Matron."

Martha chuckled. Matrons did have a reputation for being fierce.

"We have all the proof right here. Look at Miss Berry. Why, she barely has a wrinkle on her face. She's so clever. She gets to go to work every day and do interesting things with interesting people. I think I want to be you when I grow up, Miss Berry."

"You do?"

"Of course!" May laughed. "You're working on a radio serial that will be broadcast all over the country, just like *Blue Hills*. You'll be working alongside Kent Stone and Miss Katherine Connors. How lucky is that?"

"Very lucky." April nodded, wide-eyed. "I'd love to work on a serial. Working in the music department is important and Mr. Pattison is very nice to me, but your job sounds much more fun, Miss Berry."

Was she finding it fun? Not exactly. Not yet. She was still waiting for Quentin Quinn to hit his stride. Deep down, she feared it
might be a long wait.

"And who knows? One of us might get to work in television
one day if we stick around long enough." May consulted the
magazine laid out in front of her and pointed out an article she'd
been reading. "There's sure to be a need for secretaries when
it begins broadcasting in September. Can you believe television
is coming in just a few months? It feels like we've been waiting
years!"

June scoffed. "I'd love to have a television, but it doesn't matter
one jot when it begins broadcasting because my family can't afford
to buy one. I'll be standing outside my local electrical store staring
at one through the window for the next ten years, the way I'm going."

"Are they very expensive?" April asked.

May scoured the article in front of her for the details. She
looked up, dejected. "It says here the smaller models start at two
hundred pounds, but they can cost as much as three hundred if
you get the fancy model. And then you have to pay for an aerial
and get a TV license for five pounds a year."

"Five pounds? Goodness," April replied.

"Exactly." June scoffed again. "That's highway robbery, that is.
I only earn two pounds seven a week. And the two pounds goes
right to Mum."

A disappointed silence descended on the table.

"I suppose none of us will get jobs in television if we've never
even watched it." April sighed.

"Come now, it's not so bleak. There are hire purchase options
available. You know, where you pay a little each week until you've
paid off everything? I'd gladly buy a set if I had the money," May
said. "Look here! We could watch *I Love Lucy* with Lucille Ball and

Desi Arnaz, 'America's most popular family program.' And *Davy Crockett* and *The Mickey Mouse Club*."

"Are there any Australian programs mentioned?" June asked.

"Not that I can see. The article says, 'Naturally, Australian actors and actresses, too, will feature on the screens. And as more Australian talent is discovered, so the proportion of all-Australian shows will grow.'"

"Imagine *As the Sun Sets* as a television program!" April exclaimed. "Wouldn't that be exciting, Miss Berry? Miss Connors and Mr. Stone on television."

Martha hadn't heard any talk that new drama programs would be produced for television just yet. The general talk was that local drama would be too expensive to produce. New studios would have to be built to accommodate sets and there would need to be space for all the technical personnel required to put a program to air: producers and writers and cameramen and sound men and script girls and technical producers and broadcast technicians. Not to mention dressing rooms for the actors, props rooms, and space for the wardrobe department. Just thinking about it all made Martha's head spin. Radio actors didn't need costumes or makeup to cover their imperfections and highlight their assets, nor did they need cameramen to film them in pretend rooms or offices. As far as radio was concerned, actors could turn up to the studio in their pajamas and negligees and no one in the listening audience would be any the wiser.

"Lucky for me, I work in radio," Martha said. "Television needs a lot of people and so much equipment. All one needs in radio is a script, a microphone, and a voice."

"Why haven't we had television in Australia yet, Miss Berry?"

April asked. "If the Americans and the English have had it for years?"

"Very important people who get to make decisions about these things, and some in the churches, are worried that people might stop going out or reading books. They're worried it might encourage delinquency in children and might lead them to having nervous disorders if they were to watch programs featuring sadism, brutality, or horror. And it might cause eyestrain in the young ones. Not to mention distracting them from their homework."

"That's silly, isn't it? I got plenty distracted by radio programs when I was supposed to be doing homework," May said. "Especially when news of the war came on. We couldn't make a sound while Mum and Dad listened for the latest. Two of my uncles on my dad's side were serving in New Guinea and they didn't want to miss any news."

"I think everyone in the entire country was the same." Martha paused before asking May, "Did your uncles come home?"

May nodded. "We were very lucky."

Television might be all the rage, but radio had always been there when the chips were down. Newspapers came out in the mornings and the afternoons, but radio news was every hour, and it was different somehow when someone was hearing it read by a familiar voice. There was a comfort in the regularity of it, the seriousness of it. They were voices people believed in. It was an institution they could trust to tell them as much as they were able after the censors' pens had their way with news from overseas.

"Rest assured, girls," Martha said. "Whatever happens with television, there will always be a place in Australians' hearts for radio."

Chapter 11

IN WHICH MARTHA BERRY STUMBLES
ACROSS AN INCAPACITATED QUENTIN
QUINN AND COMES UP WITH A PLAN TO
RESCUE *AS THE SUN SETS.*

W hat on earth?"

Martha had just returned from lunch with April, May, and June when she was stopped in her tracks by the sight of Quentin Quinn's coat askew on the carpet by her desk.

"Mr. Quinn?"

No reply. She went to his door and pushed it open with a sinking feeling. When she peered inside, she spotted his legs jutting out from behind his desk and all the air left her lungs. Good god, had the man had a fall? Was it a heart attack? Granted, it would be unlikely for someone so young to suffer such an episode, but he had been under a lot of pressure—mostly induced by his own procrastination—and Martha had been witness to his excessive consumption of alcohol, coffee, and cigarettes.

She rushed to him and called out, "Mr. Quinn! Mr. Quinn!" Dropping to her knees, she peered into his eyes, then held a hand over his mouth to feel if he was exhaling. She'd seen the move in a picture once, but here in the real world she couldn't seem to tell. Her thoughts raced. She supposed she should check his pulse. She'd never received any first-aid training, and as she had only gleaned the sparest of medical knowledge from listening to *Dr. Paul* on the radio, she wasn't particularly well-equipped to perform a resuscitation. She inched closer to Quentin Quinn's prostrate form and pressed two fingers to the inside of his wrist. She pressed harder and moved her fingers. She couldn't feel anything. *Oh my goodness*, she thought. Perhaps he was dead! And if he was dead, what would happen to *As the Sun Sets*? There was only a week to go before they had to record the first episodes, and still there were no scripts.

Suddenly Quentin Quinn shuddered and let out a monstrous snore.

Martha fell back on her bottom in fright. If she had ever thought about using profanities, that would have been an opportune time to begin.

He hadn't suffered a random health episode. Quentin Quinn was drunk.

Martha thought about it for a moment and then put her hand on his leg, primly below the knee, and gave it a shake. His eyes remained closed. He snored again. She shook harder, until his entire body was rocking from side to side.

"Mr. Quinn? Are you quite all right?" He startled and his leg kicked out, narrowly missing her.

She got to her feet, brushed off her skirt, and walked out, closing the office door and leaving him to sleep it off. Perhaps it would help him. Perhaps he would wake with a clear head and finally get to work on the scripts for *As the Sun Sets* that were now so desperately late.

Oh, what was she thinking? Quentin Quinn was going to be useless for the remainder of the day and only halfway less useless tomorrow morning when he would no doubt turn up late again and with a thick head that no amount of coffee or cigarettes would remedy.

They still didn't have scripts and it was giving Martha Berry heartburn. More than heartburn. If this state of affairs continued much longer, she might be the one having an episode.

The trouble was, they were fast running out of time.

The serial's first week of scripts were due on Mr. Rutherford Hayes's desk by 5:00 p.m. that day. Each episode of each drama needed to be carefully vetted in case, god forbid, someone should utter the word *pregnant*, say something about politics or religion, or worse: swear.

Martha understood the rules. Rutherford Hayes answered to the general manager, Charles Moses, who himself was answerable to the board and even the prime minister, Robert Menzies. Listeners had no hesitation in the past complaining to their local member of parliament if they heard something on the radio that offended their sensibilities, and their complaints would be escalated upward to Menzies's office, and he would then roar at a public servant who would then roar at Charles Moses.

No one wanted to cause trouble with Charles Moses. Not only had he been an amateur heavyweight boxing champion, but he'd fought in the Second World War and survived two Japanese ambushes during the fall of Singapore in 1940. He'd even been mentioned in dispatches.

There'd already been articles in *ABC Weekly* and the daily newspapers about the new radio serial and its main stars Kent Stone and Miss Katherine Connors, so there was no turning back. They were on board a slow-moving train that was chugging faster and faster.

She made herself another cup of tea while Quentin Quinn snored behind his closed office door. She put the cup on her desk, took a few fortifying sips, and opened a folder marked *As the Sun Sets, Scripts, Week One*.

It was empty.

The studio was booked on Monday of the next week for four hours for the recording of the first five episodes. Actors had been hired, their contracts signed.

And as it stood, the actors had nothing to act with. They had no words to speak.

At the rate things were progressing, there was going to be fifteen minutes of dead air from Monday to Friday of the week after in the coveted slot following *Blue Hills*. Martha shivered in horror at the thought. Questions could well be asked in parliament, and then what were they to do?

What was *she* to do? Martha thought on it a moment.

Quentin Quinn's behavior wasn't just affecting his own heart and possibly his liver, but the livelihoods of others and the entire reputation of the national broadcaster.

She simply had to tell someone the truth about Quentin Quinn. Rutherford Hayes would be apoplectic, and when Charles Moses heard about it, he'd probably be apoplectic, too, or want to fight someone in a duel, and then both she and Quentin Quinn would be fired.

Well, at least Quentin Quinn might be fired. Martha hoped his ignominy might not stain her reputation. After all, he was clearly believed to be the creative genius behind the radio serial. She would be moved on to another temporary role somewhere else in the organization, a move she had become quite used to and sanguine about during her working life. Her career? What exactly was a career? There had been no path for her to tread, no trajectory with promotions on the horizon or a pay raise. She had been shuffled from producer to producer, from manager to manager, from department to department, from Talks to Music to News to Drama until she began all over again with the next crop of managers and producers.

Martha leaned back in her chair and lifted her eyes to the ceiling. She heard the snuffle of Quentin Quinn's snoring through his closed office door.

She only had one choice. She would have to summon her strength and go see Rutherford Hayes. She would have to tell him to his face every detail of the dire state they were in and that, the way things were going, there would be no *As the Sun Sets* because the sun would never rise on the new serial. That Quentin Quinn was floundering around in the dark, a man appointed to a position equal to his ambitions but far beyond his talents, and that something had to be done to rectify the situation posthaste. It was past time to be polite. She had been loyal to Quentin Quinn up to this point, but her loyalty had been sorely tested. The time for action was now. She could no longer sit idly by and watch the ship sink— and her job as a script girl with it.

That pay raise she'd successfully negotiated with Mr. Hayes would be taken away from her and she would go back into the general administrative pool, where she would have to pack up her desk and work for someone else next week and then someone else the week after. It had never bothered her before—she'd quite liked the new challenges—but something had changed. She was in on the ground of something that could be exciting and challenging.

And what of Kent Stone and Miss Katherine Connors and all the other actors who would work on the serial? It wasn't that there was a lack of work in Sydney for accomplished radio actors, but the financial rewards weren't as lucrative as people assumed. Being photographed at the theater and at movie premieres looked glamorous, but the actors worked job to job, role to role. And with television around the corner, who knew if everything Martha knew about radio would suddenly be redundant?

Her final realization was the biggest catalyst for her fury: she hadn't even received one week's pay at her new rate of one pound extra a week for being a script girl.

Was it impolite to think she was too old for such shenanigans?

"You've left me with no other choice, Mr. Quinn," Martha murmured to herself as she got up from her desk. "Far be it from me to be a tattletale, but there are jobs at stake here. And reputations." The pep talk seemed to work and as she flung open the office door and strode down the corridor toward Rutherford Hayes's office, she felt something strengthen inside her. A resolve. A determination. In her head she heard rousing orchestral music and her footsteps matched the crash of imaginary cymbals.

And then she was marching toward the desk of Rutherford Hayes's secretary, Miss Jones. Miss Jones was fiddling with something in the top drawer of her desk and when she looked up, startled, she hurriedly closed the drawer and a hand flew to her chest.

"Goodness, Miss Berry."

"I didn't mean to give you a fright, Miss Jones. Is everything all right?"

Martha waited as Miss Jones's blush faded. She didn't want to appear too familiar by demanding an explanation from the young woman. Miss Jones had always been friendly, but they were only acquaintances. Sometimes they chatted about the weather if they came across each other in the staff cafeteria, and occasionally they shared the lift when they were arriving at work or leaving at the end of the day. She had always seemed a confident and organized young woman, with her hair set in neat waves and her pale pink lipstick always perfectly applied, as befitting the secretary of someone of such importance.

Miss Jones quickly found a smile. "Everything's perfectly all right. I'm glad you've popped by. I've actually been meaning to thank you in person, Miss Berry, for leaving things so organized for me when I returned to work."

"It was my pleasure. He's really not much trouble, is he?"

Miss Jones shook her head with a warm smile. "No, he's not at all. Mr. Hayes is definitely one of the better bosses I've worked for in this place. I'm quite lucky."

"I hope you had an enjoyable time on your holiday?"

Miss Jones's cheeks flushed again. "It was marvelous. I've never felt so relaxed. And the scenery. Tasmania really is a beautiful place."

"So I've been told. I've never ventured to the Apple Isle myself," Martha replied.

"You should go. It does one good to get out of Sydney. You must surely have earned some holidays with all your years of service?"

A holiday? The thought of running off somewhere for a holiday hadn't crossed Martha's mind for a good many years, not since Violet's health and mobility had worsened. When she'd taken time off, she'd spent it at home with Violet, catching up on books she hadn't had time to read and seeing to some of the tasks every old house needed. Two years ago, she'd repainted the house throughout, in a lovely pale green called Mint. The year before, the old taps in the bathroom, kitchen, and laundry that had leaked for years were finally replaced.

"I should take a holiday," Martha said, "but at the moment things are gearing up with *As the Sun Sets* and it wouldn't be right to leave Mr. Quinn in the lurch." The way things were going, she might not have a week off until she finally retired.

"Oh yes. Everyone's very excited about it. It must be about ready to put to air."

"Yes," Martha lied through a smile. "It's all rather nerve-racking."

"Anyway, I'm holding you up." Miss Jones waved a hand as if to brush away her conversation. "Were you here to see Mr. Hayes?" She glanced down at her desk and the leather-bound diary open there. "I don't see an appointment in his diary."

"I don't have an appointment. I was hoping he might be in." Martha slipped her hands behind her back and crossed her fingers. If she was the praying type, she might have pleaded with god, any god, to give her guidance.

"I'm terribly sorry. He's out for the rest of the day." Miss Jones began to whisper. "Don't say I told you, but he's playing golf all afternoon. He said it was such a sunny day he couldn't resist."

Martha sighed and glanced at Miss Jones with an expression she hoped came somewhere close to looking like nonchalance. "Oh, never mind."

And as she turned to go, she said to Miss Jones, "I'm glad you enjoyed your holiday."

The blush returned with full force. "Thank you, Miss Berry. Oh, and did you want me to make a time for you with Mr. Hayes?"

Martha thought. When had men ever solved a problem that had been brought to them? When had they taken any problem raised by a woman with the seriousness it deserved? How many times had she heard "Ignore him and he'll stop"? Or "You should be thankful you have a job at all, what with all those blokes coming back from the war." Or "Don't worry your pretty little head about it."

There was only one thing to do. There was only one way out of this situation.

"No, thank you, Miss Jones. Forget I was even here."

On the walk back to her office, Martha glanced through open doors to see woman after woman sitting at desks working for men. Typing the words men had dictated to them. Answering phones for men. Taking messages for men. Covering up for them while they were at a long lunch or at a golf course or with a mistress. Or simply covering up their incompetence.

She reached for the handle of the door to her office and gritted her teeth at the sight of Quentin Quinn's name. Then she made herself a cup of strong black coffee, sat at her desk, and took a few fortifying sips.

She rolled three sheets of butcher paper, interspersed with two sheets of carbon paper, into the carriage return.

And began to type.

Chapter 12

IN WHICH MARTHA BERRY TYPES LIKE SHE'S NEVER TYPED BEFORE.

As the Sun Sets

Writer: Quentin Quinn

Episode One

SCENE: *Percys' Butchers. The bell above the door tinkles and we hear the chatter of women customers. In the background someone is calling, "A dozen beef sausages coming right up."*

FX: *Knife striking chopping block, bell on cash register*

JACK PERCY: *Good morning, Mrs. White.*

MRS. WHITE: *Good morning, Mr. Percy. Goodness, it's busy in here today. But then, I suppose Mondays always are at the best butchers in Sydney. Everyone runs out of meat over the weekend and they're right back in here to buy up for the week.*

JACK PERCY: *They are indeed and I'm very grateful for it. How have you been keeping?*

MRS. WHITE: *(moaning) Oh, well, I can't complain . . . but this weather doesn't help my sciatica at all. The aches and pains it gives me, I can't begin to tell you.*

FX: *Tinkle of bell*

VERA PERCY: *Well, hello there, Mrs. White.*

MRS. WHITE: *Mrs. Percy. It's very nice to see you. Don't you look lovely this morning?*

VERA PERCY: *You're very kind. I'm just popping into the shop to pick up some invoices.*

MRS. WHITE: *Invoices? Whatever for?*

VERA PERCY: *I do all the bookkeeping for the business, Mrs. White. I make sure all our bills are paid on time and that our staff get what they're owed.*

MRS. WHITE: *(harrumphs) In my day that work was left to the menfolk. What do you think will happen to the world if ladies take up all the jobs men should be doing? Women should spend their time and energy keeping a nice house and making sure there's a decent meal on the table at the end of the day, if you ask me. Your husband works so hard here, Mrs. Percy. I'm sure he's up at the crack of dawn cutting all those chops and making sausages and doing goodness knows what else. Aren't you, Mr. Percy?*

JACK PERCY: *The hours are long, Mrs. White, but I wouldn't have it any other way. And I couldn't run this business without my wife. She's a marvel at figures. Why, she always knows exactly what's in the bank . . . down to the exact pence! She pays all the bills on time and chases up people who owe us.*

MRS. WHITE: *Well . . . I never.*

JACK PERCY: *I'll fetch you your regular order, shall I, Mrs. White? Six beef sausages and a pound of tripe coming up.*

Martha turned the platen knob and the pages of script were freed from the typewriter. She picked up one of the sheets of paper and lifted it to the window so the pale light illuminated the page. It had been raining all week in Sydney and no one had seen the sun in days, so her office was dim.

She let herself take a moment to look at the words on the page. She had typed scripts before, so many times that she often typed without actually taking in the words being dictated to her by a writer or a producer or a manager who needed an urgent memo about something not very urgent being completed that minute.

But this page felt different. The butcher paper was weightier, the indentations on it more important than anything she'd ever typed.

They were her words on that page.

She read the lines, murmuring the dialogue to herself in a low voice, something she had always done after taking dictation from producers and writers to ensure sentences fell easily from the lips and sounded like a real conversation, not merely pretty and clever words on a page. She'd seen more than one actor or actress become tongue-tied over sentences that were so long and convoluted that they didn't allow the performer to take a breath. By the time they'd made it to the final word of the sentence, the listener had forgotten the first word and the whole gist was lost. Shorter sentences were better, she had always thought. More and more, that was how people spoke. In quick exclamations. In short bursts as they thought of the next thing to say. Real people didn't make pronouncements in grand soliloquies that spoke more to the writer's ego than the character. She didn't want her characters to make speeches. She wanted them to sound as if they were actually talking to each other.

Martha had always been fascinated by other people's conversations. Her journeys to and from work were the perfect place to be an observer. She'd always found that on crowded trams, passengers seemed to lose their inhibitions around strangers. She'd heard marital woes and medical ones, financial troubles and windfall gains, sobbing and laughter and admonitions and admiration. She'd heard about husbands who'd abandoned families or who'd died while clutching their chests in front of the whole family at Christmas dinner. She'd listened in on descriptions of illicit affairs and broken hearts. She had heard more about love and hate on the tram than she had ever expected to witness in her entire life.

She reached the end of the scene and let herself be proud of it. "Good," she said as she laid the page to her left. The first scene was complete.

And she had finally given Mrs. Percy a first name. Vera. After Vera Lynn because the wartime songstress had always been Violet's favorite.

Martha's thoughts were interrupted by another rollicking snore bellowing from Quentin Quinn's office. It was proof if she needed it that nothing short of an earthquake would wake Quentin Quinn. She checked the time. It was four o'clock.

Martha rolled another set of pages and carbon paper into the typewriter and sent a silent prayer of gratitude to the gloriously defiant Joyce Wiggins. After the death of Martha's old machine, Mr. Hayes had been true to his word and a brand-new typewriter had arrived on Martha's desk the very next day. It didn't help her type any faster, but it made her feel more appreciated somehow. It was portable and came with its own carrying case, which clipped on like the cover of a sewing machine, and it was the same model the newsmen toted around when they were on assignment.

As Quentin Quinn snored and snuffled, Martha found herself pounding the keyboard with a determination she'd never experienced in her entire life. Every book she'd ever read, every film she'd ever seen, every play and radio drama she'd ever listened to had led her to this moment. Words and stories and characters and all their possibilities swirled together in her head. She wasn't frightened of the task ahead. She was invigorated by it. She couldn't help but think the first stirrings had happened when Joyce Wiggins had taken one look at her and offered her cut-to-the-quick assessment.

"I bet you'd run rings around all these hopeless chaps you've worked for all these years."

It had taken Miss Wiggins exactly one minute to make that assessment. How had she done it? How had she known? What had she seen in Martha to lead her to such a conclusion? What had Joyce seen in Martha that Martha hadn't yet seen in herself?

Martha had thought about it nonstop since that day back in May. Why had she not been more furious about the way women in the organization were treated? She'd been witness to injustices just as Joyce had been, but it was as if Martha had been asleep at the wheel. She'd huffed at the unfairness but never made the next step, to take matters into her own hands and do something about it. Perhaps that was why she'd massaged the truth about the conversation she'd had with Joyce when she was questioned about it. Martha had her own frustrations over the years with the way she'd been treated, overlooked, and now, most often, ignored. But she'd never thought it was within her power to actually do something about it. She'd been brought up to be polite, and raising such issues had always been deemed far too impolite.

Until now. As she typed, she thought again of Joyce, and the Brontës writing under men's names, and Jane Austen having to hide behind the nom de plume "A Lady," and George Eliot—Mary Ann Evans—and Miles Franklin, and Aphra Behn, whose name never graced her work, and every other woman who'd had their creative endeavors thwarted and ridiculed and cast aside.

A flush crept up Martha's cheeks in a hot wave. She lifted her fingers from the keys and pressed her palms to her cheeks. Why was she only now seeing the injustice? The heat turned into rage and she swore under her breath. It felt rather satisfying.

She was a script girl now and she had everything to lose if *As the Sun Sets* should fall in a heap because Quentin Quinn was a drinker promoted way above his skill level, someone who looked down on radio listeners everywhere, who thought of them as merely following his lead as hens might do with the scattering of grain at feeding time.

No. She could not let it fail. She would not let it fail.

She thought of people all over the country for whom listening to the radio was a ritual. Women like her mother and Mrs. Ward and Mrs. Tilley, who lived for their radio programs and the characters whose voices came into their homes twice a day, five days a week. How was it that these invisible people, voices floating through the air along vibrations and frequencies, should have come to occupy such a treasured and precious place in the lives of their listeners? The characters were loved as if they were real friends. The dramas created a routine for her mother and her neighbors. They could reliably know they would feel happy, angry, and even perhaps a little bit sad on behalf of the characters they were attached to, loved, or whose antics they gasped at.

When Violet, Mrs. Ward, and Mrs. Tilley met each day for their afternoon cup of tea—a respite before the arrival of the demanding and hungry Mr. Ward and Mr. Tilley—their radio dramas were the number one topic of conversation, the glue that held their friendships together. They would rail against one character, cry for another, and hold a secret affection in their hearts for another. And there were hundreds of thousands of people across the country just like them, who needed such characters to soothe their loneliness, to fill their homes with conversation and voices.

How dare Quentin Quinn treat *As the Sun Sets* as nothing but a personal vehicle for his self-aggrandizement?

How dare he be so flippant about the older audiences and their favorite programs?

And then Martha pondered the biggest and most mysterious question of them all. How had he managed to win a position writing a radio drama when he had freely admitted to her that he'd never listened to one in his whole entire, short, privileged, barely-able-to-grow-facial-hair life?

Quentin Quinn had obviously dazzled the right people with the right words—or rather the right promises—and was so far failing spectacularly.

Martha heard herself huff and her anger flared again, creating dampness in her armpits.

She would never understand the decisions of men.

She swallowed a mouthful of lukewarm tea and kept going. As Martha typed, it was as if she'd tapped into a long-dormant wellspring. Often, when she was listening to *Blue Hills* or *Portia Faces Life*, she would try to imagine the next scene, the next tragedy that might befall the main characters. Sometimes she thought her ideas were far more interesting than the writers'. She did the same with the new novels she borrowed from the library and the short stories she read each Wednesday evening after she'd picked up a copy of her favorite magazine at the newsstand on the way home from work. What might happen to the lovers after the writer had typed *The End*? Would their happy ever after hold? Would they grow old gracefully, still as much in love with each other? Or would their affair be as flimsy as crepe paper decorations at a child's birthday party?

Martha had the story bible for *As the Sun Sets*, but it was only the barest of bones. She would put flesh on those bones and save it from being axed before the first episode had even gone to air.

She had so many ideas for *As the Sun Sets*. The Percys' daughter, Betty, might strike up a flirtation with Ernie, the new apprentice, and he might flirt back, but maybe a mysterious secret from his past would be revealed, shattering Betty's hopes and dreams. It was so interesting when couples were torn apart. One couldn't help but keep listening with bated breath to find out if the lovers would be able to overcome their obstacles or fall victim to the sorry hands of fate.

Perhaps there should be a haberdashery near the Percys' butcher shop and it might be owned by a young widow, Myrna—Martha liked the sound of that name, because she'd always loved the actress Myrna Loy—who was still grieving after losing her husband in New Guinea during the war. Women were in and out of the haberdashers all the time, picking up things like elastic for their sons' school shorts and fabric for making dresses for their daughters or themselves, or selecting balls of pastel wool for the knitting of baby layettes. It would be an interesting place for women in the show to meet and talk without the prying and judgmental eyes of men on them.

Martha would have to look up the name of a battle in which Myrna's husband might have died—heroically, of course. That would leave Myrna with plenty of scope for romance and also for the other female characters to gossip unfairly that Myrna was after everyone's husband, seeing as she was a widow.

And the greengrocers mentioned in the story bible that Quentin Quinn had so haphazardly created? She still had to come up with some characters and names for them.

She took a fortifying sip of her tea and pressed her fingers to the keys.

JACK PERCY: *I hope you've been to see the doctor, Mrs. White, about that sciatica. He might be able to do something for you.*

MRS. WHITE: *(harrumphs) What can they do? The last time I saw a doctor, it must have been years ago now, just after the war, and he told me I'd slipped a disc. It sounded so frightening I couldn't even ask him what it meant and I never went back. Probably a quack trying to get money out of me. Who can afford a back operation these days? Not me, Mr. Percy.*

VERA PERCY: *I'm sure you won't need an operation, Mrs. White. There's all kinds of new medicines and treatments available these days. I hate to hear of you suffering in such pain. Are you resting up as much as you can?*

MRS. WHITE: *Resting? (sighs audibly) Who has time to rest? But I do appreciate your concern, Mrs. Percy. Anyway, I mustn't grumble.*

VERA PERCY: *If there's anything I can ever do for you, please just ask. Nothing will be too much trouble, Mrs. White. Honestly.*

MRS. WHITE: *You really are very kind, dear.*

A yawn and then a cough.

Martha looked up from the script. She'd become so mesmerized that she hadn't realized Quentin Quinn was standing in front of her. The young man looked a right mess. His bow tie was pulled to one side like someone had yanked it, his Brylcreemed hair stood on end as if he'd stuck his finger into a power point, and, good lord—Martha blinked and tried not to look—the fly on his trousers was undone.

He rubbed a hand over his face. "What's the time?"

Martha glanced at her watch. "It's a quarter to five."

"Crikey," he exclaimed. "Where did the day go?" He narrowed his bloodshot eyes and turned to read the words Martha had been typing. "What's that?"

Martha had to think quickly. "The corrected versions of your scripts from this morning. I'd made a few errors, unfortunately, and I want the copy to be as clean as can be. For Mr. Hayes to look over. And the actors to read. I know it makes it easier when they're recording."

Quentin Quinn's eyes darted around the room. "The scripts. The scripts I wrote this morning?"

Martha nodded, forcing a smile as if to indicate that absolutely everything was fine and he shouldn't worry at all. What she might have said, if she hadn't been so polite, was what she'd heard too many times when she was younger: "Don't worry your pretty little head about that." She lifted her cup and sipped the dregs. The move gave her time to think of what to say to assuage his suspicions.

"You were quite prolific before you went to lunch. The ideas were flowing like water over a waterfall. Or, as I've heard it said so many times in this place"—she smiled—"you were on a roll."

Quentin Quinn looked down at Martha with an expression halfway between nausea and suspicion. He held out a shaking hand.

"Rightio. I'll have a check and see if you've made any spelling mistakes before I run them by Rutherford Hayes. I wouldn't want any sloppy copy to make it through to him."

"Of course, Mr. Quinn." She gathered up the typed pages, neatened them into a pile, and handed them over. She felt an ache in her jaw.

Quentin Quinn turned and walked back to his desk.

Good lord. Martha closed her eyes and blew out a breath.

She hoped he planned to zip his fly before he came back.

Chapter 13

IN WHICH MARTHA BERRY'S SCRIPTS
CAUSE GREAT EXCITEMENT WITH HEAD OF
DRAMA, MR. RUTHERFORD HAYES, AND
QUENTIN QUINN TAKES ALL THE CREDIT.

Quentin Quinn burst through the office door like a cowboy entering a saloon in the wild, wild West.

"Mrs. Barry!" he hollered, and Martha suddenly felt as faint as a barmaid in that same saloon faced with a posse of scar-faced outlaws.

"Crack open a bottle of Barossa Pearl. I have script approval!"

Relief washed over her like a wave and she sat back in her chair to let her heartbeat settle.

Her words. Rutherford Hayes had approved her words. A shiver tingled up her arms and she hoped her décolletage hadn't flushed red, as it tended to lately when she was excited. If she let it, her smile would have been as wide as the Sydney Harbour Bridge. As it was, she pulled her lips together so her face resembled something congratulatory rather than self-congratulatory.

"That's simply excellent news, Mr. Quinn."

"He loves them!" Quentin Quinn paced up and down in front of Martha's desk, bouncing on his heels. "He said, and I quote, 'Quinn. These are the freshest scripts I've seen in a long, long time. The dialogue . . .' Hang on, was it *sparkles* or *zings*? Anyway, he loved the dialogue, the characters. He thinks there's a real chance for Jack and Vera Percy to be the new Gordons, you know, the anchor couple from *Blue Hills*. The doctor and his wife."

As if Martha didn't know the Gordons from *Blue Hills*. "You must be very pleased."

She'd done it. Her scripts were fresh. The dialogue sparkled. Or zinged. She didn't care which. Something inside her sparkled *and* zinged.

"I forgot to mention, Mrs. Barry. There's going to be a photo shoot with our Betty, Marilyn Calthorpe, and Kent and, you know, that other woman."

Martha was horrified and a flush of heat crept up her cheeks. How dare he refer to Miss Katherine Connors in such a way, as if she were an afterthought? "Do you mean Miss Connors?" she asked, gritting her teeth.

He waved a hand as if he were shooing away a fly. "Yes. Her. Talk to the publicity department and let me know when it's happening. I'll need to be there, of course." He puffed up his chest like a bantam on the prowl. "As the producer, I should keep an eye on things like that. And I'm certain this will be the first publicity opportunity for Marilyn, so she'll need a guiding hand. What she says to the press and so on."

"Of course, Mr. Quinn."

Quentin Quinn almost sprinted to his desk and picked up the phone, jabbing an index finger into the dial and waiting impatiently as it spun back around after each number. Finally he was connected, and judging by the hoots of laughter and hand slaps on the desk over the next ten minutes, he was sharing his triumph with everyone he knew.

While he repeated over and over the praise that had been heaped on him ("The old man Hayes says I'm a natural. He thinks listeners all over Australia are going to love *As the Sun Sets* . . ."), Martha went to the window and stared down onto the street. Goose bumps prickled her arms and she crossed them in front of her, as if she were hugging herself in congratulations, hoping it might tamp down her racing heartbeat. Her head began to pound right behind her eyes, so hard she thought it might blow off the top of her skull. Oh, how she wanted to run down to the street and shout the news to perfect strangers. "The freshest scripts I've seen in a long, long time. The dialogue zings." Or was that *sparkles*? She didn't care. How could she? Rutherford Hayes had read *her* scripts and heaped praise on them. He would never know that he'd also heaped praise on her, even if her name wasn't on the title page and Quentin Quinn's was. She was the writer and no one could take that away from her.

She hoped listeners wouldn't compare *As the Sun Sets* to *Blue Hills*, not at first anyway, because that was impossible and Gwen Meredith was the queen of radio drama. But if the audience kept listening and liked what they heard, she would have achieved something momentous.

She had never received praise in a work context for anything she'd done. For something creative. For something she had come up with entirely on her own. So this was how it felt. Success, even if it was only the smallest beginning of it. There was still so far to go.

She hoped they had cast the right actors for all the parts. She hoped they would develop a working chemistry so they didn't want to scratch each other's eyes out after spending so much time together in a tiny studio. She'd seen it happen. She hoped that if success came, Kent Stone and Miss Connors and especially the young ingenue, Marilyn Calthorpe, didn't want to quit Australia for the brighter lights of London's West End. She'd seen that happen too many times, only for actors to return home on the boat a few years later too humiliated to tell anyone in Australia that the competition for roles was much tougher than they'd imagined it would be and that they'd ended up waiting tables or cleaning offices to make ends meet while they waited for their big break, which hadn't broken at all.

There was so much that could go wrong.

But for today, at least, something had gone right.

"Mrs. Barry, I'm heading out." Quentin Quinn slipped on his coat and took a puff of a freshly lit cigarette. "I'm off for that celebratory drink. Hold the fort, will you?"

She turned to face him. "You deserve it, Mr. Quinn." When had lying become so easy?

He gave her a curt nod before slipping out the door. She went back to the window and waited for him to emerge from the main entrance onto the footpath. When she spotted him, saw his trench coat flapping behind him as he strode down the street, and was certain he wouldn't be back in a hurry, she quietly closed the door to the main office and danced. She spun around the room like Ginger Rogers and Fred Astaire in *Shall We Dance*.

And she suddenly had a renewed appreciation for Ginger. While Fred sucked up more than his fair share of fame and always received more publicity, she remembered what one jokester had said, that Ginger did everything Fred was doing, only backward and in high heels.

Nothing and no one could take this moment away from Martha.

....

"Well, there you go. The butcher's wife has a name." Miss Connors flicked through her copy of the first week's scripts and smiled at Quentin Quinn. He nodded in recognition of his own greatness.

"So to whom am I married?" Kent Stone asked with a grin and a quirkily raised eyebrow.

"Vera," Miss Connors replied.

"How do you do, Vera Percy?" Kent bowed dramatically.

"Very well, thank you, Jack Percy."

The actors were in the studio and their discussion was being broadcast through an open microphone into the small control room, separated by a thick pane of glass. The studio, about twenty feet by twenty feet, had a high ceiling and carpet. It was padded with soundproofing material that resembled felt, and in the center of the room stood a microphone on a stand.

Nearby sat a long table filled with a variety of sound effects props. Two halves of a coconut, perfect for creating the sound of horses' hooves, sat forlornly—since they weren't making a Western, they wouldn't be needing those. A weary old cabbage and a wooden stick, useful for imitating the sound of a fist connecting with a skull, lay near them. Again, thankfully, not a scene Martha had written. Although one never knew where her imagination might take her. Next to the cabbage, a small cardboard box was filled with an old spool of recording tape, loose and tangled, which could be used to mimic the sounds of a person walking on fallen leaves. An autumn walk. How romantic. Martha made a mental note. A small, tarnished brass bell sat next to the box, and a small door in a frame of about three feet by two would be used when the characters in *As the Sun Sets* entered or left a room.

Martha stood at the back of the control room, because there were only two chairs and the spare had already been claimed by Quentin Quinn. The ashtray on the desk in front of him was already half full and an empty coffee cup sat to one side. He'd arrived that morning, the day of the recording of the first episodes of *As the Sun Sets*, with his hair neatly combed and slicked into place with hair oil and his shirt crisply ironed, sporting a new paisley bow tie. His suit bore the smell of having been dry cleaned not long before, and if she looked closely, though she really hadn't intended to, he was cleanly shaven. Martha wondered for a very brief moment what on earth might have caused this sartorial conversion before realizing the answer lay in the form of Miss Marilyn Calthorpe.

He could hardly take his eyes off her.

Seated next to him, wearing a brown woolen jumper that might have seen action in the trenches it was so old, was Handsy Hooper, the radio technician. He was a crucial cog in the wheel of recording *As the Sun Sets* and getting it to air: he controlled the faders and buttons and switches on the control panel in front of him and was responsible for ensuring the actors' voices were recorded to broadcast-quality standards.

Martha had crossed paths with Handsy Hooper many times. Too many. She loathed the man. While the idea of standing for four or more hours in the back of a cramped and dim studio seemed daunting and uncomfortable, at least it meant she wasn't sitting next to him. Who knew what he might attempt if she was squeezed in between the two men like a rose between two thorns. At least if she was standing, she could make a quick exit if he got too close.

In the crook of one arm, she held a ring binder filled with copies of that week's scripts, and in the other hand, a freshly sharpened pencil was poised to mark up the pages as they were spoken by the actors. Their task today was to record a week's worth of episodes, five of fifteen minutes' length. As script girl, Martha was responsible for ensuring the actors performed their lines as they were written (the way *she* had written them) and didn't inadvertently miss one. And there were to be absolutely no ad-libs. Word had come down from on high that the scripts had to be performed as written and approved or there was a very real risk of the drama being suspended. No one wanted an inadvertent "bloody" or "pregnant" to slip through the net. She had to listen intently to catch mispronunciations and slips of the tongue and to advise Handsy Hooper to stop recording if that happened, then listen to him complain when they would then have to begin the entire episode again.

Handsy flicked a switch, and when he spoke the actors turned to face him. "We're just getting the sound levels right in here. Keep chatting away. We'll let you know when we're ready to record. Smithy, you set to go?" The sound effects man stood to one side of the actors, his own copy of the script on a music stand in front of him. He was poised like a jungle cat about to strike. He replied with a silent thumbs-up.

"I always thought you'd make a wonderful wife," Kent Stone told Miss Connors with a wink. "Although if we were married out in the real world, we might have to dine out each evening, darling. I have the strangest feeling cooking isn't your forte."

She took a small silver compact from her handbag, opened it, and checked her makeup. She looked slyly at Kent Stone. "If you took me out to dinner every night, I might just accept your proposal."

Marilyn Calthorpe gasped and then quickly covered her mouth with a hand. "You really can't cook, Miss Connors?"

Katherine was a Miss in a way that was entirely different from Martha being a Miss. Miss Connors had relinquished her maiden name at twenty-one to become Mrs. Johnson after she'd married a Vaucluse stockbroker who was at least twice her age, but that union lasted as long as the money did. Sadly, he'd lost everything in the stock market crash of 1929 and Katherine had been forced to become used to a life to which she was quite unaccustomed. Two years later, when the economy was stronger, she became Mrs. French, after working hard to catch the attentions of the heir to a cardboard box fortune. They had a lavish society wedding with a reception at the Australia Hotel to which everyone who was anyone in Sydney was invited—even the governor—but that marriage had ended tragically when he'd drowned in Sydney Harbour six months later after falling from a yacht during a race off Rose Bay. Katherine had waited a discreet four years before exchanging vows with a prominent surgeon who disliked show business with a passion and didn't mind in the slightest that the private Mrs. Allister would continue to be known publicly by her stage name.

"Cook? Hell no," she chuckled. "I have an aversion to doing anything over a naked flame."

Marilyn Calthorpe stared at the actress googly-eyed. "I can't imagine it. I have to cook every night for the whole family."

"How many Calthorpes are there?" Kent asked with a raised eyebrow.

"Mum, Dad, and seven children. Four boys and three girls," she said. "I'm the oldest."

Miss Connors fanned herself with her script. "You poor girl." She turned to Kent. "Darling Jack. Our daughter works too hard."

"I must admit to being very nervous," Marilyn whispered to nobody in particular.

"Oh, dear girl. You'll be marvelous," Kent told her with a wink. "It's easy. Just remember, all the listeners at home will hear is your voice. Let it be real. They'll spot a phony a mile away. Relax and have fun."

"When we get it right, there's absolutely nothing like radio drama, Marilyn," Miss Connors added. "Anybody can read a script, but it's only actors like us who can bring those words to life, convince people at home that we really are these characters. Let yourself feel the emotion in the words you're about to say. You're going to be wonderful." The veteran actress then took a step closer to Marilyn and whispered something in her ear.

As Marilyn listened, her expression changed from slightly terrified to slightly less terrified. Martha couldn't hear what Miss Connors had said, but judging by the jittery smile on Marilyn's face and Miss Connors's comforting hand on her arm, it must have been warm words of encouragement. Miss Connors was all class.

Martha's doubts that the actors might not get on faded into insignificance. Kent Stone and Miss Connors were professionals in every sense of the word. Kent's vast experience on the stage and behind the microphone was something Martha admired enormously. To think he'd almost been overlooked for the role of Jack Percy. She tried not to think about her conversation with Quentin Quinn a few weeks before when they were considering who to cast as Jack and Vera Percy. He'd held up Kent's headshot and frowned. "This chap's a little long in the tooth, isn't he?"

"He's a very experienced actor, Mr. Quinn." Martha tried not to blow out an exasperated breath. "And he is up for the role of Jack Percy, the butcher, who is himself an older gentleman."

"Mmm. And surely we can't be serious about *her*?" He'd held up a glamorous photo of Miss Connors. Martha had to admit that it might be time for the actress to update her photograph. In the style of a Greta Garbo still from a movie, the black-and-white shot featured dark shadows that created heightened angles on Miss Connors's earlier, more youthful visage. Her hat and veil added mystery and her dark lips a hint of romance.

"She's a splendid actress, Mr. Quinn."

"Yes, yes, but she's playing a butcher's wife, for god's sake. Not a German spy." He'd thrown the photograph on Martha's desk in a huff and it had slipped across the wooden surface and landed on the floor, face down. Martha couldn't bear to see a legend of Australian radio drama treated in such a way and she'd hurried to pick it up.

"She's very versatile. Radio actors and actresses have to be. I'm sure Miss Connors could play the butcher's wife and any other minor female character you write."

"Now, hold on. Who's this?" And the scenario had played out exactly as Martha had anticipated it would. The only actor Quentin Quinn had eyes for was Miss Marilyn Calthorpe. She could swear he'd stared at Marilyn's photograph for a full minute, taking in every inch of her light hair—probably a platinum blonde—her big, dark eyes, long lashes, pert nose, and Cupid's bow lips. He'd insisted on a private meeting with Marilyn and had cast her that very day, without even an audition in front of a microphone.

From her vantage point behind Quentin Quinn in the control room, Martha watched him watch the young ingenue. Staring at her through the glass pane, he seemed fixated by her every move.

"Hooper," Quentin Quinn said, "we'll need a few more test lines from Betty. Miss Calthorpe, I mean. She hasn't said much."

Hooper sniggered. "Don't know where you dug her up from but I'm glad you did. She's got a set, hasn't she? Looks just like

Marilyn Monroe. But looking at her, I don't reckon her tits are as big. You seen that photo of Marilyn Monroe in *Playboy* magazine? One of my old army pals lives in San Francisco now and he sent me the first copy. I've got it right here if you want to have a look?" Hooper began rifling in a leather satchel at his feet.

Martha wished Hooper would stop talking. She also wished he would stop living.

"Not right now, old chap." Quentin Quinn turned his head just slightly, as if to remind Hooper that there was a lady in the room, and tapped his pile of scripts. "We've got a lot of work to do."

Hooper sniffed. "If you want it later, let me know. It's done the rounds of this place. I should have charged a quid each time. I'd be a rich man."

Quentin Quinn cleared his throat. "That test audio from Miss Calthorpe?"

"Miss Calthorpe," Hooper breathed into the microphone connecting the control room and the studio. "Can you count to ten, love?"

"Of course." She leaned in close to the microphone and performed the task admirably.

"I'm ready," Hooper announced.

"Right."

Then there was silence. The three actors glanced through the glass, awaiting their instructions.

Quentin Quinn stared back at them.

"Mr. Quinn? Are we ready to go?" Martha checked her watch. Fifteen minutes of precious studio time had already passed without one minute of script recorded. She knew from past experience that when their time was up, another producer would be waiting at the door—and would knock violently if they had a mind—so as not to lose one minute of their own allotted time. Studios were expensive to fit out and expensive to run, so they were kept busy from dawn to dusk and even sometimes to sunup if one of the actors turned up drunk and needed to sober up first.

"Ready to go." Quentin Quinn nervously lit a cigarette.

Martha held her breath.

Hooper flicked on his microphone so he could be heard by the actors. "Since pretty little Marilyn hasn't done this before, here's a reminder. Don't make any mistakes. I'm recording you on a wax master, which will be pressed on a sixteen-inch acetate disc. That's what's played for the broadcast of the show. If you bugger up a line, I can't stop and start the recording again. We'll have to go from the very beginning on a new wax master, which I don't need to tell you will cost money. And if you fluff the very last line, we'll still have to do the whole thing over and you won't get paid extra. Got it?"

Marilyn looked stricken. Miss Connors patted her shoulder.

"No pressure then," Kent Stone said with a raised eyebrow.

"Yes, thank you, Hooper," Quentin Quinn said with a frustrated sigh. Despite his inexperience, even he could see this was no way to encourage the actors to do their best.

"Here we go," Hooper called and held up a hand for the actors. Three fingers. Two fingers. One finger, and then he swept that finger from right to left.

He cranked up a turntable to his left and a piece of orchestral music swirled and swooped. Thirty seconds later, he turned it down slowly so the volume faded and expertly lifted the needle from the record. He then cued Kent Stone with a finger jab, and the actor moved in closer to the microphone and announced in his most perfect, dulcet tones, "The ABC presents *As the Sun Sets* by Quentin Quinn. Episode one . . . in which we meet Jack Percy, his wife, Vera, and their daughter, Betty."

Martha stood with her ring binder resting in the crook of her arm, mouthing the sentences as the actors spoke them. She would have pinched herself if she could have, but she didn't have a hand free. So she smiled instead and enjoyed every beat of her pounding heart, which was drumming like a marching band in her chest. The words and sentences she'd typed had transformed into the language of the characters: Kent Stone's rough but kind voice for Jack; Miss Connors's light and gay tone for Vera; and Marilyn Calthorpe's cheerful Betty. It really was some kind of magic. And she had waved the wand.

Her words, those she had typed herself as they flowed from her imagination like an unstoppable force, were not only there on the pages of the script but were being spoken by real actors and transformed into vibrations that were somehow being recorded directly onto a wax disc.

Was it silly for her to admit that she still didn't quite understand this radio magic?

That was the beauty of it. She didn't need to understand the technical wizardry of it. Guglielmo Marconi had and that was all she needed to know. Her job was to understand her characters and their lives. And to let Quentin Quinn believe he'd come up with the ideas.

She had absolutely no idea how she was going to pull it off.

When she stopped daydreaming, the actors were already on to the third scene.

BETTY PERCY: *Hello, Dad.*

JACK PERCY: *Hello, Betty. And how's that lovely wife of mine? Hello, Vera.*

Kent Stone and Miss Connors kissed into the air so the sound effect was caught by the microphone.

VERA PERCY: *Sit down at the table, Jack. Dinner's almost ready. And there's your paper if you want to have a read while I mash the spuds.*

BETTY PERCY: *I'll mash them, Mum. Judging by the pile of paperwork I had to clear away to set the table, you've been busy all day with the books for the butcher shop.*

VERA PERCY: *(sighs) I have. It's the end of the month and there are always bills to pay. You know, Jack? I think we sold more pork sausages this month than we ever have before.*

JACK PERCY: *(laughing) Well, I never. I know we've been busy. And people love our sausages, that's for sure. I've been thinking, love. I might take on another apprentice. I'm not as young as I was, and I could do with a hand lugging all those sheep and beef carcasses around. I'd like to teach a young bloke the trade. Give something back so a young fella can get a start in life in a good, honest job.*

VERA PERCY: *We can afford it, Jack. I think it's a terrific idea. I'm sure some young lad will jump at the chance to learn from the best.*

JACK PERCY: *I'll put a sign in the window tomorrow. See what interest that stirs up.*

BETTY PERCY: *I could make the sign, Dad. My teacher says I have the neatest handwriting in the whole class.*

VERA PERCY: *(laughing) Not for much longer, Betty. You'll soon be starting your secretarial course.*

BETTY PERCY: *Gosh. You're right, Mum. July's not that far away, is it? I'm so excited to see what kind of job I might get when I've finished. I'd really like to work in an office. Somewhere as far away from sausages and sawdust as I can get!*

The actors continued flawlessly reading their lines, page after page of Martha's script, until the end when Handsy Hooper cranked up the theme music and then faded it before he ended the recording. In the studio, Kent Stone, Miss Connors, and Marilyn Calthorpe feigned exhaustion, but their big smiles revealed how pleased they all were to have made it through the first five episodes in five clean takes. Martha slumped against the wall, letting all the tension she'd been holding in her shoulders drain out of her. She felt like a bowl of jelly, and it was all she could do to stop herself from sliding down the wall and flopping onto the studio floor.

"Marvelous!" Quentin Quinn clapped his hands together in glee. Ash from the cigarette he'd pinched between his lips scattered like snow as he moved.

Five episodes were in the can, as the radio people liked to say. It was no surprise to Martha that Kent Stone and Miss Connors had performed faultlessly, given their vast acting experience, but it was Marilyn Calthorpe who'd impressed Martha the most. This was her first dramatic role—not counting some ballet school performances at the local church hall throughout her childhood— and she had performed with excellence and professionalism. The young woman was a quick study, which meant she was smart. And Martha liked smart young women. With only a few minutes for rehearsal in the studio, along with some well-meaning advice from Kent and Miss Connors about where to stand to best effect for recording, to step up when she had a line of dialogue, and to step back to make room for the others when it was their turn, she had turned in a terrific performance.

She had captured exactly what Martha had intended for young Betty—the excitement and innocence of a young woman on the cusp of knowing great things were to come, full of anticipation about starting secretarial college and landing her first job. Martha's own experiences may have been more than thirty years old, of a previous generation, but she had never lost touch with that feeling of being on the edge of a cliff, looking on the whole entire world down below. She would give that to Betty, and so much more, if she had the chance.

Quentin Quinn went to join the actors in the studio and Martha followed him, almost bumping into Smithy, the sound effects man, on his way out with a saucepan and a lid in his hands. He gave her a quick smile and scooted off.

"Well done to you all," Quentin Quinn announced with a round of applause. Martha sensed it was for himself rather than anyone else in the room. "We've really set the scene for the show. This first week, I really wanted to focus on the Percy family so listeners will get a glimpse into their lives and learn to love them. They'll be the bedrock of the drama." He laughed and winked at Kent Stone, who seemed slightly confused at the younger man's gesture and looked to Miss Connors in bemusement. "If the lady listeners don't start swooning over perfect husband Jack Percy before too long, well, I'll eat my hat."

"In that case, I look forward to the fan mail," Kent said, checking his reflection in the studio window and primping his hair.

Miss Connors adjusted her hat. "The perfect husband? Some want the one in a million. I always wanted the one *with* a million." She passed her bundle of scripts back to Martha with a nod of acknowledgment. "And congratulations to you, Mr. Quinn. I must admit to having my doubts about you, what with you being so . . . young . . ." She looked him over from brogues to Brylcreem. "But the scripts are a joy to perform. I've never played a wife who has had so many lines—and such clever things to say too."

"And Miss Calthorpe?" Quentin Quinn turned to the young actress. "What a wonderful performance."

"Thank you, Mr. Quinn. That means a lot coming from you." She blushed and dropped her gaze to her court shoes.

"Now. I've been meaning to ask. Are you spoken for?"

The actors and Martha turned as one to look at Quentin Quinn. The recording studio fell silent.

Marilyn looked from Kent to Miss Connors to Martha with a wobbly smile. "No, I'm not." And then her smile faded. "I don't even have a fiancé. Is that a problem?"

"Perfect," Quentin Quinn announced in what could only be described as a high-pitched squeal. Silence followed. He quickly cleared his throat in an attempt to both lower his voice and regain some authority. "I mean, it's perfect for Betty. And for publicity. You're a single girl. She's a single girl. You'll be able to bring such empathy to the role."

"I hope to," Marilyn replied.

Miss Connors patted the young woman's shoulder. "You've done marvelously today, Miss Calthorpe. A true pro."

Marilyn beamed. "Do you really think so?"

"I second that." Kent reached for his hat and placed it on his head, checking his reflection again to ensure the hat sat at just the right jaunty angle. "You're a pleasure to work with, my dear."

"I couldn't ask for better parents." She giggled. "Oh, you know what I mean. To think I've been listening to you both on the radio since I was a baby. And now here I am! It's like a dream come true."

Kent and Miss Connors exchanged rueful glances and Miss Connors added slyly, "Just don't be marrying Betty off and giving her a baby anytime soon, Mr. Quinn." She visibly shuddered. "I'm far too young to play a grandmother."

They laughed together and Martha watched the easy camaraderie the cast had already established. It augured well for future episodes. For all their futures, as a matter of fact.

"Now, someone promised lunch," Kent said. "I believe that was you, Quinn."

Quentin Quinn clapped his hands together. "Of course. My treat."

Quentin Quinn opened the studio door and ushered the actors into the hallway. Just as Martha was about to join them, he stepped in front of her. "Mrs. Barry, I've left some notes on your desk for next week's scripts. Could you type them up? I'll look at them when I get back from lunch."

She watched them all leave, but not before Miss Connors turned to look back at her with a knowing expression before she followed the others into the hallway. The door closed behind her and the excited chatter of the actors faded.

Martha found herself alone in the silence.

"*Miss* Berry," she whispered to herself, her fingers clenching into fists. "It's *Miss* Berry."

Chapter 14

IN WHICH MARTHA BERRY CELEBRATES WITH THE CALENDAR GIRLS.

Miss Berry. We absolutely *love* the show!"

April, May, and June lifted their glasses—apple juice for April and sherry for everyone else—and held them toward Martha. She quickly reached for hers and the four women clinked them together.

"I'm very glad to hear it," Martha replied with a nod and a barely suppressed smile.

"What's going to happen to Betty?" April took a sip and leaned in. "You can tell me. I promise I can keep a secret."

May giggled. "That'll be a first!"

"That's not true. You're making me out to be some horrible gossip." April set her now-empty glass on the restaurant table with such great indignation, Martha was surprised she didn't break the stem of the glass.

"We're just teasing," May said and laid a hand on April's arm to reassure her friend.

"Thank you, May. But, Miss Berry, we still want to know all

about Betty! Will she have a romance with the new butcher's apprentice when he starts in the shop?"

"We promise, pinky swear," May added with hopeful eyebrows. "We won't tell anyone."

The three young women turned their pleading eyes to Martha. They were dear girls. And if they were this excited about the first two weeks' episodes of *As the Sun Sets*, what would young women around the country be thinking? That thought sent excitement racing through Martha. The hairs on the back of her neck prickled. This was much more fun than she had anticipated.

"All I will say is . . . Betty might make more appearances at the family butcher shop in the near future." Martha sipped her sherry, relishing the thick sweetness as it slid down her throat. She didn't normally make a habit of going out on a Friday night after work, but the Calendar Girls had marched into her office yesterday and demanded she make herself available to celebrate the success of *As the Sun Sets*.

"It's been weeks since we've seen you in the cafeteria at lunchtime," April had told her. "We miss you, Miss Berry."

There was no way for Martha to explain to the girls that there was no such thing as a lunch break these days. When Quentin Quinn would inevitably fall asleep at his desk—or on the floor—in the afternoons, she worked like a demon to turn his vague jottings into scripts. She had taken to packing up her portable typewriter at the end of each day and working in the evenings too. She knew that when inspiration struck—no matter the hour—she was compelled to write and would *click-clack* away on the keys until the episode was complete.

Quentin Quinn was often out of the office. There were regular meetings with Rutherford Hayes and the other drama producers and with the men in publicity. There had been a stampede of interest in the actors, especially the star-from-out-of-nowhere Miss Marilyn Calthorpe, and Quentin Quinn had made sure to attend every photo shoot for each of the local newspapers as well as for the weekly magazines and, of course, for *ABC Weekly*. He'd even been called to attend a meeting with Charles Moses himself. The general manager had requested to see the young man who was proving so successful at keeping listeners glued to their radios in the afternoons and evenings, and in such a short time too.

Martha could bear his absences. When he was in the office he was condescending and increasingly boastful. When he was out, she got more work done without being interrupted by making his cups of tea and managing all his phone calls. Yes, since *As the Sun Sets* had gone to air and was on its way to being a bona fide hit, he'd started asking Martha to make his calls for him and patch them through to his office, so he could answer, "Quentin Quinn," with an air of authority and overblown importance.

The Calendar Girls were right—it had been weeks since she'd seen them and it was too long. She'd been too busy to take a break for lunch. Most days, she was lucky if she was able to take two bites of the sandwich she'd tucked in her handbag before leaving home in the mornings.

"I've missed you all too," she told them. "Tell me, April. Is there any young man on the scene?"

April blushed, which was the only answer she needed to give. "His name is Peter Bryant and he works in the garage."

May beamed. "I introduced them. I simply knew they'd be a perfect match."

"It's early days yet. But he's very kind. And he likes collecting stamps like I do."

May winked at Martha.

"And what about you, May?"

She sighed. "Nothing much to report. My brother's getting married in October and his fiancée has asked me to be a bridesmaid." She rolled her eyes. "We can't believe he's marrying her. She's a shrew. A young one, anyway. She's already got him handing over half his pay. She says it's to save up so they can build their own home. But my parents aren't convinced. She sure does wear some nice clothes."

"But, May," June piped up. "Look at Vera Percy in *As the Sun Sets*. She does the books for the butcher shop. Surely she can't be the only woman around who understands how money works."

"My father still hands over his pay to my mother," April said. "Every pound, shilling, and pence of it."

The other women sat back in stunned silence.

"Is your father under the thumb, April?" June inquired.

May was aghast. "He doesn't go to the pub after work?"

"Oh no, we're teetotal," April explained.

"Methodists?"

"Baptists."

"Oh," June said knowingly. "It was the opposite in my house when I was a child. My dad went straight to the pub and handed over what was left to Mum when he got home. They always had terrible rows about it. I don't know how Mum managed. I really don't. Six kids. Always frightened when it came to rent day. The landlord didn't care why she barely had enough to pay the rent. He just cared that it got paid. They were hard days." June looked up from the table. "That's why I'll never get married. Who needs a husband like that? And anyway, I need this job. Almost everything I earn goes to Mum for her and the kids."

"What about your father?" Martha asked curiously.

"He ran off five years ago. Mum doesn't know where he is and doesn't want to know. To be honest, I think he's in Queensland, but Mum says he could be in Timbuktu for all she cares. She says we're better off without him. At least there's no fighting these days, unless it's the two youngest playing pirates or cowboys."

"How does your family get by, June?" Martha asked.

"There's my pay, of course, although a secretary's wage isn't much. Mum takes in washing and ironing for some of the other ladies in the street. Some of them go out to work and like having all their washing done for them. Some don't have washing machines. And some are too old to do their own."

Martha reached over and squeezed June's hand. "She must be very proud of you."

"Thank you, Miss Berry. She is. She was happy as a lark when I got this job. She was scared I might have got my dream job."

"Your dream job?"

June sighed at the memory. "I wanted to be an air hostess. During the war, I used to ride my bicycle down to Rose Bay and watch the seaplanes fly in and land on the harbor, like huge ducks. I always thought how exciting it must be to step onto a plane and disembark in an entirely different country two or three days later. Imagine getting on a plane in Sydney and getting off in, I don't know, London or Egypt or New York!"

"I'm sure it's not too late," Martha replied. "If that's what you really want to do."

"Being too late wasn't the problem. I tried. I completed the application to become an air hostess for TAA. It was quite strict. You have to be between the ages of twenty-one and twenty-seven and unmarried, both of which were no problem for me. Between five foot two and five foot six and under nine stone. I was rejected."

"What on earth . . . ?" Martha asked, but she already knew the answer.

"I'm too tall. And too heavy." June put her elbow on the table and rested her chin in her cupped hand. "I suppose the planes are small on the inside and someone like me might keep bumping their head on the ceiling, but still. I didn't think it was very fair."

"It isn't fair, June. Not at all. Do the pilots have to be short as well?"

Something lit up in June's eyes. "Exactly."

"I wanted to be a teacher," April offered up, her gaze somewhere in the distance. "I've always adored little children. How lovely would it be to go to school each day and read the children stories and teach them things? To have forty little faces staring up at you . . ." She shrugged. "But you had to be smart enough to win a place at teachers college. So I learned to type instead. My father said if I learned to type, I'd always be suitable for an office job to pass the time before I got married. He was right, I suppose."

"What about you, Miss Berry?" May asked. "When you were our age, what did you want to be?"

Martha thought on the question. She hadn't had dreams or ambitions to be anything more than the life that had been picked out for her. Girls didn't think that way back in those days. At least not girls like her. She had listened to her mother about what was best for her and that had been that.

"I really can't remember. But if I could travel back in time to when I was your age"—she smiled at the Calendar Girls and the impossibility of such a proposition—"I wouldn't in my wildest dreams imagine I would be working on a radio serial. I mean, radio hadn't arrived in Australia back then. And television's coming soon. We never could have imagined."

Dreams might be possible now, though.

Her own, in particular.

Chapter 15

IN WHICH MARTHA BERRY DISCOVERS THAT JACK PERCY IS SETTING HEARTS AFLAME ALL OVER AUSTRALIA.

Hello, Mum. Good evening, Mrs. Ward. Mrs. Tilley."

The three women sat on Mrs. Tilley's front veranda, perched on the edge of their seats like magpies waiting for old bread crusts.

"Thank goodness you're here," Mrs. Tilley exclaimed breathlessly. "We're dying to know. What on earth is wrong with Vera Percy?"

Martha felt a warm inner glow at the inquiry. It still seemed unreal to her that people were listening to *As the Sun Sets* on their own radios and were so invested in the characters she'd created.

In the first few weeks of episodes, Martha had subtly—or so she'd thought—written hints that something was amiss with Vera's health. In episode six, Vera had struggled to get out of bed to fry up Jack's breakfast before he headed off to work. Jack and Betty had been puzzled and had an early morning conversation about it while Betty made her father's breakfast. Vera hadn't missed a day of preparing bacon and eggs—Jack's own bacon, of course—since the day they'd been married. Even when Vera had suffered terrible morning sickness during her confinement with Betty seventeen years before, she'd still struggled out of bed to see her husband fed for the day.

And then, in episode eight, Jack and Betty had arrived home at the end of the day to find Vera already tucked up in bed.

Martha had wanted to create a mystery around Vera, and it appeared to have worked. Was there nothing better than keeping your listeners guessing?

"Vera? I don't know what you mean," Martha replied with a knowing smile.

Mrs. Tilley slapped a hand on her thigh and turned to Violet. "I told you that daughter of yours wouldn't spill the beans. She's a sly one, Mrs. Berry. Come on, love. Put us out of our misery. It's all anyone can talk about. Why, Mrs. Western at the grocer's today told everyone who was listening that she thinks Vera's dying of cancer. Well, then there was a big argument about that and she went away in a huff without her potatoes even though she'd paid for them!"

"She left without her potatoes?" Mrs. Ward frowned. "That's not the Mrs. Western I know. She double counts her change just in case someone tries to put one by her."

"Stan, the grocer's boy, had to run after her and give her the spuds."

Violet laid a hand on her décolletage. "Martha dear? The way Jack made her a cup of tea and some toast and took it to her in bed? Insisted she stay there until she felt better? It reminded me of your father." Tears welled in Violet's eyes and a lump rose in Martha's throat. She wished she remembered him. The sound of his voice. The touch of his hand. The cackle of his laugh.

"And then," Mrs. Ward added, "when he put a cold compress on her forehead!"

The three women sighed audibly. Martha couldn't wait to tell Kent Stone next week about all the neighborhood swooning. He'd be so pleased.

"He really does love his wife, that Jack Percy."

"Of course he does, Mrs. Ward. You can hear it in his voice, you can."

They were talking about Jack and Vera as if they were real people.

"You wouldn't believe it, Mum, but people have been sending get-well cards to Vera Percy, care of the station," Martha told them, barely containing her smile. "Hundreds and hundreds of them, from people all over Australia. They're all as concerned as you are."

"Mrs. Western better not be right about the cancer, Martha. That's all I can say," Mrs. Tilley said as she crossed her arms and grimaced. "Not only because I'd hate to think she guessed right, but you'll break our hearts, you will, if you send her off so quickly. We like Vera."

"We do." Violet nodded.

"And what will poor Jack do if Vera dies? Young Betty will grow up without a mother and in her grief might fall in love with the wrong man. And who'll do the books for the business? What if the butchers goes broke because Vera got cancer?"

Mrs. Ward snapped her fingers. "And what if he forgets to pay all his bills and ends up in prison? Oh, you couldn't, Martha!"

Martha could only marvel at what she was hearing. Her mother and her neighbors were coming up with plot lines she herself had never even imagined. Vera's death? The butcher shop struggling financially? There was so much drama in everyday life that could be mined for plots.

Mrs. Tilley was correct, of course. It was simply not the done thing to kill off a character in a new drama so soon after it had premiered. Unless, perhaps, there was a contract dispute with the actor or actress. Or they'd taken up drinking or some other unsavory pastime that might bring the serial into disrepute. No, there was no way on god's earth that Martha would dream of killing off Vera Percy. Of course, dramatic purposes were an important consideration, but Martha had grown to like and admire Miss Connors and wanted to continue working with her for as long as possible. She had brought a lovely light side to Vera's character, a tone of someone who was capable and smart in her own right yet didn't mind making her husband's breakfast every morning.

And anyway, Miss Connors had just signed a two-year contract.

Martha hadn't yet decided what was ailing Vera. In that respect, her inexperience in writing scripts was showing. At the outset, she thought it would add a mystery to the plot. When it had created so much interest, she realized she would have to give her listeners the satisfaction they were craving. It would be nothing serious, of course. Perhaps she might be lacking in vitamins and minerals. Or suffering a stomach complaint. Or migraines.

Martha had some time to decide, so she wasn't going to rush to solve the mystery too soon. She wanted the listeners of *As the Sun Sets* to keep listening. Martha wanted the program to be a success, and it would only be one if listeners were glued to their radios from Monday to Friday each week desperately waiting for the next clue about what was going on in the Percy family. It could take weeks—or indeed months—for the mystery to be revealed. Martha wanted people all over the country to wonder what Vera was hiding. She wanted them to continue listening to see how Jack was coping and if Betty might change her future plans if she faced the dilemma of staying at home to look after her mother.

It was all too exciting to think about.

"My mother died of cancer. Something"—Mrs. Ward pointed to her general abdominal area and shrugged—"down there. She never wanted anyone to know what kind of cancer it was. People were private about things like that back in the day. Oh, her death was horrible. I wouldn't want anyone to put up with what my mother went through. If Jack and Betty have to live through that . . . well, I don't know if I'll be able to hear it without crying. It might be too close to home, Martha."

Violet looked aghast. "Quentin Quinn wouldn't do that. Not when the show's just started." She paused and her eyebrows lifted. "Would he, love?"

Martha turned to Mrs. Tilley. "What do you think is wrong with Vera?"

Mrs. Tilley considered her answer. "Perhaps there's something wrong with her digestion. Gas. Or a bilious attack. Something like that."

"Lumbago," Violet added. "Or fibrositis. Some kind of rheumatism that makes her back ache. Or . . . or maybe she's just coming down with a cold or the flu. You know what it's like, Mrs. Tilley. Sometimes you just need to have a cup of tea and a lie-down. Things have got on top of her. That's all. She's doing all the cooking and cleaning and washing and doing all the books for the butcher shop. It's getting too much for her, that's all. She's not a spring chicken anymore. Betty must have been a change-of-life baby. And maybe they had problems, seeing as she's an only child."

"You could be right," Martha said with a smile. "Or you could be wrong. You'll simply have to keep listening."

Mrs. Tilley cackled. "Ooh, Mrs. Berry, she's such a tease, your Martha."

Violet beamed. "She works very hard. And she's a very clever girl."

That was something Martha never got tired of hearing.

....

After dinner, the pastoral strains of the *Blue Hills* theme filled the kitchen. Martha and Violet sat at the table in companiable silence, eating their sausages, mashed potatoes, and vegetables with a slice of buttered white bread. Martha knew not to strike up a conversation with Violet in the minutes before the program began, as she would have to wait fifteen minutes to resume it and by then Violet would have forgotten what she was going to say in the first place.

"The ABC presents *Blue Hills* by Gwen Meredith. In this episode . . ."

There was something magical about the act of listening. In imagining someone's face, their expressions, and how they moved, just by listening to their voice. Just by listening she had brought to life all the places in Tanimbla in her head. She had imagined Dr. Gordon's surgery for years, even though it only existed in Gwen Meredith's imagination and in the lines of script she wrote. In Martha's mind, the house that had been converted to a doctor's surgery had well-tended red roses in the front garden and a pathway leading in a straight line from the low front fence to the front veranda. Each window facing the street was decorated with pretty white curtains. In Dr. Gordon's consulting room, he sat in a comfortable leather chair with his window open to catch the breezes, and Martha always imagined the sounds of magpies warbling in the gum trees planted at neat intervals along the street.

Radio really was a kind of magic. Did that make her a magician? A conjurer of words rather than magic tricks? Or could words be magic in themselves?

She found herself daydreaming, tuning out of the trials and tribulations of the residents of Tanimbla and thinking more about her own characters. There were so many possibilities for what might befall them. It was in her power to take them anywhere.

Martha was pulled from her imaginings by the slight pressure of her mother's gnarled hand on her forearm. She looked up to see Violet's eyes glistening. "It's time for your show, dear."

Martha cocked an ear to hear Kent Stone's mellifluous voice announce, "The ABC presents *As the Sun Sets* by Quentin Quinn. In tonight's episode, Jack and Betty grow increasingly concerned about Vera."

BETTY PERCY: *I can't help but worry about her, Dad. It's been weeks and weeks now and Mum doesn't seem to have got her energy back. She's pale and tired and, to be honest, she gets cross with me about almost nothing.*

JACK PERCY: *I know, love. There, there.*

(SOUND *of Betty sniffing*)

BETTY PERCY: *Only yesterday she snapped at me about not mopping the kitchen floor when I'd just finished doing it. I don't know what to do, Dad. I really don't.*

JACK PERCY: *There's nothing to worry about, love. Your mother knows you do your bit around the house, probably more than most daughters. I'm sure it's nothing.*

(MUSIC *for scene change*)

JACK PERCY: *It's almost eight, Vera, love. Time for your favorite music program. Can I get you another cup of tea before it starts? Maybe a chocolate biscuit or two?*

VERA PERCY: *No thanks, Jack. If I have another cup of tea today, I'll start looking like a pot of tea leaves.*

JACK PERCY: *Betty's worried about you, Vera. She said you snapped at her yesterday in the kitchen. About mopping the floor.*

VERA PERCY: *(bursts into tears) It's true, I did. The words just seemed to fly out of my mouth without me even realizing it. Goodness but I felt terrible afterward. She went to her room, crying. Like I'd slapped her. You know I never have, and I never would raise a hand to my own child, or anyone else's for that matter. I felt like the worst mother in the world, Jack. How could I say that to our Betty? She never complains about helping around the house. And there I was, telling her off. I don't know what got into me.*

JACK PERCY: *To tell the truth, love, I've been a bit worried about you too.*

VERA PERCY: *You have?*

JACK PERCY: *Of course I have. When you've been married as long as we have . . . Vera, if I'm honest, you haven't been yourself lately. It's not just the snapping at Betty—*

VERA PERCY: *I feel so awful about that. I should apologize. And right now. Where is she?*

JACK PERCY: *Don't worry too much about it, love. She'll simmer down. Betty said something about meeting her friend Peggy at the library. Betty's keen on that new Agatha Christie book and they've got it in for her. (chuckles) I don't know where she got her love of reading from, Vera, but I'm glad she's got it. Girls these days shouldn't just be judged on how pretty they are. People should consider what's between their ears too.*

VERA PERCY: *I'm so proud of her. Remember what she was like as a baby?*

JACK PERCY: *She screamed the house down, if I remember. You didn't get a lot of sleep back in those days, did you?*

VERA PERCY: *It seems like only yesterday I was pushing her down the street in the pram. I can't believe she's nearly seventeen. And you were working all hours in the shop and trying to get enough meat in to sell when we still had the rationing for the war.*

JACK PERCY: *Do I remember those years . . . I reckon I had to stop fisticuffs breaking out on more than one occasion. And that was just between the housewives! They didn't like it one bit when they thought someone was jumping the queue. They might have got the last bit of chuck steak!*

VERA PERCY: *But we survived, didn't we?*

JACK PERCY: *We did, love. And we'll get through this, too, whatever's troubling you. I reckon you should go see the doctor. He can check if everything's all right.*

VERA PERCY: *(sighing) I don't need to see the doctor, Jack. I'm just a little tired. I'll have a cup of cocoa and I'll feel better in the morning, I'm sure of it.*

JACK PERCY: *Are you sure—*

VERA PERCY: *I'll be fine, Jack. I promise. I don't want you and Betty to worry about me. Now, how about that cocoa?*

When the music swelled to indicate the end of the episode of *As the Sun Sets*, Violet struggled up from the table and turned off the radio. She took a jug of milk from the fridge. "Think I'll make myself a cup of cocoa," she said with a smile, "just like Vera. Would you like one?"

"Let me do it, Mum. You sit down."

Violet waved away the offer. "I can do it. Stop your fussing." She let out a long groan.

A shiver of concern skittered up Martha's spine. She'd learned to be watchful of her mother's health since Violet was diagnosed with rheumatoid arthritis when Martha was still a young woman. She'd been ever-watchful for signs of increasing aches and pains or more limited mobility. Was Violet waking up stiffer in the mornings, her knees giving her more trouble? Was she better than yesterday or worse? Better than last week or last month or worse?

"Feeling tired today?" Martha tried to sound nonchalant to hide her concern.

"No more tired than usual," Violet replied. "Even I forget sometimes that I'm seventy-one years old. I don't want you to worry about me. I'm slowing down—you know that better than anyone—but there's still some life in this old girl. I even went for a little walk today. And before you chide me, it was only half an hour. But the sun was shining and the sky was so blue that I just had to, after all the winter rain we've had." Violet's eyes brightened and a smile played at her lips. "I saw something today."

"You did?"

"A new family has moved into Poplar Street. And there's something very interesting about them. They're Italian." Violet pronounced it "Eye-talian" and Martha didn't have the heart to correct her.

"How do you know they're Italian?"

"Well, for a start, they've all got that dark hair and olive skin. And they were talking to each other in Italian too. Didn't understand a word but I stopped and waved and when I said, 'Welcome to the neighborhood,' they smiled and spoke to me in Italian! I suddenly remembered that the actress Gina Lollobrigida is Italian so I said, 'Gina Lollobrigida!' and the man slapped his leg and laughed and said right back to me: 'Si, Gina Lollobrigida!'"

"Gina Lollobrigida!" Martha laughed.

"So there's the husband and wife and four little children. Three girls and a boy. The little ones were running around the garden chasing each other. It was such a sight to see."

"They sound like a lovely family."

"They really were." The kettle boiled and Violet set about making her cocoa. "Mrs. Tilley says there's lots of people from Europe coming to Australia nowadays. Not just refugees, but people who want jobs and a new life for their families. Imagine what it's been like for them, even all these years after the war. Lucky we were so far away from all that fighting. Although it was here on our doorstep, too, and that was frightening enough." Violet shook away the thought. "How was your day, dear?"

How to explain to her mother exactly how busy her day was? Quentin Quinn had spent the morning meeting with Marilyn Calthorpe. He'd called her in to discuss the role, as he was apparently keen to hear her ideas on how her character might develop. This meeting involved a quarter hour in his office and then lunch somewhere in Kings Cross. He'd left the office puffed up and proud. The look on Marilyn's face was neither puffed up nor proud. As they'd walked to the door, she'd turned and looked wide-eyed at Martha and asked in a plaintive voice, "You're not coming too, Miss Berry?"

And before Martha could reply, Quentin Quinn had piped up and told Marilyn in a condescending tone, "Secretaries don't attend meetings with the talent, Miss Calthorpe."

Martha had given Marilyn what she hoped was a reassuring smile. "I've got plenty to get on with here."

Lately, she always had plenty to get on with.

"Busy, Mum. It's always busy, but who can complain? There's

something very exciting about working on *As the Sun Sets*. I think it's the best job I've ever had, as a matter of fact."

"I can see you love it, always bringing that little typewriter home with you. I hear you click-clacking away when I'm trying to go to sleep."

"Goodness, Mum. Is it keeping you awake?"

Violet returned to the table with her cocoa. "Not in the slightest. I think it helps me go to sleep, to tell the truth. I lie there and wonder what words you're typing for Vera to say, or what Jack might say in return, and it stops me thinking about all my worries. It really does. But I do think you need to get some more sun. You're looking pale." Violet sighed. "I suppose that's what happens when you work in an office. And it's July. Where's all the sun gone, I ask you? Tell me you took a walk at lunchtime, at least. That you got yourself some fresh air."

"Of course I did," Martha fibbed and hoped her smile deflected her mother's curiosity. She found it was often necessary to outright lie—or at least omit the truth—when answering questions from her mother. Martha may have been fifty years of age, but nothing would stop Violet from worrying about her daughter. About how much she was or was not eating. About how much she was or was not sleeping. About how much sun she was getting.

"A bit of sun will always do you good, dear."

"That's very true, Mum." Martha stood. "Perhaps I'll take a walk on the weekend. If the weather's fine."

"Last weekend the weather *was* fine—not a cloud in the sky—and you spent every minute tapping away on that machine anyway."

Martha opened her mouth to protest but she stopped and clamped her lips shut. It was true. It was hard to keep such a thing secret in their little house.

"You're working too hard, love."

"Mum . . ." How could she explain to her mother how important *As the Sun Sets* had become to her? Martha had never thought it possible to actually have a career. Every job she'd had was simply a job. She had jumped from department to department over the years when one producer or manager or other had needed someone who could type and was otherwise quiet and accommodating. Docile, even. Martha didn't believe she'd ever talked back to any one of them in the twenty-four years she'd been working in radio. Funny that she had been surrounded by people whose job it was to talk, to get others to talk, to write so others could talk. But she'd never had a voice of her own.

And now, she had more than a job. It felt like the beginning of a career. She was a script girl. She was suddenly indispensable to Quentin Quinn and the drama department and to *As the Sun Sets*. If only they knew how much.

"No one's forcing me to work all the hours under the sun, Mum. I really do like it. You know how much you and Mrs. Tilley and Mrs. Ward love listening to *As the Sun Sets* to find out what's going to happen next?"

"Of course I do. It's been ever so exciting, what with Vera's secret illness and Betty going for her first job interview."

"Exactly. I find it just as exciting to write the scenes—" Martha pulled herself up. She couldn't let the cat out of the bag. Not even with her mother. Pride goeth before a fall and the immense gratification she felt in writing for *As the Sun Sets* simply had to be hers and hers alone. How could her mother, delight bursting in her chest, keep such momentous news a secret from Mrs. Tilley and Mrs. Ward? And then, bless them, it would be all over the neighborhood before the first cup of tea of the morning had been brewed.

"When I type up Mr. Quinn's handwritten scripts, I get to know before anyone else what's going to happen to the characters. And what a pleasure and a joy that is, Mum. That's why I don't mind working on the weekends and in the evenings. I find it as exciting as you do."

"Just watch yourself, dear."

"I will, Mum. Don't worry." But how could she slow down now? Her imagination had taken flight, and her head was bursting with ideas for the Percys and their neighbors and the greengrocers and other friends she'd yet to create. So far, listeners had only met the Percys and some of the customers in the butcher shop, including Mrs. White with her sciatica. But new characters would be introduced in the coming weeks, Martha knew that.

Because she had already created them.

And she couldn't wait to hear the response from listeners.

Chapter 16

IN WHICH BETTY HAS AN INTERVIEW FOR
HER FIRST JOB AND WE MEET JACK PERCY'S
NEW APPRENTICE, ERNIE WATSON.

Kent Stone, Miss Connors, and Marilyn Calthorpe stood close to
the microphone, their eyes focused intently on the control room
and Handsy Hooper.

"Just checking the sound levels. Try some dialogue, would you,
boy?"

The boy in question was the young actor who'd been cast to
play Jack Percy's new apprentice, Ernie. Cary Sullivan glanced
quickly at his fellow actors and, even from a distance, Martha
saw his Adam's apple bob as he swallowed hard. Sullivan had only
received the good news about his job—his first ever acting role—
the previous Thursday. Just as Lana Turner had been discovered
innocently drinking a milkshake somewhere in Hollywood, Cary
Sullivan had been plucked from obscurity by Kent Stone himself.

"It was his voice that struck me first," Kent had explained the
Friday before as he'd perched himself on Martha's desk. He'd

stopped by to pick up his scripts for Monday's recording. "There I was studying the menu, trying to decide between asparagus tips on toast or a crab salad, and I hear a voice asking"—he held up a hand as if the words he was about to utter might be emblazoned in lights somewhere—"'What can I get you, sir?' And I looked up to see who was the bearer of this exquisite instrument and it was Cary Sullivan." Kent shook his head, still clearly in disbelief that such a talent should fall in his lap. "His real name is Herbert Gilligan or some such, but I advised him rather quickly that such a name would never look great on a theater program, so when Quinn agreed to cast him—on the sound of his voice alone, Miss Berry—I suggested he might like something more *theatrical*. And he does look like Cary Grant. You wait and see."

"Boy?" Hooper repeated from behind his control panel with more venom than was necessary.

Cary Sullivan looked about and suddenly realized *he* must be the boy. He leaned in quickly, bumped his chin on the microphone, and began to shout to ten. Hooper roared and yanked off his headphones.

The young actor jumped back in shock and threw a panicked glance at Kent Stone.

"You're just a little too close and a smidge too loud," Kent explained. "You'll get there, young man. These checks are all about getting the sound levels just right so we're all at the same volume on the recording."

"Don't worry, Cary." Marilyn Calthorpe pressed a hand to his forearm and beamed up at him. The young man was a good eight inches taller than Marilyn, with a head of dark hair that would be the envy of all those who tried to style theirs into a quiff. His strong jaw and brilliantly bright blue eyes lit up the pale skin of his cheeks, and even when he pulled his lips together in a panic, they appeared as plump as pillows.

Kent Stone raised an eyebrow at Handsy Hooper. "Try it again. Mr. Hooper won't mind, will you, Mr. Hooper?"

"We don't have all bloody day, you know." Handsy Hooper harrumphed. Martha tried to ignore him.

"Come on, old chap," Quentin Quinn said, attempting a bonhomie no one felt around Handsy Hooper. "Give him some leeway. It's his first role. He'll get the hang of it, I'm sure."

Handsy Hooper waited for an uncomfortably long time, just to see the new boy squirm. "Speak," he finally bellowed.

Miss Connors propped a hand at her hip. "A *please* would be nice, occasionally."

Martha shot a glance at Hooper, who was hunched over the control panel. He looked for all the world like a gargoyle trapped in a dim little cave. If only he would stay there. He closed the open mic to the studio and grumbled, "And so would so-called *talent* who do what they're asked without getting all uppity. Don't they know that without me, there wouldn't be a radio program? Without me, they're reading some lines into the air that will disappear like a puff of smoke."

Quentin Quinn took a deep drag on his cigarette and mumbled something he probably hoped sounded to Hooper like agreement. The truth was, Quentin Quinn was scared of Hooper. Martha was certain of it. Although he was objectionable in almost every way imaginable, what he'd said was true. Quentin Quinn didn't understand the recording process any more than Martha did, and Hooper lorded it over both of them constantly by grumbling that the equipment was faulty or that this knob or that wasn't working that day and they may have to postpone recording. And then miraculously things would be fixed just before Martha was about to have heart palpitations.

"Rightio. Levels are good to go. Recording." Hooper counted the actors down and faded in the opening music.

Kent Stone leaned into the microphone and began.

"The ABC presents *As the Sun Sets* by Quentin Quinn . . . in which Jack Percy introduces his new apprentice and rumors abound of a new family arriving in the neighborhood."

FX: *Shop bell*
JACK PERCY: *Good afternoon, Mrs. White.*
MRS. WHITE: *Good afternoon, Mr. Percy.*

Looking on, Martha still couldn't believe that Miss Connors was able to read the lines for Mrs. White in a voice so believably different from both her own smooth tone and that which she'd created for Vera Percy.

JACK PERCY: *You're here bright and early.*
MRS. WHITE: *(laughing) Well, you know what they say. A rolling stone gathers no moss.*
JACK PERCY: *That's very true indeed. What can I get for you today?*
MRS. WHITE: *Half a pound of tripe, thanks, Mr. Percy. And four rissoles. Mr. White does like your rissoles. He says they're tastier than mine!*
JACK PERCY: *That's a compliment indeed! Now, before I get your order, I hope you don't mind if I introduce my new apprentice, Ernie Watson. Ernie, this is Mrs. White. She's one of our best and most loyal customers. I do believe she's here almost every day. Isn't that right, Mrs. White?*

MRS. WHITE: *I wouldn't go anywhere else.*

ERNIE WATSON: *Very pleased to meet you, Mrs. White. I hope you're well this morning?*

Martha's mouth gaped. It had been so long since her heart had skipped a beat that she wasn't sure it had. In the studio, the other actors snapped their heads in Cary Sullivan's direction so quickly Martha thought they might suffer a collective neck injury. Quentin Quinn forgot to take a puff on his cigarette and it hung limply between his lips, its lazy trail of smoke seemingly distracted, too, by the deep, husky, and—Martha couldn't deny it—bass-baritone bedroom voice of the young Cary Sullivan.

"That's a deep voice that boy's got," Handsy Hooper mumbled as he twiddled with a knob.

"Indeed," Martha murmured to herself because Handsy Hooper hadn't directed his comment to her, and even if he had she would have ignored him.

Ever the professional, Miss Connors didn't skip a beat and resumed her lines as Mrs. White, the slight breathlessness in her voice lending a perfect authenticity to how an older woman might react when being introduced to such a handsome young man.

MRS. WHITE: *Well, I . . . I shouldn't complain, but my sciatica plays up in this weather something dreadful.*

ERNIE WATSON: *I'm sorry to hear that. It's a real pleasure to meet you, Mrs. White. This is my first day and I'm hoping to learn all there is to know about butchering from Mr. Percy here.*

MRS. WHITE: *And you'll be learning from the best in the business, there's no doubt about that.*

JACK PERCY: *That's very kind of you to say. Now, Ernie, why don't you get the four rissoles for Mrs. White and I'll weigh up that tripe.*

Hooper played a musical interlude to indicate a change of scene.

BETTY PERCY: *Hi, Mum. I'm home.*

VERA PERCY: *Hello, dear.*

BETTY PERCY: *How are you feeling?*

VERA PERCY: *I'm fine, love. Just fine. Now, tell me, how did the interview go?*

BETTY PERCY: *Oh, very well, I think. Or terrible. (exasperated sigh) It's so hard to know! I answered all their questions and they seemed to be impressed by my typing speed—one hundred and twenty words a minute—but there are so many girls who can type just as fast as I can. I've only got a week left at secretarial college and I thought by now I'd have a job lined up. It's been so frustrating.*

VERA PERCY: *I don't want you to worry. You'll get a job and a wonderful one too. Mark my word. You've got what it takes. They'll be looking for someone with a winning smile and just the right personality to meet customers. You've got both in spades. You've learned a lot from working all those Saturday mornings in your father's shop. What's the Golden Rule?*

BETTY PERCY: *Do unto others as you would have them do unto you?*

VERA PERCY: *That's exactly right. The Golden Rule is to be polite to everyone, no matter how . . . unpleasant they might be to you. A smile cures everything, I say, especially for girls.*

FX: *Door opening and closing*

VERA PERCY: *Your father's home. I hope he brought some sausages with him!*

JACK PERCY: *Look who's here. My two favorite people. Hello, love. Here are the snags. Beef tonight. Hello, Betty. I've been wondering all day. How did the interview go?*

BETTY PERCY: *Who knows, Dad. (sighs) I tried not to be worried but I was. My hands were shaking as I was answering their questions. I couldn't make them stop!*

FX: *Newspaper rustling as Vera unwraps the sausages*

VERA PERCY: *That's nothing but nerves, Betty. I'm certain you're just right for what they're looking for.*

JACK PERCY: *When do you find out if you've got the job, Betty?*

BETTY PERCY: *The lady who interviewed me told me they would be making a decision next week and that I should wait for a letter. I'll be checking that letterbox religiously.*

VERA PERCY: *Don't you worry. I'll be waiting on the front step for the postman before he even turns into the street! Sit down, Jack. Take a load off. I'll get those sausages on.*

BETTY PERCY: *I've talked all about my day, but how was yours, Dad? Was it busy in the shop today?*

JACK PERCY: *Run off our feet, as usual, but you won't ever hear me complaining about that. The new apprentice started today.*

VERA PERCY: *Goodness. I forgot it was today. I'd better make sure he's on the payroll. What's his name again, Jack?*

FX: *Sausages sizzling*

JACK PERCY: *Ernie Watson. He seems a good lad. Very polite and eager to please. I think he's going to turn out very well indeed. He grew up on a farm out west of Bathurst and knows his way around a side of beef, that's for sure. And he's got a way with* the customers already. He was very polite to Mrs. White when she came in today, even when she started going on and on about—

JACK, VERA, AND BETTY ALL TOGETHER: *Her sciatica!*

VERA PERCY: *Oh, we shouldn't laugh. I see her hobbling around when I'm running errands or going to the post office. She's been like that for years now. It must be very painful and frustrating. But . . . she doesn't seem to want to go to the doctor to get it seen to. I can't understand that. If there was a choice between suffering so much and doing something about it . . .*

JACK PERCY: *Life's not easy for Mrs. White. Mr. White's been poorly for years too. He hasn't been able to do his job since he had that accident at work. Remember, love? When he was hit by a truck at the council depot? It was touch and go for months and months.*

VERA PERCY: *Of course I remember. It was such a shock. The first time I saw Mrs. White after that, she was in shock. I don't see him much anymore, the poor thing. Both his legs were broken—and a hip, too, I think. I honestly don't know how they manage.*

BETTY PERCY: *What about Karen and Tom? Don't they help out their parents?*

VERA PERCY: *They're both busy with their own families these days. Karen's just had her fourth—another little girl—and Tom's finally bought his own delivery truck.*

JACK PERCY: *It's not easy when you're starting up your own business. Don't we know that, Vera? You work all the hours under the sun just to make sure enough money's coming in to put food on the table and pay the rent. And if someone gets sick or needs the doctor . . . well, you never stop worrying.*

BETTY PERCY: *I understand all that, but it just doesn't seem right that Karen and Tom are too busy to help their parents.*

VERA PERCY: *Not everyone's like you, Betty.*

BETTY PERCY: *Oh, Mum. I just do what any daughter would do. Now, why don't you sit down and I'll serve dinner.*

Chapter 17

IN WHICH *AS THE SUN SETS* BECOMES A BONA FIDE HIT AND QUENTIN QUINN TAKES ALL THE CREDIT.

Martha and the Calendar Girls sat at a cafe just around the corner from work, the young women poring over a stack of newspapers and magazines. April, May, and June had dragged Martha out on the pretext of it being April's birthday, but it wasn't long before she discovered the truth.

"It's been so long since we've had lunch, Miss Berry. We thought we should celebrate by showing you these!" April waved her hands over the spread of newsprint on the table.

"We've been reading about *As the Sun Sets* absolutely everywhere," May announced. "And it's only been one month!"

April found a centerspread and turned it around so Martha could read it the right way up. "Look at this one!" she exclaimed. "'New radio drama sets hearts racing.'" She jabbed a finger at the page and looked up at Martha. "There's a lovely write-up. It mentions how Mr. Quentin Quinn came up with the concept of a city version of *Blue Hills* and he describes how he writes all the scripts himself."

June narrowed her eyes. "Are you sure? That sounds like a lot of work for just one person."

"Gwen Meredith writes *Blue Hills* all on her own," May replied. "Has done since the very first episode."

"Is that true, Miss Berry?" June asked. "Does Quentin Quinn *really* write all the episodes?"

Martha barely had teeth big enough to bite her own tongue. "Of course." Oh, how she might have elaborated so much more for the sake of the ruse. She could have said he was a genius; that he came up with the scripts so quickly she could barely type fast enough to get all the words down; that he had a finger on the pulse of what radio listeners were really after in a drama; that his characters were real and true. But she couldn't find it in her to utter a lie that big. None of that was down to him. It was all down to her. In the privacy of her own thoughts, she had wondered more than once what it would be like if Kent Stone were to announce at the beginning of every episode: "The ABC presents *As the Sun Sets* by Martha Berry. Episode four hundred twenty-three . . ."

That day would never come, of course. In trying to save the show, and her own fledgling career as a script girl, from near disaster, she had in four short weeks turned Quentin Quinn into a radio prodigy.

"Here they are. There's Mr. Quinn in the photograph with the actors." June cleared her throat and narrowed her eyes at the page. That young woman really did need stronger glasses, Martha thought. "'The ABC's head of drama, Mr. Rutherford Hayes, said that Quentin Quinn had revitalized the concept of the Australian radio serial by putting his characters in an urban setting, centered around a butcher shop, its proprietors, and its customers.' And here's a quote from Mr. Quinn himself. 'The ideas just come to me. I can't believe how easy it is to write for these wonderful characters.'"

Nothing truer was ever said, Martha thought.

"There's no mention of you, though, Miss Berry," June noted. "That's not really fair, is it? There's only you and Mr. Quinn, and you get left out."

Martha shrugged. "They're his ideas, June. I'm just the typist." Oh, how it stung to say those words. "That's the way it is."

That was the way Quentin Quinn had wanted it. Miss Connors and Kent Stone had urged Martha to join them in the photograph, but before she could even be concerned that her hair was neatly in place, Quentin Quinn had stepped in front of her.

"Mrs. Barry doesn't need to be in the promotional photographs. It's not necessary for people at home to know who my secretary is. All we need are the actors and me. The brains and heart of the show."

Miss Connors had shot Martha a glance, but Martha had quickly looked away. The last thing she wanted to do was betray the truth. She'd turned her attention to tidying a pile of discarded scripts in case her disappointment was written all over her face.

"And here he is with all the actors. Kent Stone. Miss Connors. That young Marilyn Calthorpe. Isn't she lovely? And Ernie, the butcher's apprentice." April sighed enthusiastically. "Cary Sullivan."

April said his name the way Martha might say the words *chocolate cake*. Martha had been tasked with organizing the photo shoot with the publicity department, and they'd suggested the actual recording studio would be the best place to stage the photographs. She'd called the actors together, gathered up some old scripts as props, and had even warned Handsy Hooper that he should wear a tie as he might be in the background of the photograph. Looking down at the image in the newspaper, Martha was glad Handsy Hooper had been cropped out. The actors looked like stars. Kent Stone had turned up with a face full of pancake makeup, more appropriate to the stage than the studio, but he had been right to do so because it had smoothed out his wrinkles and made his mature eyes sparkle.

Miss Connors had arrived looking as she did every other day. The woman was camera-ready the moment she stepped outside her front gate every morning, whether she was on her way to a publicity shoot or picking up bottles of milk from the front veranda. Her hair was always perfectly coiffed under her hat, with a strategically placed net veil to distract from any telltale signs of age on her face. Her lashes were long and black, her face powder applied just so, and her plump, even lips were the result of just the slightest exaggeration by her lip pencil, but one could only really tell if one was up close and the netting wasn't obscuring the finer details of her visage. Her collars were pristine and white. Her suits looked as fresh as the day they had been created by her couturier, and her shoes, mid-heel, were so shiny she might have been able to see her reflection in them if she were ever caught in an emergency situation without a compact. Miss Connors had cultivated a look and hadn't deviated from it for as long as Martha could remember. It was what made her a star.

Marilyn Calthorpe had listened intently to Miss Connors's advice and had dressed in a floral shift dress with a sweetheart neckline and a pair of flat white pumps.

"Dress like your character in the show," she'd suggested to the young actress. Martha noted with a wry smile that absolutely nothing in Miss Connors's own dress or style suggested "butcher's wife."

Marilyn had styled her hair into pigtails that framed her heart-shaped face, and the bright red lipstick she had smoothed on her plump lips wouldn't appear so brassy in the black-and-white publicity photographs.

And then there was Cary Sullivan. Next to him, Kent Stone had pulled himself up to his full five feet six inches, but there was no way on earth he would be able to match Cary unless he was standing on a box. Cary had propped himself back on one hip, one hand in the pocket of his suit trousers, and was snapped with an uncertain look on his face that hinted at an emotion that could be read as anything between confused and lovestruck. Martha wondered how many young women around the country would be cutting Cary Sullivan's face out of the magazine and sticking it to their mirrors so they could whisper Doris Day's "Secret Love" to him while they sang breathlessly into a hairbrush.

"I just adore Cary Sullivan," April whispered, sounding as if she might faint. "His voice is *so* dreamy."

"And look how handsome he is." May sighed like a swooning teenager and sat back in her chair. "He has hair just like Elvis Presley."

June scowled. "I hope he doesn't have hips like him."

"You record the show on Mondays, don't you, Miss Berry? I hope I see him next week. Wouldn't that be something?"

June scoffed. "Do you imagine that if you happened to run into him in the foyer he might fall madly in love with you or something?"

April's eyes widened. "I was hoping for an autograph, but do you think that could happen? Do you think he might ask me out for coffee? Or dinner? Or to the theater? Perhaps the Roosevelt nightclub. Isn't that where all the famous actors go? Do you think they'll let me in?"

May nodded cheerfully. "It could happen, April."

June scoffed again. "What happened to Peter Bryant in the music department?"

April glanced down at the table, frowning. "That was two weeks ago. I've just broken up with Alan from Accounts. Turns out he was also seeing Fiona from Finance."

"I can't keep up with all your beaus." June frowned.

"In that case he didn't deserve you," May said.

June shook her head. "You've been spending too much time reading those Mills & Boon books, April."

April was aghast. "Wash your mouth out with soap, June. There's no such thing as too much reading. Even if they are romances. How could you say something like that?"

"Because books are full of fairy tales. They're not real life."

"Well, encyclopedias and history books are full of real-life stories." May tidied the pile of newspapers and magazines on the table.

"I'm not talking about those," June huffed. "I'm talking about novels. No one finds love in real life the way they do in those books you read, April."

"They do too," April exclaimed with indignation, and then her shoulders slumped. "At least I hope to. One day."

"What's wrong with wanting to meet a nice young man and fall in love?" May asked. "People have been doing it for a very long time, June. There must be something to recommend it."

Martha could see something of herself in these young women. She had been a Pollyanna when she'd been April's age and couldn't say she regretted those innocent years. Was it so wrong to be an irrepressible optimist and want to find the good in everything and everyone? Didn't one have to start out in life believing people were generally good? That they would automatically do the best by others—do unto others as you would have them do unto you?

"And . . ." April tried to steady her voice. "What's so wrong with fairy tales, June?"

"They're not real, that's what." June stared at April across the table and the slightest hint of tears welled in her eyes. "You wish they might come true and they never do and you realize you've wasted so much time."

Martha wondered, not for the first time, what might have happened in June's young life to have made her so suspicious about the possibility of anything good happening to her. In her worst moments, Martha felt like June: disappointed by life and wary of what it had served up. She had lived too many years not to have been let down by people, not to have seen both the best and the worst of people's behavior. But she couldn't live her life if she were to wake up each day feeling as cynical as June. She would worry herself into a prune. And the energy it would take to purposefully turn away from the good? More than she had in her engine. Yet she couldn't be April anymore either. Perhaps she was more like May these days than she realized.

"Things don't happen in real life the way they do in books or magazines or in radio programs. Everyone's always so happy and if they ever fight"—June hesitated and caught her breath— "it's over the most trivial little thing, like a mix-up over a dinner date or buying the wrong flowers. The men are all polite and nice and . . . well, it's all rubbish. Life's not like that at all."

May turned away from June's anger and faced Martha. "What do you think, Miss Berry?" Ever the diplomat, May played the role of peacemaker between April the Pollyanna and June the cynic. Martha wondered if May was a middle child, perhaps sandwiched between an older sister and a younger one. Martha imagined it might have been complicated to grow up as the piggy in the middle, knowing that if you ever picked a side in a scrap you were sure to upset someone. May had to sit in the middle and try to make peace. Martha admired her commitment to it.

"I think, June, that you have your whole life ahead of you and you might want to allow for good things to happen to you."

June shook her head. "The only good thing that ever happened to me was getting my job and meeting April and May. Oh, and of course you, Miss Berry."

"You see?" Martha replied gently. She didn't want to scare the poor young woman away. "Good things have happened to you." But clearly not enough of them.

"Miss Berry," May asked, "do *you* think it's silly to be carried away by stories?"

Martha had been transported by storytelling ever since she could read, and the last word she would use to describe it would be *silly*. Stories were imperative. They had broadened her horizons and her outlook. D'Arcy Niland had taken her to the outback in *The Shiralee*. George Eliot had helped her understand Victorian England and its politics and art and psychology and current events. Miles Franklin's Sybylla Melvyn had exposed her to a strong-willed woman who abandoned the idea of love and marriage to be a writer. *Little Women* had put her inside the heads of four sisters and their mother in Massachusetts during the American Civil War. She had felt the sting of poverty and childhood brutality in mid-nineteenth-century London through the pages of *David Copperfield*. Jane Austen had taught her how unfair it was that an estate could be entailed away from the female line to a distant male relative because a gentleman only had daughters. She'd never been a detective, but she'd tried hard to stay one step ahead of Miss Marple and Inspector Hercule Poirot. And while she'd never traveled, she could picture Egypt and the Amazon and Machu Picchu and Paris in her mind, clear as a bell, all because she'd seen photographs and drawings in books. Books and stories had opened her head and her heart and always would.

"Books are as important to me as breathing," Martha replied. "Stories might have elements of the silly or fantastical about them, but that's what makes them enjoyable. Did you grow up reading books, June?"

June harrumphed. "There was never any time for reading in my house. Still isn't."

"I understand," May said, covering June's hand with her own. "You have a lot of responsibilities. It can be hard to find time to dive into a good book, that's for certain, when you have so many obligations."

"And anyway," June added, "I don't see my life or people like me in those books or pictures or radio shows."

A slow realization began to spread across April's face. She blushed and lowered her eyes to the magazine open on the cafe table in front of her, away from talk of love and stories that had embarrassed her friend.

"So, Miss Berry. Tell us about this Cary Sullivan. Is he a nice fellow?"

Martha, too, was glad of the subject change because the last thing she wanted was to see June in distress. "I can't fault him. He's very polite and professional for someone who has just landed his first acting job. He arrives at my office every Friday to pick up his scripts and always makes a point of asking how I am and commenting about the weather. I swear he must spend all weekend rehearsing because when he turns up on Mondays in the recording studio, he knows all his lines and everyone else's too."

"He sounds like a dream." April sighed.

June looked down at a magazine and bit her lip.

May didn't know where to look.

Chapter 18

IN WHICH MARTHA BERRY GETS A TASTE OF HOW THE OTHER HALF LIVES.

The second thing Martha Berry did after accepting an invitation to Miss Connors's Winter Soiree at Analee, her harborside mansion in Vaucluse that was so fancy it had a name of its own, was buy a new frock.

The first thing she'd done had been to decline the invitation.

She couldn't think of anything more mortifying than being forced to meet and make conversation with people so far removed from her own social milieu—even the thought of it had made her break out in a cold sweat. Although at least it hadn't been a hot sweat. They'd been arriving with a cruel regularity of late, with no warning and no mercy. She would wake in the night to find herself soaked to the skin and sometimes during the day she wished she was able to undress to her petticoats to cope with the bushfire flaming inside her. She wasn't certain which part of what organ controlled a body's temperature, but clearly its thermostat was faulty. And she wouldn't let herself imagine it was anything more serious than that because she had Violet to look after and a radio drama to write.

Perhaps she'd been working too much and had a case of frayed nerves, as the magazines liked to call it. They were quite common, the nerves. Almost every woman she knew had experienced a case of them. Mrs. Ward's mother had a bad case and Mrs. Ward had been shipped off to an aunt in Bathurst as a child while her mother recovered. Mrs. Tilley herself said she'd had a terrible bout of the nerves when her first baby arrived in a hurry and her milk had consequently gone bad because of it. Dymphna Tilley had an attack of the nerves every four weeks when her monthlies arrived, and doctors told Violet she'd had a case of the nerves in the months after her husband's infected tooth had snatched his life away.

Who knew women had so many nerves to fray? And if it wasn't nerves, it was modern tension or generalized pain or headaches. Aspro was supposed to cure nerves when one got emotionally upset, relieve things and quiet a person down.

It was all entirely ridiculous. Weren't women allowed to be physically unwell or simply exhausted or frustrated or furious without being labeled silly? Why did they have to quiet down and not complain?

She knew she would feel better if only she were able to get a good night's sleep. She tossed and turned most of the night these days, her mind racing with thoughts of where she might take Jack and Vera and Betty and Ernie in their adventures in *As the Sun Sets*. She tucked herself in bed bone-weary most days, now that she was undertaking all her responsibilities as a script girl with scrupulous care and attention *and* writing the scripts for the show, hiding the truth from Rutherford Hayes, and ensuring that Quentin Quinn continued to get all the credit for the serial's success.

The last thing she needed was to face the pressure of a group of society ladies and gentlemen who would no doubt look down their noses at her for working with the purveyors of radio nonsense.

Although she had only come to respect Miss Connors more and more during the five weeks they'd been working together on *As the Sun Sets*, most of what Martha knew about the glamorous actress had been gleaned from magazines and the daily newspaper's social pages. Miss Connors featured regularly. Martha knew about her three marriages. Her husband the surgeon who eschewed the world of entertainment but was happy for her to continue to work under her maiden name. Her childless state (something the newspapers stopped mentioning after she had reached a certain age). Her impeccable glamour. The fact that her handbag always matched her shoes and that she wore a heel—not too low, not too high—every day, including on weekends when she was picking flowers from the carefully tended rose garden at Analee. And who could forget her trademark: carefully applied deep red lipstick.

The fact that she had no children—a reality that might have given them something in common if Miss Connors hadn't been Miss Connors—had meant her career had been uninterrupted and she had become somewhat of the grand dame of Australian radio drama and theater. She was a formidable woman with a formidable career.

The trouble was that Martha felt she had absolutely nothing in common with Miss Connors and couldn't pretend that she did. Yes, they were both childless, but that was about it. They breathed in the same Sydney air, but Miss Connors's was rarefied. Martha's smelled of petrol, outside toilets, and the night cart.

She hadn't wanted to go to Miss Connors's soiree and had told her so the day she received the invitation. The actress had come to collect her scripts for the next week's recordings. There wasn't the budget to have them delivered by an errand boy, but Miss Connors had insisted she didn't mind because she came into the city on Fridays to have lunch with her girlfriends at the Australia Hotel and to shop at David Jones in the afternoon.

"What do you mean, you aren't able to attend?" Miss Connors had stood in front of Martha's desk with an inquisitorial stare. Her brown crocodile handbag hung from her elbow and Martha didn't need to see the actress's shoes to know they would be matching.

"I apologize again, Miss Connors."

"Do you have another engagement?" Miss Connors cocked her head to the side.

Martha couldn't lie. She never lied. Well. Sometimes she did but only in service of *As the Sun Sets*. "I find myself run a little ragged here at work, Miss Connors. Weekends are the only restorative time I have. I do like to spend that time with my mother." Martha always found herself up at the crack of dawn so she could visit the grocer, the butcher, and the post office before they all closed at midday. That meant two separate trips because they were in two different directions from home. And then there was the washing and the cleaning. That left precious little time for anything else. Mostly, the only other thing she wanted to do was read. And sleep. In that order.

"My dear Miss Berry." Miss Connors tugged at the fingers of her pristine white gloves and removed them finger by elegant finger. She perched herself on the corner of Martha's desk, which was quite a feat in her pencil skirt. "You have been working harder than anyone on this program. Don't think I don't see it, because I do. Quinn is too busy schmoozing up to Rutherford Hayes and romancing young Marilyn."

Martha almost bit her tongue. "I'm sorry, I don't—"

"He's been rather persistent, apparently, in his invitations." Miss Connors placed a finger in a horizontal line in the vicinity of her deep red lips. Not against them. She was far too sophisticated to smudge her lipstick for a dramatic gesture. "He's offered her guidance in the dramatic arts. Acting coaching. To improve her performance."

"I see." As far as she could judge from Marilyn's performances in the recording studio, the ingenue had settled into the role very nicely indeed. She couldn't imagine what particular advice Quentin Quinn could offer her. He wasn't an actor. Or a writer, for that matter. He was barely much of anything except a title on the door.

"She is doing rather well," Martha replied. "Perhaps it's due to his coaching."

"Mmm." Miss Connors made a noise that might have been called a scoff if Martha had uttered it. "Come, Miss Berry. Let us speak freely." She checked over her shoulder to ensure they were alone. "We both know what men in this industry are like. You've been here forever. And it feels like I've been working forever." She rolled her eyes. "Young Quentin is absolutely no different from any of them. Except perhaps a little younger, I'll give him that. Or do they seem younger the more mature I get?" Miss Connors smiled.

"Marilyn is young and quite beautiful. He is but a moth to a flame. And that is precisely why you need to come to my soiree. She needs advice and protection, Miss Berry. And you and I are in the position to provide it. The soiree will be the perfect place to do it, away from the studio. Where we might find some privacy to pass on the pearls of our womanly wisdom."

Martha's mind whirred. It was none of her business if Marilyn was of a mind to be romanced by Quentin Quinn, but it would be her business if anything that did develop went sour and she had to play go-between in the middle of a woman scorned or a man jilted, or conversely, a man scorned or a woman jilted. That kind of drama might play very well in a radio drama (she needed to take notes), but in real life it would be a nightmare. She simply did not have the energy to mediate a tumultuous relationship between her producer and the starlet. Despite every objection quivering at her nerve endings, she would be forced to change her mind.

Martha straightened her back. "You're quite right, Miss Connors. I shall come."

Miss Connors slid elegantly from Martha's desk and cocked a hip. Head to toe, she looked like a movie star. "Wonderful news. I shall add your name to the RSVP list."

"You were very kind to invite me. And here are your scripts for next week." Martha passed an envelope to Miss Connors.

"Thank you, Miss Berry. I very much look forward to seeing you on Saturday evening."

And that was how Miss Martha Berry found herself staring out at the fading evening-blue water of Sydney Harbour. Sailboats bobbed like seagulls afloat and the lights across the water at Point Piper were just beginning their evening sparkle. Martha's new frock, a deep turquoise shantung silk creation that cinched in at her waist and hugged her thighs, made it nearly impossible to walk, and the shoes she'd bought to match pinched at her toes in a manner she knew would make her feet ache for days, but she fit right in.

When she turned her back on the glittering harbor, she saw that since her arrival—on the dot of 5:00 p.m. as indicated on the handwritten invitation she had received—the terrace overlooking the tiered garden was filling up with glamorous women in beautiful gowns and men in black ties. Waiters dressed in white floated through the crowd carrying silver trays filled with champagne coupes glistening with bubbles and others with selections of exotic hors d'oeuvres. Martha had tasted a canapé filled with crab mousse and crudités and caviar on a small round cracker.

Just as she was taking her first sip of champagne, Kent Stone joined her.

"Enjoying the bubbles, Miss Berry?"

"I am, thank you, Mr. Stone. I must admit that it's not something I drink very often. If I do indulge, it's a sherry. But I quite like the sensation on my tongue."

"Sadly, I'm rather too well acquainted with the stuff myself." Kent reached for another glass and placed his empty one on a tray as a waiter glided past. As he sipped, he looked her over from head to toe. "My, you look ravishing, Miss Berry."

His warm smile made her smile back and she dipped her head in acknowledgment at his compliment. "Thank you, Mr. Stone." And perhaps the champagne had loosened her tongue, but she suddenly felt able to confide her insecurities in Kent. "I bought this dress especially for tonight. I must admit to never having been to a Vaucluse soiree before."

Kent clinked his glass with Martha's. "You've chosen well. That color makes your eyes sparkle."

If Martha didn't know Kent quite so well, she might assume he was flirting with her. But she knew Kent Stone wasn't the dating type. He had never been depicted in the social pages or the gossip columns with a woman on his arm. "A confirmed bachelor, that's me," he had often been quoted as saying. "Not one to settle down when there are so many fields to play in."

"You're being too kind to me tonight, Mr. Stone."

"There is no such thing. The old girl does throw a magnificent party, doesn't she?"

Martha nodded her agreement. "She certainly does. I've never seen a house quite as big as this. And the view . . ." Martha indicated the harbor with a sweep of her arm. "Imagine waking up to this every morning." She sighed. "I would never want to leave the house."

"Quite." Kent Stone looked over the heads of the guests. "Oh, look. There's Miss Calthorpe and Mr. Quinn."

Across the stone-paved patio, they observed a swaying Quentin Quinn stumbling after Marilyn Calthorpe, who was walking toward them as quickly as her teetering stilettos would allow. Every time Martha heard Quentin Quinn call out, "Marilyn," Marilyn's pace became a little faster. Martha could barely take in her figure-hugging navy silk gown because the look on Marilyn's face was one of trepidation, if not downright fear.

When she reached them, she stretched out a hand to grip Martha's elbow. "Good evening, Miss Berry. How lovely to find you, Mr. Stone."

"Good evening," he replied.

"I wondered if you might—"

"Well, here we all are." As Quentin Quinn sidled up beside Marilyn, pressing himself against her hip and shoulder, Marilyn's grip on Martha's elbow tightened.

"Quinn," Kent Stone said and extended a hand. "Started early, I see."

Quentin Quinn looked up and narrowed his eyes at his leading actor. "And what of it? You'll never catch me saying no when the drinks are free."

"So it seems," Kent mumbled under his breath.

Marilyn turned to face Martha. "Miss Berry, I wonder if you wouldn't mind showing me the way to the powder room?" Her eyes darted to her right.

"Of course. Follow me."

Martha shot Kent a wide-eyed look and he took the hint, stepping in front of Quentin Quinn just as Martha moved to follow Marilyn. "Tell me, Quinn. I was just about to ask Miss Berry. What's in store for Jack Percy? I have some ideas I'd like to share with you."

....

Martha and Marilyn maneuvered their way through the crowd of glamorous couples to a sitting room in which two Chesterfield sofas sat plumply, illuminated by elegant white lamps on two marble-topped end tables. Martha wondered if the rug with its swirling maroons and blues was Persian, although she'd never seen one up close so she couldn't be sure.

Martha urged the actress onto one of the soft leather sofas, and as soon as she was seated, Marilyn burst into tears.

"Oh my goodness," Martha soothed as she joined her, fishing a freshly pressed handkerchief from her handbag and unfolding it before handing it to Marilyn. "There, there." Martha didn't need to ask because she had a very good idea of what the matter was. Or rather, who. She hadn't been unaware of Quentin Quinn's attentions to the actress. Anyone could see his attentiveness to Marilyn during rehearsals. The only telephone calls he hadn't asked her to make on his behalf, to be transferred through to him because he deemed himself too important to actually dial a number himself, were those to Marilyn. But this seemed far more serious than an attraction.

"Whatever is the matter?" Miss Connors swept into the room as if she were floating. She wore a full-length dress of amber-colored silk that was so glamorous that Martha had to blink twice to take it all in.

"Come now. You can't be crying at my soiree." Miss Connors smiled sympathetically as she perched herself on the arm of the sofa. "People might think there's something wrong with my caviar."

Marilyn drew in a deep breath and was finally able to control her shuddering sobs. As she dabbed the handkerchief to her eyes, she managed a smile.

"Thank you for the handkerchief, Miss Berry."

"It always pays to have a freshly pressed handkerchief in your handbag. That was a lesson my mother taught me and her mother taught her."

"That's good advice for any girl," Miss Connors said. "Be pre-pared, as the Boy Scouts say. Although it applies to girls too. Perhaps even more so. Will you tell us what's got you so upset? A problem shared is a problem halved. That was a lesson my mother taught me." She winked at Martha.

Marilyn sniffed. "I was so looking forward to the soiree tonight, Miss Connors. I really was. I've never seen such a beautiful home. It's like a castle for a princess or something. So I borrowed this dress from my friend Dorothy and this is her handbag, too, which is why I forgot to put my own handkerchief inside. Anyway, Dorothy did my hair and I bought a new lipstick especially, and . . . and as soon as I stepped out of the taxi onto the street out front here, there he was. And my heart sank right there into my shoes."

Miss Connors met Martha's gaze and a look of recognition passed between them.

"Mr. Quinn. He was already . . . Anyway, I tried to walk right past him, but it was as if he was waiting for me or something. When he hugged me, I just stood there like a cold fish. But when he tried to kiss me, right on the lips . . . I pushed him away and ran into the party. Thank goodness I found you, Miss Berry."

Miss Connors's expression grew grim. "Oh dear."

Martha felt something harden inside her and it sat in her stomach like a stone. "We will put a plan in place, Miss Calthorpe."

"Please, Miss Berry. Call me Marilyn."

"Marilyn, I will do everything in my power to ensure that you will never be alone with Mr. Quinn." In for a penny, in for a pound. "And Hooper. And Mervin in the garage."

Marilyn's lips wobbled. "What about the acting lessons he says I need? And . . . and all the lunches? He says he wants to discuss storylines for Betty Percy, and I agree, thinking it's a work meeting, but then he doesn't talk about the show at all. I don't know what to do. I really like playing Betty. His scripts are so wonderful." She turned to Martha with pleading eyes. "This is the best job I've ever had, and I don't want to lose my job, Miss Berry."

Miss Connors stood. "I can't say I'm shocked, Marilyn. When you've been in this business as long as I have, you get to see some things. Terrible things. Cruel things. Things that end careers. But we won't let that happen to you, Marilyn. You have our word."

"I do?"

Miss Connors put a hand on Marilyn's shoulder. "You really do. You're professional. You learn your lines. You have a wonderful voice, and you are bringing such empathy to Betty."

"That's very true," Martha added at Miss Connors's silent urging. "You've seen the letters from listeners. People are crossing their fingers for Betty to get her first job. You're an inspiration to every young girl in Australia who's working hard to get where she wants to be."

"And Miss Berry and I won't let anything jeopardize that."

"What's going on here, then?" Kent Stone entered the room carrying a silver tray bearing freshly filled champagne coupes.

"Girl talk," Miss Connors said with a sudden actress's smile.

"I'm just in time then." He winked at Martha. "I've been looking for you ladies everywhere."

Martha reached for a glass and passed it to Marilyn. The poor thing looked like she could use it. "Is Mr. Quinn far behind you?"

"No." Kent Stone raised an eyebrow as he passed bubbles to Martha and Miss Connors. "He decided to leave early. At least he did after I pushed him into a taxi."

Miss Connors mouthed a silent "Thank you" to Kent Stone.

"I've seen more of this carry-on than you might imagine over the years. It really grinds my goat." Kent shook his head, exasperated. "We should report him to Actors' and Announcers' Equity. See what they'll do about protecting a member from Quinn."

"What's that?" Marilyn asked.

"It's our union," Kent replied. "I hope you're a member, Marilyn."

"Should I be?" she asked, looking from Martha to Miss Connors and back to Kent.

"Of course you should!" Kent exclaimed. "I'll sort that out for you on Monday. The union's there to help you in situations such as these."

"Oh no! I wouldn't want to make a fuss or get anyone in trouble. He's just a little drunk, that's all."

As he was every day, Martha thought.

Marilyn's taut shoulders dropped with a loud exhale. "Miss

Connors. It's nothing really. It'll sort itself out. I shouldn't keep you any longer. You have so many guests."

"Who are all no doubt quite entertained talking to one another. As they did last weekend at the Stratten-Lucas wedding and as they will at the Pacific Country Club next weekend. I'd much rather be here with all of you. We don't get much of a chance to chat, do we?"

"No, we don't." Kent turned to Martha. "Now, Miss Berry, I tried to find out from Quinn what's in store for Jack Percy. I want something meaty. Something dramatic. He wouldn't tell me a thing. Although, to be honest, I can't say he was in a position to remember much of anything. You do know what's coming, don't you? You don't have to worry about telling me. I'm the soul of discretion."

Miss Connors snorted. Martha was taken aback by it and laughed. Marilyn joined in and Kent did too.

"Why, you're the biggest gossip in Sydney, Kent!"

"That is not true," he replied with faux indignation. "Well, perhaps the second biggest. Is there anything wrong with wanting to know what's going on?"

Miss Connors sipped her bubbles. "Do tell, Miss Berry. What's in store for us?"

Martha blamed the champagne. "We'll be casting soon for a new family."

Her announcement was met with silence. Marilyn's bottom lip began to wobble again.

"Oh goodness, no, not to replace the Percys. Nothing like that at all. It was the plan all along to broaden the cast. An Italian family is going to rent the shop next door to Percys' Butchers. There'll be a husband and wife—Paolo and Carmelina Antonello—and their three sons: Antonio and . . . I haven't come up with the names yet of the two other brothers."

Martha waited while the news sank in. With furrowed brows, Kent looked to be pondering how the arrival of a new family in *As the Sun Sets* might impinge on how much airtime Jack Percy had in the serial. Miss Connors clearly was thinking the same.

In direct contrast, Marilyn's eyes lit up.

"Three sons?" she gasped. "I'd love to play a romance. Will Betty fall in love with one of them, do you think? Or perhaps . . . Oh goodness. Will there be a love triangle with Ernie and one of the Italian boys?"

Martha feigned ignorance. She didn't want to reveal all to the actors, but that was exactly what she was planning for young Betty. Precisely because the idea of an Italian Catholic migrant—Martha was already thinking it should be Antonio, the eldest—becoming romantically involved with an Australian girl would be quite controversial.

"There are a few Italians in the next suburb from me," Marilyn said. "In Leichhardt. They have a grocer's shop. You can buy olive oil in there. I've never tasted it myself, but I've seen it in the window."

"I might go and pay a visit," Martha said. "For inspiration. I mean, to pass on ideas to Mr. Quinn."

From the corner of her eye, Martha could see Miss Connors cock her head to one side. She purposely didn't meet the actress's eye. No one could know she was really writing the scripts.

"By the way, do any of you know any Italian-speaking actors?" Martha asked.

Kent Stone looked to Miss Connors. "Let me think." He clicked his fingers. "There are a few around Sydney who attempt an Italian accent."

"I'd really love an Italian speaker," Martha added. "For authenticity."

Kent Stone and Miss Connors pondered a moment. "What about . . ." Kent Stone snapped his fingers. "Did you ever work with Alex Paulson, Miss Connors?"

She shook her head. "No, but I know of him."

"That name doesn't sound very Italian," Martha said, perplexed. "Does it?"

"His real name is Allesandro Polese," Kent Stone explained. "He was born right here in Sydney and sounds as Australian as you or me. But I'm sure he could do the accent."

Miss Connors sighed. "Wasn't he caught up with all that business during the war?"

"What business?" Marilyn asked.

"He was interned in 1940. And he was still a boy too. Enemy aliens, they were called. You were only a child, but when Italy joined the war, fighting with Hitler against our diggers, Italians back here couldn't be trusted, or so the government said. Locked them up for almost five years. I think Allesandro was at a camp in Hay with his parents. Anyway, I hadn't seen him in years until a couple of months ago. He's working as a waiter at that new restaurant, Beppi's in Darlinghurst. The food was"—Kent Stone held his fingers to his lips—"*bellissimo*."

"What does that mean?" Marilyn asked.

"It means delicious, Miss Calthorpe."

Martha was intrigued. "Mr. Stone, do you think he might be interested in auditioning for a role in *As the Sun Sets*?"

"I wouldn't have a clue, Miss Berry. But I'm very happy to find out."

"I'd appreciate that."

Kent Stone winked at Martha. "Thank you for giving me an excuse to return to Beppi's."

"And don't forget to ask him if he knows anyone else who might be interested."

"I will do. Cheers." Kent Stone, Miss Connors, Marilyn, and Martha clinked their glasses together.

To Martha, it felt something like hatching a plan.

Chapter 19

IN WHICH MARTHA BERRY GETS ON WITH BUSINESS.

This line here? At the top of the page?"

Alex Paulson stood on the other side of Martha's desk with a script in his hands. His black hair was short over his ears and tall and sculpted at his crown, aided by pomade cream and a good comb. When he read the lines to himself, his thick eyebrows creased and his brown eyes hooded. He looked for all the world like Mario Lanza. The rousing sounds of "Nessun Dorma" filled Martha's head before she willed them away.

"The one beginning, 'Papa, where shall I put these boxes?'"

"Beaut," he replied and shot her a serious look. "Give me a few goes, will you, Miss Berry? I haven't acted in a bloody long time."

"No pressure at all. Take your time. If you read the part of Antonio, the eldest son of Paolo and Carmelina Antonello, I'll read Paolo."

His grave expression cracked a little and there was the hint of a smile on his face. "My nonna's name was Carmelina. My grand-mother, I mean."

"What a coincidence," Martha said. And then she realized he'd referred to his grandmother in the past tense. "Was?"

"She was killed in the war. My grandfather, too, and my youngest uncle."

"I'm so very sorry."

The war's threads looped and circled all over the world, across oceans and continents and time zones and ideologies. People were at one end or the other of chains of love and longing and agony that linked those now separated by oceans or death, sons and fathers and husbands and sweethearts and daughters and aunts and sisters. Martha had thought it was only Australians who lay in anonymous graves, their bodies having been blown to bits, in strange places thousands of miles away. But it was the other way too. Ghosts lay buried in the grounds of places people who now lived in Australia would likely never see again.

Every Australian-born family knew someone who had served, and the unfortunate ones had known one of the thirty-four thousand who'd died, the seventy-two thousand who had been injured, or, god forbid, the thirty-odd thousand who'd been prisoners of war.

But it must have been so much worse—and who would want to imagine how much worse—for those who had been living in those battlegrounds in Europe and the Philippines and Malaysia and Singapore and New Guinea and so many other places.

Alex cleared his throat and began the scene.

ANTONIO ANTONELLO: *Papa, where shall I put these boxes?*

He turned his gaze from the script to Martha and waited.

"Mr. Paulson—" She paused, hoping what she was about to ask

didn't sound indelicate or insulting. "I'm wondering if you could sound a little more . . . Italian?"

"*More* Italian?" He laughed but there was no smile to accompany it. "That's the first time anyone in Australia has ever said that to me."

"I hope you don't mind me saying, but I want the Antonello family to sound like a real Italian family. That's why I'd like to cast an Italian speaker in the role. It would be as easy as anything to find any old actor to pretend he's Italian, but nowadays, with so many new Australians here, and so many more arriving every year, I want it to sound real for them too. Australia is changing and we want to make sure we're reflecting that in *As the Sun Sets*."

Alex's face became stormy. "You mean you wanta me to sounda like-a this?"

"My goodness, no. You're not here for comic relief and neither are the Antonellos. They're going to be real characters with real dramas and problems in their lives, just like the Percys and every other character in the serial."

Under his breath he muttered, "I'll believe that when I see it."

"Please, Mr. Paulson. You have my word."

"But what about Quentin Quinn? The bloke whose name is on the door? He might think something different and then I'll end up making a joke of me and every Italian family in the country."

"Let me assure you that Mr. Quinn and I are on the same page." She crossed her fingers behind her back. "He would be here to reassure you himself, but he's been held up in meetings this morning. He's asked me to have a run-through with you and I'll pass on my notes to him. Mr. Quinn gets the final say and you'll have the chance to put your point of view across to him before you sign your contract." She hoped that was enough, but when she looked up at a scowling Mr. Paulson, she could see he was still deciding if he could trust her.

Martha looked down at her copy of the script. "Ready to go?"

ANTONIO ANTONELLO: *Papa, where shall I put these boxes?*

PAOLO ANTONELLO: *In the storeroom. At the back. Where are your brothers? They should be here. How you say . . . helping.*

ANTONIO ANTONELLO: *Tomaso is on his way back to Leichhardt to pick up Mama. She said she wants to clean the place top to bottom before we do anything.*

PAOLO ANTONELLO: *Your mama works so hard for the family.*

ANTONIO ANTONELLO: *And Mario? Who knows where he is. Probably chasing a pretty Australian girl somewhere. Blondes. It's always the blondes. (chuckles)*

PAOLO ANTONELLO: *He likes the girls.*

ANTONIO ANTONELLO: *Look around at this place, Papa. Enough of working in factories, huh? All that money we saved, the whole family, and now we're going to have our own shop. You are greengrocer. A fruttivendolo!*

"What was that word?" Martha asked.

"*Fruttivendolo.* It means greengrocer. I thought you wouldn't mind if I ad-libbed. You said you wanted it to sound more Italian."

Martha wanted to clap but she was too polite for that. "It's absolutely wonderful. And you have the accent just right. You've given Antonio a lilt of something in his voice that's just enough of a hint to listeners that he speaks another language. That's important. I don't want Antonio to sound like any other character. Radio isn't like the pictures. People will imagine what Antonio looks like by the sound of *your* voice. By the way, do you think you could do Mr. Antonello as well?"

"Sure. I'll just do my dad's voice but not so heavy on the accent."

Martha sat back in her chair and took a moment to appreciate what was happening. It had been two months now and she still couldn't overcome the excitement she felt about writing lines of script and having her words—the ones she'd dreamed up in her head—come out of an actor's mouth. "Are you sure you won't go by your real name?"

"Allesandro Polese? No thanks. At home I'm Allesandro, but when I was acting? I was always Alex Paulson and I'll stay that way. You don't know what people can be like, Miss Berry."

"I'm sure I don't." She put her script down and stood. "I'd like to recommend you to Mr. Quinn. No guarantees, of course, but if you win the part, we'll send a contract, so make sure you leave me with your address. You'll collect scripts on Fridays and we record on Mondays. It takes a little over four hours for the whole week's worth of programs, which includes a lunch break and a little time between episodes. Would that suit you?"

"Good for me," Alex replied. "I've never been afraid of having too much work."

"Wonderful." They shook hands. "I'll let you know as soon as I can. Thank you for coming in to audition, Mr. Paulson."

"Thank you, Miss Berry." He turned to leave but looked back over his shoulder. "*Ciao*," he said and winked.

When he closed the door behind him, Martha flopped down into her seat. Sweat beaded her top lip and her forehead. "Oh, for goodness' sake," she chided herself. "He's young enough to be your son."

"Three sons?" Quentin Quinn looked at the script. "I thought I said a son and two daughters." He scratched his head in disbelief. Martha was familiar with the gesture. He was never good in the morning. Especially Thursday mornings when he reviewed the scripts Martha had written from his story notes. He described them as copious. She rather thought of them as scribbled dot points on a page.

"You might remember when we discussed it that you agreed to change it to three sons, because they would all work in the green-grocers and could be potential love interests for Betty and her friends?"

Quentin Quinn shook his head. "We need at least one daughter. Three sons is too many sons. I want a daughter and I'll cast some-one who sounds like Gina Lollobrigida."

No doubt he'd want to cast someone who looked like her too.

"Easily done, Mr. Quinn. The youngest Antonello sibling will now be a daughter. We had a Mario. We could easily transform that into Maria?"

"Fine, fine," he said as he waved her away. He strode into his office and shut the door behind him with a bang. She would have to find a young actress who could play Maria, and fast. There could be an upside. She was still searching for her Carmelina. If she was fortunate, she would find an actress who could play both. Kent Stone was playing Jack Percy and having a lot of fun acting the part of the delivery driver, Stan. Miss Connors was doing a terrific job of performing Vera Percy and, when the serial needed some light relief, Mrs. White. Martha had tried not to write too many scenes in which Vera and Mrs. White both appeared, lest Miss Connors become distracted during the recording.

She added another item to her to-do list, which sat to the right of her typewriter: casting Carmelina/Maria. She had a feeling Quentin Quinn might like to cast this role. Perhaps she could visit one of the Italian community organizations to see if there were any budding young performers who might be suitable. Was it something an Italian family would allow their daughter to do? She would have to find out before she wrote any dialogue for Carmelina or Maria. For now, she had cast Antonio and Paolo, father and son.

As the Sun Sets was blossoming under her direction. Martha wondered how long it would take before Quentin Quinn realized she was stealing the show out from under him. She couldn't think about that right now. The Antonello family would have to wait.

There were scripts to write.

Chapter 20

IN WHICH MARTHA BERRY LETS THE CAT OUT OF THE BAG ABOUT WHAT'S AILING VERA.

Martha's hands hovered over the keys.

The anticipation had been building for weeks now about Vera's health, and Martha had finally decided what was ailing her already-beloved character.

Rutherford Hayes had loved the slow buildup of the drama surrounding Vera's mysterious malady—and the reader mail that continued to pour in from all over the country—and had once again congratulated Quentin Quinn for his genius. It was one more feather in his cap, which was already beginning to resemble a creation atop the head of a matron from the Victorian era. Would that he got hay fever from all the praise. And the feathers.

No, Martha chided herself. There was no point thinking that way. It was uncharitable and she knew letting those thoughts settle and grow would only make her bitter and resentful. And she didn't want to let bitterness and spitefulness settle inside her like a stone. There was too much joy in what she was doing, in the world and the characters she was creating, for her to let her feelings about Quentin Quinn ruin it. In her experience, feelings of joy came around less often than one might imagine. Even if she was not getting the credit for it, she was getting the pleasure of it in spades. She had known all along that Quentin Quinn would reap the praise and she would have none of it, at least publicly. She couldn't remember the last time she'd been recognized for her neat typing and her stellar organizational skills. Those things went unnoticed in an organization run and controlled by men. The work of women was invisible and always would be.

Nothing had changed. And nothing would change.

Vera. What was wrong with Vera? Martha was ready to put it on the page. To fortify herself, she made a cup of extra-strong coffee and slipped two honey joy biscuits from the middle drawer of her desk. They were better than cigarettes, in her experience.

She cast her eyes to the cigarette smoke–stained ceiling of her office. "Vera enters the doctors' surgery . . . ," she said and pressed her fingers to the keys.

VERA *enters the doctors' surgery.*
FX: *Bell, children coughing, general groaning*
MRS. WHITE: *Hello, Mrs. Percy. Didn't expect to see you here.*
VERA PERCY: *Oh. (pauses) Mrs. White. I hope you're well?*
MRS. WHITE: *(sighing loudly) Oh, I shouldn't complain. I'm here for my blood pressure tablets. When you have as many worries as I do, it's no surprise, is it, that my heart's playing up. Won't you come sit next to me?*
VERA PERCY: *Yes. (clears her throat) Of course. What's that you're reading?*

FX: *Magazine pages rustling*

MRS. WHITE: *I've just been looking at this magazine and all the new pictures of Her Majesty. Isn't she delightful? And so young to be our monarch. Do you think they'll have any more children? I mean, they do have a pigeon pair in little Prince Charles and Princess Anne. But it would be nice to have more princes and princesses, wouldn't it?*

VERA PERCY: *It's always a blessing to—*

MRS. WHITE: *But girls these days aren't having as many children as they used to, are they? I've only got two myself, but I'm not a queen!*

VERA PERCY: *Nor am I, Mrs. White.*

MRS. WHITE: *So what are you here for today, Mrs. Percy? Everything all right?*

VERA PERCY: *(pause) Yes. I'm quite well. Just a checkup is all.*

MRS. WHITE: *Well, I suppose we're not spring chickens anymore, are we? Everything's going to ache at our age.*

FX: *Door opening*

DOCTOR: *Mrs. Percy?*

VERA PERCY: *Hello, Doctor. Goodbye, Mrs. White.*

MRS. WHITE: *I do hope you're feeling better soon, Mrs. Percy.*

VERA PERCY: *And the same to you, Mrs. White.*

MRS. WHITE: *I don't know, Mrs. Percy. Sometimes I feel like I'm fading fast.*

FX: *Footsteps and door closing*

VERA PERCY: *(muttering to herself) Of all the people to run into. She'll have told half the neighborhood before I get home, and it'll be the talk of the shop tomorrow. (sighs)*

Martha hadn't met anyone she knew in the waiting room when she'd gone to the doctor for her appointment a few days earlier.

Three new mothers sat with their arms full of babies, squawking and cooing. A little boy sat next to a woman Martha presumed was his grandmother, his eyes full of tears, holding a heavily bandaged finger upright, blood staining through the layers of cotton. An older gentleman sat dozing, one leg missing and a crutch by his side.

The room was full of strangers, much like most of her life. It was a happy existence but a small one. Martha had her mother and their neighbors, Mrs. Tilley and Mrs. Ward, whom she knew would drop everything to help if their help was ever needed. There were the Calendar Girls at work, too, who'd become friends. She didn't have lifelong friends, the kind a person made when they were younger and who stayed close, and she had regretted that, but it couldn't be helped. Perhaps she wasn't the kind of person that friends stuck to. Maybe people found it easy to let the ties that bind slacken with her. What was it about her that meant loyalty like that was missing from her life?

The friends she'd made when she was younger had drifted away in bits and pieces over the years. Once they'd married and started having children, the distance had become even greater. She'd tried. She really had. And she was certain they had too. Maud had twins when they were both twenty-two, and one time Martha had offered to babysit when the boys were six months old so Maud could go to a doctor's appointment. She thought she might be pregnant again and needed to take the test.

Martha had found the morning a complete disaster. The babies screamed from the moment Maud left the house, and nothing Martha did could comfort the two squirming bundles. She was horrified at her seeming inability to soothe the crying babies and never again offered to look after them. Maud hadn't asked either. Martha had continued to visit for a while, for cups of tea and a slice of the sponge cake Violet made especially for Maud, but they seemed to have lost the thread that was holding their friendship together. Martha didn't know how to talk about children and Maud could talk of nothing else, especially after her third arrived. Martha didn't blame Maud. Her world had simply gotten bigger. Martha's had shrunk just a little more each time a friend married and moved away.

The same had happened with Hilda. As single girls, she and Martha had gone to cafes and shared their love of books. Their friendship was so easy at first, but Hilda was a beautiful young woman and it wasn't long before she was romanced and engaged and married. She asked Martha to be her maid of honor and Martha undertook the task with diligence and good humor. Three months later Hilda was pregnant, and Martha felt more and more like the last one standing, waving goodbye to all her friends as they sailed away to a land filled with husbands and nappies and round little tummies and golden locks and bedtime stories.

Their life trajectories had only emphasized to Martha how stuck she was in her own. She had been waiting for her life to take a turn for the better, to veer down a road that might include romance and a proposal on bended knee and marriage and children, but her path was a straight line. And after losing her precious friendships with Maud and Hilda, Martha wondered if she was simply unable to keep people close and couldn't bear the idea that she might lose another friend, so she had stopped trying to make any. She had her work. Her mother was excellent company and she had the radio and her beloved books. People lived worse lives than hers, she had consoled herself. Her father's death and her mother's poor health were constant reminders of that. And as she had proof, falling in love was no guarantee that a person would stay in love or keep that love.

So the years had passed her by and Martha now found herself, at fifty years of age, sitting in her doctor's office with a vague feeling of something being not quite right. Her monthlies had been increasingly difficult and erratic and she had started to feel lethargic, and although she'd tried to put it down to doing the work of at least three people, it felt somehow more than that. Martha had begun to wonder if she had some kind of medical problem in the ladies' department that needed to be attended to.

"Miss Berry?"

Martha stood quickly and her handbag tumbled from her lap onto the floor. She hurriedly picked it up, smoothed her tweed skirt, and followed Dr. Gordon into his office.

Now, it wasn't *the* Dr. Gordon from *Blue Hills*, but she wished it was. Her doctor was in his early eighties. His bald head was shiny and mottled, and she was surprised he still had all his teeth.

Teeth. Her father hadn't been able to afford to see a dentist and had died because of it. She was at least grateful she had the means to pay.

Dr. Gordon checked a piece of paper on his desk while the thin wire reading glasses that were perched on the very end of his nose threatened to slip off onto his desk.

"Mmm. I see." He turned to her. "I haven't seen you in a long while, Miss Berry."

"I've had no need, Doctor. I've generally been in very good health."

"What seems to be the problem now?"

Martha felt a blush of shame creep up her cheeks and redden her décolletage. She hated that she flushed when she was embarrassed, but it had become worse lately. Sometimes, even when it was cool, she had become inexplicably hot, as if the door to a furnace had been opened somewhere in her vicinity so that the heat blasted her from head to toe.

"I haven't been feeling well."

"In what way?" He turned back to the paper on his desk, picked up a pen, and waited as if he was about to take dictation.

"The tiredness, firstly. It comes over me like a wave."

He looked her up and down. "You're not a young woman anymore, Miss Berry. You might simply be overdoing things. I see you're a Miss."

"Yes." Why did it always sound like an accusation?

"You've never married?"

What did that have to do with the price of eggs? She shook her head. "No."

"Any sexual intercourse?"

Her breath caught. Suddenly a sweat broke out on her top lip and her forehead seemed drenched. Without thinking, she began to fan herself.

"There's no need to be prudish, Miss Berry. I ask because I need to investigate all the possibilities. Including that you might be expecting."

"Expecting?" When Martha realized how loud her reply had been, she cleared her throat by way of apology. "I'm not expecting, Doctor. There's absolutely no possibility of me being in the family way."

He looked her up and down. "I see. But stranger things have happened. I'm sure you've heard of a change-of-life baby."

Of course she had. Mrs. Hargreaves down the street had been pushing a pram well into her fifties. And in her fifties she'd looked seventy, which was no recommendation at all for having a child so late in life.

"Yes, but I can assure you, Doctor, that's not the case with me."

"Are you not having intercourse?"

She shook her head. The blush creeped higher until she was sure her cheeks were aflame.

"I see. How are your menstrual periods?"

Martha knew he was a doctor, but would talking about her intimate bodily functions with a man always feel this uncomfortable? "I used to be as regular as clockwork, but lately things have changed. To tell the truth, that's why I'm here to see you. Something might be wrong. Down there."

He turned to face her. "Do you sometimes feel inexplicably hot?"

Martha mopped her brow with the handkerchief she'd been clutching. "Yes."

"Sweating, I see."

"Yes."

"Sleep?"

"I've been restless. Perhaps that's why I feel tired. It's been very busy at work."

That last sentence seemed to go completely over his head. "I think you've hit menopause."

"Menopause?" Had she read about it in a magazine? She wasn't sure.

"I believe you ladies call it 'the change.'"

What? She'd been waiting for her life to change and now her body had gone and done it without her even knowing.

"Sadly, for a female, the charmed days of your womanhood are now in the past. You'll likely feel dull and unattractive from now on. That's the cycle of life, I'm afraid, Miss Berry. There's no cure. It's something that happens to women and you'll have to bear it."

"Oh."

"When did your mother go through it?"

Her mother? If Violet had suffered as Martha was now, she had never mentioned it. They simply didn't talk about such things. "I don't know."

"Perhaps you should consider giving up work, if things get too much for you. That'll help with your tiredness."

Martha was simply too polite to point out to him that she was thirty years younger than he was, and he still believed he had the vitality to turn up to work every day and cure people's maladies.

"So there's nothing to be done?"

"No. An aspirin might help if you experience any stomach cramping along with a period. A hot water bottle. The usual."

"How long will I feel this way?" Martha asked.

"It can go on for years in some women," the doctor told her as he wrote on a page of her medical file.

At her desk, Martha sat back in her chair. She'd left the surgery with nothing more than the equivalent of a "there, there" and a pat on the back. In the days since, she'd been thinking about what her doctor had told her.

Years. The menopause. Of course it was. But why did she know so little about it? Why had she worried herself sick over the past few months for fear that she was growing something troubling in her abdomen? Why didn't women talk about things like this with each other?

And then the heat in her chest turned into a pounding in her heart and a rage she could barely contain. She hit the keys with a new ferocity.

VERA PERCY: *I beg your pardon?*

DOCTOR: *It's the change of life, Mrs. Percy. (chuckles) That's what you ladies call it, anyway. We doctors prefer to use the medical term menopause. It's the time in your life when you stop having your monthly periods.*

VERA PERCY: *But I'm still having them, Doctor. Sometimes not for months and then . . . Well, they've been quite difficult to deal with. I've been too worried to leave the house just in case I get caught out. Are you sure there's nothing wrong?*

DOCTOR: *I've looked at your blood tests and I'm certain there's nothing else for you to be worried about.*

VERA PERCY: *I thought there was something wrong with my . . . downstairs.*

DOCTOR: *Menopause happens to every woman, Mrs. Percy. It's perfectly natural. But if sleep is a problem, try to rest. Lack of sleep can be an issue for all of us as we get older.*

VERA PERCY: *I've been waking in the night . . . two or three times . . . to go to the toilet.*

DOCTOR: *That's quite common.*

VERA PERCY: *How long will this last, Doctor?*

DOCTOR: *I wish I could be specific. It could end next week, or it could go on for years. You'll have to bear with it, I'm afraid.*

Martha sat back in her chair. Her breath was heavy and a sweat had broken out on her top lip. She dabbed it with a handkerchief. Then she rolled the page out of her typewriter, set it on the stack to her left, and looked on the pile of scripts with a satisfied sigh.

Chapter 21

IN WHICH VERA'S DIAGNOSIS SETS THE CAT AMONG THE PIGEONS.

Quinn!"

Head of Drama Rutherford Hayes's voice bellowed down the corridor before Martha even heard his footsteps. When he appeared at the door, she managed to find an expression of poised equanimity.

"Where is he?" Mr. Hayes demanded. His face was as red as beetroot, and he was waving a sheaf of paper in his right hand.

"Mr. Quinn is still at lunch."

He looked at his watch. "It's half past two!"

"With the actors." Quentin Quinn had made it a tradition to entertain the key cast members every Monday after they'd finished recording. Martha was beginning to believe it was his favorite time of the week, and although she was never invited, Kent Stone and Miss Connors had lived up to their pledge never to leave Marilyn Calthorpe alone in Quentin Quinn's company. They had become her constant chaperones.

"I've just listened to today's episode of *As the Sun Sets*." He glowered. "More like *As the Sun Sets on My Career*. And Quinn's!" He stopped pacing and leaned over Martha's desk with gimlet eyes. "*Why didn't I see these scripts before they went to air?*"

That was a very good question with a very complicated answer. The truth was that Quentin Quinn had, as the Americans were fond of saying in their movies, gone AWOL on the Thursday and Friday of the week before, and Martha hadn't been able to find hide nor hair of him. She had written every script as she usually did, but they had sat unchecked on Quentin Quinn's desk. When she'd turned up the previous Monday, hoping against hope that he might have come in on the weekend and gone through them, she'd been sadly but not unexpectedly disappointed. There was not a red pen mark on them anywhere, and with the actors set to arrive in just five minutes, she'd had no choice but to copy them quickly and give them to the actors as they were assembling in the recording studio for their half-hour rehearsal.

There had simply been no time to do anything else if the show was to make it to air.

"Today's program . . ." Mr. Hayes was pink in the face and so angry he could hardly speak. Martha had a sinking feeling her masquerade was about to be unmasked.

Mr. Hayes attempted to straighten his tie and flatten his hair. "I've just been roasted by Charles Moses, who in turn has been roasted by the top dog in the prime minister's office because the PM was too busy to roast Moses himself. Do you have any idea what Quinn has done?"

Martha sat mute. Any answer she provided would give the game away.

"For goodness' sake." He came to a halt and shouted at her. "*Menopause?* No one wants to listen to a middle-aged woman at her doctor's hearing about . . . women's private business. It should stay at home . . . not be broadcast throughout the country. All over Australia, farmers and farmers' wives were sat out there today, innocently eating their lunch and talking about wheat prices or wool prices or the rain or who knows what else, and when the music for *As the Sun Sets* started up and they were expecting more of the same kind of drama . . . and then they get *menopause*. I'm surprised they didn't all choke on their sandwiches."

The men might choke on their sandwiches, but Martha knew exactly what the women would be thinking, and it was something along the lines of *That's me. That's exactly what's happening to me.*

"I don't know how on earth he thinks he can get away with this."

"Shall I ask Mr. Quinn to come to your office when he returns?" Martha asked, trying not to betray any emotion at all. If she was looking at herself in the mirror, her expression might resemble that of a carnival clown, its smile frozen in perpetuity.

"As soon as he sets foot in this office, send him to me." Mr. Hayes turned to leave but then looked back over his shoulder. "And tell him he will need to mount a very good argument as to why I shouldn't sack him on the spot."

....

"Now?"

Quentin Quinn blinked at Martha. He smelled like beer and an overflowing ashtray, and if Martha wasn't mistaken, the red stain on his shirt appeared to be some kind of casserole gravy. It was twenty minutes past three and he didn't know how lucky he was that he hadn't just run into Rutherford Hayes.

"Mr. Hayes came by earlier insisting on seeing you when you

returned to the office." She got up from her desk and crossed the room to turn on the electric kettle. She checked the glass jar next to it and was reassured to find it was half full. Good. Quentin Quinn would need plenty of caffeine if he was to sober up. For if Martha was to save *As the Sun Sets*, she would have to make him look and sound as presentable as she could, given he'd spent the past three hours at the pub, and give him the ammunition he needed to defend the show to Rutherford Hayes.

She didn't give a jot about his career—which he had not taken remotely seriously from the day he'd won the job—but she cared about her own. More than cared. She wanted this show to survive. She needed it to.

"Mr. Hayes wants to see you to discuss today's episode."

Quentin Quinn looked around the room, confused. He hiccupped. "Remind me, Mrs. Barry, what happened in today's episode?"

"Vera went to the doctor today to discuss her health issue."

"Right. Cancer, isn't it?"

"No, Mr. Quinn. We've begun a very important and groundbreaking storyline for Vera." The kettle boiled. Martha heaped two teaspoons of coffee granules into a cup, thought about it a moment and added another, before filling it with hot water. No milk for him today. It needed to be strong and bracing. He needed to be sober enough to mount just the right argument to Rutherford Hayes to save his job. And hers.

"Groundbreaking?"

"The scene in which Vera goes to the doctor."

"Oh." Quentin Quinn scratched his head.

She pushed him into the chair positioned on the other side of her desk before urging his coffee into his hands. "Here. Drink this." She waited impatiently while he sipped at it. She checked her watch. With the mood Rutherford Hayes was in, she had to act quickly. He might well reappear at the door any minute.

"Faster, Mr. Quinn. Please."

"You've made it too hot, Mrs. Barry. I'll burn my tongue."

Martha waited while he blew across the top of his coffee like a child might with their cup of hot chocolate before bed. For goodness' sake. "Listen carefully, Mr. Quinn. Vera goes to the doctor's surgery and runs into Mrs. White, you know, the one who complains about her sciatica all the time."

"Of course," he replied. He rubbed his eyes and yawned.

"So in the scene, Vera is telling the doctor all about her symptoms and he advises her she is experiencing the menopause."

Quentin Quinn looked up at her in confusion. "The *what?*"

"It's something women go through when they're in their fifties. They stop having their monthlies . . . you do know what monthlies are, don't you?"

Quentin Quinn screwed up his face. "I grew up with a mother and three sisters. I know what the monthlies are. All those rags on the line for all the neighbors to see. And they all seemed to have them at the same time. Made my life a misery. Ugh," he groaned.

"So menopause is when that stops happening. This is what the doctor tells Vera. She's been scared something serious is wrong with her. Perhaps even cancer. But it turns out it's not cancer and, well, she'll be fine in the long run."

"I don't seem to remember writing anything about the menopause."

"Of course you did."

"No." He scowled. "I don't think so."

"Mr. Quinn." Martha's mind raced. "I could show you my notes from your dictation if you like, but they're all in shorthand. And unless you can read shorthand—"

"You mean all those squiggles and lines you write down with your pencil? How on earth can anyone read that nonsense?"

"I can. I trained in it. Like almost every other woman in this place. Now, when Mr. Hayes gets angry you must—"

"He's angry?" Quentin Quinn was suddenly distracted from his doubts about the authorship of the scripts and bolted upright, spilling half his cup of coffee all over Martha's desk. Without blinking, she went to the kettle, took the folded tea towel from under it, and blotted up the coffee while she continued trying to convince Quentin Quinn he was the real author of her work. Oh, how that stung.

"The important thing to stress to Mr. Hayes is that this story-line of Vera's will speak to women all over the country. They're our listeners, the women who suffer in silence. They're the women who don't share this news with their mothers or their sisters or their work colleagues. Or even their friends, because women have been taught not to talk about what ails them. And because of that, everything seems more mysterious and un-knowable. Women suffer in silence, Mr. Hayes. That's what you should tell him. We are doing the women of Australia a great service by bringing this health issue, which happens to every woman, out into the open. We are shining a light on the dark, mysterious corners of womanhood, Mr. Hayes. That's why Vera's story is groundbreaking."

Quentin Quinn looked up at Martha as she stood over him. He was concentrating hard on the movement of her lips and he seemed to be miming every word she spoke a moment after she spoke it. It was the most peculiar thing. He was actually *listening* to her. He was taking in what she was telling him as if what she was saying was important. She knew she had given him no choice, but it was her good fortune that he was still inebriated enough to be told what to do and to listen like a schoolboy reciting his times tables.

He swallowed the coffee. She made another cup.

"'We're going to educate women, Mr. Hayes,' you'll tell him. Vera's storyline will resonate with listeners and, more importantly, they'll learn something from it about their own lives and their own health. The same thing will happen to your own mother—if it hasn't already—and your wife and your sisters. What could be more important?"

"Groundbreaking," Quentin Quinn murmured. "'What could be more important?'" he repeated, glassy-eyed.

He stood on wobbling legs and Martha pressed his shoulders until he sat down again. Martha tried to find some strength. And then there it was, in George Eliot's words: *"When a woman's will is as strong as the man's who wants to govern her, half her strength must be concealment."*

"Just one more cup of coffee and you'll be good to go."

....

Fifteen minutes later, Martha walked two paces behind Quentin Quinn as they made their way to Rutherford Hayes's office. Quentin Quinn appeared to have sobered up a little and she'd straightened his tie and insisted he put on his suit jacket to cover the casserole stain. She'd thrust a comb into his hand and ensured he looked into the small compact mirror she always carried so he could tidy up his hair.

He hadn't asked her to go with him to see Mr. Hayes, but Martha followed him anyway. There was too much at stake to let him make the argument by himself.

When they presented themselves at the reception desk, Miss

Jones smiled warmly at Martha and then stared at Quentin Quinn. "Mr. Quinn. Miss Berry."

"Good afternoon, Miss Jones," Martha said. "I believe Mr. Hayes is expecting Mr. Quinn."

Miss Jones's eyes widened. Martha didn't need any explanation to know what Miss Jones was trying to tell her. It was a warning somewhere between *beware* and *run for your life*.

The door to Mr. Hayes's office was suddenly thrown open and the head of drama stood at the door bellowing, "Quinn! Get in here!"

Quentin Quinn took a moment to come to grips with what was going on and glanced at Martha. She gave him a little nod and lifted an arm to indicate he should proceed. She followed ten steps behind him, as if she were Prince Philip and he Queen Elizabeth.

Martha closed the door behind them. Quentin Quinn walked to Mr. Hayes's desk and slumped into the leather chair opposite Mr. Hayes.

"I didn't say you could sit down!" Mr. Hayes shouted.

Quentin Quinn sprang to his feet and swayed slightly from side to side. "Of course, Mr. Hayes."

Martha held her breath, preparing herself to catch Quentin Quinn if she needed to.

"As far as I'm concerned, you should be on your hands and knees begging for your job. What the blazes were you thinking? The bloody menopause? I can't even say the word without feeling uncomfortable." Mr. Hayes suddenly turned to Martha. "What on earth are you doing in this meeting, Miss Berry?"

She had anticipated his question. "Mr. Quinn asked me to come along to take extensive notes so he can put in place any and all of your suggestions for how he might go forward with *As the Sun Sets* from this point on."

"Well. Good. There will indeed be extensive suggestions going forward from this point on. Starting with this storyline about Vera Percy's you-know-what."

"May I sit down, Mr. Hayes?" Quentin Quinn asked, and Mr. Hayes waved a hand in the general direction of the chair as if he couldn't be bothered if Quentin Quinn did or didn't sit down. Quentin Quinn fell back into the chair with a slump and covered his mouth just in time to smother an audible burp.

"Vera's you-know-what," Quentin Quinn replied. "About that."

Mr. Hayes lifted his pipe from his crystal ashtray, and he was so distracted by Vera Percy's menopause he put it in his mouth without lighting it.

Mr. Hayes huffed. "Now, Quinn. This storyline. You need to put a stop to it. Pretend Vera was having a fever dream or something. I don't know how many episodes you've written featuring this direction, but they are all to be scrapped."

Quentin Quinn opened his mouth to speak and sucked in a deep breath so fiercely that all the color drained from his face.

Martha swung into action. She began to fan him with her notebook as she explained to Mr. Hayes, "A bad oyster at lunch, perhaps."

"He'd better not vomit in my office. Miss Jones!" Mr. Hayes bellowed.

"He's hyperventilating. Slow down, Mr. Quinn. Deep breaths. One. Two. That's it."

Miss Jones appeared at the door. "Yes, Mr. Hayes?"

"This chap's about to . . . Get something, will you?"

A moment later, she reappeared at Martha's side and discreetly handed her a metal rubbish bin. Martha patted Quentin Quinn's back gently, keeping him in his seat in case he felt the need to stand up or, god forbid, say anything further.

"He might not be able to speak at the moment," Martha began, "but Mr. Quinn did mention some things to me about the scripts in question that I'd like to pass on to you. He believes Vera's storyline will intrigue our women listeners, Mr. Hayes. And more importantly, they'll learn something from it about their own lives and their own health."

"What a load of poppycock. Ladies go see their doctor if there's something the matter. They don't gossip about it with their girlfriends."

"Perhaps they should," Martha shot back and then caught herself. "Mr. Quinn certainly believes that our medium—radio, the greatest of them all—can entertain *and* enlighten. If Vera's storyline can give women information about their own health, haven't we achieved something?"

Mr. Hayes stopped blustering and looked at Martha intently.

"Just think, Mr. Hayes. The change of life has happened or will happen to half of all Australians. Your grandmother, your mother, your wife. Even your daughters one day. What could be more important than letting them know that what is happening is normal, that it happens to every woman? Isn't that what radio is for? Isn't that what a public broadcaster should aim to do? Enlighten its citizens?"

Mr. Hayes held an index finger to his chin and tapped it. Ten times. Martha counted.

"Well. Since it's already gone to air, we'll have to stick with it."

She finally breathed out.

"With one change, and this is nonnegotiable. No one—and I mean *no one*—can say the word *menopause. Change of life* is, however, acceptable."

Quentin Quinn pushed back against Martha's hand and sat up straight. "Glad you agree, Mr. Hayes."

And then he lurched forward and vomited all over his shoes.

Chapter 22

IN WHICH MARTHA BERRY LEARNS MORE THAN SHE EVER IMAGINED ABOUT MRS. TILLEY'S UTERUS.

The change!"

Martha would recognize that cackle anywhere. Mrs. Tilley was standing by her front fence, her apron flapping in the breeze, a scarf wrapped tight around her curlers. Mrs. Ward was by her side, her curlers covered too. Martha glanced up to see Violet sitting in her regular spot on the wicker chair on Mrs. Tilley's veranda.

"Hello, Mum. Good afternoon, Mrs. Tilley. Mrs. Ward."

"Hello, love," Violet said. She put a hand against her cheek. "We can't believe it's the change. That's why Vera's been poorly. The poor dear."

"So you listened today then?"

"We hung on every word," Mrs. Ward said. "We finished our cheese and pickle sandwiches and then made another cup of tea while the serial was on. Poor Vera."

The three women murmured their agreement. Martha swung

open the low gate, walked up the little path, and took the three steps to the veranda.

"And Jack Percy! Isn't he an angel. Being all understanding and sending Vera to bed with a cup of tea and a hot water bottle." Mrs. Tilley harrumphed. "But honestly, Martha. He's not like any husband I know, being so understanding and all. I didn't get any quarter from my hubby when I was going through it. At least that doctor she went to see was nice. Not like the ones I know. He actually talked to her and explained things. Mine just told me I'd have to put up with it and that was that."

"Same here," Martha added. "Mine told me I'd be dull and unattractive from now on. A woman's lot, basically."

Martha sat on the top step of the veranda.

Violet tut-tutted. "Watch where you're sitting, Martha, love. That cold concrete will give you piles."

"It's only for a minute, Mum."

"Now if you want to talk about piles," Mrs. Ward piped up, "I got the worst ones after I had my Merle. Agony, they were. I could barely sit down for months."

Violet leaned forward in her chair. "You're going through the change, love?"

Martha nodded. "I've been a bit tired so I went to the doctor to see about it."

"So you told Mr. Quinn all about it and he put it in the serial? Is that how it works?"

"Yes." Martha nodded, careful not to meet her mother's eyes. Oh, Martha was going to be caught out in a lie now. It was ludicrous to think a fifty-year-old woman would be discussing her downstairs problems with a young man. A young man who was her boss. She moved quickly to explain. "The younger generation is different these days, Mum."

"I'm not surprised you're tired," Violet said. "You've been working all hours on that serial. Nights and weekends too."

"I love my job. I'll be fine. Now that I know what it is, I needn't worry so much."

"I know, I know. But I don't want to see you worn out. I'd like to have a chat with that Mr. Quinn. Tell him not to work you so hard." In the spaces between those words, Martha heard what was really worrying Violet. The guilt that her own daughter had to care for her. That she couldn't do her share of the things that kept a household of two women going. That every meal was prepared by Martha. Every piece of washing was wrung through the mangle by Martha. Every wet mop, every clean mirror, every scrubbed pot, every dirty plate and cup and saucer had Martha's hands on it, not Violet's swollen, knobby, and aching ones. What Martha couldn't convince her mother to believe was that none of it was ever a chore. Wasn't it what mothers and daughters did for each other?

"Cup of tea, Martha?"

"No, thanks, Mrs. Tilley. I'll have one after dinner when we're listening to *As the Sun Sets*."

"But you already know what's going to happen!" Mrs. Ward laughed.

Martha felt herself laughing along. "I know, but it still feels exciting to hear it coming out of the radio."

"I've been thinking about that Vera Percy all afternoon," Mrs. Ward continued, her gaze turned to the cloudless Sydney twilight. "I don't think I've ever talked about the change and what it was like. Not with anyone. In my day, you didn't talk about things like that, especially not out here on the veranda in front of Uncle Tom Cobley and all. But things should change, Martha. We women hide away with our problems. Everyone tells us that it's embarrassing or shameful so we never talk about it. It's a bit of a relief to find out that the problem you think is yours and yours alone is one a lot of other women have too. It takes a load off, you know?"

This was magic to Martha's ears. And it was only the beginning of what she had planned for Vera. And the other characters she was going to introduce in the next few weeks.

"You know," Mrs. Tilley said, shaking her head. "I was telling your mum and Mrs. Ward that I still get the hot flashes. Even all these years later."

"It's a woman's curse, isn't that right?" Mrs. Ward sighed. "To be honest, I feel a bit lucky. My monthlies were as regular as clockwork, except when I was expecting, of course, and then one day—I think I was fifty-five because it was about when Merle turned thirty—my monthlies stopped and that was it."

"Makes me green with envy, that does," Mrs. Tilley said.

Martha checked her wristwatch and sprang to her feet. "It's five minutes to six!"

Mrs. Tilley and Mrs. Ward moved as fast as their aging bones would allow, and Martha reached a hand toward Violet to help pull her gently to her feet. She was slowing down, Martha realized, a little more each day.

"I wouldn't want to miss my serials," Violet said. "Even though I heard it all at lunchtime. Twice is nice, don't you think, dear?"

Chapter 23

IN WHICH MARTHA BERRY SEES CRACKS START TO APPEAR IN QUENTIN QUINN'S CHARADE.

INT: *Vera Percy runs into Mrs. White on the street outside the butchers.*

FX: *Background chatter and traffic noises*

MRS. WHITE: *Oh, hello, Mrs. Percy.*

VERA PERCY: *Good morning, Mrs. White. How are you today?*

MRS. WHITE: *I shouldn't complain, but this weather and my sciatica? Not a good mix, I'm afraid.*

VERA PERCY: *I'm so sorry to hear that. I really must—*

MRS. WHITE: *As a matter of fact, I'm glad I've run into you, Mrs. Percy. What do you make of this new shop here?*

VERA PERCY: *I'm quite excited about a new business opening up on our street. It hasn't been the same since old Mr. Turbill died, has it? Mrs. Turbill just seemed to lose her zest for life when he passed.*

MRS. WHITE: *Poor old thing, Mr. Turbill. He never was the same after the first war. Mrs. Turbill's an angel for looking after him the way she did. Rest in peace, I say.*

VERA PERCY: *It'll be strange not to have a tobacconist here, though, not that Mr. Percy has ever smoked. And I never took it up either.*

MRS. WHITE: *Goodness knows nobody likes a lady who smokes. But the young women these days . . . I blame the war, I do. It made women . . . mannish. Wearing trousers and smoking . . . I'm glad things went back to the way they were after the war. The men came home, back to their jobs and back to their homes, and the women became housewives and mothers again, the decent ones at least. I can't speak for all those young ladies . . . or at least they call themselves ladies . . . who are still running around the town like flibbertigibbets.*

VERA PERCY: *Let's not forget those whose husbands didn't come home, Mrs. White. They had to find ways to support themselves and their children. That must have been a terrible struggle.*

MRS. WHITE: *Oh . . . Yes. Of course they did. What a pity the Turbills didn't have any children of their own to take over the business.*

VERA PERCY: *The good news is, Mrs. White, a family business will be taking over the premises. A greengrocer, I believe.*

MRS. WHITE: *A greengrocer? We could certainly do with one of those. It's quite a walk over to Thompsons' and with my sciatica, that walk gets too much. And sometimes, Mrs. Percy, their bananas are very expensive. But I don't know what to make of the name on the window. It looks like something Italian. (she pronounces it Eye-talian)*

VERA PERCY: *Antonello. You're right. It does sound Italian. How exotic.*

FX: *Sound of bustling and a dropped box*

ANTONIO ANTONELLO: *Mi scusi. I'm so sorry, I wasn't looking where I was going. Are you all right, madam?*

VERA PERCY: *Quite all right, thank you. Although I'm not sure about that box. It sounds like something inside might have broken.*

ANTONIO ANTONELLO: *Please forgive my manners. I am Antonio Antonello. This is my family's shop. Frutta e verdura.*

VERA PERCY: *It's very nice to meet you, Mr. . . . . Antonello? I'm sorry. I'm not used to saying foreign names.*

ANTONIO ANTONELLO: *An-ton-ello. Like yellow.*

VERA PERCY: *Antonello.*

ANTONIO ANTONELLO: *That's right!*

VERA PERCY: *I'm Mrs. Percy. My husband, Mr. Jack Percy, owns the butcher shop right next door. And may I introduce you to Mrs. White. She's a very loyal customer of all the businesses on this street.*

ANTONIO ANTONELLO: *How do you do, ladies?*

MRS. WHITE: *I won't even try to say your name, young man. (laughing)*

ANTONIO ANTONELLO: *Please. Call me Antonio.*

MRS. WHITE: *Oh, I couldn't.*

ANTONIO ANTONELLO: *I insist.*

VERA PERCY: *When will you be opening the doors?*

ANTONIO ANTONELLO: *In two weeks, we hope. We're painting the shop inside and outside, make it fresh.*

VERA PERCY: *No one wants to buy their carrots and peas in a place that smells like tobacco, do they, Antonio?*

FX: *Chatter fades*

KENT STONE: *Tomorrow on As the Sun Sets . . .*

Martha and Quentin Quinn watched on as Handsy Hooper played the theme music and then ended the recording when the orchestral strains finished. With a groan and something muttered under his breath, he got to his feet to stretch out his back and announced, "One down, four to go."

In the recording studio, the actors stepped back from the standing microphone and smiled at one another. It was always such a relief when they made it through an entire fifteen-minute episode without fluffing a line and having to start all over from the beginning.

"They managed to get through that without a hitch, Mr. Quinn," Martha noted. "Miss Calthorpe made a slight deviation from the script in scene three at the job interview, but she covered it so well even I had to check twice. Such a professional."

Anything Martha could say to divert Quentin Quinn from the idea that Marilyn needed extra acting lessons was worth a try. Since the soiree at Miss Connors's, Martha and the other actors had lived up to their pledge never to leave Marilyn alone in Quentin Quinn's company. It was easy when they were recording because the studio was full of people and Martha was close by in the control room monitoring the scripts, the actors in the studio, *and* Quentin Quinn and Handsy. *Good lord*, she thought with a weary sigh. Would it always be her job to look out for the behavior of every man she worked with?

"Yes, she is. Coming along nicely. Give me a minute, Hooper," Quentin Quinn announced. He threw open the door to the control room and strode out with a barely concealed arrogance, roughly brushing past Martha in his eagerness to get into the recording studio. The scripts she'd been holding on her clipboard to mark off each line of dialogue as the actors performed it correctly were knocked to the ground in a flutter as he passed.

"Very good, very good." He applauded, bowed dramatically, and walked to the actors standing in a loose circle around the microphone. From the control room, keeping as safe a distance as possible from Handsy Hooper, Martha watched with growing suspicion.

"Wonderful episode. Just wonderful. Miss Connors, I don't know how you manage to have a conversation with yourself—you as Vera, then as Mrs. White, then Vera again—but you do it so seamlessly people at home would never know."

Miss Connors primped her perfect chignon, but Martha noted the look of suspicion in her eyes. "Thank you, Mr. Quinn."

"And, Kent? You continue to give us such gravitas as Jack. That scene where you're comforting Vera? Nice stuff indeed." He then turned to Marilyn and Martha felt her insides tighten. "Marilyn. You're getting Betty *almost* right." He held up a hand and pinched his fingers together as if he were adding salt to a casserole. "I think you need another one-on-one class. Just so you can really nail Betty's naivety. Her vulnerability."

Miss Connors's head jerked up and she looked across the standing microphone to Smithy at the props table, who had already busied himself with his wilting cabbage to avoid getting caught up in production drama. Miss Connors and Martha exchanged a knowing glance.

"And our newest cast member. Mr. Paulson. May I call you Alex?"

"Of course, Mr. Quinn," Alex Paulson replied.

Quentin Quinn slipped into the space between Alex and Marilyn. "Terrific start. Just terrific. I do have a note, though."

"A note?" Alex appeared confused.

"Yes," Quentin Quinn said. "I think you need to tone down the Italian just a little bit."

"Tone down . . . ?" Alex cocked his head to the side.

Quentin Quinn laughed and slapped him on the back as he tried to catch the eyes of the other actors. His manner was making Martha's stomach churn with indignation. Everything about his performance, his show of authority over Alex, screamed jealousy.

"It's a radio term, my friend. You'll become used to such expressions and feedback when you've had more experience. The thing is, old chap, you're sounding a little too 'new Australian,' if you know what I mean."

Alex's shoulders rose almost imperceptibly, but not so little that Martha didn't notice his chest puff up in barely concealed umbrage.

"You want me to sound a little less Italian." He looked to Martha. They locked eyes. She had told him the exact opposite when she'd cast him.

"You have the accent just right. You've given Antonio a lilt of something in his voice that's just enough of a hint to listeners that he speaks another language. That's important. I don't want Antonio to sound like any other character. Radio isn't like the pictures. People will imagine what Antonio looks like by the sound of your voice."

From forty feet away, Martha shook her head at him, a mute pleading for him not to reveal what they'd discussed.

Alex was silent for a long moment before a look of understanding flared in his dark eyes. He shot a casual glance at Quentin Quinn and shrugged. "Sure. Whatever you want, Mr. Quinn."

Quentin Quinn clapped his hands together. "And next time, don't say anything in Italian. I don't know what it was you said, but we don't want to confuse the listeners. If they hear something unfamiliar, they'll turn to the person next to them and ask if they heard it too and what was that he said, and before you know it a whole scene has gone by and they will have lost the thread of what's going on."

"Rightio, mate," Alex replied, and Martha couldn't be bothered to hide her giggle.

Kent Stone stepped forward, casting a quick glance at Quentin Quinn before averting his eyes, as if he was dismissing the young producer's comments and very presence. "If I may put in my two pence worth, Alex, I think that was a fine scene. You really brought a sense of joie de vivre to young Antonio. In your hands, I really heard the excitement of a young man who has just arrived in a new country, who's left all the troubles and the war behind him and sees the future laid out in front of him, bright as a new pound note."

"Thank you, Mr. Stone. That's very kind of you to say. And coming from you, an actor of such experience. I'm honored."

"I couldn't agree more," Marilyn added with the brightest smile Martha had ever seen. She deftly stepped around Quentin Quinn as if he were a dog's droppings on the footpath and moved closer to Alex, laying a delicate hand on his forearm. "There's an Italian greengrocer shop right near where I live. I hear Italians all the time in my suburb and the young ones sound just like that, Alex. I can't wait until we have more scenes together, and I think it was so romantic when you said those words in Italian."

"Yes, yes." Quentin Quinn puffed up his chest in an attempt to appear taller. Martha could almost see the steam coming out of his ears. "Just mind what I said, Alex, all right? Stick to the script as it's written."

Martha wasn't the only one taken aback at the tone of Quentin

Quinn's voice and the snarl on his lips. He ran a hand through his hair and announced, "Twenty minutes, everyone," before storming out of the studio.

FX: *Sizzling frying pan and cutlery on china*

VERA PERCY: *Hello, love.*

JACK PERCY: *Hello, dear. I don't know what you're cooking, but it smells delicious. (kissing sound)*

VERA PERCY: *Oh, Jack. Not when I'm in my apron!*

JACK PERCY: *I'd kiss you if you were dressed as a washerwoman.*

BETTY PERCY: *Hi, Dad.*

JACK PERCY: *Hello, Betty, love. How was your day?*

BETTY PERCY: *(sighs) I'm still waiting to see if I got the job. It's so frustrating having to wait each day until the post comes and not getting a letter. Do you think they'll write to me if I don't get the position?*

JACK PERCY: *They should, love. You'll find out soon enough. And if they don't choose you, well, they didn't deserve you in the first place.*

BETTY PERCY: *Thanks. I feel better already, Dad. Sit down, won't you? I'll put the plates out. There's your paper.*

VERA PERCY: *You were busy today when I popped in, Jack, so I didn't get a chance to tell you. I met the young Italian man from next door. The greengrocer. His name is . . . let me remember so I get it right . . . Antonio. Antonio something.*

BETTY PERCY: *His last name is something?*

VERA PERCY: *Of course not, silly. It's something long and complicated, and as hard as I try to remember, I can't think what it is. Anyway, he seems such a polite young man.*

And quite charming too. Hardworking. He says he and his father will be opening the shop in a fortnight.

BETTY PERCY: *Tell me everything about him, Mum. Is he hand-some?*

VERA PERCY: *(laughing) He looks just like Mario Lanza!*

BETTY PERCY: *Dreamy. (sighs)*

Chapter 24

IN WHICH VERA PERCY'S CHANGE OF LIFE
CHANGES RADIO FOREVER.

When Martha arrived at work the next Monday, after a long and tiring weekend in which she'd plotted and planned what was next for her characters—for she thought of them as *her* characters now—she was greeted by a huge cardboard box on her desk.

It was piled high with so many letters that they had cascaded onto her chair and the carpet like the foam of an overflowing pint of beer.

"What on earth?" She quickly hung her hat on the coatrack, removed her gloves, and set her handbag on a hook next to her hat. She scooped up some of the mail from the carpet and tried to form the letters into a pile on her desk. That was when the name on one of the envelopes caught her eye. *Mrs. Vera Percy.* Martha tore open the envelope and unfolded the page, her heartbeat picking up and pounding so hard she couldn't stop shaking. She took a deep breath to steady herself so she could focus on the neat loops and swirls of the handwriting on the page.

Dear Mrs. Percy,

I'm writing to let you know that things will get better.
I went through the change four years ago and I barely
made it through the day without having to put on a fresh
housedress at least once. Oh, the perspiration. Even in
the middle of winter! You might try a cold compress on the
back of your neck. I found it provided some relief.

Martha smiled so wide her cheeks hurt. She lowered herself
into her chair and plunged her hands into the box, randomly
picking out letter after letter, tearing open the envelopes in
anticipation of discovering what the next listener might share.

And in that early morning quiet, before the footsteps of busy
people doing important work echoed up and down the corridor,
before the bustle of staff going about their busy jobs, before her
first cup of tea of the day, and hours and hours before Quentin
Quinn usually arrived at the office, Martha read and read and read,
ignoring the paper cuts from tearing open so many envelopes.

Dear Mrs. Percy,

I've never mentioned this to another living soul, but I
started the change two years ago and it's still dreadful. I
long for the days when I enjoyed a decent night's sleep and
I could get up in the morning and not be exhausted before
I've even done any household chores.

Martha made herself a cup of tea and continued reading.

Dear Mrs. Percy,

You are so fortunate to have a husband as understanding
as Mr. Percy. When he told you to make sure you rest

and he went to the kitchen and cooked dinner for you?
Well, my first thought was that the kitchen is no place
for a husband, but then he was so caring that I must
admit to bursting into tears. When I went through the
change, my husband gave me no quarter. He insisted on
marital relations, even though it hurt and was the last
thing I wanted. In the end, he said I wasn't the woman he
married, that I was shriveled up and barren, and he left
me for his secretary.

"Oh no," Martha said to herself. "What an awful, awful man.
You're so much better off without him"—she checked the name on
the back of the envelope—"Mrs. Cleeves."

Martha wasn't aware how much time had passed until a knock
on her door and the arrival of April, May, and June alerted her to
the fact that it was lunchtime.

"Miss Berry?" It was April.

"What's all this then?" June demanded, and the three young
women went to Martha's desk, their mouths agape.

Martha looked up at them, but the tears in her eyes made them
nothing but blurred smudges of brown and blue. Where, oh where
was her handkerchief? There were no words to explain how she
felt at the kind words and comfort in all the letters she'd read that
morning, at what listeners had revealed about themselves and
their own struggles with their bodies, their husbands, their lives.
Martha had dared put her own experiences into Vera's mouth and
the women of Australia had listened. Martha felt heard. They
believed they were offering words of comfort and support to the
fictional Vera Percy, but Martha greedily took them for herself.

*You are not alone. You will get through this. You don't need to suffer
in silence.*

"Are you quite all right, Miss Berry?" May stepped closer and put a comforting hand on Martha's shoulder.

Martha knew that if she were to attempt to speak she would sob instead, so she simply plunged a hand into the cardboard box and randomly selected a handful of unopened letters, passing them to the three young women.

"I haven't seen this much mail since one of the news announcers accidentally said the b-word on air," June told them.

"B . . . bastard?" May asked, whispering the word in case anyone were to walk by the open door and hear her profanity.

"Bloody," June confirmed with a knowing nod. "One of the newsmen snuck into the studio with a lit match just as the newsreader was going live to air and set his script alight. Consequently, he said, 'Bloody hell!' when he shouldn't have."

"Goodness," April said, a look of concern in her wide eyes. "Imagine everyone around the country hearing *that*." She slipped a finger carefully into the flap at the back of an envelope and pulled out a letter. "'Dear Writers of *As the Sun Sets*,'" she read out loud. "Ooh, it's been scented with lavender." She held the letter to her nose and sniffed. "'I want to commend you for the sensitive way in which you have portrayed Vera Percy's menopause diagnosis. I am a nurse and I believe this is something the medical profession doesn't talk about nearly enough with their women patients.'" April's eyes were wide with surprise. "Isn't that wonderful! A nurse!"

"Listen to this," May announced. She cleared her throat and pulled her shoulders straight, as if she might be about to perform a recital.

"'Chin up, Vera. I know what you're going through. With a husband like your Jack, you'll sail through. Make sure that Betty cooks every now and then so you can have a rest. She's old enough now to help you more in the kitchen.'" May shook her head and laughed. "'PS: I hope Betty gets the job.' Oh, how funny. This one thinks Vera and Jack and Betty are real!"

They laughed in unison and then May pulled her lips together. "Of course, that's because she sounds like a real person, doesn't she?"

June huffed. "She's a character in a radio serial. Played by Miss Katherine Connors. How can people not know that when it's announced at the end of every episode and there are pictures of Miss Connors in all the magazines?" She rolled her eyes and opened her letter. "'Dear Mrs. Percy: My name is Jemima Smith and I'm fourteen years old. I'm pretty sure my grandmother is going through the change, too, but she never talks about it. She's looked after me since my mother died. Sometimes when she cries for no reason, I think it's about something I must have done, like not wiped the dishes carefully or something. Now I understand.'"

The women fell silent. Martha's mind whirred. She had set out to explain something that was happening to her, something that had seemed so individual and private. Yet it had struck a chord with so many women, young and old. There were hundreds and hundreds of letters in the box on her desk. Would each tell a different story?

Martha dug out another one.

"'Thank you. I finally understand what my wife is going through. Sometimes, there's nothing better than some under-standing and a cup of tea to settle her. And I learned that from your program.'"

"What about this one?" June added. "'How disgusting. No one wants to hear about women's business on the radio. Absolutely shameful.' He's not happy."

April searched a pile of letters, flipping them over to see the return addresses on the back. "They're from all over Sydney, Miss Berry. Bondi. Potts Point. Marrickville. Crows Nest. Everywhere!"

"This is incredible!" May laughed. "The show is so popular! You must be so pleased."

Pleased wasn't the right word for what she was feeling. Martha was still too much in shock to really comprehend her reaction. She had typed words right there at her desk, which had been read into a microphone by actors and transmitted over the radio to households all over Australia, and people had listened. More than listened. They saw themselves in Vera and Jack and Betty. Her own experiences were real. There was a validation in that, too, that she couldn't deny made her happy. More than happy. Ecstatic.

And then the truth hit her like a cyclone, almost bowling her over.

How it burned that Quentin Quinn would get all the credit.

"This deserves a celebration!" April announced.

May clapped her hands together. "Let's have sandwiches *and* scones for lunch. With jam and cream."

"No scones for me," April said, shaking her head. "I'm watching my figure."

June rolled her eyes.

"Will you have some, Miss Berry?" May asked.

"I'll tell you what, girls." She took her handbag from its hook on the coatrack. "I'm going to skip the sandwiches and go straight for the scones."

When Quentin Quinn finally arrived in the office at two o'clock that afternoon, Martha was at her desk, full to the brim with scones and delectable whipped cream and strawberry jam. The

Calendar Girls had insisted on paying for Martha, which she found very touching, and had even insisted she take the two left-over scones home, wrapped in a clean handkerchief, for Violet. It was a very touching gesture that, after the events of the morning, had Martha in tears once again.

But she was back at her desk, still sorting through the letters, wondering how on earth she would find time to reply to them all.

"Mrs. Barry?"

She looked up. Quentin Quinn seemed clear-eyed and bright. His tie was still neatly knotted at his neck and nothing about him looked ruffled. She couldn't remember the last time she'd seen him appear so put together.

"Good afternoon, Mr. Quinn."

"Are these all letters?" He picked up an envelope and read the sender's address. "I didn't authorize a competition or a giveaway. They must have the wrong department."

"They're not in response to a competition or a giveaway. They're from listeners."

A look of concern flitted across his eyes. "What did we do to offend people?"

"Nothing at all. Quite the opposite, in fact." Martha handed him a letter. He stared at it as if it might be radioactive.

"People like *As the Sun Sets*. Very much, as a matter of fact. Especially Vera's recent storyline."

"Oh yes." He screwed up his face. "Don't remind me. My mother called me about it. It's all she and her friends at the gardening club can talk about. Poor Vera. Vera this and Vera that. Anyone would think Vera Percy was the star of the show." He tut-tutted. "I couldn't get off the telephone fast enough. Who on earth wants to discuss that kind of thing with their mother?" He threw the letter back on Martha's desk without even opening it.

His casual disparaging of his mother, of their listeners, and of her set something rumbling inside Martha. It rose up in her throat and she ground her teeth to stop it from blurting from her lips. How unfair for him to be so dismissive of the very listeners who had made his program such a success! How dare he dismiss the very real lives of the women who listened to his serial?

Her serial. She would be damned if she would let him take the credit, even if that battle was one that would only rage inside her, silently, fiercely.

"Listeners like Vera Percy very much," she managed to say, straining to keep her voice calm. "They're as concerned for her as your mother is."

Quentin Quinn rolled his eyes. "I think we need to have a fire at the butchers. Make it arson. That'll bring some of the focus back on Jack. All he's done the past few weeks is be a simpering fool over his wife. I don't know how we went down that road. I still don't remember writing those scenes. No man I know acts like that. I can't see why women are so enamored with him, Mrs. Barry."

He strode to his office and slammed the door behind him.

Martha startled in her seat. "Of course you wouldn't."

<hr />

In the days and weeks that followed, the stream of mail from Sydney's suburbs and towns became a torrent from around the country as post arrived from places as far-flung as Townsville and Mount Gambier and Perth, from Melbourne and Hobart. Listeners offered prescriptions for herbal teas and potions for Vera to settle her symptoms. One woman had insisted her husband sit at the table at lunchtime and listen to Vera, "or I swore I'd never cook him dinner again."

It wasn't long before word of the deluge found its way to Rutherford Hayes, and as Martha had predicted, Quentin Quinn became the showman once again, basking in all the glory of the success of a storyline he had neither conceived nor written. When he received a letter of congratulations from the general manager, no less ("Mrs. Moses simply loves it"), he stood by Martha's desk and gloated as if his success wasn't the result of her assistance, the stellar performances of the cast of actors, and, yes, even Handsy Hooper's work.

It was often said that success has many fathers while failure is an orphan. In Quentin Quinn's world, the opposite was true. Just as he viewed the success of *As the Sun Sets* as down to him alone, Martha knew in her heart that the minute anything went wrong, he would readily share the blame with others.

She was beginning to dislike him more and more.

Chapter 25

IN WHICH MARTHA BERRY DISCOVERS HER SECRET IS OUT.

Miss Berry?"

Martha turned toward the door of her office at the sound of Kent Stone's voice. She would know it anywhere. She heard it in her head now when she was writing scripts. It was a strange thing, she'd discovered, to have not just the characters' thoughts in her head, but the actors' voices too. Kent's deep voice was gravelly around the edges when he played Jack Percy, smooth as the finest whiskey when he was speaking the episode intros and outros: "Next week on *As the Sun Sets* . . ."

"Mr. Stone. Miss Connors. How lovely to see you. Do come in." Martha shot to her feet. She couldn't think what had precipitated this unexpected visit. It was Tuesday. A day like any other. Quentin Quinn was who-knew-where and Martha had spent the morning largely ignoring his dot-point scrawls on his episode notes ("Vera and Jack fight about the break-in, she says he could have been killed, etc.") and writing scripts. She had disregarded everything he'd said about plotting a break-in at Percys' Butchers and was crafting a scene in which Ernie the apprentice asked Betty to the pictures. Martha had in mind that when they joined the queue to buy popcorn and Fantales on their date, they'd run into Antonio Antonello with a group of his friends and there might be awkward conversations for everyone. If listeners wanted a break-in, they could get that kind of entertainment from one of the dramas on the *Caltex Theatre* show. *As the Sun Sets* was about people and their lives, their romances, and their challenges. It was about family and love and hope and heartbreak.

"Thank you, Miss Berry." Miss Connors seemed to float into the office instead of walk, and as she elegantly removed her snow-white gloves, finger by finger, she gave Martha a sisterly smile. Martha had worked closely with the veteran actress for almost three months now and continued to wonder at her equanimity and poise. Never a hair out of place. Never a lipstick smudge on her teeth. Every word she spoke was said with intent and purpose. Miss Connors possessed a grace and a class that were about something more than simply money. Of course, she always wore the latest fashions and Martha had continued to admire her matching shoes and handbag—today they were black patent—but there was something more. Miss Connors had a confidence that was about more than wealth or privilege or a beautiful home with harbor views. There was some kind of steel in her spine, a confidence in knowing oneself, in being on such firm ground that no one could knock her over or unsettle her.

"Busy as ever, I see?" Miss Connors said, casting an inquiring eye over Martha's desk as Martha resumed her seat. "It's said that you can tell a lot about a person by the way in which they work."

Martha looked at her own desk and interpreted it through Miss Connors's gaze. Her typewriter sat squarely in front of her chair. To her left she'd assembled a pile of butcher paper interleaved with sheets of carbon to ensure that when she typed there were extra copies of the script. In the platen a piece of paper flopped lazily, as if the type on the page had made it heavy. To the left of the typewriter sat three piles of perfectly typed scripts. One for Martha. One for Quentin Quinn. And one for Rutherford Hayes. The head of drama had doubled down on his demand that he see all the scripts before they went to air, and after the fuss that was created when the now-notorious menopause episode had gone to air, Martha knew she couldn't get around him anymore. There was a pencil, sharpened to a point, a clean coffee cup, and a small green vase filled with fresh flowers that Martha had picked that very morning from Mrs. Tilley's garden. One listener had advised that the floral scents calmed some of the symptoms of the meno-pause, and Martha was trying the suggestion to determine if it was helpful. The jury was still out, but she liked the perfume and they looked pretty on her desk.

"What would you say about Miss Berry's desk, then, Katherine?" Kent closed the door to the hallway and sauntered over, a hand casually slipped into the pocket of his trousers. He really did look like a movie star. What a pity he'd never gone to Hollywood, Martha thought. He would have been leading-man material a decade earlier. Perhaps a decade and a half.

"Miss Berry's desk? Oh, this tells me everything I need to know about our Miss Berry. A tidy and organized desk reveals a tidy and organized mind."

Martha paused. "I don't like things to be disorganized. As my mother always says, a place for everything and everything in its place."

"Yes, quite," Miss Connors murmured as she sat down oppo-site Martha.

Kent perched on the edge of the desk and leaned forward

slightly as he looked intently at Martha. Her heart skipped a little beat. He looked like he was posing for a publicity photograph. The actors stared at Martha without saying a word, making her feel just the slightest bit nervous, so she filled the silence.

"I must admit to being surprised to see you both here this early in the week. We work as fast as we can here on *As the Sun Sets*, but we don't have scripts for next week yet, I'm afraid."

"Oh, we know that," Miss Connors said.

The two actors exchanged glances.

"We're here about something else." Kent raised one eyebrow. Martha wasn't sure how he did that so successfully. She'd practiced it at home in the mirror but could never make the other remain in place. That was why he was the actor and she was the scriptwriter. The script girl.

"Something else?" A shiver skittered up Martha's spine and her imaginings took her to the worst possible place. They hated her scripts but they believed they were complaining to her as a colleague about Quentin Quinn's writing when, unbeknownst to them, of course, they would really be saying they hated *her* scripts. And perhaps they were leaving because they found the storylines trite and clichéd and had landed roles in the West End. Or Broadway.

Martha glanced at her empty coffee cup and wished it was full.

"Yes," Miss Connors said. "We've come to talk to you about something else."

"Please bear with me. Bear with us, I mean. I'm sure we can do better," Martha suddenly blurted. Something behind her eyes started pounding and, oh goodness gracious, another hot flash was making itself felt in every pore of her body. Why now? She leaped to her feet, strode to the window, and jerked it open. The sounds of Kings Cross below cranked up like someone had been at the volume knob on a radio. As she leaned half in and half out of the window, she felt sweat beading on her brow and wondered how indelicate it would be to wipe it away. Where was her handkerchief?

"We'll work harder on the scripts. Make them punchier. Add some more emotion. We'll make *Blue Hills* look like . . ." She racked her brain. "*Songs of Praise*." She crossed herself even though she wasn't Catholic. "We'll create tighter cliffhangers. Cut out some of the scenes that don't really add anything to the ongoing story. We'll create some drama between Jack and Vera so you can both exhibit your acting chops. It won't all be about Betty and Antonio, I promise. Or Betty and Ernie. Please be assured that we're even thinking of creating a storyline for Mrs. White, Miss Connors. So she's not just a cardboard cutout of a neighborhood gossip, but someone with real problems of her own." Martha was talking so fast she hardly knew what she was saying. "And, Mr. Stone? We had a thought to burn down the butcher shop in a suspicious fire. That'll create quite the mystery, won't it?"

The flush finally dissipated and Martha stepped back from the open window. Kent Stone and Miss Connors were staring at her as if she'd gone mad.

Perhaps she had. What on earth had she promised? Burning down the butcher shop? That had been Quentin Quinn's ridiculous idea. How could they burn down the one place that was central to the whole drama? And a storyline for Mrs. White? If listener letters were anything to go by, they wanted less of the old busybody, not more. Although Martha had a sneaking suspicion that people secretly loved her, or loved to hate her because she could say things no one else could. And didn't everyone know a Mrs. White?

"Miss Berry." Miss Connors reached out a hand. "Please come

sit down. You'll do yourself an injury if you stand too close to that window. Shall I boil the kettle?"

Much to Martha's surprise, Miss Connors reached for Martha's empty cup and took it to the kettle. She turned back to Martha while waiting for it to boil.

"Are you having a tropical vacation, my dear?"

Martha was puzzled. "I don't have any holidays planned."

Miss Connors laughed. "That's not what I meant."

"Ladies." Kent Stone held up his hands in mock defeat. "At least wait until I leave the room. It's bad enough I have to play sympathetic old milksop Jack Percy when it comes to these ladies' things. And now I have to do the same in real life?" He winked at Martha good-naturedly. "It's more than a thespian can bear."

Martha returned to her desk feeling absolutely discombobulated. When her legs turned to jelly, she flopped down in her chair. She was certain she looked a fright. She held her palms to her cheeks and felt the flush of redness still there. She was clammy, and when she perspired from her head, the roots of her hair curled and turned into a terrible frizz.

"Here you are." Miss Connors placed a cup of coffee in front of Martha, who received it gratefully.

"We're not here about the scripts, Miss Berry," Kent Stone told her. "At least not in the way you're thinking. And for goodness' sake, let there be no more talk of burning down the Percys' shop, please? I'll have to spend episode after episode weeping over some thoroughly burned chops. How dull." He smiled at Martha and she let herself laugh.

"We absolutely adore your scripts, Miss Berry." Miss Connors smiled.

It took Martha a moment to process what she'd heard.

Your scripts.

Her stomach plummeted into her shoes.

"We don't want you to change a single thing about them," Kent Stone added. "Except for perhaps the name of the writer on the front page."

Where was that buzzing coming from? Martha looked about her office. It sounded for all the world like a swarm of bees had flown in. She shot a glance to the open window. No bees. The sound began to drown out her hearing and she was certain Kent Stone and Miss Connors were saying something to her, but she couldn't make out a word. When the roil of nausea hit, she rose from her chair, clutching at the edge of her desk for a moment before her legs turned to jelly again. She lay on the carpet as elegantly as she could.

"Miss Berry!" Miss Connors leaped to her feet and ran to the door. She flung it open wide and called out, "We need a doctor!"

"It's all right. It happens sometimes. Low blood pressure." Martha let her eyes flutter closed. She placed her hands gently on her stomach, palms down, to check if it was still rumbling traitorously. She heard running footsteps and then the scent of a man's cologne wafted over her.

"Hello, old chap." That was Kent Stone.

"Stone. I was just passing by on my way in to see Rutherford Hayes about some business and I heard Miss Connors here calling. Hello, Katherine. It's been forever." There were kissing noises—air-kissing noises, because Martha knew Miss Connors wouldn't smudge her lipstick for a kiss, not even from Cary Grant.

She felt the nudge of a knee at her hip.

"Hello there. Are you quite all right?"

Was she unconscious and in some kind of dream? She would know that voice anywhere.

It was Dr. Gordon from *Blue Hills*.

Chapter 26

IN WHICH MARTHA BERRY AND THE ACTORS HATCH A PLAN.

Honestly, I couldn't possibly eat another piece of cake. But thank you, Miss Connors."

Martha sat on a linen-covered sofa in Miss Connors's sunroom. The fabric was white with swirls and loops of blue paisley and there were two matching cushions propped at each end. It was long enough for four people to sit on and take in the view of the harbor. Outside, the blue waters twinkled in the afternoon sunshine and a surprisingly warm breeze wafted through the windows, rustling Martha's hair and tickling her cheeks. If she closed her eyes, she might easily imagine herself on a tropical island somewhere in the middle of the Pacific.

"Another cup of tea then? Surely you need some sustenance, Miss Berry. Why, you fainted right there on the floor of your office."

Next to Miss Connors, Kent Stone slapped his cheek. "You gave us all such a fright that I nearly fainted myself."

Miss Connors hovered solicitously near Martha. Her immaculately painted lips were pulled into a tight line and she stood with her arms crossed. She hadn't left Martha's side since the two actors had insisted that Martha needed an immediate rest and whisked her away from the office in a taxi for the short journey to Miss Connors's Vaucluse home.

As it turned out, Dr. Gordon from *Blue Hills* hadn't been much help at all, what with not actually being a doctor in real life. But the sound of his voice alone had revived Martha enough that she was able to get to her feet. She'd felt better immediately when she looked up into his handsome blue eyes. In all the years she'd been working at the ABC, she hadn't actually met him. In that moment, all her fears about her ruse being revealed had vanished from her mind, and a very different kind of roiling in her stomach took over and her heart beat so fast that she thought it might burst out of her chest. Miraculously, she was eighteen again. And what a delicious feeling it was. She had forgotten how attraction felt, how it seemed to light a fire of thrilling excitement inside her and make her feel sick all at the same time.

"You're too kind, Miss Connors, but truly, I'm feeling quite all right now. My doctor says I have low blood pressure and the best thing to do when I'm feeling lightheaded is to lie down immediately. I was nowhere near fainting."

"Really?" Kent Stone sat on an armchair opposite Martha. There was that eyebrow again.

"Yes, really, Mr. Stone. I'm fine."

Miss Connors sat next to Martha and patted her blanketed foot. "Are you sure I can't call my doctor? He makes house calls, you know. He's very discreet."

Martha found herself laughing at her predicament. There she was in a mansion, lying back, her shoes sitting neatly on a Per-

sian rug, her knees covered with a blanket as if she were a con-
valescent, a pillow propped behind her head, and two famous
actors concerned for her health. Would anyone believe this had
ever happened?

"I don't need a doctor. And I think it's time I went home. I don't
want my mother to worry, and she will if I'm not home in time for
the encore evening broadcasts of *Blue Hills* and *As the Sun Sets*."

"You're not going anywhere." Miss Connors pointed at her
accusingly. "You conveniently fell to the floor of your office before we could have our conversation."

Martha swallowed hard. She was hoping they'd forgotten.

The sound of a doorbell ringing had Miss Connors on her feet.
"There they are now."

Martha turned to Kent Stone. His eyebrow was still poised
in midair. She wondered if he sprayed it with hairspray in the
mornings before he left the house to help keep it in place. That
eyebrow deserved to be on television when it began broadcasting
in Australia.

"*They?*"

"We called Miss Calthorpe and Mr. Paulson and told them you
were unwell. They insisted on coming to see you."

"Oh no, they shouldn't have!" Martha tossed the blanket aside
and got to her feet. "This is ridiculous. I'm perfectly well."

"Miss Berry!" Marilyn's trilling voice filled the room like bird-
song. "We were so worried when Miss Connors called to tell us
what had happened. Are you all right?" The young actress looked
sweeter than ever. Her hair was swept off her forehead and sat
in sumptuous curls at her shoulders—very Lauren Bacall—and
Martha noted how easy it was to appear young and fresh-faced
when you were *actually* young and fresh-faced. Beside her, Alex
Paulson held a bunch of red roses wrapped in tissue paper.

"We hope you're feeling better, Miss Berry."

Her jelly legs returned and she sat down again. "That's too kind of you. Thank you." Martha gratefully received the flowers, inhaled the sweet perfume of the deep red petals, and then set the arrangement on the low coffee table in front of her.

"Really, you've all overreacted. But then, I suppose you are actors and you know a good drama when you see it." The assembled thespians smiled at her.

"Quite." Kent Stone nodded.

"You're dissembling, Miss Berry. *You're* the one who knows a good drama," Miss Connors said. "We know. All of us do." She nodded elegantly as she crossed one leg over the other and held her fingers together like a bridge. "I guessed from the very first casting meeting we had. There was something about you. And something about *him*. Call it women's intuition."

Marilyn Calthorpe nodded.

Alex Paulson winked.

Kent Stone's eyebrow remained fixed in its astonished place.

Martha sat back on the sofa and let her shoulders slump. "I had no idea it would end up like this. I really didn't. Rutherford Hayes offered me the role as Quentin Quinn's secretary to give him a guiding hand. To let him know what we needed to get done and by when, that sort of thing. There are a million little tasks to cross off a list when you're making a radio program. People at home must think it's as easy as a company of actors standing in front of a microphone, but it's not. As you all well know."

The actors nodded, although Martha wasn't sure if they really had any idea of the work it took to ensure scripts were ready for them to read come recording day. They only saw the tip of the iceberg. Martha had been rowing like mad for months to make sure that iceberg didn't break apart and sink. All without a life jacket. Or a boat.

"Quentin Quinn came to the show with so little experience." She spoke so quietly they all leaned in just a little to hear her better. "It was never my plan to write the scripts. Not in a million years. But when it became clear to me Mr. Quinn was failing to write even a single line . . . I couldn't let the whole thing fail."

Kent tut-tutted. "Quinn is absolutely clueless. We know you've been carrying the show since the beginning. No one who drinks that much could possibly write scripts like that. Why on earth the department believed it needed to bring Quentin Quinn on board will always be a mystery to me. Thank goodness you stole the show out from under him."

"You're wrong, Mr. Stone. I didn't steal the show out from under him. I *rescued* it."

"Of course you did, Miss Berry," Miss Connors said.

"Thank goodness you did," Marilyn added.

"Who knows what would have happened to us all if you hadn't grabbed the bull by the horns and kept this ship sailing?"

Martha was glad she was the one writing scripts and not Kent Stone.

"Without you, there would be no *As the Sun Sets*. We know that for certain. There would be no kindhearted Jack Percy—one of the best radio roles of my life. Without you, I'd probably be recording advertisements for Lux Soap Flakes and Johnson's Baby Powder. 'Best for baby. Best for you.' And waiting for the next job. If there was going to be one." He shivered. "It doesn't bear thinking about."

"And I'd still be answering telephones for a living." Marilyn sighed. "I love this job so much, Miss Berry. I can't thank you enough for all you've done for me. I love my storyline and your scripts are so easy to learn. You manage to write the way my friends and I talk. Modern. You know?"

Martha took that as an enormous compliment. Hadn't George Eliot said that the finest language is mostly made up of simple unimposing words?

Alex Paulson nodded. "Miss Berry, if it wasn't for you and your idea to write an Italian character, I'd still be looking for extra work as a waiter."

"And," Miss Connors said, "Kent and I know you were instrumental in casting us as Jack and Vera. If you hadn't pushed for someone of my . . ."

"Vintage?" Kent Stone raised his eyebrow playfully.

"Experience," she replied. "Well, I'd be rattling round this big house all day waiting for my husband to come home."

"Surely shopping and lunching fill in some time during those long dreary days, my darling Katherine?" Kent Stone teased.

Laughter filled the room and Miss Connors smiled knowingly at Martha. "Your fingerprints are on every line," she continued. "I've worked in theater and radio for more years than I care to admit, and no one—no one, Miss Berry—has ever written as convincing a female character as you have in Vera. From the day I read my first lines, I knew Quinn wasn't writing them. What does he know of life? What experience could he bring to a serial like *As the Sun Sets*?"

"He's still so wet behind the ears," Kent Stone added. "If he should be writing for radio at all—and there is a debate to be had about that—he should be on a show like *Children's Hour* or . . . or *The Argonauts*. Something for younger people. He might have more in common with them, at least."

Alex perked up. "I still have my green and silver badge with *Argo* on it. Demosthenes 14, I was."

Kent screwed up his face. "It's all Greek to me."

Martha and Miss Connors laughed while Marilyn simply looked confused.

"You don't know *The Argonauts*?" Alex asked her incredulously.

She shook her head. "My father doesn't like us girls listening to the radio much. Or reading. He said it would give us ideas above our station."

"Does he know you're working on the show?" Alex asked.

"No," Marilyn replied. "We've managed to keep him away from all the magazine and newspaper articles. He only reads the racing pages anyway. If he found out, he'd surely make me quit. He thinks actresses are no better than prostitutes."

A collective gasp filled the room.

"He may be your father, Miss Calthorpe," Miss Connors said, "but I hope you're not offended when I suggest he sports some rather old-fashioned attitudes."

"Oh, I know he does. If he knew about Alex and me, he'd—"

"What?" Martha blinked. The lovers blushed. Alex reached a hand toward Marilyn and they entwined their fingers. Of course. How had Martha not seen it? She'd been too busy creating a fictional love story between the two to realize that art was mirroring life.

"We wanted to keep it quiet," Marilyn said. "Especially with Mr. Quinn the way he is." Martha knew exactly how Quentin Quinn was. She wouldn't put it past him to kill off Antonio Antonello—or make him guilty of setting the fire that may or may not damage Percys' Butchers in the storyline she was still refusing to write—just to get rid of his real-life love rival.

"And we didn't want the newspapers to find out," Alex added. "Because of Marilyn's father."

"He'd pop a gasket if he found out I was dating a Catholic."

Martha sucked in a deep breath and tried to remember every-thing the actors were saying. She had enough material from this one afternoon alone to keep the show going for years.

"There's only one thing to do," Kent Stone said.

"Go to the union?" Marilyn asked. "I joined up, Mr. Stone."

"Me too," Alex said, directing a loving gaze toward Marilyn.

"Good work, you two. But no, this dilemma doesn't call for the assistance of our equity brothers and sisters." Kent tapped a finger on his chin.

"What are you suggesting, Mr. Stone?" Martha asked.

"Why, we should go to Hayes, tell him the truth about what's been going on. Then he'll fire Quinn."

Martha's stomach lurched. "I couldn't possibly admit that I've been writing the show!" she exclaimed. "Quentin Quinn would have me sacked for . . . for insubordination."

"This isn't the army," Miss Connors said with a smile.

"But my revelation will make him look like a fool. And no offense intended to the men in the room, but in my experience men don't respond well when they're made to look the fool."

Miss Connors's gaze drifted into the distance. "Let's think about this. If Quinn is exposed and he decides to be foolish enough to engage in an act of retribution against you, how would that serve his best interests? If you were fired, Miss Berry, who would write the scripts for *As the Sun Sets*? Quinn certainly can't and he's bound to be found out as the hollow man he is."

"But if it becomes known that it's been me all along, he'll be humiliated. He'll make my life a misery."

"Men are so predictable, aren't they?" Kent Stone said with a sigh. "There's only one thing to do. We'll have to find a way to get rid of him."

Martha gasped.

Miss Connors sighed. "He doesn't mean *kill* him." She turned to Martha and said, "Bless. We mean he has to be moved on to something else. That's the surefire way to get rid of an incompetent man. Promote him."

Martha wondered if everyone in the room was as perplexed as she was.

"That way, you can be promoted to head writer, Miss Berry, and assemble a team around you to help with producing the program. You've been working yourself to the bone doing the jobs of two people, and it's clearly catching up with you. Today's fainting spell, for instance."

"How many times do I have to explain it's my low blood pressure?"

Kent Stone sighed. "Yes, yes. Miss Berry, you deserve to have your experience and talents recognized. You deserve all the credit for *As the Sun Sets*, not Quentin Quinn. We have to think of something. His drinking is only getting worse. His manners are becoming intolerable. And his behavior to Miss Calthorpe has simply been beyond the pale."

Martha turned to Marilyn, horrified. "I thought we'd put things in place so you wouldn't ever have to be alone with him?"

Marilyn nodded in reply. "You did and I appreciate it, Miss Berry. But he calls me at home, which makes things very awkward with my father. I'm polite, of course, but that only seems to encourage him. He asks me to dinner and insists I need private acting coaching with him. I can't think what I've done to make him behave this way. I'm so worried that if I come right out and ask him to leave me alone, he'll fire me."

Alex's shoulders broadened as if a wind had blown in from the harbor and puffed them up like sails. "Over my dead body."

Marilyn leaned into his shoulder and Alex slipped an arm around her.

Martha couldn't believe she was about to say what she was really thinking. She brought her fingers together to form a steeple.

"So. How do we get rid of Quentin Quinn?"

Chapter 27

IN WHICH QUENTIN QUINN'S STAR CONTINUES TO RISE.

As the Sun Sets. Producer Quentin Quinn's office."

Martha still couldn't help but cringe a little every time she said it. She had been answering the telephone with a simple "Miss Berry speaking," but as the program had become more popular, Quentin Quinn had insisted on putting himself front and center. In doing so, Martha found herself relegated further and further away from having any formal role in the program. Or, in fact, any identity at all.

"Good afternoon. Is that Miss Berry?"

Martha rolled her eyes. "This is she."

"It's Miss Armitage from the general manager's office."

Martha slowly rose to standing. A shiver of fear skittered through her, turning her legs to jelly. What had they done? What had gone wrong? Why was the general manager's office calling?

"Hello, Miss Armitage. How may I help you?"

"I have Mr. Moses on the line for Mr. Quinn."

Martha crossed herself. Thank goodness Mr. Moses's sponta-
neous phone call hadn't come earlier in the day. Quentin Quinn
had arrived back from lunch possibly only half-inebriated and
had closed the door behind him.

"Yes, of course. I'll put you through."

Martha connected the call. "Mr. Quinn?"

"What?" he growled.

Martha gritted her teeth. He'd also begun answering her in
this abrupt way as if he was in the midst of making a thousand
decisions and her interruptions were an annoyance, not part of
her job and his.

"It's Mr. Moses's office, Mr. Quinn. The general manager is
wanting to speak to you."

There was a thump and a clang and then static on the line. Had
he dropped the receiver? "Mr. Quinn?"

"Put it through, Mrs. Barry."

Twenty minutes later, Quentin Quinn threw open the door to his
office and strode over to Martha's desk with more energy than
she'd ever seen him exhibit this late in the afternoon. His cheeks
were ruddy, which was nothing new, but his eyes were bright and
clear, which was new. He fumbled in his trouser pocket for his
pack of cigarettes, managed to light one with trembling fingers,
and then took a long drag, exhaling his smoke in a cloud. He
watched it drift toward the ceiling with barely concealed joy on
his face.

"Is everything all right, Mr. Quinn?"

Martha's first reaction had been one of sheer relief. She often relived her meeting with Rutherford Hayes, when he'd castigated her for putting scripts to air without his approval.

Quentin Quinn put his cigarette between his lips, clamped them firmly shut, and jogged back to his office to fetch his coat. "Everything's fine and dandy. More than fine and dandy. It's . . ." He laughed. "Well, it's bloody marvelous, as a matter of fact." He slipped his arms through the sleeves and fixed his lapels. "I'm heading out. I'll see you tomorrow. Get to work typing up those scripts, will you, Mrs. Barry." He turned to leave.

Martha ground her teeth together and felt the ache in her jaw. "It's Miss Berry, Mr. Quinn. Miss Berry."

He looked back over his shoulder. "What was that?"

"Nothing," she murmured. "Nothing at all."

....

At the end of the day, Martha stepped outside the building onto the street and into pelting rain. Early September in Sydney was changeable, to say the least. If the forecast had been for a wet evening, she hadn't seen it but was relieved she made a habit of carrying her umbrella in her handbag every day, just in case.

She stood for a moment under the eaves of the tobacconist shop next door to the building and watched the rain pummel pedestrians on their way home. She would stop only a moment. She didn't want to keep her mother waiting for dinner, even if it meant arriving sopping wet and then having to hear Violet's concern about catching her death of cold because she'd let herself get rained on. No matter how old she was, Martha would always be Violet Berry's daughter.

"Miss Berry?"

It was Penelope Jones, Mr. Hayes's secretary.

"Miss Jones. I hope you're well?"

Miss Jones's pretty blue eyes lit up and sparkled. "I'm very well, thank you. And you?"

"About to get soaked on my walk to the tram, but never mind."

"The same." Miss Jones chuckled. "But I like the rain. It makes everything in the city feel so clean." She hesitated and cast a furtive look around.

"I hope you don't mind me saying, but . . . it's about Mr. Quinn."

Martha's ears pricked up. "Yes?"

"I understand Mrs. Moses, the general manager's wife, is a committed listener of *As the Sun Sets*."

Martha was thrilled and let out a little laugh before stifling it. "Is that right? What wonderful news." That might explain the phone call earlier that afternoon. Martha tucked away that useful piece of knowledge. It could come in handy one day. "It will do us no harm to have fans who have the ear of the general manager."

"I understand she's particularly fond of Vera Percy and what she's going through."

If only Martha could show more than the mildest excitement. If only she could scream to the rooftops that she was behind the storyline that had the whole of Australia talking.

"We've had so many letters about it. It seems to have struck a chord."

Miss Jones took a sideways step closer to Martha and lowered her voice. They had to avert their umbrellas to make space. "I enjoy it very much too. As does my mother. It's all she can talk about these days, and she never stops asking me about the program, Miss Berry. You've created something wonderful."

Martha swallowed. "Mr. Quinn is very talented."

There was a look in Miss Jones's eyes that said more than her words. "Yes, I understand he is."

Did Miss Jones suspect something? Martha wondered how much longer her secret would remain hidden. The actors had already guessed, but any plan to get rid of Quentin Quinn hadn't moved along further than that conversation at Miss Connors's house. No one wanted to upset the apple cart by letting the cat out of the bag, as Kent Stone might have said. *Goodness me*, Martha thought. She was even beginning to think like him. Surely everyone was on too good a wicket to spill the beans.

"Miss Berry." Miss Jones laid a hand on Martha's arm. "I think there's something you should know."

She knew. She definitely knew. Martha couldn't breathe. "Yes?"

"I tell you this in the strictest confidence, you understand."

"Of course."

Miss Jones glanced from left to right and then over both shoulders. The two women weren't in the best location to be sharing such confidences as anyone from the office could walk by at any moment. Miss Jones leaned close and whispered in Martha's ear. "Mr. Moses has offered Mr. Quinn a job in television."

Martha blinked. "Television?" She wished there was a bus stop nearby because she desperately needed somewhere to sit. "Oh."

"They want him to create a new police show. Like that American program *Dragnet*. But then again, these things do change. Anyway, the hope is that Quentin Quinn will do for television what he's done for radio with *As the Sun Sets*."

The ground under Martha's feet suddenly shifted and she felt as if she was plunging somewhere dark and unknown. Who would replace Quentin Quinn? How quickly would the new producer discover that in effect she had been running the show all along?

How quickly would she be exposed? And then how quickly would she be sacked? Because surely no one would want a script girl who had usurped her producer and hoodwinked everyone into thinking Quentin Quinn was behind the success of *As the Sun Sets*.

In that moment of stark realization, Martha saw her career as script girl disappear in a puff of smoke. Perhaps her whole career. For if she wasn't working at the ABC, what would she do?

"The government is concerned that Australian television will be full of imported American programs like *Perry Mason* and *I Love Lucy*. Which means the board is concerned too. No one wants Australian children picking up American accents. That's why they're looking to create local programs as fast as they can."

"I see." Martha had obviously failed to hide her perplexed expression, because Miss Jones smiled and whispered, "Among other things, I see the agenda for board meetings. And let's just say, Mr. Hayes likes to discuss the agenda items. In some detail." Miss Jones was the fount of much information. "Anyway, I wanted to tell you because all the girls in the office simply love *As the Sun Sets*. We'd hate to see it go because the right producer and writer couldn't be found. What do you think will happen with Betty? Will she choose the dashing Italian or the dependable butcher?"

Martha shrugged. "I couldn't possibly say."

"Of course."

"Would you mind me asking, Miss Jones, has there been any discussion about what might happen to *As the Sun Sets* if Mr. Quinn does indeed move to television?"

Miss Jones shook her head. "Not that I've heard. I'll let you know, though, when I do. I can't imagine it will end. The board knows how popular it is. Mr. Hayes has been keeping them up to date. It's a feather in his cap as well as Quinn's." Miss Jones folded her umbrella.

When Martha looked up to the fading blue sky, she realized it had stopped raining.

"Look at that," Miss Jones said as she, too, turned her gaze up-ward. "Every cloud has a silver lining, Miss Berry."

On her walk home from the tram, Martha was too distracted to avoid the puddles and arrived home with wet shoes and cold feet.

She changed into her nightgown and dressing gown, and once her feet were ensconced in her warm slippers, she cooked a quick dinner of lamb chops with mashed potatoes and peas and carrots while the reassuring voices of the *Blue Hills* characters filled the kitchen, and she and Violet settled at the table to eat while *As the Sun Sets* continued.

While Violet listened intently, even though she'd heard the same episode that afternoon over lunch, Martha's thoughts couldn't be confined to the kitchen. In the space of one hushed conversation on a busy street, her world had turned on its axis.

So the wunderkind Quentin Quinn was going to television. Her first thought had been an unkind one, perhaps. They could have him, she'd thought. She couldn't worry about whether he might succeed or fail on his new show. She had found during her working life that men of the ilk of Quentin Quinn—those who attracted attention early, who were employed because they were the right sort of fellow from the right sort of school or university, or from the right sort of club—were given opportunities that weren't open to others. That was why, she supposed, a council streetsweeper would always remain a council streetsweeper, why the ladies working in the kitchens of cafes and in laundries and in offices and shops would remain there, stuck somehow, with no old friend available to see their potential. Men like Quentin Quinn were always promoted past their level of competence. What was he good at? She wasn't sure he had any competencies beyond knowing the right people and hoodwinking them all. For women, it was the exact opposite. Martha had never believed she'd been given the chance to achieve what she was truly capable of. Until *As the Sun Sets*.

And now she was in danger of having it all taken away.

Would Rutherford Hayes believe her if she revealed she had been writing the scripts all along?

And how hard was she prepared to fight to prove it?

Chapter 28

IN WHICH BETTY PERCY IS ROMANCED BY NOT ONE BUT TWO YOUNG MEN.

FX: *Tinkle of bell*

ERNIE WATSON: *Hello, Miss Percy.*

BETTY PERCY: *Hello there, Ernie. I'm wondering if my father's here. I've brought a message from Mum. About dinner tonight. She's after half a dozen sausages for a new recipe she's trying out. Sausage casserole with pineapple.*

ERNIE WATSON: *Crikey, that sounds delicious! I'm sorry to say Mr. Percy's not here. I believe he's popped out to see one of his lamb suppliers. I can organize the sausages for you if you like.*

BETTY PERCY: *If you're sure it's not too much trouble.*

ERNIE WATSON: *Nothing's too much trouble for you, Miss Percy.*

BETTY PERCY: (stumbles) *Oh . . . How . . . How kind of you to say.*

ERNIE WATSON: *Anything for the boss's daughter, of course! Was that beef or pork Mrs. Percy was wanting?*

BETTY PERCY: *Beef, please, Ernie.*

FX: *Rustling of paper*

ERNIE WATSON: *I hear the new job's going well.*

BETTY PERCY: *(laughs) I suppose Dad's been telling you all about it?*

ERNIE WATSON: *He fills us in every morning on what you did the day before. "Betty had to make four pots of tea for her boss." Or "Betty had to go to the shops and get just the right kind of biscuits for her boss."*

BETTY PERCY: *Oh no! I can't believe he's telling you all that! It makes it all sound so silly. Making tea and fetching biscuits. I do so much more than that, you know.*

ERNIE WATSON: *I'm sure you do. It's a bit like working here. People must think all I do is stand around all day, looking handsome and flirting with the customers.*

BETTY PERCY: *I don't think that. My father's the butcher, re-member. I know how hard you all work. And I'm well aware of the occupational hazards in a job like this. You'll be lucky if you have all your fingers after you've been butchering for a few years. Sausages and chops don't make themselves, do they, no matter how dangerous!*

ERNIE WATSON: *No. No, they don't. Look. Don't be upset at Mr. Percy. He's just so very proud of you.*

FX: *Tinkle of bell*

BETTY PERCY: *Customers. I'd better be off. Nice to see you, Ernie.*

ERNIE WATSON: *(calls out) Miss Percy! Don't forget your snags!*

SCENE BREAK

FX: *Footsteps*

BETTY PERCY: *Oh, I'm so sorry! I didn't mean to run into you. I was off with the fairies.*

ANTONIO ANTONELLO: *No, no. It's all my fault. (pause) "Off with the fairies"? What does this mean?*

BETTY PERCY: *It means I wasn't concentrating on the man coming out of the doorway of his shop. I'm Betty Percy. That's my father's shop right there. He's Jack Percy, the butcher.*

ANTONIO ANTONELLO: *Si. Miss Percy. I have met your father and your mother. My name is Antonio Antonello. This is my family's shop.*

BETTY PERCY: *It's very nice to meet you, Mr. Antonello.*

ANTONIO ANTONELLO: *And you too, Miss Percy.*

BETTY PERCY: *I'd best be going. Mum's waiting for her sausages.*

ANTONIO ANTONELLO: *Watch out for those fairies! (a pause) Mamma mia. Bella donna.*

....

A week after her secret had been exposed, Martha sat back in her chair and tried to shrug off the ache in her shoulder. She was at the kitchen table at home on a Wednesday night, and her typewriter, a notebook and pencil, a cup of hot chocolate, and a half-eaten plate of biscuits were her only company.

Violet had gone to bed not long after dinner, *Blue Hills*, and *As the Sun Sets* (in that order), pledging to read for a little while before turning out the light, but Martha knew her mother. Violet was too tired most days to even hold up a novel in bed, and sleep overcame her fast enough that she would have barely made it through a page, even if she wanted to. Martha didn't begrudge her mother her early bedtime. She wished she could fall asleep as easily, but every attempt to drift off was derailed by a mind that pulsed with ideas and characters and dialogue and what-ifs and scenarios so strange she wasn't sure where they had come from. She found herself dreaming of Jack and Vera and Betty. Of Ernie. Of Antonio and his family. Which reminded her: she was still looking to cast an actress to play Antonio's mother, Carmelina.

Yes. She picked up her pencil and scribbled a note to remind herself.

A yawn escaped her and when she turned to check the clock hanging on the wall above the stove, she was surprised to see it was half past ten. How was it that the time flew by so quickly when she was writing, that her characters were able to take her into their worlds so forcefully that she started to hear them talking in her dreams?

There were just a few lines to go before the end of the scene she'd been working on, and she wanted to finish it before she lost her train of thought. She lifted her fingers and pressed them to the keys.

Betty would make a choice, but not yet. Not before she'd been torn every which way by the attentions of two different men.

Martha smiled to herself. The journey getting there was going to be wonderful.

Chapter 29

IN WHICH MISS JONES REVEALS HER TRUTH TO MARTHA BERRY.

I s it true?"

Martha unwrapped her cheese and pickle sandwich and looked across the cafeteria table at April. May and June were also staring at her.

"Is what true?" Martha took a bite.

The Calendar Girls exchanged glances and May leaned in close. "People are talking about Miss Jones—you know, the one who works for Rutherford Hayes? Well, they're saying"—May leaned in even closer and dropped her voice to a whisper—"that she's going to be an unwed mother."

Martha almost choked on her sandwich. "May! How could you repeat such a thing?"

May looked contrite. "I've only told April and June, I pinky swear, Miss Berry. When I heard the story, I didn't know what to do. I mean, naturally I knew I shouldn't repeat it. That goes without saying. I needed April's and June's advice about what to do with the secret. I was thinking how awful it would be to be talked about in such a way and . . . and that someone should tell her."

"Honestly," April said. "She hasn't told another soul, have you, May?"

"Of course not. Especially not when it's something so . . . so . . ." May looked stricken.

"Vicious?" June narrowed her eyes and shook her head. "It's that horrid Miss Carver in Payroll. Looks like she's at it again."

Martha didn't like to think ill of people, but June was right. *Horrid* was the perfect word to describe Miss Carver. She was perhaps the most conniving person Martha had ever had the misfortune to meet. The young woman—who'd barely been at the ABC more than two years—had made it her business to know exactly what was going on and with whom. Martha remembered the rumors Miss Carver had spread about her. She could hardly think about them without experiencing the same shame and embarrassment she'd felt when she first heard she'd been the subject of the young woman's latest campaign of terror.

The previous year, Miss Carver had told Pam from Payroll that the real reason Martha "flitted from job to job" at the broadcaster was because she simply wasn't good enough to hold down a steady position. Then she'd added fuel to the fire by proclaiming quite loudly in the cafeteria—within Martha's earshot—that Pam had been found stealing from staff pay packets and had spent the ill-gotten gains on purchasing a new rabbit coat for herself. Neither story was true, but Pam hadn't been able to withstand the ignominy and had left for a secretarial position at Sydney's water board.

It had always been Martha's natural tendency to give people the benefit of the doubt, to allow that a person might have a reason for acting the way they did, perhaps stemming from sadness or anger at a wrong done to them from which they hadn't recovered. At first, Martha had tried to be sympathetic to Miss Carver's catty comments and her tendency to spread entirely malicious and cruel gossip about the people she toiled with every day between nine and five o'clock. George Eliot had written that it was a narrow mind which could not look at a subject from various points of view, and Martha had always seen the common sense in the words. But no matter how hard she tried, she could make no such rationalizations work with the horrid Miss Carver.

"I wish the cat had got her tongue when she was a young girl and never let go. Please don't pay any mind to what you've heard. People like her are best ignored."

"But . . ." May twisted her fingers around each other into a tangle. "Shouldn't someone tell"—she mouthed "Miss Jones" before continuing—"of the rumor?"

"Mmm." Martha could sense the dilemma. She knew what it was like to be the subject of Miss Carver's scuttlebutt. But on the other hand, wouldn't Miss Jones be mortified if she found out such a rumor was circulating?

June looked as if she were about to burst a blood vessel. "I'd like to give that Miss Carver a piece of my mind."

May put a hand on June's arm. "Don't even attempt it. She'll simply turn her attentions to you and invent some rumor or other, some totally baseless story, and spread it like a bushfire. How on earth does she do it?"

"I know exactly how," June said through gritted teeth. "I've seen it with my own eyes. She waits in the lift until it's full, like at lunchtime or at the end of the day when everyone is leaving, and pretends to whisper but isn't really whispering. And everyone hears exactly what she wants them to hear and within twenty-four hours the rumor has spread through the whole building. Or it might take until Monday if she drops her bombshell on a Friday afternoon."

April was horrified. "That can't be. That means she's doing it on purpose."

"Of course she's doing it on purpose." June huffed. "She takes joy in hurting people. It's horrid."

May turned to Martha. "What should we do, Miss Berry?"

....

When she returned to her office, Martha made a discreet call to Miss Jones to ask her if she was available for a cup of coffee after work on the pretense that she was planning a trip to Tasmania and wanted to ask Miss Jones which tour company she had booked through, where she'd stayed, and so on. Miss Jones had readily agreed, which was how they came to be sitting in Repin's Coffee Inn on Castlereagh Street watching the rush hour crowd bustle by. Martha had chosen a cafe a good distance from the office to protect them from running into anyone they knew.

Martha halted Miss Jones midconversation, when the young woman was marveling at the beauty of the southern Tasmanian wilderness, and announced, "I didn't really ask you here to talk about Tasmania."

The color drained from Miss Jones's face. "You didn't?"

Martha shook her head. "Forgive me for not being honest about my intentions in having coffee with you. I have something far more important to bring to your attention. How can I put this? It's a rather delicate matter."

Miss Jones put her face in her hands and gasped. "You know, don't you?"

This was all happening rather more quickly than Martha had thought it might. Did she imagine she might have to wrestle a confession out of the young woman? She hadn't been sure at all how the conversation would go, if she was honest.

"Please, Miss Jones. You don't have to confirm or deny anything to me. It's really none of my business, nor should it be anyone else's. But someone has made it her business, which I find totally appalling, just so you're clear. I just thought you should know, that's all, what people are saying."

"It's true." Miss Jones revealed her tear-streaked face to Martha. The poor young thing. Finding oneself in that kind of predicament was hard enough without the rumors.

"Do your mother and father know?" Martha asked.

"Of course they do. They were there."

Martha parted her lips to speak, but nothing came out. This situation was not making sense at all.

Miss Jones slowly undid the metal clasp on her handbag. She reached into it and pulled out a small white box. She snapped it open, took out a plain gold band and another with a small glittering stone on it, and slipped them onto . . . the ring finger of her left hand.

"You're married?" Martha breathed a sigh of relief. She'd been trying to find the final jigsaw puzzle piece in this conversation with Miss Jones and it had finally slipped in place. At least that might help with her delicate situation. Miss Jones wouldn't be the first woman in history to be married *after* a baby was conceived. But . . . *wait a moment*, she thought. *Married and still working?*

"There," Miss Jones said defiantly as she held up her hand, ring side out, as if she were making a point to Martha. "It's true.

I'm not really Miss Jones anymore, but I could hardly go by my new name at work, could I? I'm Mrs. Ross, if you must know. Tasmania wasn't a holiday. It was my *honeymoon*."

"You're married," Martha said to herself in a murmur, almost as a confirmation. "Please accept my warmest congratulations." But as she said the word, as she formed a smile, she knew that the beginning of married life would signal the end of another.

"I don't like to leave it at home, but I can't wear it to work because . . ." Miss Jones shuddered. "Because of the stupid law. And do you know what the worst thing is, Miss Berry? I've wanted to shout from the rooftops that I'm married to a wonderful man. But I've been forced to lie. And I feel terrible about it. But not as terrible as knowing I would have to resign as soon as anyone finds out. I needed to hang on as long as I could. For the money. Dennis and I are saving to buy a house. Not that my wage helps much—I mean, he earns so much more than I do—but we're scrimping and saving every pound we can for a deposit. We're in a little flat in Cremorne at the moment. And it's lovely but it's not ours. And anyway . . . there won't be enough room for all of us when the baby comes."

Miss Jones placed a gentle hand on her stomach and then turned her red eyes up to Martha.

"Congratulations," Martha said softly. "That's simply wonderful news. You and Dennis must be so happy. Not to mention your parents."

Miss Jones's bottom lip began to quiver. "It happened a little more quickly than we planned, if I'm honest. On our honeymoon."

How to broach the subject she had come to raise with Miss Jones?

"That's actually what I wanted to talk to you about. It's difficult to say, Miss Jones, but you should know. While I can hardly see any sign of it at all, there are rumors circulating that you are expecting."

Martha could see her mind whirring. "But how could they? No one even knows I'm married. I haven't told a soul. This is what I've been most frightened about. Someone finding out and revealing the truth. You can't know how many sleepless nights it's caused me, ever since Dennis proposed. Why can't I be a wife and a working woman, Miss Berry? Why?"

"I wish I could quash the spiteful stories, but I can't. I thought you should know what's being said, no matter how undoubtedly hurtful it is."

Miss Jones slumped back in her chair and stared into space. "I can't think how . . . unless someone heard me in the bathroom. That must be it. I've been suffering from terrible morning sickness. Well, all-day sickness, if I'm honest." Miss Jones went white again. "They think I'm . . . oh my goodness, Miss Berry. People must think I'm having a baby out of wedlock!"

Martha nodded gravely. "Yes."

"I know who it was. I know exactly. Miss Carver. She asked me if I was feeling all right and I had to hurriedly invent something so I told her I must have had too many sausages for dinner the night before. Thinking back, I remember the look on her face. A sort of smug expression. She's horrible, Miss Berry. Simply horrible."

Martha was silent. She wasn't in a position to confirm or deny anything, not having heard it from Miss Carver herself. But Miss Jones was right. Miss Carver was mean and haughty and, unfathomably, she seemed to take great delight in humiliating others by revealing things she had no right to reveal. Only last year, she had let it be known that one of the staff in the orchestra department wasn't a spinster who lived with her spinster friend,

but that the two of them were indulging in Sapphic passion.
Once people rushed to the dictionary to find out what she meant,
the staff member resigned. Martha remembered her leaving in
tears, her dear friend comforting her as she left.

Martha had been too polite to say anything back then and had
watched in silent horror as once again the inevitable results of
such gossip played out in someone else's real life. But slowly, the
politeness was being leached out of Martha like color from a shirt
washed too many times.

"These are my choices," Miss Jones said. "Admit I'm married
and resign. Or pretend I'm having a baby out of wedlock and be
forced out anyway. I love this job, Miss Berry. I'm very good at it.
Mr. Hayes praises my work all the time and I'm proud of what I
do. Why should I have to hide?"

"I don't believe you should, but that's the law when it comes
to the Commonwealth Public Service." And so many other work-
places in the country.

Miss Jones bit her lip. "It might be, but that doesn't mean it
isn't ridiculous and so unfair."

"I don't disagree with you, Miss Jones."

"What should I do?"

"I can't decide for you, Miss Jones."

"That's just it, Miss Berry. I can't decide for me either. Men
have decided, haven't they? That I must no longer work when
I'm married, as if putting a ring on my finger somehow means
I'm not important anymore. As if working will keep me away
from baby-making and child-rearing and being a good house-
wife. It's infuriating, Miss Berry, it really is."

"I can't help but agree with you," Martha said.

"I have a cousin in England who married and didn't have to

resign. Over there, they got rid of this stupid nonsense just after the war."

Martha could do nothing else but agree with her again. It *was* infuriating. It was such an arbitrary wastage of female talent. Over the years, Martha had often felt as if she would be the last woman standing. She had worked with so many smart and capable young women who'd fallen in love and married, a natural next step, and then been forced to leave. No married woman was eligible for employment, either permanently or temporarily, in the Commonwealth Public Service. Or state government. And once married, every woman was deemed to have "retired" from the date of her marriage.

There was a provision that a woman's employment might be possible "in special circumstances," but how many men deemed any woman exceptional enough to fit that category? How much had been lost to the nation because these married women could no longer work at the broadcaster? What might they have been able to contribute, to accomplish, if they'd been allowed to stay? What might radio sound like if there were more Gwen Merediths creating radio drama? If there were women reporters in the newsroom who might be able to bring their perspectives to stories and news items about matters of importance to everyone who was listening, not just men?

"What will you do?" Martha asked.

"If I am now the subject of such gossip, I'll have to tell Mr. Hayes as soon as I see him. I don't see I have any other choice. I'll probably be gone by the end of the week. He'll have to find someone to replace me."

It was the sad truth.

"I do appreciate you telling me what you've heard, Miss Berry.

Really. At least I might get to tell Mr. Hayes before he hears it from somewhere else."

"I'm so very sorry," Martha replied. "You're very capable, and I know you'll be dreadfully missed by Mr. Hayes. And by me."

Tears welled in Miss Jones's eyes and she dabbed at them with a handkerchief. "That's very kind."

Martha nodded her goodbye—what on earth else was there to say?—and stood to leave. When she looked at Miss Jones—Mrs. Ross—and saw tears streaming down her cheeks, all she could think was what a terrible waste.

Chapter 30

IN WHICH MARTHA BERRY STUMBLES UPON A CRYING APRIL AND ANOTHER DARK SECRET IS REVEALED.

April. Whatever's the matter?"

The next morning, Martha took the stairs from her office to the cafeteria—it was often a better bet than waiting for the ancient lifts, which creaked and groaned in a very sinister manner—and was shocked to find April there, hiding in the dim light. She was sitting on one of the cool cement steps, her knees bent, her head lowered. Her hands covered her face, and her hair, usually coiffed just so into a low bun at her collar, had come loose. Blonde strands hung down her back, tangled and knotted.

"Miss Berry, no need to t-trouble yourself. I'll be fine, honestly I will."

Martha gently took April's shoulders and tried not to react at the smudges of the young woman's favorite plum-colored lipstick on her left cheek, the trails of watery mascara down her face. "Let's get you tidied up. You need a good strong cup of tea and a sit-down." Martha slipped a folded handkerchief from the pocket of her suit jacket and pressed it softly to April's cheeks, dabbing at the slurry of mascara. Slowly, April's sobs turned to sniffs and then, in a shuddering exhalation, her breathing returned to normal.

"Thank you, Miss Berry."

"There's no need to thank me. Come to my office. You'll have some privacy there, at least."

After the stress of the latest round of auditions the day before, Quentin Quinn hadn't yet appeared at work that morning and Martha had assumed he might go directly to lunch instead. She was quite used to having the mornings to herself and found that when she didn't have to fetch him his endless cups of coffee and tea, which he drank alternately with two cigarettes in between each cup, she was able to get so much more work done. She knew she and April would have some privacy. They made their way down the corridor, April's head discreetly lowered, and Martha closed the door to her office to stop passersby from looking in and asking questions.

"Now sit yourself down. I'll boil the kettle and I have a pot and a jug of milk here." When the pot had brewed and Martha had poured two cups, she passed one to April and fetched Quentin Quinn's chair from behind his desk. She sat.

"How's that going down?"

Finally, a smile. "Just what I needed, Miss Berry. Thank you."

They sat in silence. Soft voices emerged from the radio in the corner of the room. Martha found them soothing when they were turned low, as if there was a friendly conversation going on somewhere close. Martha thought of her mother at home, who would likely be listening to the same programs, waiting for *Blue Hills* at one o'clock. She would be on to her third or fourth cup of tea and might have tucked into a few custard creams by now.

"Would you like to tell me what happened?"

April smiled weakly. "It's nothing. Honestly. I simply over-reacted."

Martha waited. "So something did happen then?"

"It was . . . a misunderstanding. Mr. Hooper. He . . . I must have given him the wrong idea, that's all."

In that moment, Martha wished she had it in her to swear as freely as all the men who worked around her did.

She reached for April's hand. "Mr. Hooper doesn't need any-one to give him wrong ideas. He has more than enough of his own."

The door swung open and May and June burst in.

"Oh, April!" May exclaimed.

"What on earth?" June muttered through gritted teeth. "Ann from Accounts called and told us she'd seen you go into Miss Berry's office and that you seemed to be crying. She's very concerned."

April looked at Martha. "Oh goodness. I don't want anyone to know."

"Don't trouble yourself, April. I've known Ann for twenty years. Your secret is safe with her."

"Who was it this time?" June demanded, her hands propped on her hips. She looked as if she was ready for fisticuffs.

Martha blinked. Had she heard correctly? "This time? You mean others have—"

June groaned. "Come on, Miss Berry. Look at her. What do you expect?"

"June!" May said, shocked. "That is no excuse and you know it."

June had a tendency to speak before she had fully thought through her feelings and emotions. "I didn't mean . . . I'm sorry, April. What I meant to say was that men are men, and we all know what they're like."

"I wish someone had told me. I was asked to take a parcel down to studio four. I knocked and he said come in." April covered her face with her hands and began to cry again.

"And then what happened, April?" June asked gently when April couldn't seem to form her words.

"When I opened the door, he was . . ."

Her friends waited.

April closed her eyes, as if by doing so she might be able to shut out the memories. "He was sitting in his chair and the top of his trousers was sort of gaping open, and at first I thought he might have spilled his tea on them. So I said, 'Are you all right, Mr. Hooper?' and then I realized he wasn't actually patting down the front of his pants. He was doing something to his . . ."

A moment of silence pressed on them all. Each knew what the other was thinking. Martha knew she had to be the one to say it. "His penis?" Martha scared herself at how cold her voice sounded in the quiet of her office, with the three women around her almost forgetting to breathe.

"Yes. I think so. I've never actually seen a man's . . . you know . . . before. I'm not even allowed to say the word at home. I'm a respectable girl, Miss Berry, really I am."

"Of course you are," May told her, and crossed herself.

"What did you do then?" June's cheeks were glowing beet red in fury as she reached out and covered April's right hand with hers.

"I didn't know what to do. I was so shocked I sort of froze on the spot."

"And what did he do, April?" May's eyes were filled with tears.

Martha raised a hand. "There's no need to badger poor April. She's been through a terrible thing, and it's important we let her tell us in her own time."

May looked downcast. "Yes, Miss Berry."

"He jumped up from his chair and grabbed me. My breasts." April took in a deep breath and her eyes widened as if she'd suddenly found her anger. "And then he pushed himself against me—"

"With his . . . whatchamacallit . . . still hanging out of his trousers?" June gasped.

"It wasn't hanging. It was straight and it poked me right in my stomach."

May and June gasped, horrified.

Martha took a moment to find the words she had hitherto been too polite to say out loud. "That disgusting piece of filth."

The three women looked at Martha, their mouths gaping.

"I'm sorry, girls. I don't know where that came from." Martha held their gazes. "But he is a disgusting piece of filth."

"Too right he is," June replied.

All May could do was nod.

"It was horrible," April said, her voice a whisper. "I pushed him back, I must have, because he sort of stumbled and fell back in his chair and . . . and then I opened the door and ran out of there as fast as I could. When I got back to my desk in the music department, everyone was laughing and pointing at me. Except for Bridie and Karina. It was as if the men all somehow knew what had happened."

Martha's jaw suddenly ached. "Of course they knew, April. Why do you think they sent you to take the package to Handsy Hooper? They'd called ahead to the studio to let him know you were coming."

May began to tremble. "Do you mean they think that behavior is something to laugh at? That's simply dreadful."

April burst into agonizing sobs. May handed over her handkerchief, and April's tears transformed it into a wet mess before

June retrieved hers from the cuff of her sleeve and proffered it too.

Martha's mind whirred and then something snapped. She knew in an instant what it was: It was the weight of her own guilt. She should have tried harder to make his behavior known all those years ago when it had happened to her. Twenty years ago, when she was thirty, Handsy Hooper had cornered her in the tearoom at the end of the day. She'd stayed late at her desk to type up some notes for her boss, a memo he'd needed urgently for a meeting first thing the next morning, and she'd told him it would be no trouble because back then, before the war, her mother had still been able to prepare dinner, so Martha hadn't felt the need to leave on time.

She remembered that she had been standing at the sink rinsing out her teacup because she never, ever left a dirty cup or saucer or plate for another woman to clean. She'd just hung up the tea towel and was holding her cup and saucer in her hand when the lights went out. She'd blinked and glanced to the windows to check if there'd been a blackout on the street. When her eyes had adjusted to the dim illumination bleeding through the windows, she heard strident footsteps, and before she could turn to see who it was, he'd thrust into her from behind and reached around to grab her breasts.

She'd dropped her cup and saucer and they'd shattered on the linoleum floor. It had all happened so fast. His meaty hands had grasped her breasts, squeezing her so violently that bruises in the shape of his fingerprints appeared that night. It had been so quick. He hadn't been out for a tender caress of a woman's skin or the scent of her perfume. Martha still wasn't sure where the idea to fight had come from, but in those days she'd worn a small heel and she'd managed to dig one into the top of his foot and jabbed backward with an elbow. When he'd yelped and loosened his grip in surprise, she'd run.

Oh, how she hated him. He'd wanted to shock and hurt and scare her.

And she had been shocked and hurt and scared.

And humiliated. That, most of all. She was a colleague and all she was to him was a pair of breasts and a female body to grab and grope. And for twenty years, she'd had to work in the same building—sometimes in a control room ten feet by ten feet—and pretend it had never happened. She'd reported it to her boss but was told to forget it, that he hadn't meant anything by it, that it was just horseplay. Handsy hadn't had to pretend it never happened. He had lorded it over her, sneering and muttering whenever she was nearby, as if he was saying, "I know you liked it." That idea sent shivers up her spine whenever she was within one hundred feet of him. Always had. It was an episode she'd tried to forget and almost had. Until now.

"Handsy Hooper's been doing it for years," Martha said. "He did it to me too."

The young women gasped in shock.

"Twenty years ago," she said.

May sniffed loudly. "The man who lives next door?" She looked around to check that they were alone. "He says terrible things to me when he thinks no one else can hear. About what he wants to do to me. The f-word and everything."

"God forbid," Martha murmured.

June lowered her head and stared at her shoes. "It was my uncle."

All the air seemed to have been sucked out of the room. Martha could hardly breathe. "Oh my goodness, June." Martha grasped for June's hand and watched as silent tears spilled down her rounded cheeks. "I told the priest and he told my mother and father, and my mum slapped me so hard for telling lies that I had a red face for a week. It was her brother, you see."

"What happened to him?"

"He died in the war. In Italy. When my grandparents got the telegram and rushed around to tell Mum, it was the best day of my life. Everyone else was crying. I wanted to dance a jig right there in the living room. My two sisters, the same. We couldn't cry, no matter how hard our parents wanted to make us."

"Oh, June." April embraced June in a hug. "I'm so sorry." Then she stood and took a deep, shuddering breath. "I think I'll put the kettle on."

Chapter 31

IN WHICH BETTY PERCY FINDS HERSELF IN
A VERY UNCOMFORTABLE SITUATION WITH
HER NEW BOSS, MR. ROGERSON.

That night, as Martha sat at her kitchen table with her portable typewriter, fury bubbled up inside her.

Her heart pounded and the reverberations reached right down into her fingertips, which struck the typewriter keys with a surge of violent anger. She had to do something. She had to say something in the only way she knew how. If politeness had held her back for her first fifty years, the truth was going to win out from now on. Too many women kept too many secrets. For too long women had buried their ambitions and their intelligence, succumbed to the law of the land made by men, and put up with behavior and situations no man had a right to impose on them. They had made excuses and apologies for the bad behavior of some men, had covered up for the failings of other men, and had silently labored and toiled without complaining. Because it was their lot. Because it was what women did. Because that was the way of the world.

Not anymore.

If Martha couldn't change the real world, she vowed in that moment to change the world for the women of *As the Sun Sets*. Scene by scene, page by page, episode by episode.

FX: *Typing*

BETTY PERCY: *(talking to herself) Now where is that invoice?*

MR. ROGERSON: *Betty! (he calls from a distance) Where's my dry cleaning?*

BETTY PERCY: *(footsteps) Your dry cleaning, Mr. Rogerson? I don't believe you—*

MR. ROGERSON: *Come in, come in.*

FX: *Door closing*

BETTY PERCY: *I don't believe you brought your dry cleaning in today. I can make a note to remind you when you leave this afternoon, so you don't forget to bring it in tomorrow.*

MR. ROGERSON: *(chuckles) My, my. You're a very organized young lady, aren't you? I knew that the minute I agreed to make you my secretary. How long have you been with me now?*

BETTY PERCY: *Two weeks, Mr. Rogerson. I'm very grateful for the opportunity.*

MR. ROGERSON: *Of course, of course. I pride myself on giving lovely young ladies a start in life, a little diversion on their way to becoming a good wife and mother. I rather see myself as practice for a husband.*

BETTY PERCY: *Oh . . .*

MR. ROGERSON: *Yes. A pretty young girl like yourself can learn a lot from a more experienced man like me. If you can learn how to make me happy, Betty, there's no doubt it will come naturally to you when you find a husband. Yes, yes. You'll make someone a very lovely wife one day.*

BETTY PERCY: *Oh . . . That's very kind of you to say.*

MR. ROGERSON: *It's the little things, Betty, that make a husband happy. Like wearing a pretty dress. There's nothing a man likes more than seeing a young lady make an effort to look attractive, to show off her figure when he comes home from work tired from his hard day at the office. He wants to be reminded why he's working so hard. Do you like pretty things, Betty?*

BETTY PERCY: *Oh . . . um . . . yes. I'm just like every other girl in that respect, I should think.*

MR. ROGERSON: *Every girl likes pretty things. It's as natural as wanting to be liked and wanting to be happy. Tell me, Betty, is there a young man in your life who buys you pretty things?*

BETTY PERCY: *No, not at the moment.*

MR. ROGERSON: *That can't be true. (laughs) I can't believe such an attractive young girl like you, with your figure and your looks, hasn't been snapped up yet. Although I'm relieved, if I might say. This way, you can devote all your time to me. Don't tell your father, Betty. He might be jealous that he's no longer number one in your affections.*

BETTY PERCY: *If that's all, Mr. Rogerson. I have to type up that invoice you've been waiting on.*

MR. ROGERSON: *That's all for now. I know you're not far away if I need you.*

From the control room, Martha watched as Marilyn Calthorpe and Kent Stone acted out the scene. She'd provided the scripts to both of them the Friday before and had invited them to stay for a discussion of what she had planned.

"In this scene," Martha had explained, "Betty's boss, Mr. Rogerson, becomes far too familiar, Marilyn, and makes completely inappropriate comments to her. I want Betty to react as any young woman would. With politeness. She's been brought up to respect her elders and not talk out of turn."

"I won't have to stretch myself too far," Marilyn had told Martha. "Men take one look at me and say all sorts of things, the kind of things that would get their mouth washed out with soap if their mother heard. Especially men in the street." She sighed. "Or men in shops or at the chemist or, honestly, anywhere I go. Even in the library. I've tried ignoring them, but that makes it worse. Their shouts get louder and the comments more awful. I've learned to smile back at them as if I appreciate their insults and just keep walking. It honestly gives me a headache. Sometimes I feel it would be more pleasant to simply stay at home in my dressing gown."

Kent put a kind hand on Marilyn's. "Trust me. Men can be awful." Martha wanted Kent to voice the odious Mr. Rogerson, as he was someone Marilyn knew and trusted. When she'd asked him, he'd agreed with a nod and not another word had to be spoken.

"But you're not awful," Marilyn said emphatically. "Nor is Cary or Alex. You're all perfectly lovely."

Kent had squeezed her hand. "And so are you. I simply don't know what to do about my own sex."

In the studio, Kent was as professional as Martha knew he would be. He slipped into Rogerson's leery, deep-voiced growl as easily as he might put on his velvet slippers at the end of the day. As his character's voice grew more sinister, Kent maintained a distance from Marilyn on the other side of the standing microphone, realizing without knowing it that he didn't need to physically intimidate Marilyn to make her reaction authentic. Marilyn was also doing a marvelous job and was reacting just as

Martha had hoped she would, using a cheery politeness in her lines at first, and then, as Rogerson's words grew more personal, she allowed a brittle kind of fear to crackle in her voice. It gave Martha goose bumps.

To her left, Handsy sat at the control panel, paying very close attention to every word Marilyn uttered.

"Ugh," he groaned, and when he slipped one of his hands under the desk, Martha closed her eyes and turned away. He was a truly grotesque human being who had so little self-awareness that he would never recognize his own abominable behavior in Mr. Rogerson.

Throughout her life, Martha had heard suggestions from men about how she should live, how she should act, how she should look, and how she should be. Appear respectably dressed at all times, with neat and ironed clothes, but take care not to look too pretty lest the boss's wife think you're out to steal her husband. Always check your lipstick in the mirror just in case it's smudged onto a tooth and you look slatternly. Perfume must be worn every day, not so little that it doesn't leave a scent but not too much lest you reek like the Coles perfume counter: cheap. Pants are only suitable for those with straight legs, small feet, and not too much development 'round the posterior. Heels too high look sluttish and no heels at all looks too casual. Make the best of your looks. Dress according to your personality. Don't dress according to your personality.

Nowadays, though, none of that mattered to her. She was old in most people's eyes, and as long as she was attired respectably enough that she didn't look like a mad old woman wandering the streets with her stockings at her ankles and her hair matted up like a backstreets Medusa, she was able to pass by without attention or comment.

In the studio, Smithy the props man closed the small door and clattered a cup on a saucer held close to the microphone. Kent shook off the odious Rogerson and let a smile overtake his face as he transformed into Jack Percy. It was a sight to behold. From behind him, Miss Connors stepped up to the microphone to join Kent and Marilyn.

VERA PERCY: *Hello, Betty. You're home late.*

BETTY PERCY: *Sorry, Mum. I missed my bus and had to wait for the next one.*

VERA PERCY: *Never mind. I've kept you some dinner in the oven. Corned beef and mashed potatoes. Your favorite. Let me get it for you.*

BETTY PERCY: *That would be lovely. (sighs) Although I can't say I'm all that hungry. I've had a rotten day.*

FX: *Newspaper rustling*

JACK PERCY: *Hello, love. What's this I hear about a rotten day?*

BETTY PERCY: *Oh, don't worry, Dad. Really. I've let myself get a bee in my bonnet over nothing. Nothing a nice meal of corned beef and mash won't fix.*

JACK PERCY: *When you've helped your mother with the dishes, come join me in the living room. There's sure to be some nice music on the radio that'll settle your mood.*

BETTY PERCY: *I will, Dad.*

FX: *Footsteps*

VERA PERCY: *So tell me all about this rotten day, Betty.*

BETTY PERCY: *Oh, Mum. (starts sobbing)*

VERA PERCY: *There, there, Betty. It'll be all right. Sometimes all you need is a good night's sleep. Everything will feel better in the morning. You'll see.*

BETTY PERCY: *I don't think a good night's sleep will fix this problem. It's Mr. Rogerson, Mum. He's . . . (sobs)*

VERA PERCY: *Did something happen to him? Is he all right, Betty?*

BETTY PERCY: *He's . . . He's simply horrible. The way he looks at me, at my legs and at my . . . I can't even say it. And today he was saying how pretty I was and asking me if I liked pretty things.*

VERA PERCY: *Are you sure he wasn't just being friendly?*

BETTY PERCY: *No. Oh, I'm not sure. Perhaps I gave him the wrong idea. Maybe I've smiled too much or been too attentive. He was asking if I had a boyfriend and when I told him I didn't, he said he was glad because I could devote all my time to him. It was horrible, Mum. Just horrible.*

VERA PERCY: *(voice hardens) Oh, Betty. I'm going to get your father . . .*

FX: *Chair scraping*

BETTY PERCY: *Oh, please, Mum. Don't tell Dad. It's so humiliating. I don't want him to know.*

VERA PERCY: *He could go have a word with this Mr. Rogerson. Tell him he's not being an honorable boss. That he should keep things on a strictly professional basis with the young girls in his office.*

BETTY PERCY: *Please don't. I just want to forget it ever happened. Is my dinner ready?*

"Don't know what Betty's got her knickers in a twist about."
Martha had been so intently focused on the actors' performances that she'd blessedly almost forgotten she was alone in the control room with Handsy Hooper. Quentin Quinn had asked her

to oversee that day's recording because he—as he put it—had some urgent business to attend to. She figured he was in meetings with the television people sorting out the size of his new office.

"What was that?" she asked through gritted teeth. As Marilyn and Miss Connors stepped back and Cary stepped forward to join Kent for a scene in the butcher shop, Handsy grunted, and from the corner of her eye she could see his face turned to her. She felt bile rise in her throat.

"He's her boss. He can ask whatever he likes. Do whatever he likes. And what's wrong with saying she's pretty, tell me that?"

Martha studied her copy of the script and put a pencil line through the scenes the actors had completed.

"Cat got your tongue, hey?" Handsy Hooper grunted. "That's because you know I'm right, Miss Hoity-Toity. Well, guess what I've heard on the old grapevine?"

"Did you say something?" she said archly.

"You heard me, Miss Berry," he snarled. He was clearly enjoying this. "I heard you'll be gone the minute Quinn takes up his new job in television. Word is he doesn't want to take you with him."

Martha channeled Kent Stone and attempted to raise one eyebrow. "Is that so?"

"It's just what I've heard."

She gritted her teeth. "We're at the end of the episode. Cue the music."

Hooper startled and dropped the needle on the record before turning up the volume. As soon as he'd stopped recording, she opened the door, stepped out into the corridor, and slammed the door with as much force as she could muster.

And then she let out a swear word she'd never used before in her life. And it felt very satisfying indeed.

Chapter 32

IN WHICH MARTHA BERRY PUTS HER CARDS ON THE TABLE AND PLAYS HARD.

Miss Jones—for she would never be Mrs. Ross to Martha—called Martha just before lunch the next day to let her know that Mr. Hayes was seeking a meeting with her as soon as possible. Martha finished her cup of tea in one big slurp, checked her reflection in the mirror lest she look untidy, and arrived at his office precisely four minutes later. It was never good to be tardy when the head of drama had requested a meeting with you.

"He's waiting," Miss Jones said with a wink to Martha and a nod to Mr. Hayes's office. "Don't worry," she whispered.

Martha still had memories of the Great Vera Menopause Incident and tried to blink them away.

"Before I go in, how are you feeling? Still queasy?" Martha asked.

Miss Jones pointed to a bread-and-butter plate filled with plain cracker biscuits. "I'm told these help, but so far all evidence is to the contrary."

"How long until you leave us?"

Miss Jones wiped fresh tears from her eyes. "Mr. Hayes has pulled some strings with personnel, and I'm here until he finds someone to replace me."

"That won't be easy, Miss Jones. All the best. Truly."

Miss Jones teared up again at Martha's well-wishes. "And to you, Miss Berry."

Martha smiled and took a deep breath for courage as she knocked on Mr. Hayes's door. There was a muffled, "Come in," and she opened it.

"Miss Berry. Thank you for coming so promptly." Rutherford Hayes stood politely and waved a hand. "Please take a seat. Would you like a cup of tea or coffee?"

"No, thank you."

Mr. Hayes returned to his seat before taking a long puff on his pipe. "The thing is, Miss Berry, and I won't beat around the bush, I find myself unexpectedly without a secretary." He paused and looked to the ceiling as if he were about to embark on a philosophical lecture and he was thinking about the best way to start. "The usual way of these things being announced is for a girl to let everyone know she's engaged and then determine a date for the marriage sometime in the near future, which has always given men like me time to consider a replacement. It's happened with lots of girls over the years, unfortunately. They get swept off their feet by a chap and don't want to come back to work."

Martha couldn't be polite about such a situation. "Isn't it more that they aren't allowed to work once they're married, rather than them choosing to stay at home, Mr. Hayes?"

"Yes, yes, of course," he replied, as if he understood the point Martha was making. Martha doubted it. What man could understand the wrench of finding love and losing a career all at the same time? "That goes without saying. Miss Jones is a marvelous young woman. Always two steps ahead of me. Knows what I'm thinking before I even have to ask for it. I'm very sorry to lose her. Although, even if being married wasn't an issue, she would have left anyway when the baby arrived. Damn shame." Mr. Hayes took a puff and rested his pipe on the cut-crystal ashtray on his desk. "The thing is, Miss Berry. You did such a sterling job when you filled in for her that I was rather hoping I could tear you away from your position as script girl on *As the Sun Sets* to be my secretary."

Suddenly there was a strange buzzing in Martha's ears. Mr. Hayes's lips were moving and she studied them as a scientist might study a bug under a microscope, trying to make out what he was saying and wondering why no sound was coming out of his mouth, and then the buzzing became a pounding heartbeat that rose up in her ears like a throbbing bass drum was being played in an invisible chair right next to her, beating so hard inside her skull that she thought it might crack in two.

His secretary.

"Your *secretary*?"

Mr. Hayes leaned forward and rested his elbows on his desk. His suit jacket had leather elbow patches. She'd never noticed them before. A look of concern furrowed his brow.

She heard, ever so faintly, "Miss Berry? Are you quite all right?"

She drew in a deep breath to see if it helped. It did, a little. "You're asking me to be your new secretary." She had to hear it again to confirm she hadn't imagined the whole thing.

"Yes." Mr. Hayes cleared his throat and smiled proudly because he was a man and of course he would think there was no greater compliment for a woman like Martha, an older woman, a single woman, a woman who had missed out on so much in the way of a life, than to be asked to be the secretary to the broadcaster's head of drama.

"I must admit, and Miss Jones recently reminded me of this, that you might have been overlooked all these years you've been working here. Your light may have been buried under a bushel, as they say. But having worked closely with you for those two weeks when you-know-who was in Tasmania—on her honeymoon, it turns out—I have come to a new appreciation of your talents, Miss Berry. We're going to be very busy during the next twelve months. There are plans for a new series of Charles Dickens adaptations for the evenings and we have writers working on some children's plays too. It'll only get busier and I'll be needing someone with experience and maturity to help me in this role."

"No!" Suddenly Mr. Hayes's office door was flung wide open. Martha and Mr. Hayes startled and turned to find Miss Jones standing in the doorway, her hand fisted on her hip. A look of fury had narrowed her eyes and pinched her mouth into a tight line.

"What on earth?" Mr. Hayes said. "Miss Jones? What are you doing?"

"Forgive me for bursting in like this, but I couldn't help over-hearing your conversation."

"The door was closed, Miss Jones," Mr. Hayes replied, perplexed.

"Well." She huffed. "I had my ear pressed to the door. You simply cannot make Miss Berry your new secretary."

"Whyever not?"

"Because she's too good to be your secretary, that's why."

Mr. Hayes looked like he'd been slapped across the face. Verbally, perhaps he had.

"For goodness' sake, Miss Jones. Come in and shut the door."

She obliged and sat in the chair next to Martha. Martha could do nothing but stare at this fierce young woman and marvel at her.

There was not a shred of politeness in her demeanor and Martha envied it. What would her own life have been like if she had Miss Jones's tenacity? What would her life have been like if she'd been born in 1936 and not 1906?

Miss Jones turned to look at Martha and it was all Martha could do not to burst into tears. Her world was spinning backward on its axis. Until *As the Sun Sets*, no one had ever spoken up for her like this, defended her, fought for her. How was it possible that Miss Jones and the cast had become her fiercest allies and champions?

Mr. Hayes shot to his feet and flapped his hands. "Settle down, Miss Jones. It's not healthy for you to get so excited in your present state. Not to mention you almost gave me a heart attack, bursting in the way you did."

"I apologize, Mr. Hayes, but I simply had to before Martha said yes to your offer."

Miss Jones and Mr. Hayes turned to stare at Martha.

"Were you going to accept my offer?" Mr. Hayes asked.

Martha stared at him. Her mother's words echoed in her head. "You could have gone to university, Martha. You were smart enough. You're still smart enough. Things were different for girls like you back then."

And then she heard George Eliot. "It's never too late to be what you might have been."

Martha looked at Mr. Hayes and Miss Jones in turn. "I was going to say thank you but no."

Mr. Hayes looked from one woman to the other as if he'd been baffled by the opposite sex his entire life. He put an elbow on his desk and rested a palm on his forehead. "Dear, oh dear."

Miss Jones beamed. "The thing is, Mr. Hayes, Martha absolutely must stay where she is. With *As the Sun Sets*."

"Whatever for?" Mr. Hayes replied. "We'll be bringing in a new producer and writer and anyone can be a script girl. But not everyone can fill your shoes, Miss Jones."

"That's very flattering, but you have to know what's really been going on. She's the one responsible for the success of *As the Sun Sets*. Not Quentin Quinn. He's fooled everyone from the very beginning. Miss Berry picked up the pieces, chose the cast, and has written every single script."

Miss Jones reached a hand to one of Martha's and squeezed it. "Miss Berry has been the heart and soul of *As the Sun Sets* from the very beginning. Haven't you?"

Martha had already said no to Mr. Hayes's job offer, so what else did she have to lose? If she'd imagined a moment like this, she would have thought she'd be so nervous she'd be unable to utter even a syllable. But suddenly the pounding in her head eased and her hearing was as clear as a bell. A warmth blossomed inside her, and for the first time in a long time it wasn't a hot flash.

"Is this true, Miss Berry?"

"It's been me all along, Mr. Hayes. I've written every word of every script. I cast the show and I even chose the theme music. I worked from the basic storyline that Mr. Quinn outlined but ignored the parts that were, frankly, ridiculous."

Mr. Hayes simply stared at Martha, openmouthed. Miss Jones's grip on her fingers became more reassuring.

In for a penny, in for a pound. "From the very first week, Quentin Quinn's problems with alcohol were evident to me. We were weeks into production and he hadn't written more than a few minutes of the first show. I didn't want to see it fail, not after we'd assembled such a wonderful cast and after I'd been given the opportunity to work so closely on a new program."

"Quinn's a drinker?"

How on earth could Mr. Hayes be shocked by such news? "Sadly, yes, and while I have little respect for the young man in a professional sense, I am worried for his health."

"That time he vomited right here in my office." It was a statement, not a question.

"He would rattle off a few ideas to me about what direction he wanted the drama to go in, and then, while he was at his long liquid lunches, I would write the scripts and let him think later they were his words. Those who drink too much often don't remember what happened before they became inebriated. I've worked with enough men to know that to be true."

Mr. Hayes slapped himself on the forehead and then winced. "Your revelation explains one thing. That damned Vera Percy storyline. I didn't even think about how a twenty-five-year-old chap could know so much about what an older woman was going through. I assumed he was simply an excellent dramatist."

"She's the excellent dramatist, Mr. Hayes." Miss Jones couldn't contain herself. "Miss Berry is walking in the footsteps of the magnificent Gwen Meredith. She should be celebrated and promoted. What a coup for the broadcaster to have two wonderful series written by two wonderful women! Imagine the publicity possibilities!"

"I could see no choice but to let Mr. Quinn—and everyone else—continue to believe it was him all along. It seemed easier than exposing and humiliating him. I could see no winners in that scenario."

"She must stay with *As the Sun Sets* as the writer and producer," Miss Jones interjected with some urgency. "We can't let the show be handed over to someone new who might want to make all sorts of changes or even bring in his own script girl. We want it to stay just as it is. Our listeners wouldn't hear of it, Mr. Hayes, not when they love Jack and Vera and Betty and Ernie and the Antonello family so."

"Was that your idea, the Italians?" Mr. Hayes asked.

Martha nodded. "I believed the inclusion of a migrant family might help build bridges with real migrants who are coming here in droves from Europe. All they are trying to do is find a safe place in which to raise their children, but there doesn't seem to be much understanding, at times, of that. And since the show is set in Sydney, I believed it was realistic."

"Quite. So you're saying you've covered for Quinn all this time?"

"Since the day he started. If I can speak honestly, Mr. Hayes, I do believe he was thrown in at the deep end without a tightrope." There he was in her head. Kent Stone.

"I bear some responsibility for that, is that what you're saying?"

"That's not for me to judge, Mr. Hayes. All I've ever cared about is making *As the Sun Sets* the best serial it can be for our loyal listeners. I didn't set out to lie or usurp Mr. Quinn's role. I did what had to be done to ensure the show went to air."

"I don't understand what happened to him." Mr. Hayes was perplexed. "He came so highly recommended. My own son went to university with him and said he was a powerhouse, writing and directing two productions a year when they were students. I thought Quinn could easily whip out a weep-while-you-sweep drama at his tender age. I mean, it's not much work to write for women, is it? They'd listen in no matter what we put to air. Out of habit."

Martha fought the sudden urge to slap someone. Mr. Hayes's son had recommended Quinn for the position? *That* was his qualification?

There was a long moment of silence. Miss Jones squeezed

Martha's fingers so hard she was beginning to feel pins and needles in them.

"I do believe, Mr. Hayes, that habits could easily be broken if *As the Sun Sets* didn't meet the high standards our listeners expect. And there are alternatives on the commercial stations. *When a Girl Marries*, for instance."

Miss Jones sighed. "'. . . dedicated to all those who are in love and to those who can remember.' It's such a wonderful show."

Mr. Hayes shuddered. "The last thing we want is for listeners to be turning to the commercial stations. You've created a dedicated legion of fans, Miss Berry."

Pride swelled in Martha's chest, and this time it didn't cometh before a fall. She deserved the praise and let herself feel it. In secret, despite all the odds, she had created a successful radio program. It was her dialogue that zinged. Or sparkled. She didn't care which. That letter that Quentin Quinn had framed, the one personally signed by Charles Moses? It should have *her* name on it, not Quentin Quinn's.

"I have," she replied.

"And I believe one of your most dedicated listeners is Mrs. Hayes. And Mrs. Moses. And the wives of many of the board members too. If I tinkered with anything on their favorite show, I'd never hear the end of it."

"There's no need to tinker with anything," Miss Jones said abruptly and finally let go of Martha's hand as she began to gesticulate. "Let the television people make the announcement that Quentin Quinn is going to be creating a new police drama and that his protégé, Miss Martha Berry, will be taking over the show. You could simply say that Miss Berry has been an integral part of the behind-the-scenes work on the serial and Mr. Quinn has left detailed instructions for storylines going forward. You can even say that Quentin Quinn will still be overseeing the program from his new role, if that helps. And then surely there could be an article in *ABC Weekly* featuring Miss Berry." Miss Jones lifted her hands in the air and stretched her arms out wide. "'The ABC's new woman radio star.'"

"That's quite good, Miss Jones." Mr. Hayes reached for a pencil and scribbled something down on a notepad by his phone before looking up, a wistful expression on his face. "You're going to be missed."

"When the ridiculous marriage bar is lifted, I'll be back. If you'll have me."

Mr. Hayes sighed and smiled. "In a heartbeat."

"Wait a moment," Martha said. Mr. Hayes looked up from his notepad. Miss Jones looked to Martha with wide eyes. "I haven't said yes."

"I assumed that was a given," Mr. Hayes said. "Not that I have a choice, it seems, but you're an excellent choice, Miss Berry."

That pride in Martha's chest swelled and flooded over her in a wave. "I have certain conditions that will need to be met."

"Name them." Miss Jones pointed to Mr. Hayes's notepad. "Take notes, Mr. Hayes."

For the first time in her life, Martha was in a position of power and she was going to use it. "I'd like you to announce that *As the Sun Sets* will continue with me as the producer and writer and that I'll have an all-woman team behind me."

Mr. Hayes dropped his pencil.

Chapter 33

IN WHICH QUENTIN QUINN RIDES OFF INTO THE SUNSET.

M rs. Barry?"

Martha didn't feel the need to grind her teeth or take a deep breath or swallow away feelings of annoyance at Quentin Quinn anymore. Since the day he'd arrived, he'd failed to call her by her name. Now, in the short time they had left together, she had resolved to fail to hear him unless he addressed her correctly.

She continued typing her memo to personnel. It was titled "New staff on *As the Sun Sets*." It was of the utmost importance. There was no time to waste now that she'd had agreement from Rutherford Hayes. She had to ensure he approved her request before someone else got in his ear to change his mind or before he forgot. It wasn't that he was a careless man—far from it. It was just that he had a hundred different requests every day for more staff and more budget and more studio time and more actors and more musicians, so she had to make sure her request was still top of mind when she slipped the memo across his desk.

Once word had gotten around that there was to be a change at the head of *As the Sun Sets* and that there were staff vacancies, applications had flooded in from, it seemed, every young woman in the organization. Some had even knocked on her door to plead their case personally. One of them had been the horrible Miss Jane Carver.

The day before, the young woman had walked into Martha's office without so much as even a knock and sidled up to her desk.

"Miss Berry?"

Martha had looked up from a script to find Miss Carver's supercilious smile leering down at her. She stood so she would be face-to-face with her.

"What can I do for you, Miss Carver?"

Miss Carver put an envelope on Martha's desk and nodded toward it. "I understand you'll be looking for new staff to work on *As the Sun Sets*. I wondered if you would accept my application. I've been a secretary here for more than two years now and I know the ropes. I have an excellent typing speed and I'm extremely proficient at shorthand. I believe I'll be an asset to the program."

Martha kept her face blank. She would rather have Quentin Quinn back than work with this young woman. And in that moment, Martha decided that perhaps someone should point out to Miss Carver the error of her ways.

"Thank you for your application, Miss Carver, but all the available positions have been filled." Martha picked up the envelope and handed it back without even opening it. "And if I might give you some words of advice."

"Advice?"

"I've been at the ABC a long time. Twenty-four years, as a matter of fact, and there's much I've learned. People here are judged by their actions, Miss Carver. One will never feel truly satisfied in one's work if one has to walk all over people to get ahead. Spreading rumors and false information may be satisfying in the short term, like drinking a very sweet cup of tea perhaps, but it'll do no good in the long run. It'll rot one's teeth."

Miss Carver looked at Martha in confusion for a moment until the penny dropped. Her lips curved up in a sneer.

"I don't know what you're accusing me of, but—"

Martha moved swiftly, rounding her desk, taking Miss Carver by the elbow, and ushering her out into the hallway. She closed the office door behind her with a slam.

No, Martha thought as she looked back on the satisfaction of rejecting Miss Carver. She knew exactly where to look for new staff. The Calendar Girls.

She had April in mind for the new receptionist role and May to step up as script girl. A peacemaker like May was perfect for running interference for Martha when she was caught up writing or producing or attending meetings. And June? She had big plans for June too.

"*Mrs. Barry!*" Quentin Quinn shouted again from his office.

Once again, she failed to hear him. She took a little delight in the agitation in his voice. When he finally stomped to her desk, she continued to type.

"I would like a cup of tea."

Martha stopped typing. Quentin Quinn was red-faced and looked slightly wild. Was he nervous about taking up his new role in television? If he was, he would never let it show. Martha took a good look at him, examined his expression. Was it nervousness or impatience? The polite thing to do might have been to jump from her chair and rush over to the kettle, urging him to return to his office and assuring him she would bring the cup of tea promptly, and did he need any more assistance with packing up his office?

But Martha was done with being polite. She was done with being overlooked and underestimated by men like Quentin Quinn, those young enough to be her son yet who acted as if she were the child.

"I beg your pardon?"

"A. Cup. Of. Tea." He enunciated each word with a hiss. "I haven't left yet so I am still your boss. You must still answer to me and fulfill my requests, Mrs. Barry."

"It's *Miss* Berry, Mr. Quinn. As I have pointed out to you many times before."

"Miss. Mrs. What difference does it make?"

Martha got to her feet. Standing like this, she looked down at the top of his head. He must have found it suddenly intimidating because he took a step back.

"Because if I were a Mrs., I would not be allowed to hold any position in this place. I would be barred from working here. So it's Miss. And I am proud to be a Miss, Mr. Quinn. And I would appreciate it if you would finally, even on your last day, get it right."

"*Miss* Berry then."

"Yes, Mr. Quinn?"

"I would like a cup of tea while I pack up my things. If you don't mind."

"Certainly."

....

There really wasn't that much to pack. He insisted on taking the ring binders that held his copies of the scripts with him, no doubt as some kind of souvenir of the beginnings of his brilliant career in the broadcasting arts. His ashtray, a collection of notebooks and pencils, and his framed letter from General Manager Charles Moses.

Martha had organized for a trolley to be delivered, and she piled the boxes on it and directed the deliveryman to Quentin Quinn's new offices in a just-renovated part of the building where the new television staff were being housed. The radio employees were inundated with rumors about the facilities that had been created for the television drama department. Freshly painted offices, important-size desks, a generously stacked stationery cupboard, and all the tea and coffee they could drink. It was often difficult to unpack fact from fiction, truth from professional jealousy when the shiny new thing garnered all the attention. It made everyone in radio feel like overlooked spinsters, something Martha had been quite resigned to accepting as her lot in life. Until *As the Sun Sets* had given her a voice.

And she had so much more to say.

"Well, that's it." Quentin Quinn slipped on his suit jacket and patted his pocket to ensure his cigarettes were inside it. "I'll be off then."

Martha moved to the side of her desk and clasped her hands in front of her. "I believe it's traditional to say break a leg, Mr. Quinn."

He looked at her for a moment and then reluctantly let out a little smile. "Thank you. If anything comes for me here, I expect you'll send it on to my new office in the television department? I don't know yet who my secretary will be, but I'll ensure she makes contact with you."

"Of course." *Pity the poor woman*, Martha thought.

"Right." Quentin Quinn nodded and walked to the door. After a moment, he turned back. "You know, you remind me of my mother."

"I'm sure you mean that as a compliment."

"You are both the most incessant nags. Both of you believe you've had something to do with the success I've had in my career."

"Whatever gave me that idea?" Martha replied.

When Quentin Quinn laughed, Martha joined him.

"Break a leg, Miss Berry."

And then he left.

Chapter 34

IN WHICH MARTHA BERRY, PRODUCER AND
WRITER OF *AS THE SUN SETS*,
EXERCISES HER POWER.

I couldn't possibly." April gasped and then held her breath for so long that Martha feared she might faint.

"You can and you will. I would very much like you to come work with me on *As the Sun Sets*. I need someone smart and polite to answer the phone and the hundreds of letters we get every week. I simply can't do it all anymore and I won't have to. I've negotiated with Rutherford Hayes to have two staff working for me."

April flopped into the chair at Martha's desk. "I don't know, Miss Berry. I have great respect for you, and I simply adore *As the Sun Sets*. But what would I say to all those people who call on the telephone asking about the show? And . . . and the actors! I couldn't possibly talk to famous people!"

"Whyever not? They're just people."

"No, they're not. They're fancy and rich. What on earth would I say when, I don't know, Miss Connors calls?"

"You will say, 'Welcome to *As the Sun Sets*. April Atkinson speaking. How may I help you?'"

April giggled. "I learned that at secretarial college. That's not what I mean. I mean . . . oh, I don't know what I mean."

Martha put her elbows on her desk and leaned forward. "April. You are more than capable. I know you don't believe it, but you are a very smart young woman. I don't know who put it into your head that your only role in life is to look pretty, but it's not. You are so much more than an ornament." April simply stared at Martha as tears welled. "I'd love to have you on my team. Please say yes."

"Mr. Pattison will be very disappointed in me for leaving the music department. He didn't even like it when I took my annual leave. There was so much to do when I got back that it took me weeks to catch up."

"April, you mustn't put any disappointment he might experience before your own career. You're a young woman with every opportunity ahead of you. Both at work and in life."

"But . . . I won't be able to work for you forever, Miss Berry. I'll have to resign when I get married, and then where will you be? You need someone more reliable than me."

"Is there some news I've missed out on, April? Are you getting married?"

"No, not at the moment. But I might." Her shoulders sagged. "I hope to, one day. All my life, that's what my father told me I must do. Get married to secure my future and produce grandchildren. I suppose I listened to him when he said that was all I could do. But it's the way the world works for girls like me, isn't it? What would be the point in working so hard to get ahead if it'll all be for nothing?"

As much as Martha hated the fact of it, April had a point. Would this young woman take the advice of someone old enough to be her mother, who might have accumulated some wisdom about the world and what it did to women with ambition? She had been surrounded her entire career by women who'd had their jobs snatched out from under them the minute they married. The choice couldn't have been clearer: marriage or work. And never the twain should meet. How could they not have felt cheated?

"The national broadcaster isn't the only place in Sydney that makes programs for the radio. The government is very strict about married women working, but some private businesses don't give a hoot. With the experience you gain here, you could work anywhere you choose. Married or otherwise."

April's eyes widened. "My mother went back to work after she had me and then my two sisters." April drifted into a memory. "As soon as we were all at school, she put on her stockings and her suit and went back to the office she'd worked in before. It's an accountancy firm. Her boss told her he hadn't been able to find anyone half as good to replace her, and he welcomed her back with open arms. She always said if she stayed home one day longer she would have gone mad." April snapped out of her reverie and met Martha's gaze. "I suppose she didn't like having children. Being stuck at home with us all day."

"Perhaps it was more that she liked being more than one thing. She loved being your mother, but she also loved being a working woman." Martha thought. "What did your father say about it?"

"He was furious. But Mum didn't listen to him. She likes having her own money and not having to ask her husband for a few pounds when she wants to buy a new suit for work." April chuckled. "Perhaps that's why he's been so hard on me, Miss Berry. Because he couldn't make his wife do what he wanted her to do. I do believe I'm more like my mother than I thought. I like being a working woman too." A new determination filled April's voice that Martha hadn't heard before. "I like walking into the building every morning and accomplishing things. Fixing things that Mr. Pattison, god bless him, has forgotten. Typing up letters for him to sign. Putting records away. Ordering new ones. Doing all the things he forgets to do."

"Exactly," Martha said. "I want you to bring all those skills to this position, to help me make *As the Sun Sets* even better. Will you say yes?"

The smile on April's young face was all the answer Martha needed.

"It's never too late, you know," Martha added, "to be what you want to be."

Martha picked up the receiver of the telephone on her desk and slipped it between her shoulder and her cheek. She'd been changing the typewriter ribbon and her fingers were smudged with black ink. The things were as fiddly as kittens.

"Martha Berry," she answered.

"Miss Berry, it's me, Miss Jones. Mrs. Ross. Mr. Hayes is wondering if you could stop by his office."

"Right now?" Martha looked down at her inky fingers. A passerby might have assumed she'd just been arrested and was in the process of having her fingerprints taken.

"If you are free." Miss Jones's voice dropped. "Handsy Hooper has arrived in high dudgeon. Mr. Hayes wants to put the two of you in a room to sort things out."

Martha settled her nerves. She had been waiting for this. "I'm on my way."

Less than five minutes later, her hands scrubbed clean in the ladies' room on the way, Martha crossed the reception area outside Mr. Hayes's office and stood before Miss Jones's desk. The secretary cocked her head to one side in the direction of the closed door, but it wasn't really necessary. Handsy Hooper's shouts could be heard loud and clear through the walls. He was yelling at such a volume she might have heard him down on the street if she'd been walking by the building.

"How long's he been going off like this?" Martha asked.

Miss Jones checked her watch. "Ten minutes. And that's not including the phone call early this morning and the succession of supportive visits from his colleagues."

"The other technicians are standing by him?" Martha couldn't believe what she was hearing. They all knew what he was like, the things he'd done to women. They'd all witnessed his crude behavior and his lewd jokes.

"He's put the word out that all the men are going to be sacked and replaced by girls."

"That is the most—"

Mr. Hayes's door swung open. Hooper's shouting grew louder and over the top of it Mr. Hayes said, "Miss Berry?" He waved her in and she followed. Had he rolled his eyes at her or was she imagining things?

Mr. Hayes closed the door behind her. Handsy Hooper was pacing up and down in front of Mr. Hayes's desk like a rat in a cage. Martha was surprised he hadn't worn a rut in the carpet. When he saw her, he stopped, lifted an arm, and pointed an accusing finger at her. His lips curled into a sneer and his eyes were narrow with fury. "What's *that woman* doing here?"

"Please, Mr. Hooper. Take a seat. I'm sure we can settle this if we all keep calm."

Martha glanced around the room. The office was large but not that large, and Hooper stalked from wall to wall like a cornered jungle cat. She suddenly felt uneasy and remained standing near the door.

"We can settle this all right," Hooper snarled. "You just tell that woman that she's got no right to take me off the show. Any show. She's not the boss of me." He hooked his index fingers into the belt loops of his trousers and hoicked them up, as if the move might make him appear taller. "You tell her, Hayes, that I don't answer to her. Or any woman."

"Please, Hooper. Calm down," Mr. Hayes implored.

"Calm down? That woman's got me sacked. And you've let her. Why should I calm down?"

"You're not sacked. For goodness' sake, stop characterizing it that way. Now I'm not going to say it again. Sit down in that chair or I will march around my desk and shove you into it. Understood?"

Martha had never heard Mr. Hayes speak in such a way and clearly neither had Hooper, for it shocked him into silence and then, a moment later, submission. When Hooper finally lowered himself into a chair, every limb still quivering, she moved the empty chair that was positioned next to his and placed it at a distance at which she felt safe.

"Now, Mr. Hooper. The new producer of *As the Sun Sets*, Miss Berry, has simply requested that a girl be trained up in the technical aspects of the recording studio." He threw a glance at Martha, clearly on the hunt for moral support. "Seeing as it attracts so many female listeners."

She had June in mind for the role. The young woman brooked no nonsense from anyone and had the right amount of gumption. And, behind her fears, she was smart as a whip. Martha believed June was a scared young woman who needed prodding out of her shell, rather like a hermit crab. And Martha believed she was just the right person to do it too.

Hooper flared up again. "You tell me how a listener in Townsville or Tasmania can tell if it's a man pushing the buttons or a girl. It makes no difference."

Martha had heard every possible argument over the years as to why women weren't suited to undertake technical roles in radio production—the equipment was too heavy for their delicate frames, or production work was too complex for women who weren't naturally scientifically minded—and had decided that times needed to change. If a woman could work an oven, she could press buttons and turn knobs and fit wax cylinders to a recording device. One hardly needed the strength of Tarzan or the wisdom of Solomon to perform that role. And anyway, hadn't women proved during the war that they could ably take over the tasks once thought to be the sole domain of men?

Martha saw her opportunity and took it. "That's my exact point, Mr. Hooper. A listener in Townsville or Tasmania can't tell if it's a man pushing the buttons or a girl. It makes no difference at all. I believe being a technician is a skill any girl can master, if someone like you can."

Hooper acted as though she wasn't even in the room. "That woman doesn't tell me where I work."

"No, but I do, and once your replacement has been trained up, you're moving to sports."

"I'm not moving anywhere," Hooper bellowed.

Martha slowly got to her feet. She had spent her entire career babying men and she'd finally had enough. More than enough. She positioned her hands on her hips and glared down at Handsy Hooper. As Miles Franklin said, "It's a sign of your own worth sometimes if you are hated by the right people."

"As a matter of fact, you are, Mr. Hooper. The truth is, every woman in this place is absolutely sick and tired of the disrespect you have shown us. It's not just the snide looks and the insults muttered under your breath that you think no one else can hear. We've heard every single one. You have touched just about every woman in this place in the most inappropriate manner. You have groped our bottoms and pinched them, pressed against us in doorways and lifts, in staircases and kitchens and, yes, even in studios. And we are mightily sick of it. I will not have that happen on my show. When I accepted Mr. Hayes's offer to write and produce it, I made that very clear to Mr. Hayes, which is why you are being moved elsewhere. Your own behavior has caused this chain reaction, Mr. Hooper. You have only yourself to blame."

He turned to Mr. Hayes, his eyes bulging. "Are you just going to sit there and let her say rubbish like that?"

There was a long silence. "Yes," Mr. Hayes replied calmly.

"You mean to tell me you're going to let that woman, that dried-up old prune spinster, that . . . lesbian . . . surround herself with girls? You know what people will say about that, oh yes you do."

Mr. Hayes pressed his palms to his desk and slowly rose to his full height. He wasn't an especially tall man, but he seemed to suddenly tower over Hooper.

"Mr. Hooper. If I hear one more word along those lines, by George I'll . . . If I hear you spreading such malicious gossip anywhere inside this building or out, you will be summarily sacked. You have my absolute word. Now I suggest you pull yourself together and leave. And before you do, Miss Berry deserves an apology."

Hooper finally met Martha's eyes. She saw a look of pure contempt but didn't blink. He would never again see her scared.

"I do apologize, Miss Berry." He slowly looked her up and down and stormed out. Mr. Hayes and Martha cringed as he slammed the door so hard it rattled the building's old windows.

Martha sat, half in shock, half in a furious rage that had her heart thudding against her ribs. Mr. Hayes lifted the receiver on the telephone and politely asked Miss Jones for two cups of coffee. He put the receiver down and sighed.

"Well, that was uncomfortable." He chuckled and Martha joined him, grateful for something, anything, to break the tension still lingering in the room like stale cigarette smoke.

"People never like being confronted with their own failings," Martha said.

"Is that all true? About his behavior?"

Martha nodded. It was time to tell the truth. "Every word. He did it to me. Years ago. And he's worse with the younger women." Was it her place to tell Mr. Hayes about April's recent experience? She decided it wasn't.

"I expect he thinks it's a bit of fun," Mr. Hayes said, shaking his head in disbelief. "A workplace joke."

Martha's righteous anger flared. "And I suppose women and girls just don't have a sense of humor."

"What I mean is, what men think of as horseplay might be interpreted differently, that's all."

"If it was horseplay, wouldn't he indulge in it with all his colleagues, not just the female ones?"

Mr. Hayes thought on it.

"Tell me, Mr. Hayes. Has Hooper ever grabbed your breast so hard you discover bruises when you get out of the bath?" Martha blushed with the awkwardness of speaking so intimately about her body, but she was not going to hold back any longer. Hooper's behavior had to be made public. He must not be allowed to get away with it any longer.

Mr. Hayes was silent.

"Or has he squeezed up against you as you walk through a doorway, getting so close that you can feel his arousal pressing into your stomach?"

"Good god, Miss Berry. Why didn't you say something? Or why didn't the others? If it's been going on so long, why did none of the girls say anything to their superiors?"

"I did. A long time ago. I was told that I should ignore him and he would stop."

"He didn't, I assume?"

"No. It emboldened him."

"I have daughters of my own out in the workforce. To think there might be men acting in the exact same way to them . . . It's unfathomable. I'm certain they would have told me if anything like that had happened to them."

"I suggest you ask them, Mr. Hayes. You might be shocked at what you hear."

"Well, at least I hope I've proved to you that I can be sympathetic to a woman's troubles in the workforce."

"It's appreciated, Mr. Hayes. Truly."

He sighed. "Times are changing, aren't they, Miss Berry? I don't know if things were better back in the day or just . . . easier. Perhaps I'm too old for this job. Who'll want a head of radio drama when television takes over and people watch all those American shows in the evenings instead of crowding around the wireless and listening in to adaptations of Charles Dickens or Agatha Christie?"

Martha had thought about that too. Times were moving fast and who knew what changes television would bring? All she needed to know was that she had her own little corner of radio in which to make a difference. That would be enough.

"There will always be radio. I'm sure of it. And if you want to be in touch with what young people are thinking," Martha said as she stood and tucked in her chair, "ask those daughters of yours. Or their daughters. I find the opinions of young people entirely enlightening."

"Of course I will!" May skipped to Martha and threw her arms around her in a tight hug. "I'd love to come work with you, Miss Berry. A script girl? Whatever does that mean? Oh!" She giggled and then let go. "Never mind. I don't care as long as you're my boss. I can't believe it! A woman boss!"

"And a pay raise," Martha said. "Don't forget about that."

"Wait until I tell my parents. And my granny! They'll be over the moon."

Martha had to smile at May's enthusiasm. She could only wish she'd had a woman boss when she'd begun her career in radio. If she had, she might have had dreams of a real career much earlier in her working life. She might have been inspired to branch out, to try new things, perhaps to come up with an idea for a new serial and write the scripts. So many years had passed in which any ambition had been thwarted. She wouldn't let the same happen to the Calendar Girls. They were young. She would make sure they had chances that had been denied her. She didn't have daughters to shepherd through life, but she could help April, May, and June rise to their full potential.

That was what Martha could pass on to the next generation: the hope of something more.

Chapter 35

IN WHICH AUSTRALIA FINDS OUT THAT THE
CREATIVE MIND BEHIND *AS THE SUN SETS*
IS NONE OTHER THAN UNASSUMING SCRIPT
GIRL MISS MARTHA BERRY.

Martha?"

Martha gripped the telephone receiver. She would know that voice anywhere. It was Mrs. Tilley from next door. A lightning bolt of fear streaked up Martha's spine and gave her an instant headache. "What's happened, Mrs. Tilley? Is Mum okay?"

"Stop your panicking. She's perfectly fine. Although you nearly gave her a heart attack, that's what."

Nothing was making sense. "A heart attack?"

"Well, we're all sitting here in my living room listening to *Blue Hills*—Mrs. Ward made an apple cake for after our egg and lettuce sandwiches with that nice dressing she makes too—and the music plays and we all look at each other and nod because we never say anything when *Blue Hills* ends and *As the Sun Sets* begins—not a word in case we miss something—and then all of a sudden, we hear the music and then, knock me down with a feather, Kent Stone says your name! Right there on the radio! And that's when your poor mother almost had the heart attack."

Martha opened her mouth to speak but could hear a jostling down the line and then a crack as someone dropped the phone and the receiver swung against the wall in the hallway of Mrs. Tilley's home. She could see the floral runner and the black-japanned floorboards underneath, the telephone table with its small vinyl-covered seat on one side.

Kent Stone had just announced, "The ABC presents *As the Sun Sets*, created by Quentin Quinn. Written by Martha Berry."

Of course, if she'd been allowed to write what she really wanted to, Kent Stone's announcement would have been: "The ABC presents *As the Sun Sets*, in which we find out for the first time that the creative mind behind the drama is none other than Script Girl Miss Martha Berry."

At least that was how Martha might have written it if it were happening in the serial. Talk about a plot twist.

Instead, the announcement of her ascension wasn't an announcement at all, not really. The broadcaster had arranged for a story to go out to the newspapers just as Miss Jones had suggested, that the young creative mind behind the success of *As the Sun Sets* was heading off to the bright lights of the new medium of television to create an Australian drama featuring an all-Australian cast for local audiences.

Mr. Quinn will be preparing scripts and casting actors for a homespun police drama that will feature stories ripped from the headlines about Australia's own criminal underworld.

Martha had smiled to herself when she'd read the article, set out on a whole page in *ABC Weekly* along with a photograph of Quentin Quinn posing behind a typewriter with a pencil positioned behind one ear. He was acting the part of a newsman, just as he'd acted the part of a writer when she'd worked with him. *Good luck to him*, she thought without any malice. It was someone else's job to cover for his inadequacies now.

"Martha dear? Is that you?" Martha couldn't make out whether her mother was laughing or crying. Perhaps both. "You wrote today's episode, Martha?"

"I did, Mum."

Violet sniffled and then laughed. "Oh my goodness. Oh my goodness. Am I going to hear your name on the radio every day?"

Martha laughed too. "Yes, Mum. Twice a day, in fact."

The phone jostled again. "We're so proud of you, Martha. Who can believe it? Little Martha Berry from next door with such an important job."

"Thank you, Mrs. Ward. That's so kind of you to say. But I wouldn't have this job in the first place if it wasn't for loyal listeners like you and Mrs. Tilley and Mum. And people all over the country."

She heard, faintly, "For goodness' sake, give the phone back to Violet."

"It's me again, dear. We'll celebrate tonight when you get home."

"Of course we will, Mum. I'll see you later."

Martha hung up and sat back in her chair, letting her gaze drift to the ceiling. Thank goodness her mother was all right. Perhaps a little too much excitement for one day, but that was completely understandable. She was proud of her daughter and Martha let herself feel that pride. It was almost too much for Martha too.

She'd taken care not to trouble Violet with the machinations of Quentin Quinn's promotion to television, the rumors about what might happen to her in the wake of his departure and her subsequent promotion. Every episode of her own drama would have made her mother worry as intensely as she worried about Vera's health and Betty's romantic entanglements.

Martha couldn't contain the shiver of excitement that tingled every toe and every finger.

Why did it feel as if she had waited her whole life for this moment?

Every disappointment, every setback, every knockback she'd ever had had somehow brought her to this day. This momentous day. Up until now, her life had been a series of what-ifs. What if she'd fallen in love? What if she'd married? What if she hadn't answered the newspaper advertisement for secretaries at the national broadcaster way back in 1932? What if her father hadn't died? Might she have stayed longer at school and taken up a real career? Or gone to university?

Her father. Would he be proud of her if he were still alive? Would he have shed a tear or two just as Violet had over her success? Would he have bragged to his mates down at the pub that his daughter was writing for a radio serial? Or would he be disappointed that she'd never been chosen by a man, that she'd never married, that she'd never given him grandchildren? Would she have been a disappointment to a simple man who'd only ever wanted to live a simple life?

There was a knock at the door to her office and Martha looked up as she wiped away her tears.

"Come in," she called and the door was thrust wide open. Kent Stone, Miss Connors, Marilyn Calthorpe, Cary Sullivan, and Alex Paulson walked in. Kent held aloft a bottle of Barossa Pearl. Miss Connors was carrying something wrapped in gold and bearing a ribbon almost as big as the package itself. Marilyn held a cake tin in her hands. Cary was juggling six champagne coupes, and Alex held a basket of fruit overflowing with apple-green grapes and plump strawberries and oranges as big as tennis balls and bright yellow bananas. On top lay a bouquet of flowers.

"May we come in, boss?" Kent Stone asked, and all Martha could do was nod and stand to greet them all.

The actors laid their offerings on her desk and crowded around her, chatting excitedly. She hadn't yet moved into Quentin Quinn's old office. She was still at her secretary's desk, with her typewriter and her stack of scripts and her carbon paper to one side, her teacup and saucer and a vase filled with flowers from Mrs. Tilley's garden on the other.

"We thought today was worthy of a celebration," Miss Connors said as she slipped an arm around Martha's shoulders and squeezed tight. "To our new producer and writer. Miss Martha Berry!"

"Hold on a minute," Kent added quickly. "We haven't cracked the Barossa Pearl yet." Cary set out the glasses and Kent popped the cork before expertly pouring an even amount into each glass.

"You've done that before!" Martha laughed.

He winked at her. "Once or twice."

"Miss Berry!" Three voices echoed her name and Martha looked up to find April, May, and June had joined in the celebration.

"Congratulations!" April said and hugged her. "I can't wait until next week when I start. I told Mr. Pattison that I absolutely, positively had to begin my job next Monday, even after he begged me to stay. I simply said, 'Miss Berry needs me urgently.' And I've been practicing. Welcome to *As the Sun Sets*. April Atkinson speaking. How may I help you?"

"Why, that's perfect, April," Martha replied. "And I can't tell you how glad I am that you'll be here so soon. Ever since we aired the episode with Betty's horrible boss, Mr. Rogerson, you won't believe the letters we've been getting. Hundreds and hundreds of them, all from women telling me how something similar happened to them. If I was inclined, I'd have inspiration for a year's worth of episodes. The evil that some men do has to be read to be believed."

"Poor Betty," May said. "Do you think she'll ever tell her father what's been going on?"

"You'll find out before anyone else," Martha said with a smile, "now that you're my script girl."

"How can I ever thank you for the opportunity you've given me?" May asked. "My mother and father are so proud of me they're fit to burst." Martha could imagine they would be. Not only did May have a new job, but she'd received a pay raise too. It wasn't much, but more than a general secretary was earning. And every little bit helped.

June stepped forward cautiously. "Miss Berry?"

"Yes, June?"

"I can't thank you enough for recommending me for the technician's training position. It's been one week, and I'm getting the hang of it already. At first I thought I wouldn't have a clue about what to do with all those faders and knobs, but it's easier than I thought. When I told Mum, she said it sounded like a telephone switchboard. That's the job she used to do before she had kids."

"You'll be brilliant, June. You're very clever. I always saw that in you. I know you're the only girl in the training program, so if any of the blokes give you any trouble, you've got friends to talk to. Who'll believe you." Was June grinning? Turned out there was a first time for everything. "Wait a moment," Martha said. "Are those new glasses?"

June nodded and pushed them up her nose. "First thing I did with my extra pay."

April came in close and reached for Martha's hand. The Calendar Girls suddenly looked no longer like girls. They were young women. The world was their oyster.

"I don't know how we can ever repay you, Miss Berry."

"I know how," Martha told them.

They regarded her with wide-eyed curiosity. "When you're my age, give a young woman a job."

"I won't be able to. I'll be married and I won't have a job," April said, despondent at the idea of being unable to fulfill Martha's wishes.

"Don't you worry about me. I'm never getting married," June announced. "So I'll do it, Miss Berry."

"Good to know."

"What about you, May?" April asked.

"Maybe I'll start pushing for things to change. Why shouldn't women who are married keep their jobs? I'm sure someone's trying to do something about that, and I want to help."

"Now there's a plan," Martha replied, her heart bursting with pride.

"Oh, we forgot to show you!" April presented an envelope to Martha.

"Open it!" May urged.

Martha lifted the flap and pulled out a thin piece of card. On it in neat block letters was written:

MISS MARTHA BERRY
PRODUCER AND HEAD WRITER
AS THE SUN SETS

"I asked the chaps in the art department to make it," June said, beaming. "It's temporary, just until you get a proper one. But we thought it was about time your name was on the door."

Martha felt suddenly unable to catch her breath. Tears swam, rendering the sign blurry, and she hurriedly wiped her eyes so she could read it over and over. Her name was on the door. Not a man's name. Not Anonymous or A Lady. Her own name. She could finally claim her work as her own.

"I don't know what to say." Martha looked at all the people in the room. Her friends, as she'd grown to think of them: April, May, June, Kent Stone, Miss Connors, Marilyn Calthorpe, Alex Paulson, and Cary Sullivan.

"I believe the usual thing is to say thank you." Kent Stone waved his arm with a theatrical flourish.

Martha's sob choked the words in her throat at her first attempt, but she took a deep breath, filled her lungs with air and happiness and pride, and then laughed. "Thank you!"

"You're welcome," April trilled and then the Calendar Girls engulfed her in a warm embrace.

During the tumultuous past few weeks, a new sign was the last thing she'd thought about. She'd been far too busy doing the work that went with the title to even think about it. Six months before, her first instinct would have been to tell the young women that she didn't need her name on the door.

Now, she knew the power of its symbolism. For them and for her. Gwen Meredith had trod the path so Martha was able to follow in her footsteps.

Perhaps one day one of these three remarkable women might walk in hers.

Chapter 36

IN WHICH TELEVISION ARRIVES AND
CHANGES THE WORLD FOREVER.

SEPTEMBER 16, 1956

Quiet! Quiet!"

Martha and the cast and crew were gathered in the *As the Sun Sets* production office to watch the first television broadcast on TCN-9. April and May had brought scones and a cake. Kent and Miss Connors had brought champagne, which they were drinking out of Vegemite glasses—much to Miss Connors's consternation— June had fixed a cheese plate, Cary brought along some beer, and Alex arrived with a stick of salami and some olives in a glass bottle. Everyone had stared at them with some trepidation before tucking in and declaring them delicious.

Martha hadn't had to do a thing except borrow a small television set from Rutherford Hayes. It sat on a tall, wheeled trolley, and she'd pushed it down the corridor and into her office just before everyone had arrived. He'd ordered the television in anticipation of the first broadcast but had been suspicious of it and had never even turned it on to watch the test pattern. He considered it disloyal to pay so much attention to the new medium and had told Martha he would spend his Sunday evening at home listening to the Budapest String Quartet and the Tanunda Town Band and would then end the night with the special Sunday night celebrity concert on 2BL by Victoria de los Ángeles.

June was alternately jiggling the aerial and the volume knob. She was ensconced in her radio production training and Martha understood she was already running rings around the other male trainees. It was dark outside and the lights from the nightclubs and businesses of Kings Cross flickered through the windows.

June clapped her hands together. "There, that's it." She stepped back and admired the slightly blurry image. It flickered and turned to snow and then looked a little clearer. And then flickered to snow again. "No one move!" she commanded. And no one did.

Martha checked the clock on the wall. "Thirty seconds!"

A hush fell over the room.

And then a man in a dark suit appeared. He was wearing a bow tie and a pocket kerchief. His hair was slicked back neatly as if he were a nightclub crooner. Behind him was a map of the world and he was standing in just the right place to obscure Australia.

There was a collective intake of breath as they watched the man smile and announce, "Good evening and welcome to television."

A cheer went up around the room. Kent Stone and Miss Connors made sure to clink their Vegemite glasses with everyone before a collective ceremonial sip, and when the first program started with a live musical performance, Marilyn and Alex began to dance. April and May joined them, and June continued to fuss with the television aerials, hoping for a clearer picture. They were all fizzing with excitement, just like lit firecrackers. How could they not be? They were seeing the bright new world come to life before their eyes. How exciting it must be to know they would be a part of it.

Martha, Kent Stone, and Miss Connors sat on the edge of Martha's desk and watched the young ones celebrate.

"That Bruce Gyngell's a lucky chap," Kent Stone said. "Imagine having that on your résumé! The first man to appear on Australian television." There was a hint of envy in Kent's expression but it lasted only a moment. Martha knew he was far too generous a performer to begrudge another man his chance in the limelight.

"The bow tie was a nice touch," Miss Connors said. "He's quite handsome, isn't he? Just the sort of man people at home will flock to at the end of a busy day."

Kent upended his glass and reached for another bottle, refilling their glasses. He lifted his toward the young staff and actors. "I fear you're right, Katherine, darling. Viewers will want their television personalities to be young and handsome. Or young and beautiful. There'll be no place for thespians like you and me in this brave new world. I'm afraid we're a bit too long in the tooth for television."

"Oh, that can't be right," Martha said quickly. "While I would never countenance losing either of you from *As the Sun Sets*, actors of your experience and talent are sure to be offered roles when production really gets going on local television shows. I'm sure of it."

"Perhaps we might be cast in Quentin Quinn's police show," Kent said and raised an eyebrow with a smirk.

The three of them burst into laughter so loud that the young cast and crew turned to look at them with bemusement.

Martha sipped her Barossa Pearl and shot her colleagues a wry grin. "How lucky was I that Quentin Quinn scored a plum job in television? And it all happened so quickly. I don't know who possibly could have had a hand in it." Bubbles fizzed on her tongue.

"You don't?" Miss Connors raised both eyebrows. Kent Stone raised one.

"We barely had time to come up with a plan before he was already gone. There was no treachery involved on our part whatsoever. All I know was that he was called to a meeting with the general manager and he came back looking like a boy in a candy shop."

Miss Connors and Kent Stone exchanged glances.

"I'm assuming there's something you haven't told me?" Martha asked.

Miss Connors regarded Martha over the rim of her glass. "Did I ever tell you, Miss Berry, that my husband plays golf with the general manager's next-door neighbor? And that the general manager's wife and the next-door neighbor's wife are very, very good friends?"

Martha could begin to see the outline of where this was leading and held back the desire to laugh uproariously. "I wasn't aware."

Kent Stone stood and bowed dramatically. "Miss Connors, our queen, worked her magic."

Martha should have known never to underestimate a woman.

"I may have merely mentioned that the young wunderkind behind *As the Sun Sets* should be snapped up by the television department before one of the commercial stations got him first. That Sir Frank Packer was hunting for talent. Remember how he stole Bruce Gyngell from the ABC? And look at Bruce now."

"And isn't it funny how rumors spread?" Kent raised that single eyebrow again.

"We were desperate to get rid of him and save you, Miss Berry. We think you're wonderful, you know that. But it was in our best interests too. Television's here. We're 'long in the tooth' as Kent so delicately put it. And we both love Jack and Vera Percy. It was an easy decision and so surprisingly easy to pull off."

Kent Stone and Miss Connors clinked their glasses again and then clinked Martha's.

"I don't know what to say," Martha said, shaking her head in disbelief. She knew this was how the world worked, so she shouldn't have been surprised. It was *who* you know, not *what* you know and, up until *As the Sun Sets*, she simply hadn't known anybody who would stand up for her, praise her, fight for her.

She felt quite overcome. "To *As the Sun Sets*."

Her cast and her staff and her crew turned to her as one and called out in response, "To *As the Sun Sets*!"

And then Kent Stone climbed up on Martha's desk, much to the shock and amusement of everyone in the room, and held his arms out wide. "To our Miss Berry."

When she went to sleep later that night, their applause was still ringing in her ears.

Author's Note

Martha Berry, her friends, her colleagues, the actors, most of the ABC personnel mentioned in this book, and even the serial *As the Sun Sets* are entirely fictional. However, some real people do feature.

The writer Gwen Meredith was a legend of Australian radio drama. In 1934 she began working for the broadcaster, writing radio plays, serials, and commentaries. For five years she wrote *The Lawsons*, a serial about the plight of rural Australians during the war. In 1949 she created *Blue Hills*, which ran for 5,795 episodes over twenty-seven years. It was claimed that at its most popular, half of Australian radios tuned in at 1:00 p.m. each afternoon across the country to listen to the trials and tribulations of the people of the fictional town of Tanimbla. She also wrote a number of novels based on the *Blue Hills* characters. The legend goes that she wrote every one of those 5,795 episodes. She was awarded an MBE in 1967 and an OBE in 1977 for her services to the arts.

Charles Moses was general manager of the ABC for thirty years until 1965. Like my fictional Martha, he came to the ABC in the year it was founded, 1932, his tenure interrupted only by his years of army service in the Second World War—he served with distinction in Singapore and Malaysia, achieved the rank of major, and was mentioned in dispatches. He was knighted in 1961. He supervised the establishment of Australia's first national television network in time for the 1956 Olympics, but (according to my husband) his real claim to fame should be that he was the star commentator for the famous "synthetic" broadcasts of the 1934 Ashes Tests from England, featuring Bradman and Ponsford's prolific run-scoring (Bradman scored 758 in the series; Ponsford 569). Sitting in a studio in Australia, he would tap a pencil against a hollow piece of wood and describe the play while reading telexes from England, making it sound as if he was really at the match. The ABC's listenership doubled within one year. Against the wishes of some other managers, he backed the establishment of *Four Corners*, a foundational program in Australian journalism.

The character Joyce Wiggins is fictional, although she was inspired by the real-life Joyce Belfrage. A producer, she infamously threw her typewriter out the window of her office in 1963 in frustration at her treatment by the ABC. I have borrowed that story and tweaked it slightly, giving her action to the fictional Joyce Wiggins, and in 1956, not 1963.

I began my career in 1984, when I won a journalism cadetship in the ABC's Adelaide newsroom, so I have a fierce loyalty to the broadcaster. You might notice it within the pages of this novel. At that time, commercial broadcasters believed listeners didn't like hearing women on the radio (one of them told me himself). Things have changed markedly since then, which can only be a good thing.

The "marriage bar," the policy that prevented the continued employment of married women, wasn't lifted in the Australian public service until 1966. Gwen Meredith, and a few women considered truly exceptional, were employed anyway when it suited, but the vast majority of women at the broadcaster had to resign when they married.

The following books were particularly useful to me when I was writing this book:

Kylie Andrews, *Trailblazing Women of Australian Public Broadcasting 1945–1975* (London: Anthem Press, 2022).

Jacqueline Kent, *Out of the Bakelite Box: The Heyday of Australian Radio* (Sydney: Angus & Robertson, 2022).

Richard Lane, *The Golden Age of Australian Radio Drama: 1923–1960* (Melbourne: Melbourne University Press, 1994).

Acknowledgments

Last year I celebrated ten years as a published author, and I can't really find the words to describe what a dream come true the past decade has been. There have been way more highs than lows, new friends whom I treasure, old friends who have cheered me on every step of the way, and pinch-me moments when I've hit the Australian top ten and even the *USA TODAY* bestseller list.

To still be published, writing the stories I find fascinating, seems like a miracle.

Thanks, as always, to the people who keep me grounded, entertained, laughing, fed, wined, and chocolated: my dear friends. You know who you are. (And if I mentioned you all, I'd be sure to leave someone out and then I'd feel mortified.)

To my writer friends, who are very dear to me. You also keep me grounded, entertained, laughing, fed, wined, and chocolated. Honorable mentions go to Bronwyn Stuart, Amy Matthews, Lyn Ward, Penelope Janu, and Tricia Stringer. Thanks for those weekly check-ins, Tricia. This book wouldn't ever have been finished without you!

To my husband, Stephen, and sons, Ethan, Ned, and Clancy. We live a loud and raucous life and I wouldn't have it any other way. And yes, you rank *slightly* higher than Maisie, the golden retriever, who looks at me adoringly and stays lovingly by my side all day, every day. Maisie is simply the best. (Dog people will understand.)

To my mum, Emma Purman, for dumplings, cakes, lunch dates, and all your love.

To Jo Mackay for reassuring phone calls and simply being brilliant at what you do. I'm so lucky to have found you.

To Annabel Blay for your thoughtful edits and eagle eye. My books are always better once they've passed through your hands.

To Jo Munroe for the spark of an idea that led me to this story. Genius!

To the team at HQ HarperCollins, including Jim Demetriou, Sue Brockhoff, Nicolette Houben, Eloise Plant, and everyone on the sales team, in the warehouse, and in the "Book Cover Department," which is what I embarrassingly called it when I'd forgotten its proper title, the design studio (I swear my hair was pulled so tight into its 1950s-style bun that it fried my brain a little): Mark Campbell and Darren Holt and especially cover designer Christine Armstrong. It's always such a joy to open the email and see your work. I always cry when I see the cover for the first time and this one was no exception.

And finally, to my readers. You make it possible for me to be an author, something the fifteen-year-old me with a fantastic dream never thought possible. If you've ever felt like Martha in your workplace or even at home, this one's for you.

Never forget: it's never too late to be what you might have been.

Discussion Questions

1. There was grave concern that the advent of television in Australia would destroy society. What were some of the concerns, and do we have any similar worries with technology today?

2. Many women of Australia paused everything to listen to the latest episode of *Blue Hills*, and later, *As the Sun Sets*. Do you have a show or podcast that you stop everything to tune in to (or stream when a new episode releases)? One that you can't wait to discuss with your friends? Why do you think some shows are able to do this?

3. Martha rescued Quentin, and several of her previous supervisors, due to their incompetence. How have you navigated coworkers, or perhaps a supervisor, who was not meeting the demands of the job?

4. Martha found herself in a predicament. Episodes of *As the Sun Sets* were due but there were no scripts. What do you think you would have done if you had found yourself in Martha's position?

5. Martha used *As the Sun Sets* as a conduit to bring to light issues that were taboo to discuss (workplace sexual harassment, menopause, racism). Have you read any books or watched any shows that have done something similar? What was the issue and how did the medium (show, movie, book, podcast, etc.) handle it?

6. Women's rights have come a long way since 1956. But are there any issues presented in the book you see women still reckoning with today?

7. Who was your favorite character and why? Which character bothered you the most and why?

8. What did you think of the ending and how Martha used the Calendar Girls and others to rectify some wrongs?

9. What do you see in Martha's future? The Calendar Girls? What about Quentin, who moved on to the world of television?

10. If you could create a radio serial of fifteen-minute episodes, like the ones in the book, what would it be about?

LOOKING FOR MORE GREAT READS? LOOK NO FURTHER!

HARPER MUSE

*Illuminating minds
and captivating hearts
through story.*

Visit us online to learn more:
harpermuse.com

Or scan the below code and sign up to receive
email updates on new releases, giveaways,
book deals, and more:

@harpermusebooks

About the Author

Photography by Catherine Leo

VICTORIA PURMAN is an Australian top ten and *USA TODAY* best-selling fiction author. Her most recent book, *A Woman's Work*, was an Australian bestseller, as were her novels *The Nurses' War*, *The Women's Pages*, *The Land Girls*, and *The Last of the Bonegilla Girls*. Her earlier novel *The Three Miss Allens* was a *USA TODAY* bestseller. She is a regular guest at writers' festivals, a mentor and workshop presenter, and was a judge in the fiction category for the 2018 Adelaide Festival Awards for Literature and the 2022 ASA/HQ Commercial Fiction Prize for an unpublished manuscript.

To find out more, visit Victoria's website, victoriapurman.com. You can also follow her on Facebook or Instagram (@victoriapurmanauthor) and X (@VictoriaPurman).